AN ALTERNATE EARTH—
WHERE $E = MC^2$
IS THE SYMBOL OF LOVE!

"You have come too late," Almayer told Einstein. "The President has sent for me to ask me the same question he asked you."

"And what was your reply?" asked Einstein, pale with fear.

"Have you any doubt on that score? Could you believe that I would lend myself to researches that might be turned into floods of human blood? I, who am a disciple of Gandhi? I have told him that *the atomic bomb is a scientific impossibility!*"

"Fantastic and original . . . Boulle has an unmistakably origina' ....ancisco Chronicle

"Pierr......... ......n into limitless space" .... Kansas City Star

Recent SIGNET Science Fiction

☐ **DO ANDROIDS DREAM OF ELECTRIC SHEEP? by Philip K. Dick.** An original and satirically funny tale by one of science fiction's most original authors, this book is about Rick Decard, a cop with an unusual beat and an unusual assignment—to kill six androids. (#T3800—75¢)

☐ **THE PUPPET MASTERS by Robert A. Heinlein.** Americans desperately fight for survival against an invasion of monsters from outer space. (#T3572—75¢)

☐ **DOUBLE STAR by Robert Heinlein.** A jobless actor is shanghaied to Mars for the most dangerous performance of his career. (#P3669—60¢)

☐ **REVOLT IN 2100 by Robert Heinlein.** A novel and two stories set 100 years in the future, when the U.S. is ruled by a terrifying dictatorship. (#P3563—60¢)

☐ **THE DOOR INTO SUMMER by Robert Heinlein.** The engrossing story of a man propelled into the future, who then seeks revenge in the strange world of 2000 A.D. (#T3750—75¢)

THE NEW AMERICAN LIBRARY, INC., P.O. Box 2310, Grand Central Station, New York, New York 10017

Please send me the SIGNET BOOKS I have checked above. I am enclosing $_____(check or money order—no currency or C.O.D.'s). Please include the list price plus 10¢ a copy to cover mailing costs. (New York City residents add 5% Sales Tax. Other New York State residents add 2% plus any local sales or use taxes.)

Name_____

Address_____

City_____State_____Zip Code_____
Allow at least 3 weeks for delivery

PIERRE BOULLE

Time Out Of Mind
and other stories

TRANSLATED FROM THE FRENCH BY
XAN FIELDING AND ELISABETH ABBOTT

A SIGNET BOOK
PUBLISHED BY THE NEW AMERICAN LIBRARY

Copyright, ©, 1966, by Pierre Boulle

All rights reserved. No part of this book may be reproduced in any form or by any mechanical means, including duplicating machine and tape recorder, without the written permission of the publisher, except by a reviewer who may wish to quote brief portions in connection with a review for a newspaper, magazine, radio, or television. For information address The Vanguard Press, Inc., 424 Madison Avenue, New York, New York 10017.

Library of Congress Catalog Card Number: 66-26792

Translated from the French *Contes de L'Absurde suivis de* $E=mc^2$

This is an authorized reprint of a hardcover edition published by The Vanguard Press, Inc.

SIGNET TRADEMARK REG. U.S. PAT. OFF. AND FOREIGN COUNTRIES
REGISTERED TRADEMARK—MARCA REGISTRADA
HECHO EN CHICAGO, U.S.A.

SIGNET BOOKS are published by
The New American Library, Inc.,
1301 Avenue of the Americas, New York, New York 10019

First Printing, March, 1969

PRINTED IN THE UNITED STATES OF AMERICA

CONTENTS

TIME OUT OF MIND 7

THE MAN WHO PICKED UP PINS 36

THE MIRACLE 43

THE PERFECT ROBOT 64

THE ENIGMATIC SAINT 76

THE LUNIANS 112

THE DIABOLICAL WEAPON 141

THE AGE OF WISDOM 150

THE MAN WHO HATED MACHINES 165

LOVE AND GRAVITY 204

THE HALLUCINATION 220

$E = MC^2$ 230

TIME OUT OF MIND

My name is Oscar Vincent. I am unmarried. I own a small bookshop in the Montparnasse district. I have just reached the age of fifty. I fought in the war like everyone else. I feel that war is a necessary experience for a man.

I read a great deal and am particularly interested in the latest literary, philosophical and scientific works. I sometimes ponder on the problem of existence, and this suffices to satisfy my appetite for mystery. I admire the cleverness of the scientists who have succeeded in splitting the atom. I am thrilled whenever I reflect that I was born in this century.

It was fortune alone that plunged me into the midst of events out of the common run. I neither bless fortune nor do I curse it. I am something of a fatalist. But I should very much like to know how I am going to extricate myself from my present plight.

It all began on the evening of 7 August 1949. I was sitting outside on the terrace of La Coupole, watching the crowds go by and drinking a cold beer, as I am in the habit of doing during the summer months. At this time of day, as usual, a newspaper lay open in front of me and from time to time I read a few lines when I got tired of looking at the passers-by.

I felt things were not going at all badly.

It was at this moment that the Badarian insinuated himself into my life with a forcefulness that testifies to his personality.

For several minutes my attention had been drawn to a person who was now passing my table for the third time, scrutinizing the customers. He was dressed in a red Roman toga; this detail struck me, but what struck me more was a strange and absolutely 'novel' quality in his countenance—maybe the nobility of his features? Maybe the majestic width of his brow or the Olympian curve of his nose? Maybe his golden complexion, which I had never seen before in any living creature? He was well below average height and reminded me strangely of an Egyptian god who had donned a Latin toga as a jest.

I observed him closely. He walked slowly past me, hesitantly, as though he was lost in the town and did not dare to ask the way. Eventually he appeared to make up his mind and sat down at the table next to mine. When the waiter came to take his order, he indicated the glass of beer which stood in front of me with a gesture which signified 'the same'. He looked helpless. I noticed that I was not alone in being diverted by his presence; not far from me sat a little bald-headed man in glasses who could not take his eyes off him.

The man with the golden skin took a gulp of beer and pulled a dreadful face. He sat silent and pensive for some time, then turned to me.

'O friend,' he said in a solemn voice, 'would you be so kind as to tell me in which century we're living?'

'I beg your pardon?' I replied.

'I should be very grateful,' he went on, 'if you would tell me the number of the century.'

The manner in which he expressed himself was not calculated to diminish the stupefaction into which I was plunged by this question. The stranger had spoken in Latin. I happen to be conversant with this language, so that I had no difficulty in understanding him and replying. Our whole conversation therefore took place in classical Latin, of which I give here a rough translation.

I thought at first he might be a practical joker. Yet his tone of anxious courtesy precluded this hypothesis. A madman perhaps? I decided to enter into the spirit of the game and humour him.

'O citizen,' I replied, 'with the greatest pleasure. We are living towards the middle of the twentieth century. To be more precise, in the year nineteen hundred and forty-nine.'

His features betrayed painful astonishment. He looked at me reproachfully and said:

'O friend, whatever induces you to make fun of a stranger exiled in an era which is not his own? I know perfectly well we are not in the year nineteen hundred and forty-nine, as you have deceitfully told me, since I left the kingdom of Badari about eight thousand years ago and at that time we had already reached the year ten thousand.'

I have always been told that one should not contradict madmen. This one's quirk no doubt was to believe he belonged to another epoch. I remembered having read an article on the recent discovery by M. Brunton of the vestiges of

Badari, an ancient city, and being fascinated by the astonishing civilization revealed by the excavations. Evidently some similar material had unbalanced this fellow's mind. I replied slowly and in the same tone:

'O stranger, I do not deny the prodigious ancientness of the marvellous Badarian civilization. All the same, I call the gods to witness, I had not the slightest intention of making fun of you. My words simply meant that we were in the year nineteen hundred and forty-nine of the Christian Era. As you are well aware, O sage, time is relative. That is why we may well be in the twentieth century in relation to the birth of Christ and in the year eighteen thousand or thereabouts in relation to the genesis recognized by the men of the erudite and illustrious city to which you refer.'

These words restored his composure. He fell into a deep reverie and appeared to be engaged on some complicated calculation.

'Friend,' he said at last, 'I apologize for having doubted your good faith; but you find me confronted with a difficult problem. I am going to prove my trust in you by telling you a secret. I do not think that the learned academy which sent me here can take umbrage at this. Moreover, I see in your features the sign of that simplicity of mind which to us is a guarantee of trustworthiness. Forgive my candour; it is customary with us Badarians. I must tell you, then, what you would have already guessed if you had been a little more quick-witted: I am travelling through time. My name is Amoun-Kah-Zailat. As I said, I come from the famous city of Badari which I left a few moments ago according to my time, that's to say about eighty centuries ago by terrestrial reckoning. I am a professor of the royal college and I have been entrusted with the mission of trying out the time machine which has just been elaborated by that erudite body. Preliminary tests have already been carried out by one of my colleagues. They took him up to the Roman period, which we now know fairly well, and which explains why I am perfectly at home in Latin. I donned the clothing of that period as I thought that the toga, like the language, might have been preserved throughout the ages; but I see I am mistaken. I aimed my machine on departure at a date situated twenty thousand years in the future; that's the extreme limit we can hope to reach. In the course of this journey I realized this length of time was too great to be accomplished in one lap. I decided to make an intermediate landing and touched down here a few minutes ago in an age which I calculate to be about eight thousand years from our own; but I am not sure of my figures and should like to be enlightened on this point.'

9

I was beginning to believe—however extravagant this might seem—that he was speaking the truth. During his conversation the doubts I had entertained as to the soundness of his mind gradually yielded to a feverish excitement which perhaps only showed the unsoundness of mine. This, I said to myself, is a genuine, authentic Badarian, a member of the race whose existence was intimated by Brunton in his book *The Badarian Civilization.* What a miracle to have picked on me of all people to witness this adventure! A journey through time! Could it be that the fictions of Wells were being actually fulfilled? A thousand questions rose to my lips. The stranger went on:

'I understand your surprise, O my son. No doubt you are completely unaware of the marvellous Badarian civilization. It is probable that in the course of the eighty centuries that have elapsed on Earth during the few minutes my journey lasted . . .'

This hypothesis, even expressed in Latin, exceeded by far what I was able to listen to in cold blood. I asked the stranger to come and sit at my table and allow me to offer him a drink as a token of welcome to this century. He accepted with pleasure. I asked him what he would like. He replied that nothing in the world would induce him to dip his lips again into the horrid beverage which the slave had just set before him but that his palate had been pleasantly titillated a few days previously (a few days by his reckoning, that is) by a ruby-coloured liquid brought back from the Romans and which the latter called *vinum.* I ordered two bottles of the best Burgundy. He took a gulp, made an appreciative gesture and said solemnly:

'This beverage is pleasant and comforting. I shall take a few bottles with me when I go back.'

As for me, I drained four big glasses one after the other and begged the Badarian to go on with his story.

'As I was saying' Amoun-Kah-Zailat went on, 'in all probability, in the course of the eighty centuries that have elapsed on Earth during the few minutes of my journey, the brilliant Badarian civilization must have been annihilated. I understand your astonishment, for it is equally likely that our marvellous discoveries have been lost. The Romans were already ignorant of them. In particular, the ingenious machine for exploring time was unknown to them. I do not think it has been re-invented since.'

I assured him that the practical possibility of a journey through time had never revealed itself to us.

'O Amoun-Kah-Zailat,' I said, 'this displacement in duration strikes me as being one of the most astonishing achieve-

10

ments of mankind and I realize we are still children in spite of our recent advances in science. All the same, our century is not as ignorant as you suppose. The Badarian civilization is by no means unknown to me. Though extinguished in the memory of mankind, it has lately been studied by our experts. Recent excavations have revealed this glorious past. I must tell you that your city was destroyed over six thousand years ago and buried in the sand. Today our hardy pioneers are digging the ground and uncovering the ruins.'

'Can this be so?' said Amoun with great interest.

'They have come upon remains of pottery, bronze daggers and skeletons with twisted limbs. But not a vestige has been discovered of these marvellous inventions you have mentioned. We thought you were an agricultural people. We knew you could carve statues in ivory with incomparable artistry, that you could work mother-of-pearl and chase bronze; but no one ever suspected you of this scientific knowledge, the effects of which are apparent to me today.'

'That's not surprising, come to think of it. The crude objects you have just mentioned were obviously capable of withstanding the wear and tear of centuries; but our greatest masterpieces were executed in materials far more refined than brass or copper. . . . Haven't you ever heard of waves and radiation? Aren't you people capable of transmitting energy by these invisible means?'

I told him we were and that we had even achieved some splendid results in this field. With self-satisfaction I described our radiotelegraphy and television apparatus.

'Well, then,' he went on, 'as you see, the essential element of your machines is not perceptible. Supposing that in a few years the secret of this transmission by waves is lost and a future conqueror discovers the remains of these contrivances of which you seem so proud. It will be impossible for him to understand their use. He'll think they're fetishes or decorative objects. That's how your men of science argue when they unearth fragments of vases and pieces of metal carved with symbols that are incomprehensible to them. . . . But I see you're still at the lisping stage of human knowledge. With us, the conspicuous characteristic of our latest mechanical discoveries is their apparent simplicity. The one that brought me here, for instance, is based on a very complex system of rays but its material structure is reduced to a minimum. Here it is. It's not surprising that such a commonplace machine should pass unnoticed.'

He took out of his pocket a small lustreless white object more or less ellipsoid in shape. A keyboard consisting of various buttons and levers projected from it and this appeared to

11

constitute the entire mechanism. I then noticed that the little man in spectacles whom I mentioned before was leaning forward in an intensely interested manner. He was sitting not far from us and must certainly have overheard part of our conversation. The Badarian hastened to put the object back in his pocket.

'I need hardly tell you, my friend, that this is an exceptional proof of my confidence. This thing is more precious to me just now than all the sacred vases of the royal treasure. I do not intend to linger in your epoch. I want to reach the twenty-thousandth year which I have chosen as my target and then go back home. . . . But you were saying that the divine city of Badari is no more?'

'Don't you know?' I said, after pondering deeply. 'While you were travelling through time, did you not observe its decline and the long wear and tear of the centuries? Did you not witness your own death? Did you not see your ashes packed away in one of those richly coloured urns which we admire so much today?'

'To facilitate our conversation,' said the Badarian, 'I feel I ought to tell you something about our methods. You will thus avoid asking a lot of questions which, if you don't mind my saying so, my friend, seem rather stupid to me. . . . But since we have made each other's acquaintance, could you not tell me your name? This fashion of addressing people by such terms as "O friend" and "Stranger" is laborious. That's another inheritance from the Latins.'

'My name,' I said, 'is Oscar Vincent.'

'Yes. . . . Good. . . . After all, if you don't mind, I think I'll go on calling you "Friend". . . . Well, as I was saying, your conception of time travel is puerile. Listen.'

We sat facing each other in the balmy atmosphere of this Montparnasse summer evening. I was so intrigued by his story that I had forgotten all about dinner. It was nine o'clock. The bottles were empty. I was about to have them replenished when the little man in glasses rose to his feet and, to my intense stupefaction, addressed us in Latin.

'O citizens,' he said, 'do not take offence if I take the liberty of interrupting your conversation. Do not accuse me of discourtesy if I happen to have overheard what you have said. Ever since your arrival I have been struck by your bearing, O ancestor. I could not help hearing your opening words. I was so astounded that I listened to the rest. Do not blame me, but bless the providence that decreed this meeting and the incomprehensible attachment which men feel for the past, which prompts them still, in this day and age, to teach Latin in their schools. In this day and age! . . . I should say in *my* day and age, for, O noble strangers, we are not of the same epoch. Miraculous though it may appear to you, my friends, I must tell you that you see before you another time traveller. But I, on the other hand, belong to your very distant future. Neither of you can have an inkling of my existence, for I shall only be born in ten or twelve thousand years; I cannot be more precise about the date, for, like you, O my ancestor Amoun, I have landed in this age by mere chance, after perceiving that the duration of two hundred centuries for which I had regulated my machine necessitated an intermediate landing.

'My friend, you have before you Dr. Djing-Djong, one of the greatest scientific brains in the Republic of Pergolia—but, alas, you know nothing about the Pergolian Republic, for the land on which this glorious country will come into being is still covered by the ocean which you, O Parisian, call the Pacific. I must tell you I have been entrusted . . . I mean, I *shall* be entrusted by the Pergolian Academy with the mission of undertaking a voyage of exploration into the past, making use of our latest invention: the machine for exploring time. We shall fix its duration for two hundred centuries of terrestrial time. According to my calculations, I had counted on reaching the famous Badarian era which our learning has revealed to us. A trivial incident forced me to touch down here. I am now delighted, however, since I am thereby enabled to make the acquaintance of two different epochs at once.

'I arrived five days ago, reckoning by your time, O Parisian. I exchanged my Pergolian clothes for those of your day and age, which are less conspicuous, and here is my machine.'

He revealed an oval object similar to Amoun's.

'O divine Djing-Djong . . .' I began.

But I had to break off, so deep was my emotion. I signalled to the waiter, asked the Pergolian to be seated, and had just enough presence of mind to ask him what he would like to drink. He told me that he found the beverage known as 'brandy' satisfactory in every way.

'It resembles,' he added, 'a liqueur of ours, of which I used to partake regularly. I mean, of which I *shall* partake. To tell you the truth, I am not yet accustomed to living ten thousand years behind my epoch and I must ask you to forgive me for these confusions between the past and future tenses. If you don't mind, I shall have a brandy and a little soda water.'

I ordered a bottle and a siphon. I examined the newcomer in silence. He was rather short, dressed fairly decently in a

13

black tail coat, and completely bald. A satanic flame glittered in his eye, and I should certainly have noticed the abnormal size of his skull if my attention had not been fully occupied by the Badarian. The latter had not said a word since the little man's intrusion. He looked somewhat vexed.

I took a big gulp of brandy and recovered my composure a little.

'Gentlemen . . .' I began. 'Forgive me, Gentlemen . . . I mean: O Most Learned Ones! You, the most famous of Badarians and you whose renown eclipses—or rather *will* eclipse—that of the most illustrious Pergolians, this evening marks the greatest event in my life, and I thank Providence for enabling me to witness such marvels. I blush for my unworthiness when I think of your immense wisdom, Amoun-Kah-Zailat, and the wisdom that will be yours, Djing-Djong. But take pity on the obscurantism of this century which is, I now realize, a sort of dark Middle Age. Enlighten me further, I beg you. You, Badarian, who lived eight thousand years ago, you have been dead for at least seventy-nine centuries—how can you be here, before my eyes?'

'There's nothing I should like better than to satisfy your curiosity, but you ask questions which testify to a rare simplicity of mind. Allow me to begin at the beginning, as I was about to do when this Pergolian sage interrupted us . . . and you, O my distant descendant, listen to my story, after which I shall be glad to hear yours.'

Dr. Djing-Djong having nodded in assent, the Badarian went on:

'Several centuries ago our scientists had already realized the theoretical possibility of accelerated displacement into the future. One of our physicists had indeed demonstrated that time, far from being uniform, was variable for individuals situated in different systems, depending on the relative speeds of these systems. . . . But I don't know if I am making myself sufficiently clear for your intellect, Parisian?'

'Go on. This theory is by no means unknown to me. One of our scientists has made a similar discovery.'

'The possibility (theoretical, I repeat) of living in a time different from time on Earth was therefore acknowledged, but its practical achievement necessitated a speed approaching the speed of light. I shall take an example which will be comprehensible to you: it's the one we give to our schoolchildren. A traveller leaving this planet at a speed of a hundred and eighty-one thousand two hundred and thirty-five miles a second and coming back after having lived for two years will find the Earth older by two centuries. . . .'

'I know,' I said, feeling proud of my knowledge, 'Professor Langevin made his name . . .'

'All right, but don't interrupt me. I shall now teach you something you don't know.

'This fact remained in the realm of theory until the discovery was made of a ridiculously simple process by means of which a body could be subjected to a speed approaching that of light without suffering the slightest damage. From then on travelling through time was a feasible proposition, but only in one direction. We could despatch messengers ahead of our epoch. They merely had to be launched into space and rapidly brought back to Earth. I'm expressing myself schematically. In point of fact, once the subject had left, he escaped our control completely since he was already outside our time. He was therefore given very precise instructions in advance and subjected to special training.

'A dozen individuals were "projected" in this manner and we have only just recovered the first, whose voyage had been calculated so that he should return to Earth after a duration of twenty-five years of our time, and a few seconds of his. He was in perfect health but was extremely surprised to find one of his sons as old as himself. As for the other travellers in this initial series, we do not know what has become of them, for we have not yet recovered them.

'In point of fact, if you have followed my explanation carefully, you must notice a huge gap in these initial tests. Our envoys were quite able to reach any terrestrial future epoch, but were incapable of travelling backwards in time. The invention was incomplete. Our traveller could benefit from all the advances in human knowledge achieved by mankind in the course of his voyage but he had no means of communicating this knowledge to his contemporaries . . . until the latter, having caught up with him, had become as knowledgeable as himself. This was not good enough. All the greatest brains in Badari therefore devoted themselves to the problem of the return.

'I pride myself on having contributed to the discovery which enables a complete cycle to be accomplished. We at last possess the means of retracing our steps through the centuries, which some scientists considered impossible, believing time to be irreversible. It is not. I shan't go into all the technical details—you wouldn't understand them, Parisian. As for you, Pergolian, your presence here proves that our invention has been rediscovered. When I want to return to Badari, I shall merely have to press a button on my machine. I shall then launch myself at a complex speed in accordance with an imaginary dimension of time and space. I shall traverse time

15

in a negative sense and rejoin my epoch. All our tests have been conclusive and, as I told you, an envoy has already brought back some extremely interesting material on the Roman Empire.'

I listened to these words with deep attention. Djing-Djong merely gave an occasional nod of approval. When Amoun-Kah-Zailat had finished, he exclaimed:

'What admirable Pergolian wisdom to have rediscovered these marvels! Your story, Badarian, leaves little for me to explain. We too have found—shall find—the means of reaching fabulous speeds. We too shall discover the principle of complex displacements and imaginary dimensions. The only difference between your adventure and mine, O Ancestor, lies in the direction of the voyage. We shall decide to accomplish it in the past. And so, after a careful regulation of my machine, I shall fly back into the Badarian era, bringing with me the enthusiastic hopes of all the Pergolians. I shall set off in twelve thousand years. I arrived five days ago after a voyage of a few hours . . .'

I could endure the terms 'complex speed' and 'imaginary dimension', but this constant mingling of present, past and future made my senses reel. I ordered another round of drinks.

'Forgive me, friend, for interrupting you,' I begged, 'but you must give me time to adapt myself. Don't proceed too quickly with your revelations. . . . Let's see, now,' I went on, trying to collect my thoughts, 'you claim, Amoun-Kah-Zailat, that you can retrace your steps through the centuries and return home at the age of your departure?'

'Exactly.'

'And later on, if you die, your displacement will still last in the future. The men of this century—myself, for instance—will thus have seen you after your death?'

'Without a shadow of doubt,' said the Badarian.

'Why not?' interjected Djing-Djong. 'After all, you're seeing me now, before my birth.'

'That's true,' I muttered pensively, 'I hadn't thought of that. . . . But then, who is to say that you're not dead *now* . . . or rather, I was right, you are most certainly dead.'

'O Parisian, it's good wine you have here, but your skull is as thick as an aurochs'. Yet it's quite simple. For you, I am dead. But for my own time, I am very much alive since I am living. My death is in *my future,* even though it is in *your past.* I shall die, in other words, some eighty centuries ago according to your reckoning. There's no contradiction in this.'

'Yes, yes. . . . But suppose you make a journey of only two

16

years into the future (I mean two terrestrial years). You spend a few days in that epoch, then return to your own and never leave it again. . . . As far as I can see, two years later you'll find yourself back in the very time in which you have already lived . . . in which you will live two years before . . . I mean two years afterwards.'

'That's undeniable, and this meeting with oneself is one of the more intriguing aspects of this sort of adventure. It's obvious that with an enclosed cycle of feeble amplitude, and by subsequently living normally again in terrestrial time, I must inevitably come face to face with myself, as I am facing you now at this moment.'

'Oh, what a thought!' I cried in dismay. 'But you, Djing-Djong, when you're born. . . . When you will be born. . . . When you have been born, if you return to this country, will you recognize the Paris you have visited . . . which you will visit, yes, some twelve thousand years before your birth?'

'I don't think so,' said Djing-Djong. 'You keep forgetting that I *shall be born* for you, but that I shall already have *been* born for myself, since here I am. At this moment I am merely rejuvenated by two or three hours and since I am sixty years old I was born sixty years ago according to Pergolian time.'

We went on discussing these matters on the terrace of La Coupole. With the help of the brandy, I managed not to cut too poor a figure, albeit making a sorry muddle of my tenses. It was a balmy night. Montparnasse had recovered its picturesque pre-war atmosphere. In the crowd there were foreigners belonging to every race and wearing every kind of clothing. A Badarian in a toga was not in the least conspicuous.

'Nobody,' I reflected, 'can have an inkling that the most extraordinary event in history is taking place . . . has taken place, will take place . . . and that it is I, Oscar Vincent, to whom it has been granted to witness this adventure. What admirable consideration on the part of Providence!'

Overflowing with gratitude to Destiny, I diffidently asked my visitors if they would like to try a wine that was rather popular with us and I ordered two bottles of champagne. We clinked glasses. Amoun-Kah-Zailat deigned to express his satisfaction. He said:

'It's a strange sensation, friend, to be suddenly transported eight thousand years ahead of one's epoch. I shall not malign your century, Parisian, even though it seems to have reached an inconceivable degree of ignorance. But the air is balmy, the light gentle, and I feel an unaccustomed sensation of warmth. I render homage to your sense of hospitality and thank you in the name of my learned colleagues. . . . What are my erudite Badarian colleagues doing at this moment? What were they doing, that is, eighty centuries ago? They were anxiously awaiting my return. They will not be disappointed. The harvest I shall reap will mark a date in the history of science. . . .

'But I cannot linger over the somewhat material pleasures of your epoch, my friend; I have a mission to accomplish. I shall set off again towards the target I have set myself: I shall reach your epoch, Djing-Djong. It is possible, Pergolian, that if I land in your country, it will be during your lifetime. It is therefore possible that I shall meet you again there, but you will not recognize me, having not yet lived through our present meeting. I hope that you will receive me as courteously as our Parisian friend and that the art of wine-making will not have been lost.'

'Rest assured, O Ancestor; but you're deluding yourself with a wild hope. You cannot meet me again in Pergolia, for if you do run into me (forgive this somewhat inelegant turn of phrase) it was in my past, and I would know it. Yet your face is not familiar to me.'

'That's true, O future sage, I had overlooked that detail. . . . But the time has come, Parisian. Can you do me a last favour? I'm reluctant to take off in the midst of this crowd; a departure into time cannot pass unnoticed. Will you show me a quiet spot from which I can launch myself without creating a scene?'

I got up to accompany him. I made Djing-Djong promise to wait for me at La Coupole, for I intended to have a further talk with him.

'I shan't move,' said the Pergolian, 'until you come back. I don't plan to resume my journey until tomorrow. As for you, Ancestor Amoun, I wish you a pleasant voyage. But haven't you any message to send to your brethren if, as is possible, I also land in your century?'

'Tell them that you met Amoun-Kah-Zailat on your way, that everything is all right and that I shall be back soon. *Vale!*'

We strolled for a short distance along the boulevard, then I led Amoun down a side street in the direction of the Luxembourg. As we walked along, the Badarian said:

'Forgive my hasty departure, friend, but I don't like the look of that little Pergolian. I suspect him of harbouring evil designs. I have a foreboding of a dastardly plot. The huge wealthy country of Badari has always aroused the envy of her neighbours. In the past we have dealt with countless enemies. What is going to happen when our prosperity becomes

18

known to future nations? If they are as learned and powerful as ourselves, as seems to be the case with the Pergolians, would it not be a great temptation for them to undertake an expedition in time to conquer us and seize our treasures? I don't like the shape of Djing-Djong's skull at all—or his puny limbs. To me, who have made an intensive study of the relations between the physical and the moral, these are so many signs of evil. . . . Parisian, I'm going to confide in you, because I feel you won't betray me. My own voyage, albeit inspired first and foremost by a disinterested scientific spirit, is also partly an intelligence mission. Having discovered the greatest secrets of the Universe, and prompted by a justifiable appreciation of our worth and glory, we wish to make the benefits of the Badarian civilization known to the nations of all times. I am afraid of the Pergolian plans, which are liable to conflict with ours.

'My mind is made up. I am going to regulate my machine so as to reach that fellow's epoch. I shall spend several weeks in it to find out what is being plotted there. Then I shall return to Badari and report to His Majesty our King. We shall then take whatever measures are necessary.'

We were in an empty street. He took from his pocket the machine for time travelling and proceeded to regulate it carefully.

'Everything is ready,' he finally declared.

'But,' I said sadly, 'can it be that after such a brief appearance you are leaving me with no hope of return? Am I to lose you for ever after you have dangled such marvels before my eyes? You have scarcely told me anything about this brilliant Badarian civilization.'

'You may perhaps see me again sooner than you think,' said Amoun-Kah-Zailat with a smile. 'I promise to touch down here on my way back.'

'And how will I know where and when to find you?'

'Have confidence, friend, in Badarian wisdom. . . . Now, stand back a few paces.'

He carefully wrapped his toga round him, made a gesture with his hand which I interpreted as a sign of farewell and pressed a button on the machine. There was a purple flame, a white flash, a long whistling sound like a rocket, and a trail of light which appeared above my head, rising into the cloudless sky. This lasted for a very short moment, then everything lapsed once more into darkness and silence. I was alone, hanging on to the railings of the Luxembourg in my emotion.

I remained a few seconds leaning against the bars. Scarcely had I succeeded in mastering my feelings than a fresh flash pierced the darkness. A second trail of light appeared in the sky and, in front of me, on the very spot he had just left, but now clothed in a tight-fitting black costume, my friend Amoun-Kah-Zailat re-appeared.

'What on earth is happening?' I exclaimed. 'In heaven's name, what does this sudden return mean? As you see, I'm delighted, but what accident disturbed your plans? What went wrong with your machine?'

He gave a condescending smile.

'There has been no accident, Parisian. Everything's working perfectly. Didn't I tell you I would touch down here on my way back? As you see, I've kept my word. I'm back from Pergolia after spending a whole month in that country, which I don't like at all, and very glad I am to find myself again in the warm atmosphere of Paris.'

Once more I could not conceal my stupefaction.

'But you left me only a few seconds ago!'

'Exactly. What's so miraculous about that? How many more times must I tell you that from the moment I launch myself into space my duration is not the same as yours. I reached Pergolia in less than an hour, which corresponded roughly to eleven thousand terrestrial years. I spent about a month there, as I intended—incidentally, I suffered a great deal from the filthy food and insipid drink I was given in the year twenty-nine thousand one hundred and fifty-three—then I retraced my steps in time, having regulated my machine so as to touch down here, as I promised. Since the day and hour of our first meeting had struck me as agreeable, I tried to get back at the same point. I succeeded without too much trouble. Here I am. I have lived in fact for one month. You have spent ten seconds of your life, and the Earth, relative to myself, eleven thousand years in the positive sense and eleven thousand years in the negative sense. All this is crystal-clear. I hesitated to return a little *before* my departure. I didn't do so in order to spare you unnecessary emotion, for I can see you are not absolutely accustomed to this relativity of time.'

'I understand,' I said in a daze, 'I understand. Thank you for waiting a few moments. But did you really reach the year twenty-nine thousand one hundred and fifty-three, as you call it? Did you see . . . Will you actually see . . . Listen, for pity's sake, let's agree to use only the past tense, even if it's illogical! Did you really see the Republic of Pergolia, a representative of which country is waiting for me at this very moment in front of a bottle of champagne?'

'Have no doubts on that score. I saw it, and I bring back grave tidings from there. The situation is serious. I shall tell you my adventures. . . . But could we not sit down in one of those establishments where they serve the drink to which I am still partial after a month? Let's keep Djing-Djong waiting, he's an infamous rascal.'

I looked at him. He was dressed, as I have said, in a close-fitting costume which accentuated his god-like figure. I took him to a little bar in Saint-Germain des-Prés, hoping that his garb would pass unnoticed. And indeed no one paid the slightest attention to him. I ordered some drinks. He went on:

'Yes, my son. Pergolia, which has reached a fairly high degree of knowledge in the physical and mathematical sciences, is certainly not the country in which I should choose to end my days. The inhabitants are unsympathetic and know nothing about the pleasures of life. Furthermore they are scoundrels who, as I had suspected, are preparing a war-like expedition against the radiant Badari. But let me tell you my adventures. They are pretty strange.

'As you know, I had aimed at the Pergolian era, according to Djing-Djong's directions, and such is the perfection of my machine that I landed exactly in that epoch, in the very capital of the Republic, which is called Bala and which is the most horrid city on which a noble Badarian has ever set eyes.

'I mingled with the population, taking care not to reveal my true identity. I managed to exchange my toga for these Pergolian clothes which offend my aesthetic sense. I learnt the language of the country in a few days, then I tried to insinuate myself into the society of scientists, who form a real aristocracy over there. My luck was in. I succeeded in being engaged as a servant to a doctor of the Pergolian Academy. There I learnt I had reached the city of Bala—O scientific marvel!— not only in the era of Djing-Djong but, mind you, at the very moment this fellow *was returning from his voyage through time*. I must remind you that the use of the past tense is a concession which grates on my nerves. I should say, at the moment this fellow will have returned. This remark is intended to counter your objections in advance. You remember that when I visualized the possibility of meeting Djing-Djong over there, he deliberately pointed out that if he had already seen me he would have remembered the fact? Well, I did met him in Pergolia, but it was *after* our meeting here, *after* his expedition into the past to Badari and *after* his return. He therefore could not possibly have any recollection of this incident which is still in the future. Do you follow?

'Go on,' I said, gulping down a big glass of neat brandy.

'Where was I? . . . Ah, yes. Well, I was there when Djing-Djong got back. There was an unforgettable moment when he realized—weigh each of my words carefully—when he realized that, having encountered each other twice in your century (for we shall be seeing him again presently) he did not know, at the time of our second meeting, that we had already met in Pergolia by my reckoning, or that we would be meeting each other by his reckoning eleven thousand years later, while I did know it and was able to draw up a plan of battle!'

'What! What!' I exclaimed.

'I admit it requires concentration to understand our respective positions, but pray make an effort. As I said before, we shall be seeing him presently. I know this, because he told me so in the year twenty-nine thousand one hundred and fifty-three, in a fit of temper. At that moment he himself will not be aware that the instant of his return to Bala has already been lived by me. But when, over there in Pergolia, this meeting, which for me has already taken place, takes place for him, then he will understand that today I knew all the circumstances of this future conjunction, and that he has been bamboozled. . . . That is what happened and he bitterly resented it. I don't know whether I'm making myself clear?'

'Go on. I see more or less what you're driving at.'

'Well, Djing-Djong came back from his expedition. Naturally, I first of all concealed my presence. I managed to listen from beginning to end to the report the rascal made to the Pergolian Academy at a conference which was held at my employer's and which I attended, hidden behind a piece of furniture. O my son, what perversity inspires these men and what a terrible danger threatens Badari!

'To begin with, I felt a certain satisfaction at hearing from his own lips that my own voyage had ended successfully . . . I must tell you that Djing-Djong had in fact reached Badari shortly after *my return*. At this point I doubt whether you can fully grasp the strangeness of the situation, and I admit my own thoughts are a bit confused. Never mind . . . Well, I had the satisfaction of hearing my rival describe an act which I had not yet accomplished and an event which he himself has not yet lived today. I'm condensing the story to make it easier for you. Everything worked out perfectly. But let me get back to Djing-Djong's report. . . .

'He described the beauties of the Badarian civilization, the good fortune of that prosperous city, the wisdom of its small population. He evoked the vast empty spaces surrounding it and compared them to the meagre expanse of the Pergolian countryside. That's where the shoe pinches. With their ridiculous mania for reproducing their species instinctively without thinking of the future, this nation has become as over-crowded as rats were, in my time, in certain foreign countries. The soil cannot feed all the inhabitants. What I suspected is only too true, alas. Their accursed scientists have conceived a plan which is as cunning as it is diabolical: to send an army into the past in order to conquer Badari.

'Djing-Djong's report has encouraged them. Mass-production of the machines has started. An intensive course of training is being given to legions of conquistadors. At this very moment the vanguard of the army may be on its way. . . . But no, I'm not the one who's raving! Pergolia will not exist for another eleven thousand years. Djing-Djong has not yet left. He is waiting for you on the terrace of that establishment where we were sitting just now, a month ago. My son, I feel exhausted. These voyages demand a manner of thinking which imposes a severe drain on the best balanced minds. All this is becoming extremely complicated. . . . But let me continue.

'Well, I attended the scientists' conference in hiding and listened to the doctor's report. He showed them some marvels filched from our museums by his dastardly hand. He described several experiments he had made. He described how he had had carnal intercourse with Badarian women, from sheer scientific curiosity, to create a hybrid race. It was horrifying. At the mention of these heinous crimes I lost my composure. I sprang out of my hiding-place; I rushed at the wretched little doctor and upbraided him for his villainy. He recognized me, realized what I told you just now and, pointing me out to his colleagues, cried: "Here is the man I keep meeting all the time, in every epoch and in every place! Here is this Badarian who dared to launch himself into duration twenty thousand years ahead of me! I ran into him twice in the twentieth century of the Christian era. He has come here to spy on me while, all unknowingly, I am waiting over there, in the city called Paris, sitting outside on a café terrace. But he, the rogue, before I see him here before my eyes, went back to Paris after discovering my plans. He will try to wheedle a poor little imbecile whom he has won over to his cause. With the help of this fellow Oscar Vincent, he will try to get me drunk and steal my machine. But Providence is on the watch and I have frustrated their plans, since I am here after having fulfilled my mission in Badari.

' "And that's not all, Pergolians! I testify that I keep running into this accursed ancestor in every epoch, in the past, in the present and in the future! Our lives are so intertwined, my past with his future, my future with his past, that the gods themselves can't make head or tail of it any longer! I encountered him again in Badari after he attended this secret meeting and outwitted me, as you will see presently. He then

23

discovered by subterfuge every detail of our great project and went out of his way to frustrate it. He boasted over there of having outwitted me, as he will have the honour of doing in front of Your Excellencies! Well, may Destiny be fulfilled. Die, you wretch! I know you are going to turn this dagger I am pointing at you against my breast; but since this scene is inscribed in time, I am compelled to try to kill you, knowing it is I who will succumb. Die, then, wretched murderer." And he flung himself on me, raising his dagger.'

'What!' I cried.

'Please, Parisian, don't interrupt me. It's complicated enough as it is. But let me tell you, he spoke the truth. I'll explain the theft of the machine to you presently. Concerning the murder, nothing was more accurate.

'Well, he flung himself on me, with his dagger raised. Fortunately I am far stronger than he is and I was on my guard. In the twinkling of an eye I had twisted his arm and seized the weapon.

'"So, you wretch," I cried, waxing indignant in my turn, "do you think I too am not exasperated at having met you, at meeting you and having to meet you the whole time and all over the place? Do you think it amuses me to serve as an instrument of Destiny? Do you think it's for pleasure that I shall indulge in the ridiculous farce of robbing you of your machine, knowing full well that I shall fail, since I see you here before me! Die, you wretch, since it is thus ordained!"

'With these words I plunged the dagger into his heart. He uttered a loud cry and gave up his foul ghost to the Devil. . . .

'Yes, my son, I am a criminal, but I feel not the slightest remorse; moreover, I acted in self-defence. My only regret is not having put an end to the career of that sinister person. Alas, I have to see him again, here, in Paris . . . and in eleven thousand years, on his return to Pergolia, where I shall stab him to death. . . . And afterwards I shall have to go back to Badari . . . see him yet again. . . . Do you know my voyages have inspired me with subtle notions about time? I am beginning to perceive that it's not quite as simple an element as we thought. . . . But I must finish my story.

'Well, so then I killed little Djing-Djong—would that I had done so earlier! There was a fine shindy in the learned assembly. All those little pen-pushers rushed at me, uttering fierce cries and stupidly waving their puny fists. I would willingly have brained a few of them, but they outnumbered me and I should not have come out of their epoch alive. I preferred to beat a dignified retreat. Thanks to the length of my legs and the superiority of my lung-power, I managed to get away. I went into hiding in the town. I stayed there a few days longer to find out what the members of the Pergolian Academy were plotting. Djing-Djong's death has not discouraged them; they have not abandoned their plan. Strife is imminent between Pergolia and Badari. War is inevitable. Having discovered what I wanted to know, I hastened to make my imaginary way back. The rest you know.'

I had listened to this strange story in silence, with the help of a few drinks to withstand the Badarian's extravagant disclosures without flinching. The space all round us was packed with couples jerking and twisting to the rhythm of a strange music. Amoun-Kah-Zailat watched them with an amused expression and manifest pleasure.

'I love the incoherent commotion of your century,' he said with a sigh. 'Would that I could remain in it longer and rest my mind. Alas, it's time to be off; duty calls me elsewhere.'

I asked him what his plans were.

'Well, now, every weapon is justified against a treacherous foe. I have decided to get hold of Djing-Djong's accursed machine by subterfuge. You will help me; we'll play a fine trick on him. I shall tell him that for some reason or other I have postponed my departure and we shall spend the rest of the night drinking. I shall make him consume some heady beverages. I have noticed that he is partial to the strong drinks they serve in your country. Inebriated, he will be at my mercy, and I shall be able to purloin his machine. Then he will be a prisoner in your century, and Badari will be saved.'

Some anomaly in his reasoning offended my common sense.

'There's nothing I'd like more than to help you,' I said, 'but didn't you say this plan would fail? That this destiny would not be fulfilled? Is it really necessary to indulge in this simulacrum of an act which we know must be abortive?'

'Who said anything about a simulacrum? What we are going to live through is an actual event which exists as I have described it. Although I know perfectly well what is going to happen, from having heard Djing-Djong describe it, it is not in my power to alter the course of destiny. Are you really so innocent as to be unaware of the rules of scientific determinism? This is precisely what will happen: Doctor Djing-Djong will get the better of us. He has already deceived us: the object he showed you and which you saw him put back in the right hand pocket of his tail coat is not the machine; it's merely a copy, designed to frustrate thieves. When he sees your anxious expression and notices your concern, he will suspect our scheme. Furthermore, I shall commit an unforgiveable error. I am going to tell him that I have not yet left,

25

but I shall forget I am wearing Pergolian clothing. He will thus guess that I have already completed my voyage and will be on his guard. He will pretend to be drunk. I shall get hold of the fake machine, in the belief that I have seized the proper one. Then, displaying the real contrivance, which is in the left hand pocket of his coat—but which we do not know to be there, mind you—he will cry out in triumph. . . . But what is the good of these predictions? You'll hear him yourself. It is not possible for me to avoid this event. I must tell you, however, that I still have freedom of choice; it would be rather hard to explain, but our greatest philosophers have come to this conclusion. I am still absolutely free to act as I wish, but I intend, I decide now, to accomplish the fatal act, the theft of the machine. Come on, and don't forget to keep his glass filled!'

I meekly got up, paid for the drinks and accompanied the noble Badarian towards his destiny.

Everything occurred as had been foreseen and determined. We rejoined Djing-Djong just as La Coupole was closing. I took my guests to a night-club. Over our drinks, we chatted of things past and things future. The little Pergolian imbibed with a chuckle all the mixtures I insidiously prepared for him. Towards three in the morning Amoun-Kah-Zailat, judging him to be drunk, cunningly filched what he thought was the infernal machine. But Djing-Djong suddenly sobered up and cried:

'Poor fool! Let me tell you I had suspected your scheme and have hoodwinked you like the whipper-snapper you are in spite of your years. You say you never left the Montparnasse district, and I see you dressed in Pergolian national costume! Don't think you have fooled me. I humoured you to see to what lengths your deceit would go. What you're holding in your hand is merely a piece of lifeless metal wrought by an artisan in the divine city of Bala and which I had brought with me in the event of such accidents. As for you, stupid Parisian in whom I trusted, we shall meet again before long. . . . You ignorant and deceitful creatures, here is the real machine!'

Fumbling in the left hand pocket of his tail-coat, he produced an oval object and clasped it in both hands.

'And now I, Djing-Djong, whom nothing can prevent from pursuing his voyage, bid you farewell. *Vale!*'

There was a purple flame which dimmed the lights in the night-club, a white flash, a long whistle, then silence. The doctor had disappeared.

'Ouf!' said Amoun-Kah-Zailat. 'That painful scene is over at last. I can't say I'm sorry. It is disagreeable for a noble

Badarian to hear himself being called an imbecile and an ignoramus by one of his distant descendants. It's over and I'm much relieved. Let's have another drink and put our heads together.'

I was sitting alone on a stool at the bar of the night-club, trying to sort out my thoughts. It was four o'clock in the morning. Amoun-Kah-Zailat had just left to organize the resistance of his people against the Pergolian invasion. The barman looked at me curiously.

'Hail, Oscar Vincent, O perfidious Parisian,' said a shrill voice in Latin.

I turned round. There stood Doctor Djing-Djong. I was no longer astonished by anything.

'Sit down,' I said to him. 'You're no doubt going to tell me that you have spent several months in Badari. That doesn't surprise me in the least. I hope you have forgiven me for helping our ancestor to play a good trick on you. Your superior brain surely cannot be offended by such puerile pranks. But what is this strange garb I see you wearing?'

These last words alluded to a brightly coloured cloth wound round the little scientist's body.

'This is the only dress of the Badarians. As you have guessed, I have just made a prolonged visit in that era and I'm on my way back to my country. I forgive you because of your stupidity, Parisian, on one condition . . . But first of all stand me a drink because I'm tired after my journey and I feel depressed. I have just learned from the lips of Amoun-Kah-Zailat that the wretch stabbed me to death in Pergolia, and the prospect of having to live through that event is not particularly pleasant.'

He took a big gulp and went on:

'I need your help. This is my plan. Amoun believes he knows it, but he doesn't know everything. . . . Incidentally, he no longer knows anything at all since he's dead. I succeeded in getting rid of him before my departure. . . .'

'Come now . . .' I stammered. 'But he himself is going to kill you in Pergolia!'

'That's why I forestalled him. When he informed me of my demise, I saw red and was unable to control myself. I picked up a hammer which happened to be within reach and smashed his skull in. It's not of great importance. I . . .'

I seized my head in both hands.

'Forgive me,' I begged, 'but when he passed through here an hour ago he must have known he was . . . was going to his death. Yet he never said a thing.'

'Not at all. This event was in his future and also in mine. I know it now and I could, at a pinch, tell him about it in Pergolia, but I feel I shall do nothing of the sort.'

'Oh dear!' I exclaimed, distressed by my friend's demise.

'Let's not discuss that fool any longer. I only hope that his death and my own will rid me of his presence for ever. Alas, there's no chance of that!'

'No chance of that?'

'Think it out for yourself. . . . But enough of this idle chatter. Listen to my plan. First of all, let me tell you that I indulged in certain experiments during my visit to Badari. I had brought with me a few samples of seminal fluid from the finest specimens of the male Pergolian population. I selected a few females and succeeded in fertilizing them. The result surpassed my hopes: the children born of a Pergolian man and a Badarian woman are admirably constituted and appear to be remarkably intelligent. Here is a means of creating a superior race. . . .'

'I beg your pardon, but how long did you stay in Badari?'

'About a dozen years. . . . As I was saying, these experiments in cross-breeding were a complete success. Moreover, I did not confine myself to this artificial insemination; I went to work personally, with equal success. Did I tell you that the Badarian women were extremely attractive? But that's a mere detail. . . . I conceived a tremendous scheme. As you know, the scourge of my beloved Pergolia is overpopulation. Well —make an effort to understand—I am arranging for the overflow of my compatriots to travel back in time. I take them to Badari. They settle down there, multiply, breed with the natives. Little by little, thanks to our natural qualities and large numbers, the Badarian race declines, wastes away, disappears. There remains nothing but the divine Pergolian race which perpetuates itself into the future . . . and its descendants *recreate* our Pergolian race twenty thousand years later. What will happen then? I hardly dare think. These voyages backwards in time give rise to unusual situations, and we may have to modify the process of thought . . . and even that's not all. Up to now the radius of action of our machines has been limited to twenty thousand years. Think of the day when we shall be able to reach epochs even further back in time! To arrive at the era of the appearance of life on Earth! To correct, yes, correct the blunders of Nature! Yet, my friend, this will come to pass, therefore it *has* to come to pass. The Pergolian will leave his mark on the origins of the Universe. The world as it now exists has been fashioned by our genius. It will be granted to us to *be the cause of what has been achieved*. This is the greatest triumph of Science. But to get back to our Badarians . . .

'There's no time to lose. That accursed Amoun is still capable of playing a dirty trick on me in spite of my demise. I'm going to return home as quickly as possible. I shall have time before my death to give my instructions to my colleagues. We shall forthwith despatch an advance guard to occupy the territory. The population of Badari is less than ten thousand souls. To conquer them and reduce them to slavery, fifty or so Pergolians equipped with our famous death ray will be sufficient. Fifty well armed soldiers. They will touch down in your century. You will receive them. You will provide them with food and drink so as to maintain their morale at its highest level. That's all I ask you to do.'

'But,' I objected, 'how do you expect a poor bookshop owner like me to give hospitality to a whole contingent?'

'That's up to you. If you refuse, so much the worse for you. You have no idea, Parisian, how little the life of a twentieth-century human being counts for a man who has just committed a crime eight thousand years ago and who will be killed eleven thousand years hence by the hand of his victim. . . .'

I raised no further objection. What could I do in the face of force except comply? I agreed to do what he said, even though the memory of poor Amoun made my acquiescence painful.

'At least,' I said, 'tell me the exact date of the arrival of your thugs.'

'Here they come now,' said Dr. Djing-Djong.

A shower of shooting stars whizzed through the ceiling of the night-club. Fifty Pergolians with bald heads and clothed in black costumes materialized before my eyes. They were everywhere. The last to arrive, finding no chairs, sat down on the bar.

'Here they are,' Djing-Djong went on. 'As I wanted to be sure you would not betray me, I chose the present moment as their date of arrival. Order a round of drinks for them.'

I was extremely embarrassed. The expenses of the evening had more or less drained my purse. I burnt my boats and ordred champagne all round. The barman, who had impassively witnessed the arrival of the company, started lining up the glasses. Djing-Djong picked up a bottle and drained it in one gulp, after which he became more friendly.

'You're not such a bad fellow, Parisian, after all,' he said. 'I shall retain a pleasant memory of you and your country. But it's time for me to be off to prepare the departure of these soldiers you see here and to brave the dagger. Long live Pergolia. Farewell.'

He flew off into the incipient dawn, leaving me in the

midst of fifty spindle-shanked little mannikins who kept looking at me and chuckling. I did not know what to do. The barman damped a pencil stub in the corner of his mouth and
totted up the bill. I drained my glass and prayed to the gods.
A fresh shower of shooting stars raced across the room. I hid
my face, realizing that something quite extraordinary was
about to happen.

I opened my eyes. Fifty Badarians were there: fifty hefty
stalwarts with gleaming golden skin barred the entrance of
the night-club. Clothed in a sumptuous robe of brilliant hues,
with an angry frown on his face and his nostrils dilating
aggressively, more superb than ever, their leader Amoun-
Kah-Zailat stood by my side.

'Have no fear, friend,' he said. 'Badarian wisdom is watching over you. The hour of battle is at hand.'

'I thought you were dead,' I muttered.

'So I was. I see Djing-Djong must have told you about this
adventure. But listen to this: a few minutes after that traitor
had taken me by surprise and shattered my skull, one of my
disciples had the idea of trying out an experiment. He placed
in my hand, which was still warm, the contrivance I use for
travelling through time, after fitting it with an automatic device for starting and stopping. It had been regulated for a very
short voyage into the past. The experiment succeeded and I
found myself two weeks back, alive and kicking, in Badari.
These two weeks enabled me to make all my preparations. I
guessed that the Pergolian army would touch down here. I
equipped several Badarians to come and encounter them, and
here we are. A great battle is going to take place in your era.'

At these words I realized at last how all this was going to
end, and from the depths of my despair I found the courage
to plead my cause.

'O indomitable Badarian,' I cried, 'you whom death itself
cannot stop, is this murderous combat really necessary here
and now, when we happen to be at peace and on the road to
perfection? You said yourself that you found this epoch and
this country agreeable, and you still have not plumbed our
wisdom! Let me reveal a few aspects of it, to discourage you
from your scheme.

'What characterizes this century is science, and scientific
subtlety. In Physics, for instance, we have just demonstrated
that all the laws established before our time were false; furthermore, we have also established that no such laws could
exist and that the behaviour of the Universe was a matter of
chance. We do not know how to create matter, but we have
recently discovered how to destroy it.

'In the science known as Mathematics we have succeeded

in bestowing a definition on the indefinable, based precisely on its property of being indefinable, which reveals a quite exceptional ingenuity.

'As for Morals, we have come to recognize, after a lengthy evolution, that the natural process of procreation, by means of which we reproduce our species, was not in itself completely amoral or utterly condemnable, which shows that our wisdom is matched by our intellectual audacity. Still better— and this will likewise give you an idea of our Logic—we have maintained with equal vehemence firstly that Good was Good and, afterwards that it was Evil. If there exists on this Earth or in the heavens another point of view, rest assured, Amoun-Kah-Zailat, it will not escape us and we shall one day adopt it.

'Perhaps it is under the heading of Metaphysics that our research has been crowned with the most striking success. In this realm, having recognized that God and the World are equally inconceivable, we have built up more or less every possible theory to combine these two entities. I only have time to mention them briefly: we first of all asserted that God had created the World; next, that the World was created by itself; after that, that these two incomprehensibles were fused in one, which was likewise incomprehensible; next that only the one or the other existed; and finally, making the most audacious intellectual effort in the whole of our history, we rounded off the series by conceiving a world that had created God. We have a genius, I tell you, a positive genius for expediency and improvisation when it comes to elements that escape us!

'We have proved our worth in many other fields. In Literature, for instance. . . . Alas, I haven't time, I can see, to describe all our perfections. But, I beg you on bended knee, allow our destiny to be fulfilled in peace and go and join battle a few centuries later.'

I ended in tears, so deeply was I moved by this evocation of our own merits. But my Badarian friend showed nothing but impatience.

'That's impossible, my son,' he said, 'because this battle, which you deplore, is situated in your epoch. You ought to be proud to live through this adventure, which can be compared only to itself in the infinite unfolding of duration. I need hardly say that my troops have been specially trained. None of my recruits is unaware of the art of cunningly displacing himself in time to discover the secret thoughts and accomplished acts of the enemy. But you'll see with your own eyes.

'The hour has come, Badarians,' he went on in a sonorous

voice, addressing his troops. 'Forward into time and into space.'

A loud clamour broke out, which was answered by growls from the Pergolians and a chuckle from Djing-Djong who had come back by means of some miracle or other. The battle took place before my eyes and those of the barman, who imperturbably went on totting up figures.

It was an unimaginable scuffle. I was surrounded by clouds of shooting stars that changed into warriors clothed alternately in a variety of costumes. I realized that each soldier, to deceive his enemy, was making feints into the past and into the future.

I saw the Badarians disappear all of a sudden, then come back armed with flints and dressed in bearskins. They had probably made a small mistake and gone a little too far back in time. At this spectacle the Pergolians vanished in a puff of smoke and reappeared armed with long spears, drawn up in a square which I took to be the Macedonian phalanx. Whereupon the Badarian unit changed into a motorized squadron.

There were some singular encounters. I saw the noble Amoun-Kah-Zailat clad in a Greek tunic, then imprisoned in a medieval suit of armour and astride a caparisoned charger. I saw him, before my eyes, in the uniform of an American soldier; but in a flash he was replaced by a babe in swaddling clothes. Another error, no doubt. He disappeared at once and came back in the guise of a hideous skeleton. His claw-like fingers fastened on little Djing-Djong who was crowned by a shaggy bonnet. But the doctor made a gesture and turned into a huge ape from some prehistoric age, whose eyes glinted like those of the Pergolian scientist. Whereupon Amoun-Kah-Zailat changed into dust.

Strange-looking corpses littered the floor of the night-club, rose to their feet, cursed one another in outlandish tongues, wrestled together, shrank in size, grew bigger, turned into monsters, foetuses, groups of atoms. Ray clashed with ray, wave with wave. Rivers of blood flowed through the room, coagulated and disappeared in the same moment.

I saw . . . but how describe the indescribable? I could not bear it a moment longer. To drown all these horrors, I seized a bottle which had escaped the carnage and drank without drawing breath.

The storm eventually died down. The rays gradually faded away. The monsters finally dissolved. The room was empty and desolate. The silent barman began sweeping up the broken bottles. The warriors had vanished into thin air—all but my friend Amoun-Kah-Zailat who was sitting beside me. He said:

'Give me a drink, my son, it was a hard tussle. Furthermore, my thoughts are extremely muddled. The enemy has dispersed into time, so have my soldiers. As for me, I believe I have been killed a dozen times or so, but I had the infinite pleasure of slaughtering Djing-Djong in forty different centuries. However, this need not prevent us from broaching your good wine.'

'And the result?' I enquired with bated breath.

'Oh,' he said in an embarrassed manner, 'it's hard to say. I hesitate to give an opinion.'

He suddenly looked weary, aged, disillusioned. A change began to take place in his physical appearance. His face grew less proud, his bearing less noble.

'Listen,' he went on slowly. 'This is the truth, as it is beginning to dawn on me. You knew about Djing-Djong's plan to transport part of the Pergolian population to Badari? Well, we halted the vanguard, but the *main body* of the troops selected an earlier period for its displacement. Long before I exist, Badari was occupied by these creatures whom I no longer dare call wretches.'

He fell silent. I was not dreaming. He was visibly ageing. His face puckered and wrinkled before my eyes. What ultimate miracle was I about to witness? Or was I going mad? Where had I seen this satanic grin, these eyes glinting with malevolence, these thin lips? He went on:

'So Djing-Djong's plan will succeed, has already succeeded; and so there has occurred what his subtle mind was able to foresee, but which I cannot yet grasp completely in the confusion into which I have been plunged by these adventures.

'The Badarian race has disappeared; the Pergolian race has taken its place. Parisian, kneel before the fantastic mystery of life! The Pergolians have become the Badarians; but in the course of history the Badarians have in their turn become the Pergolians. They are at one and the same time our ancestors, ourselves and our descendants, we are their forefathers and also their offspring. There is absolute reciprocity, and therefore identity. They are *we*, I tell you, and we are *they*, who are flourishing in Badari.

'Each of the two units you saw represented a different aspect of the same reality. Each warrior fought against his own *self*, and I, Amoun-Kah-Zailat, am none other than the Pergolian scientist Djing-Djong. I engender myself in the future and come to life again in the past. . . .''

The transformation was now complete. It was Djing-Djong who now sat drinking by my side. I felt dazed and bewildered. These events had shattered my nerves and unbalanced my mind.

I staggered out of the night-club. The faint light of dawn illuminated the ancient district of Montparnasse where I had lived so peacefully. Djing-Djong had followed me outside and kept chuckling, knowing full well what was going to happen. I could not endure his presence any longer. I simply had to escape from this nightmare.

At my feet, in the gutter, I caught sight of a whitish ellipsoid. One of the warriors had dropped his machine. I picked it up and examined it curiously. My attention was drawn to a couple of buttons. The Pergolian scientist explained with surprising consideration that one was for starting, the other for stopping.

'This device is regulated for the past,' he said with an engaging air. 'Have a try. Just a short voyage. Press the first button and, almost simultaneously, the other. You'll find yourself only a few hours back. It's not difficult.'

Such was my haste to get away that I did not think twice. I had no inkling of the Machiavellian scheme that lay behind this obliging attitude. I closed my eyes, and it was only after making the fatal gesture that I cursed the gods and mankind.

I felt a fierce vibration. I was seized with nausea. Stars flashed past my eyes, then with a violent jolt, I found myself back on Earth.

And at that very moment I realized what had happened. The world had grown twelve hours younger. I was living the evening before, in the same frame of mind as at the beginning of the adventure. I was about to pass through this infernal night all over again and, since I was going to relive it in every detail, *inevitably, when dawn came, I would pick up the machine and press the button.* I would then go back in time and again relive this night . . . again and again, for ever and ever. My little gesture had fettered me to this fatal cycle.*

I opened my eyes and looked round me.

I was sitting outside on the terrace of La Coupole, watching the crowds go by and drinking a cold beer, as I am in the habit of doing during the summer months. At this time of day, as usual, a newspaper lay open in front of me and from

* A keen-minded observer has pointed out that, if events repeat themselves for me exactly as they happened, I must at every stage of the story know the stage that follows. This is indeed the case. I am aware of every detail of the cycle through which I am living from past eternity into future eternity. If I did not reveal this until now, it was to hold the reader's interest. Besides, I had to begin somewhere, hadn't I?

O.V.

time to time I read a few lines when I got tired of looking at the passers-by.

It was at this moment that the Badarian insinuated himself into my life. . . .

THE MAN WHO PICKED UP PINS

This scandalous story is, alas, only too well known: a worthy but impoverished young man goes to one of the high and mighty of this world—a businessman or a banker—and applies for a job. At first he is turned down flat. As he makes his way towards the door, the tycoon sees him stop all of a sudden, with his eyes fixed on the floor, then bend down, carefully pick up a pin and stick it in the lapel of his coat. Whereupon, moved by this gesture, the banker calls him back, congratulates him, kisses him on both cheeks, takes him on as his partner and gives him his daughter in marriage together with half his fortune, a yacht, half a dozen aeroplanes and a racing stable as a dowry.

A humorist has satirized this stupid episode and described how he spent one morning surreptitiously scattering pins in the path of several tycoons, then ostentatiously picking them up as soon as they were in sight, and how never once did any of them pay the slightest attention to his gesture. But it is not enough, in my opinion, to ridicule this character and the sickening moral of this parable. The man who picked up pins deserves a far harsher punishment. I very much hope that one day he will be hung and made to expiate his heinous crime in an everlasting hell along with his two sorry acolytes, the imbecile who trusted him and the hypocrite who reported this anecdote for the edification of the masses. It is a duty to reveal him in his true light and to stigmatize this sample of a pernicious species which is gradually poisoning our civilization.

Let us begin by his more harmless vices: first of all, it is clear that he is a useless creature without the slightest spark of genius. He must have a mind devoid of all thought, a heart insensible to all noble desire, a soul powerless to embrace the smallest dream, to bother about a pin on a carpet and to react by bending down and picking up such a trivial object. He acts in this manner only because the gods have denied him the gift of being stirred by any other enterprise. Secondly, he is a servile creature, a toady, a dog that licks the hand that beats it. He had just been contemptuously rebuffed and, instead of slamming the door behind him on his way out, he cringes and goes down on his knees.

But all this is a mere trifle. There is something far more serious. In point of fact the man who picked up pins is an abominable impostor. Whatever spirit you attempt to attribute to his act, you will find it execrable.

Was he simply trying to make the banker believe that the sight of untidiness was intolerable to him, that he merely wished to remove a blemish from the carpet? This in itself would betoken vile presumption. A pin has never been a defilement to a carpet. A pin on a carpet cannot in any way suggest untidiness. If there had been a hundred pins, perhaps, but this is not the case. The story clearly states: *one pin*. In fact, one pin on a carpet is not of the slightest importance—except if it happens to be the bedroom carpet on which one walks barefoot. But the room in question is not a bedroom; the story again clearly states that the banker received the young man in his office. A pin is not a dirty object. It is not incompatible with hygiene. It is far less dangerous than dust which, I am sure, impregnated the carpet. And yet the young man did not pick up dust. Oh no! because dust cannot so easily be seen.

But we have not yet plumbed the depths of his villainy. The really perfidious intention of this rogue, you may be sure, is to bestow a cosmic importance on an utterly insignificant act. His gesture presumes to suggest to the infatuated monarch enthroned behind his desk that only a superior mind can bend down in this way to pick up a pin. And it succeeds. The banker's gullibility is on a par with his dishonesty, and even more nauseating perhaps. Think of it: the tycoon has something tantamount to a revelation. He suddenly feels he has the soul of a philosopher. He is prepared to argue that a pin can cease to be a pin.

He swallows all the balderdash suggested by the impostor. He is now convinced that the act of picking up a pin is a transcendental act—which is a lie and cannot be sufficiently denounced. The act of picking up a pin will always be a contemptible, base and ridiculous act. If only the young man has picked up twenty-five pounds of pins he might have resold them and bought himself something to eat, or else melted them down to make some useful object or work of art. But in his situation a single pin can be of no use to him whatsoever. If again it was a *special kind* of pin, say a safety-pin—but

37

even this hope is denied us; the story states it was an ordinary tiny pin—if it had been a safety-pin, however, and if his braces had snapped, the safety-pin might have helped to hold up his trousers. But try and mend a pair of braces with an ordinary tiny pin.

Besides, his braces had not snapped (or else he was not wearing braces but a strong leather belt). If his braces had snapped, he would certainly have lost his trousers by bending down to pick up the pin; and the story says nothing of the sort. Furthermore, if he had merely bent down to pick up a pin for the purpose of holding up his trousers because his braces had snapped, you may be sure he would never have charmed the banker or found a chronicler. This episode would never have come to our ears in spite of its obvious import and far loftier moral. This is the way the world is: had the man bent down to pick up a useful object for a specific purpose, he would never have drawn the attention of anyone at all.

But in the fact of picking up the pin for the sake of the pin, the financier discovered—and with what rapture—a sort of diabolical religion, a pseudo-philosophy, the logic of which is based on denial of the obvious, its metaphysics on the dogma that the *entire importance of the world derives from insignificant details,* and the moral of which teaches that the mind will raise itself to the essential truths by fastening exclusively on these minute details. But in fact what is important in the world is to earn millions of dollars or massacre hundreds of thousands of people, build cathedrals or discover a cure for cancer, swim the Channel, cross the Atlantic in a barrel or outer space in a rocket, construct a machine capable of reproducing itself, foretell what the Universe will be like in ten centuries' time or discover what it was like seven thousand years ago. It is to write the *Odyssey* or *The Fall of the House of Usher.* It is not to pick up a pin. And the act of picking up a pin is in no way a first step, impulse or spur towards wealth, war, the constellation Andromeda or *The Fall of the House of Usher,* as the rogue who bends down on the carpet insinuates.

Yet this is exactly what the sanctimonious banker swallows, hook, line and sinker, his eyes gleaming with the cosy sense of his perspicacity. And in the first place he believes the young man to be capable of making a fortune. He has noted the care with which the latter stuck the pin in the lapel of his coat, and heard a voice whisper in his mulish ear: 'There is no such thing as a small saving.' This is another outrageous distortion of the truth. Certainly there are small savings, just as there are big savings. And even though you might not know it, O makeshift philosopher, there are also *medium* savings. The saving of a penny is a *small* saving, and the saving of a pin is paltry and ridiculous. When he has repeated his gesture three hundred and sixty-five times, your hero will merely have picked up three hundred and sixty-five pins, which still represents a contemptible capital. He will have wasted precious time and effort which he might have employed in making more important savings—*real* savings, mark you, if this be his bent—or, better still, he might have made some intelligent speculations which would have brought him in *real* wealth. Moreover, he might have contracted lumbago and spent far more money on doctors and chemists than the cost of three hundred and sixty-five pins. Even for the purpose of making a fortune, since this is what interests you first and foremost, his method is therefore heresy. When he has squandered half your money, sold his yacht, his racing stable and your daughter's jewellery, he will sponge on you until you are utterly ruined, O perspicacious banker, you who know how to choose your right-hand men! In actual fact the man who picks up pins can be guaranteed to finish up as a picker-up of cigarette-butts.

You will assert that money is not everything, that it is only of incidental interest to you. Your vision reaches far beyond mere material success. I know. You have swallowed any amount of this sort of tripe. You believe that in certain ill-defined matters of which you have vaguely heard (here you lump together literature, science, philosophy, painting and art in general) you believe that in these exceptional realms, of whose existence you are occasionally dimly aware, you believe that 'genius nowhere reveals itself so much as in minute attention to detail'.* This phrase, which you read by chance one day, which is the symbol of blithering stupidity, this insolent adage fathered for the satisfaction of the mediocre, struck you as so fine, so profound, that you inscribed it in letters of gold in your office.

Without any difficulty, if not without disgust, one follows the sluggish workings of your mind which you are pleased to consider so acute. One readily divines the sacrilegious confusion which insinuates itself into your feeble grey matter, a confusion which the rogue who picks up the pin deliberately tries to induce. In making this gesture he obviously has Newton in mind. He says to himself: 'Newton discovered the law of gravity by watching an apple fall to the ground. That is how genius proceeds, by fastening on details. Therefore if I pick up a pin, the banker will believe that I am going to dis-

* Péguy.

39

cover the law of gravity.' And this is precisely what happens. It is an absurd argument, as you can see; but nothing is more difficult to refute than this sort of argument. I intend to set my mind to it, however, for one cannot allow such impudent insinuations to spread with impunity.

Firstly, in the case of Newton, it was a question of apples, and an apple is not a pin. There are fundamental differences between an apple and a pin. Secondly, the pin does not fall to the ground. It has *already* fallen, a long time before—several days, maybe several weeks before, since a pin may very well escape a vacuum cleaner handled in a slovenly manner. I have myself witnessed a case of a pin remaining on a carpet for a month. There it lies, then, on the carpet, motionless, *inert*. Where is the connection with an apple which *falls*? Finally, Newton never picked up the apple, because he was a real genius and knew perfectly well that the act of picking up an apple is a sterile act. He merely watched it fall and meditated thereon. Meditating is just what the man who picks up pins is incapable of doing despite the visible efforts he makes to persuade us to the contrary. If he had really had the law of gravity in mind, after picking up the pin he would have flicked it up at the ceiling. He would have flicked it up twice, ten times, a hundred times and watched it fall.

And then . . . then? This takes the cake. Then, *even* if we assume, with an indulgence bordering on weakness, that he had had the wits to make this experiment, *even* if we obligingly concede, against all the evidence, that he had flicked the pin up at the ceiling, even in that case, mark you, he would *not* have invented the law of gravity. Why not? Quite simply because, by virtue of its shape and on account of air resistance, a pin does not fall from the ceiling at the same rate of acceleration as an apple on the ground. He would therefore have invented a false law. Kepler would have deduced therefrom that the trajectories of the planets were lemniscates and not ellipses. Einstein would never have discovered relativity, and all our knowledge of matter would be inaccurate. Our overkindly assumption, our extreme concession, is therefore to no purpose. In fact it is utterly unlikely. He never flicked the pin up at the ceiling. The story admits of no ambiguity on this point. He stuck it into the lapel of his coat; he did not remove it from there. He stuck it in *carefully,* mind you, carefully, that's to say his impoverished intellect was completely absorbed by the pin, and by nothing else.

Whereas to anyone in his right senses it is as plain as a pikestaff that genius consists in scorning small details and fastening straight away on the essential, the tycoon blithely swallows this unwarrantable enormity, to wit that, on the contrary, genius is to be recognized by its attention to the insignificant. And, to him, not only is the man who picks up pins a potential Newton, he is also of the stuff that artists are made of—a great writer, for instance. To the financier, a great writer is a man who attaches no importance to the *subject*, who starts working from material details like words, full-stops and commas, without previously taking the slightest pains to pursue a general idea. He is to be recognized, he believes, by the very triviality of the subject he chooses, and the greatest of all is the writer who starts with a mind completely blank. 'There are no good subjects for the novelist',* he has read in some *Digest* or other. And indeed the fact that such monstrosities have been written and typed out, read by so-called educated people, then printed and published in thousands of copies, without anyone having the urge to make a bonfire of them, this fact is, if not an excuse, at least an explanation for the obnoxious vapours that cloud the banker's brain. It is understandable that he should say to himself, fascinated by the man who picks up the pin: 'Here is a new Proust.'

A great businessman, an artist of genius—and that's not all. The banker labours under many another illusion, especially the one which induces him to give his wretched daughter in marriage to the man who picks up pins. He is convinced that 'happiness derives from the small things in life'. This is yet another pearl he has fished up from one of his *Digests,* under the heading of Philosophy, and which takes second place only to 'genius nowhere reveals itself so much as in minute attention to detail' and 'there are no good subjects for the novelist' in the list of repellent falsehoods that are wantonly propagated by obstinately wayward minds. What derives from the 'small' things in life, my dear banker, is not happiness, it is the *small,* paltry, mean satisfactions of those who have foisted this claptrap on the world, of those who have earned a reputation for profundity and originality by systematically denying the obvious, for the gratification of feeble minds like yours, and their shameless exploitation by the creatures who pick up pins. Happiness, in point of fact, derives from *big* things, like vast wealth, like genius, like anything else substantial. It consists, on the contrary, in despising small things. A man who picks up a pin and sticks it carefully in the lapel of his coat is as incapable of assuring his wife's happiness as a drunkard or a rake.

The story is silent on this point, but I can easily visualize and also describe the home life of the man who picks up

* Alain.

pins. From his wedding-day on, he has no other thought in his head, no other desire in his heart, than to force his wife to emulate him. To educate her along these lines, to *train* her, will be in his eyes a sacred duty. And if she has no vocation, no particular bent for picking up pins, maybe he will not resort to threats and blows, but only because he has discovered a more odious method of coercion. He will place a saucer on the bedside table in their bedroom and with a sigh deposit in it all the pins his luckless spouse has neglected to pick up, but which his eagle eye has been careful not to overlook. She will be subjected without respite to the torture of the infernal saucer of pins. She will gradually decline and waste away. She will suffer from dreadful nightmares. In the daytime she will trudge from one room to another, with a glazed expression and her eyes fixed on the carpet. And one night, in a fit of despair, she will seize one of the pins from the saucer and plunge it into her wretched husband's eye. Whereupon he will leap out of bed, find a hatchet with the help of his one sound eye and bury it in her skull. That is what the home life of the man who picks up pins will be. That is how happiness derives from the small things in life.

Picker-up of pins, I loathe you. I hold you chiefly responsible for every decline, every setback of mankind. Through your fault literature has become insipid, poetry is dead, philosophy shoddy, and the film industry produces nothing but duds. Through your fault thousands of people are today dying of starvation, and thousands of others are homeless. Through your fault we have not yet reached the planet Mars. You are capable of every villainy, every crime in the calendar.

I hope I have unmasked you by showing that, despite the apparent harmlessness of your gesture, it inevitably leads to disaster. One begins by picking up pins; then one ruins one's benefactor, next, one indulges in scandalous 'sayings'; after that, one murders one's wife with a hatchet; and one ends up by inventing the New Novel. Such is the ineluctable concatenation of Evil.

THE MIRACLE

1

The priest slowly climbed the steps which raised him above
the heads of the congregation, praying God to grant him true
eloquence: the eloquence that reaches souls. Having reached
the pulpit, he collected his thoughts for a moment, made the
sign of the cross and embarked on his sermon.

Father Montoire owed his reputation as a preacher to the
persuasive warmth of his language as well as to the strin-
gency and subtlety of his reasoning. He appealed with equal
facility to the simple faith of the humble and to the intelligence of educated men. Having made an extensive study of
scientific and philosophical subjects, he continued to take an
interest in various intellectual pursuits and was abreast of the
latest developments in the field of human knowledge. On
these he based many of his unexpected, striking arguments
which, through their plausibility and originality, attracted the
attention of a well-informed élite. Several inveterate materi-
alists could be cited who had been won over by his reasoning
after vainly seeking the truth all their lives. But he also knew
how to bring doctrine within the comprehension of the un-
educated. When his critical mind had analysed the most complex modern theories and revealed that they all tended to
substantiate religious truth, he appealed to the masses of the
faithful and infected them with the ardour of his face in a
direct and stirring language.

He had a great reputation, and the ecclesiastical authorities
regarded him as a future pillar of the church. In spite of the
high regard in which he was held, he had never abandoned
his reserve of manner and led a simple life. He had no desire
to be transferred to a post more in keeping with his merits,

but officiated in a small church where his sermons always attracted a large congregation.

'Brethren,' said the priest, 'today I want to speak of miracles, those rare and wonderful manifestations of the infinite power of a God who sometimes deigns to reveal His material presence to our coarse senses.

'I shall take this opportunity to demonstrate the fallacy of an opinion which was widespread in the last century and which some people still promulgate although it has been rejected by all men of real erudition: I refer to the so-called conflict between religion and science, between faith and reason. There has never been a greater error than contrasting the one with the other.

'We true believers are aware of the reality and even the necessity of miracles. I say "reality" because it would be folly to cast doubt on the countless testimonies which bear them out, testimonies from infinitely varied sources, including the most erudite and the utterly illiterate. I venture to add "necessity", because we are unable to conceive that God in His mercifulness should refuse to grant us an occasional sign within our scope of understanding, by bridging the gulf that separates His perfection from our lowliness.

'But today I wish to appeal to those who have been but superficially touched by grace and whose minds demand rational explanations. Well, for the benefit of such as these, even for the most demanding of them, science, true science, which is never at variance with religion, has recently put forward excellent reasons for believing in miracles and shed a blinding light on their august significance. . . .'

He paused, lowering his gaze to the pews nearest the pulpit. There he saw Doctor Faivre, a celebrity in the medical world and an old school friend of his. They were still on friendly terms, even though the doctor was an unbeliever and made no bones about it. They often had long arguments, at the end of which Faivre, who respected every creed, would acknowledge the priest's subtlety of mind without, however, discarding his own scepticism.

He had come to hear his friend out of curiosity, as he sometimes did, and was listening to him with interest. Their eyes met. Father Montoire was glad to see him there and, raising his voice, continued:

'The great natural laws, my brethren! There was a time when men, in their pride, believed they had identified and codified, absolutely and completely, the few phenomena that impinge on our imperfect senses; they presumed to see in these mechanical rules the epitome of universal reality. Listen to what Laplace had to say in the last century:

'*An intellect which at a given moment could assess all the forces with which Nature is animated and the respective situations of the creatures of which it consists, that is if it was sufficiently great to submit these data to analysis, could by the same token apprehend the movements of the largest bodies in the Universe and those of the most insignificant atoms; to such an intellect nothing would be uncertain, and past and future alike would be present before its eyes.*

'And he added that God was a hypothesis for which he felt no need. The stubborn minds of that time refused to admit the possibility of a single exception to the order which they were beginning to perceive. They were drunk with their own discovery—Nature—and these laws, which should have revealed God's majesty to them, they considered sovereign in themselves. Those who still acknowledged a God insulted Him by limiting His power.

'Brethren, we have had to revert to a humility more in keeping with our condition. The most materialistic science, concerned exclusively with facts and experiment, is now obliged to recognize its inability to understand everything and explain everything. As a famous doctor recently said: *The rigid framework which contained the scientific knowledge of fifty years ago has proved too restricted to contain all the facts. . . . From now on, and probably for ever, we must cease conceiving the Universe as being regulated by concealed mechanical devices . . . these imaginary devices, which, all things considered, are somewhat childish, have all been shattered.**

'You see how far we have progressed from the mechanical determinism of Laplace! But to come back to the question of miracles, which is our concern today. Modern science has been forced to admit the possibility of *exceptions* to laws it had believed to be immutable. Those who have delved most deeply into matter no longer dare state that a given cause in given circumstances will necessarily produce a given effect. They speak only of very great probabilities. On closer inspection they have perceived that these laws in themselves are not incompatible with phenomena which are inconceivable to common sense. They have recognized that nothing exists in the essential composition of water, nor in the movements to which its molecules are subjected, that prevents its transformation to another liquid or into an entirely different substance. Avatars of this sort, albeit most improbable, are possible.

'Mind you, brethren, this improbability is vast. It makes our minds reel. I have no intention of minimizing it. On the contrary, I want to underline the theoretical possibility of

* Charles Fabry.

45

such events, which proves the wisdom and far-sightedness of God, no less than their *prodigiously exceptional* character which enhances His greatness when He brings them about. Granted, our Creator wanted to subject nature to harmonious laws, and any departure from their rhythm, we know and feel, necessitates such an extraordinary concatenation of circumstances that it cannot be brought about without some deliberate external impulse. Mathematicians have demonstrated that if matter were subjected solely to the laws of probability, there would not be the slightest chance of such a departure occurring except over a length of time out of all proportion to that of our Universe. This exception, which is nevertheless conceivable, which is nevertheless compatible with the established order, God has reserved the right to call forth on occasion. That is what we mean by a miracle.

'What is this "anti-chance" we hear so much about in modern publications, which, by a process of *selection,* is said to be able to bring about inconceivably improbable redistributions among the infinitely possible combinations of atoms? What is this "demon", invented by Maxwell, which is said to have the power of producing a distribution of heat contrary to common sense? Mere words, my brethren, behind which men have concealed what was beyond the bounds of their comprehension: the Supreme Will, which alone is capable of giving the impulse It wants to Its creation. . . .'

The priest developed this theme, which he knew was more likely than most to convert certain people—in particular Doctor Faivre, who never took his eyes off him. He rounded off this first part of his sermon by evoking the mystery of life and enjoining the congregation to meditate on its awe-inspiring character.

'How can we not believe in miracles, my brethren, when we have before our eyes creatures whose very existence is a permanent wonder? As recently as last century it was possible to believe that the haphazard interplay of physico-chemical reactions was enough to account for their structural development over a long period of evolution. There too, on close inspection, scientists have had to acknowledge the error of their ways. The composition of a simple cell is certainly not incompatible with natural laws; its spontaneous generation is *possible,* just as the metamorphosis of all matter is possible, but it presupposes such an improbability that all men of good faith refuse to acknowledge it today. What are we to say, then, of those billions and billions of elements of which the body of a living creature is composed? And what are we to say of the genesis of the soul? Each is a living proof of divine omnipotence. Each is a miracle, a monument whose countless stones, miraculous themselves, are assembled and organized by these exceptional departures from the laws governing matter and from the laws of chance.'

Finally he brought his eloquence within the comprehension of the ordinary people. He recalled some of the most famous miracles and concluded by extolling the virtues of those whom God had selected to bring them about.

'Consider, my brethren, His lofty vision and sovereign impartiality. He takes no heed of worldly differences in the choice of His elect. In His eyes faith is the most sublime qualification. It can move Him, whether it comes from a learned doctor of the Church or from a humble shepherd.

'Blessed are those whose faith needs no reinforcement by proof. Blessed are the meek. They know, without thinking about it, that our Lord can do anything. It is often to one of these, as I say, that He delegates a grain of his miraculous power. Amen.'

Father Montoire stepped down from the pulpit amid murmurs of approval from the congregation. Doctor Faivre came to see him in the sacristy and congratulated him.

'Did I convince you?' asked the priest.

'You would have, if I ever could be by words. Alas, I have never witnessed a miracle.'

2

A few days later the priest spent the afternoon in church hearing the confessions of a crowd of penitents, of whom there was always a large number eager to seek his absolution. He finished late, said a short prayer, and headed towards the sacristy across the deserted nave.

'Father!'

He stopped and perceived a woman of apparently modest condition standing by the aisle leading to the sacristy. She had waited for him there, being unable to summon up the strength to overcome her timidity until he was on the point of leaving.

'Father, please!'

He was moved by the pathos in her tone and retraced his steps. She held out a letter with a trembling hand.

'For you, Father, from Doctor Faivre.'

'From Doctor Faivre?'

She was so agitated that she could not utter another word. She lowered her eyes, twisting the corners of her shawl nervously. Father Montoire spoke to her kindly.

'I can't read it here. The church is too dark. Come with me.'

He wanted her to go ahead of him. She held back and made a gesture. He then noticed that she was not alone. A figure could be seen in the half-light.

'My son,' she said in a low voice.

'Come along, both of you,' said the priest, intrigued.

She went up to her son who was standing motionless, as though incrusted in the wall. He did not move until she seized his arm. Father Montoire saw him feeling his way with a stick. He ushered them into the sacristy and, without asking any question, switched on the light to read the letter.

'My dear friend,

'Please don't think this request is made in a spirit of irreverence. You know me well enough to realize that I treat serious matters seriously, and this is a serious matter. I have done my utmost to dissuade this worthy woman, Madame Courtal, from coming to see you. I have finally yielded to her entreaties and given her this letter of introduction. She is an old family servant of ours and deserves to have some interest taken in her misfortune.

'She absolutely insists on bringing you her son Jean, a young man of twenty-five who was blinded in the war. Medical science can do nothing for him. He is incurable. She has known you for a long time; she hears all your sermons. After the last one she got it into her head that you can cure her son and wants you to pray God to perform this miracle. I find it extremely difficult to pass on her request. Please don't hold it against me but do everything in your power, without disheartening her, to make her see reason. I can do no more myself. There is not the slightest chance of a cure. Furthermore, his wound has deprived him of his senses. He's a simple-minded soul, and lives only by his mother's love and care. Once more, I beg you to forgive me.'

Father Montoire felt disconcerted and perplexed. The woman's pleading eyes questioned him anxiously. The blind boy stood stiff and motionless and seemed insensible. Since the priest hesitated to speak, she fell on her knees.

'I beseech you, Father. I know it was wrong of me to come and ask you this, but you alone can do something for him. The doctor says it's impossible, but doctors are often wrong. I had no hope left, and then, when I heard you speak about miracles and show so clearly that God could do anything, my faith was restored. I seemed to see a light. I felt that our Lord could cure my child if you would consent to ask Him in the proper way. I was once taught that He performed miracles, but no one made me understand it as clearly as you. Father, forgive me for being so bold, but you must pray to God on my behalf; I don't know how. You must ask Him to restore my son's sight.'

'My good woman,' the priest murmured, deeply moved.

He was overwhelmed by this touching faith and did not know what to say in reply. He uttered a few inadequate words of consolation.

'My good woman, this is a terrible misfortune for your son and for you. . . . The good Lord has put you to a severe test. But who can tell whether He does not reserve the greatest blessings for those He has so cruelly stricken. I promise to pray for your child; but, alas, I possess no miraculous power. I am only a humble creature like yourself.'

'I beg you on my knees, Father. I am sure, if you really will do it, God will listen to you. They say you have converted a lot of learned gentlemen who were unbelievers, because you know the words that stir them. . . . And those who have cured the sick never realize their power beforehand. You said so yourself, Father.'

He made her get to her feet again. He could still think of nothing to say to her—he who was usually so eloquent—and reproached himself for being at a loss for words. 'It's true,' he thought, 'the elect are unaware of their gift until the moment it is revealed to them. Have I the right not to try? But how can I entertain such thoughts! I'm out of my mind. . . . And such a desperate case as this! Faivre asserts there is no chance of a cure. . . . Yet how can I reject her plea? How can I, without having first tried everything, discourage a faith so simple and sublime—I who have preached trust in His infinite mercy? She would tax me with hypocrisy and, with her plain down-to-earth common sense, would turn away for ever from the Church and its priests.'

He finally came to a decision.

'My dear woman,' he said, 'I shall pray to our Lord to look down upon your son's affliction, but on one condition. As you are well aware, miracles are extremely rare events. The probability of their occurrence is remote in the extreme. . . .'

His speech was still imbued with the erudite language of his sermon. He rebuked himself for not using simpler words to suit the occasion.

'God has allowed your son to be blinded. As with all His acts, there is a reason that escapes us. I shall beg Him to reconsider His decision, but you must promise me that if He does not heed my prayer—which, alas, is all too likely, since I am unworthy—you must promise not to lapse into despair and to hold no bitterness in your heart. His designs are impenetrable, and it is not for us to judge Him.'

She thanked him and promised. His consent was all she had comprehended. She took him by the arm and exhorted him passionately.

'At once, Father; you must pray at once! And in the church; at the foot of the altar. I am sure it will work better there.'

She was transfigured. Her faith inspired her with an authority which made him feel diminished. Dominated by it, he yielded and immediately regretted it, feeling ashamed, as though he was being a party to some sinful farce. But already she was leading off her son, who followed her like an automaton. She made him kneel down in front of the altar, then stepped back a few paces and stood erect and motionless, her fingers locked in an attitude of prayer. Father Montoire shuddered, sickened by a bitter mixture of pity and qualms of conscience. He reflected: 'Poor woman! What a cruel disappointment on top of such misfortune! What a terrible disillusion awaits her! God alone will judge if I am committing a sin or an act of charity.'

He in his turn knelt down, buried his face in his hands, again asked the Lord forgiveness for his temerity, and besought Him in a low voice:

'Thou to whom no living creature is without significance, Thou who canst raise the dead and destroy the living, take pity on this distress. Though I scarcely dare, even on bended knee, I beg Thee to cure this sick man. I know I am unworthy of asking this favour of Thee, but I humbly beseech Thee, if it be Thy will, give Thou a sign of Thine omnipotence and Thy mercy.'

He remained on his knees for a long time, his lips murmuring the same words over and over again. Beside him, the blind man had not budged. The woman's anguished look was fixed upon them. Finally he rose to his feet with a heavy heart. She did not move. She was expecting something more from him.

'Ought you not to touch his eyelids?' she said, trembling. 'And say a few words out loud to him, as Jesus did?'

He was overwhelmed by a wave of despair and realized, to his shame, that he would once more have to give in to her. He no longer had the strength or the courage to desist. He would stretch his plea to the point of sacrilege. He laid his trembling hands on the lifeless eyelids.

'My God, I beg thee as an exceptional favour, heal this unfortunate.'

And he added in a loud voice, addressing the blind man:
'See thou the light.'

He turned away to hide his tears, tormented by remorse

and aware of having reached the extreme limits of human misery.

Thereupon a sudden gleam appeared in the blind man's eyes. A living light abruptly transfigured his features. He raised his hands to his transformed face and lowered them again, crying: 'Light!' Then, unassisted, before the startled eyes of his mother and the priest, he slowly made his way towards the candles which shed a faint glow at the far end of the church.

Had the sky fallen about Father Montoire's head, he would not have experienced such utter stupefaction. He stood petrified, speechless, gasping, his brain in a whirl. The woman, her features contorted, clung to the communion table in the throes of a nervous tremor. She watched with bated breath as her son turned round and walked up to her. He had recovered his senses along with his sight. At last she found the strength to stretch her arms out to him, and they embraced, weeping.

'I knew it!' she stammered. 'I knew God would hear you. God bless you, Father . . . this happiness is beyond bearing! I shall light candles. . . . I shall go to Mass every day. I'll make a pilgrimage. . . . You can see, Jean, you can see! Thank him, oh thank this saint to whom you owe this miracle. How can we show our gratitude? Here's all the money I have for your poor. I'll give you more. . . .'

She was out of her mind with joy. The priest murmured, almost incoherently:

'I'm not the one you must thank. Only the Almighty can perform miracles.'

'My God, wretch that I am!' the woman cried. 'I have not yet flung myself down at His knees.'

She prostrated herself before the altar, with her forehead in the dust.

'Yes, on your knees,' said the priest absently.

He appeared not to have come to his senses completely. He looked at her, crumpled on the floor, as though he was a stranger to this scene.

'On your knees,' he repeated in a toneless voice.

Then, recovering himself:

'We too on our knees, my son, to thank the Lord for this conspicuous favour.'

They remained for several minutes on the cold flagstones. Mother and son prayed feverishly. The priest tried to dismiss a host of contradictory sentiments from his mind to make room only for gratitude. He found it painfully difficult to concentrate, even for a simple act of thanksgiving. At last he slowly rose to his feet. The woman followed suit and her son looked all round him, as though in a daze. She seemed to have recovered her composure. They remained silent for a moment, then Father Montoire anxiously enquired:

'You're quite sure he . . . he couldn't see beforehand?'

'I'm quite sure! I've wept enough and cursed our misfortune! I was going out of my mind. I didn't tell you this, Father, but I was ready to appeal to the Devil. I went to fortune-tellers. I can't tell you what I haven't tried. . . . Wretch that I was not to have trusted in Him, in Him who can do everything, as you proved in the pulpit, Father!'

'Yes, everything, absolutely everything, as I proved in the pulpit,' he echoed automatically. 'But tell me exactly, word for word, what Doctor Faivre said.'

'I can tell you now. In his opinion there was no hope at all. He made this clear to me little by little, so as to spare my feelings, for he's a kind man. I can't remember his reasons. He said something about burnt tissues . . . but that's all over now. He's going to be very surprised when he sees him. You were in the right, Father, and all the doctors were wrong. I still remember your words. You said that scientists today can no longer assert that miracles are impossible.'

'Yes,' the priest again replied in the same absent voice. 'I was in the right.'

She kept gazing at her son's transfigured features with an awe that was suddenly mingled with apprehension.

'You can see all right, Jean? As you did before? Tell me what you see.'

'Yes,' said the priest excitedly, as though he was waking from a dream. 'Tell us what you see. Tell us what you feel. Tell me what you felt at the moment I touched your eyelids with my hands, at that very instant!'

'I see the light,' the young man replied, 'as I used to before. I felt a shock, and I had the sensation of waking after a long sleep. I can't explain it any better. Beforehand, everything was black inside and outside. And then it was as though there was a shower of light before my eyes, and also within me.'

'My God, can this possibly be?' muttered the priest. 'This has every appearance of a miracle. . . . My good woman, you must go to Doctor Faivre at once for him to examine your son.'

'We'll go there straight away, Father.'

'I'll also go and see him,' said the priest, pensive once more. 'I want his candid opinion. He'll give it me. He's an objective scientist and a man of sound advice. He'll tell me what interpretation should be put on such an extraordinary event.'

He had a feeling of vertigo and longed for his visitors to leave. Their gratitude made him feel uncomfortable. He had an imperative desire to be alone and commune with his conscience.

Mother and son left at last. He tried to compose himself in silence, at the foot of the altar. But he could not overcome the uneasiness that was growing within him and conflicting with his thoughts as well as his prayers. Presently he left the church, after instinctively drawing away, almost with repulsion, from a cripple who stood at his usual post, by the door, holding out his hand in supplication.

3

Father Montoire spent a feverish night, turning over in his mind every phase of the event. In the morning, unable to find relief, he decided to go at once and confide his trouble to his superior.

The bishop received him as soon as he arrived and gave him a cordial welcome.

'We were delighted,' he said, 'to hear that your last sermon was spoken of in such glowing terms, not only by the faithful but by a section of society which is generally not very interested in our endeavours. It's a joy for me to offer you my sincere congratulations.'

'Monseigneur, do not look on me as a preacher whose humble merits may have been praised. I have come to inform you in all humility of a supernatural event which took place yesterday evening in my church and to tell you the deep disturbance into which it has plunged me.'

'A supernatural event, my son?' said the bishop, raising his eyes.

'Everything seems to point to it, at least, Monseigneur. It has upset me so much that I no longer know what to think of it. I dare not define it for fear of committing a sin.'

'A sin?'

'Yes, Monseigneur, but I cannot decide which, my confusion is so great—pride or lack of faith.'

The bishop looked at him curiously.

'My son, the wisest minds sometimes have a momentary weakness. Tell me the cause of your trouble and, with God's help, we shall find a remedy.'

'This is how it came about, Monseigneur. I was preaching a few days ago, as you already know, on miracles, an article of our faith. I was trying to the best of my ability to find the right words to convince the unbelievers and the indifferent. Yesterday, after confessions, I found a woman and her blind son waiting for me. She begged me to ask God to perform a miracle to cure her child. I hesitated. It seemed to me to be wrong. I could not make up my mind, but finally, out of pity, though much against my will, I consented. At the sight of her tears I even ventured to lay my hands on the sick man's eyes and ordered him to see. I repented immediately afterwards, as of a sin of pride. Well now, Monseigneur . . .'

Feverishly reliving the scene of the previous evening as he evoked it, the priest shivered at the recollection.

'Well now, Monseigneur, at my touch, under my fingers, the marvel occurred. The blind man saw the light. He now sees. He and his mother are overflowing with gratitude, but I don't know what to make of it. I have come to beg you for advice.'

The bishop looked at him with growing astonishment and pondered for some time before replying.

'My son,' he eventually said, 'if anyone else but you—whose prudence and wisdom I know—had told me such a tale, I confess I should have entertained the most serious doubts. You know that signs of this sort are extremely rare; that is what makes them so precious. The Church demands the most positive assurances and a wealth of testimonies before giving an opinion. Granted, our Lord *can* bring about a supernatural event. It remains to be seen when He wishes it and whether it is not tempting providence to ask Him to look down upon a particular case.'

'Monseigneur, that's exactly what I said to myself before praying to Him.'

'Consider, moreover,' the prelate continued, '—and on this subject there is nothing I can teach a scholar like you—that the sources of error are legion and that the shrewdest minds are sometimes apt to be deceived by appearances.'

'That too is what I keep telling myself ever since yesterday, Monseigneur. But the woman had been sent to me by my friend, Doctor Faivre, one of the ablest physicians alive. His diagnosis was categorical: the sick man could not be cured —and what room is there for doubt, Monseigneur, when the marvel occurred before my eyes, under my hands, and with no one's intervention?'

'I must stress the point, my son,' the bishop continued with great authority. 'Miracles are truly *exceptional* facts. In these matters it is our duty as churchmen to adopt a ruthlessly critical attitude, even more so perhaps than anyone else. Remember that the enemies of the Church, yours and mine, are always on the watch for possible errors on our part, and ready to turn them to our own confusion. These errors can come about in any amount of ways. In the first place, there is always the possibility of deception. . . .'

'That was my first thought,' the priest confessed. 'But deception seems impossible in this case.'

'Let us therefore dismiss that hypothesis. There are still many other natural explanations. A great physician, you say, had condemned this poor soul to spend his life in darkness? As you know yourself, science is not infallible. It is probable —and this is the most reasonable view to take—that he made a mistake in his diagnosis, taking a temporary affliction for an incurable disease. Does not medical history abound with examples of such confusions? In that case it would not be necessary to invoke the particular intervention of the Almighty. . . . You must not think, my son,' he added indulgently, 'that a profusion of qualities and talents such as yours is sufficient to bring about such a rare phenomenon as a miracle . . . which is one of the most awesome manifestations of our Lord and one of the most firmly established articles of our doctrine.'

'Do you really think, Monseigneur, that it would be a sin of pride, in this particular case, to believe in a miracle?'

There was a strange note in his voice. It was as though an affirmative answer would have relieved his conscience. The bishop looked vexed and pondered further.

'I cannot give you a definite opinion at once, my son, but, to be quite frank, I fear so. Set your mind at rest, however. I can see you are sincere, and outward appearances have deceived wiser men than you. The saints themselves have sometimes been the victims of hallucinations! I think we shall have to wait for further testimonies, besides yours and that of two innocent souls, before being able to entertain—and then only with the utmost caution—the possibility of direct intervention. Just think, my son—under your hands! In your church!'

'Yes,' the priest echoed contritely. 'Under my hands, in my church, in this day and age! I have thought about that too all night.'

'And what about the man himself? You told me he was not in possession of all his faculties. Was he not himself the victim of an hallucination? A fit of temporary insanity?'

'He can see,' said Father Montoire almost dejectedly. 'He can see and he has recovered his reason. This very morning I received a long message from him describing his joy and assuring me of his eternal gratitude.'

'I advise you to meditate further, calmly and dispassionately,' the Bishop went on after a short silence, 'and if necessary have a good rest. You look overwrought. Above all, wait for Doctor Faivre's conclusions. When he has examined the young man again, you'll see he will admit he made a mistake in his diagnosis at the outset. Go in peace. I shall pray to God to restore your serenity.'

As he left the bishop's residence, Father Montoire made a thorough examination of his conscience. The event having receded a little in his memory, he was beginning to doubt his own senses. His superior's words of wisdom had calmed him a little. He managed to convince himself that he had been deceived by appearances and felt deeply relieved in consequence. He decided not to postpone his visit to Doctor Faivre any longer.

'After all,' he reflected, as he rang his friend's front-door bell, 'at the foot of this business there are physical and material facts. The important thing is to study them carefully before coming to any conclusion.'

As soon as he saw the priest's cassock in the waiting-room, Doctor Faivre rushed over towards him, and, with a muttered apology to his patients, ushered him into his office ahead of them. His manner contrasted strangely with his usual composure. He gave his friend no time to explain his action.

'I've been waiting for you impatiently. You've come, I assume, about Jean Courtal. His mother brought him round here yesterday evening. It's the most extraordinary case I have ever come across in the whole of my career, and I still haven't recovered from the shock. Now listen: you know that science is often mistaken. I am not one of its fanatical apostles. I have sometimes made mistakes myself and I've always admitted them. In many cases all we medical men are able to say is "perhaps" or "probably".'

The doctor paused, then went on somewhat solemnly:

'In this case, however, there is not the slightest chance of a mistake, I swear. On his discharge from hospital, where all the doctors considered him incurable, I took a personal interest in Jean Courtal, since his mother, as I told you, is an old family servant of ours and her despair had touched me. I had him examined by several of my colleagues, the most qualified experts alive. No case was ever investigated with such meticulous attention. Well, we all came to the same opinion: the boy *could not see*. There was an absolute material impediment. I don't want to go into long explanations now—I'm saving that for the report I intend to submit to the Academy —but he could not see, I tell you! The essential organs of sight had not only been affected, they were actually destroyed; they didn't exist.

'I have just notified two of these colleagues, who have a clear recollection of their examination. They are as impressed

56

as I am. As doctors, we can say only this: no scientific explanation can be given for this cure. I leave it to you, as a priest, to draw your conclusions. But in the face of this event, which to my comprehension is *impossible,* I am forced to acknowledge supernatural intervention and to state: this is a miracle.'

'A miracle!' exclaimed Father Montoire.

He was unable to suppress a protest. He still had in mind the words of the bishop and the objections of his own instinct. The doctor, who was more and more perturbed, paid no attention but continued excitedly:

'Yes, a miracle. No man in his proper senses could deny it. You can count on me to produce the most convincing testimonies. In the face of such a wonderful cure, I can conceive of no other cause than Him whom you serve, of no other instrument than the power of faith which attracted His attention to a luckless creature.'

'The power of faith,' the priest echoed mechanically.

'There's a great deal more I could say. For me, this sign has been a revelation. I must confess I'm a changed man and I can see I shall have to revise most of my opinions. Up to now I've been what is commonly called a free-thinker—not an atheist but a sceptic. No proof seemed to me sufficiently convincing, and I did not believe in the possibility of discovering the truth in the realm of metaphysics. I feel I must make honourable amends. Today I am in the throes of such emotion that I can't express myself clearly. I must first of all sort out my thoughts. If I may, I'll come and see you in a few days and have a long talk with you.'

The priest looked at him with amazement, unable to ward off a feeling of dread. He stammered a few words of thanks. In a confused way he realized that this conversion ought to be regarded as a further example of divine intervention, but he could not praise the Lord as he should have done and felt himself plunged again into agonizing uncertainty.

He made his way home on foot. As he walked along, he kept recalling the scene which haunted him. His priesthood and studies had accustomed him to spiritual self-examination. He called upon all the resources of religion and his own experience and intelligence in an attempt to reach some conclusion which would satisfy both his heart and his mind. Once again he went over every detail of the marvel and reviewed all the circumstances, recollecting with merciless lucidity the qualms of conscience that had assailed him.

'The woman begged me . . . I yielded against my will, out of pity and weakness. At the moment I held out my hands and called upon Thy holy name, O God, I asked for Thy forgiveness as though for a sacrilege. I cannot hide anything from Thee. . . . Did I have faith? Alas, not for a second did I acknowledge that Thou mightest vouchsafe my prayer!

'His face was expressionless, his eyes lifeless—not a glimmer of reason. And all of a sudden his eyelids started quivering under my finger. . . . There was no other intermediary apart from myself. And at the moment his eyes came to life, at that very moment, I who have preached to convince sceptics, who have invoked the deepest arguments of heart and reason to provoke confidence in Thine infinite power—in Thy very presence I doubted. Now once more I beseech Thee, make me aware of this miracle, which stirs no embers in my soul!'

4

Father Montoire slipped out of the church furtively but was recognized by the crowd of cripples who were on the look-out for him. This was the moment for which they were waiting, to fasten on him and beg him to invoke God's mercy on their behalf.

Three months had elapsed since the healing of the blind man. It had been whispered abroad that the priest performed miracles. Every evening, whatever precautions he took to pass unnoticed, he was harassed by dozens of unfortunates who had been waiting several hours for him to appear. Each day his torment became more unbearable.

This evening the agony that seized him at the sight of suppliant cripples was intolerable. They clung to his cassock and refused to let go. They were not content with words of consolation, not satisfied with promises of prayer. Each of them clamoured for the priest to take him by the hand and lead him to the foot of the altar, where the Almighty had manifested Himself. Each of them demanded that he lay his hands on his affliction, order him to be cured and call upon Providence to witness his personal distress.

He tried to turn away from them. Could he, without impiety, be party to a ceremony which still seemed to him to be a criminal parody? Dare he again imitate the sacred gestures of Christ and the greatest of His elect? The boundaries between superstition and religion seemed to him to be less clearly defined. Would he have the audacity to repeat ten or twenty times more the procedure that filled him with terror and which his superiors censured?

The bishop had let him know that these manifestations were not viewed with a favourable eye. After Doctor Faivre's conclusions, which had been confirmed by his most learned colleagues, after the report forwarded to the Academy, in which the physicians submitted proofs of a supernatural cure, the prelate's scepticism had been only feebly shaken. He had referred the case to Rome where, after being received with suspicion, it was now being thoroughly examined in view of the priest's reputation and the weighty scientific attestations. While waiting for the papal decision, the bishop maintained the greatest reserve.

The priest raised his head and tried to slip away. The plaints of the cripples grew more urgent. He was now assailed by different scruples, and the sting of doubt pierced through to the deepest levels of his conscience.

Supposing, after all, God had really chosen him, unworthy though he was, to magnify His glory? Supposing it was a true, an authentic miracle? How then could he refuse to repeat, for the sake of these simple trusting souls, the gestures and invocation which had already brought about Divine intervention? To shirk the issue was a token of the basest ingratitude. Was it not tantamount to denying God's goodness? Was this not the sinful course?

Reluctantly he yielded once more to supplications that were past bearing. He seized one of the unfortunates who was walking on crutches. He dragged him into the church, flung him down at the foot of the altar and stretched out his hands, uttering the presumptuous words. No sign was given. The supernatural power had not revealed itself again since the healing of the blind man. The priest stood ashamed and distraught, his hands laid on the lifeless leg. Already the others were jostling one another to take his place.

They all filed past. Chained to his original miracle, he had to follow this Via Dolorosa to the end. He laid his hands on every sore and every deformity. He had developed a horror of this place at the foot of the altar. At the sight of each fresh woe he had to make a superhuman effort not to curse the artless, senseless trust of these creatures; not to reproach them, as though for an outlandish absurdity, for this blind faith that caused him such unbearable torment; to explain, with feigned benevolence, that miracles were exceptional favours; not to proclaim his sham out loud when, at the moment of the laying on of hands, he perceived a gleam of desperate hope in their eyes; and to dismiss them with a few words of consolation when, having failed as he expected, he saw their features darken and their faces suddenly grow pale with distress and resentment.

He had managed to control his expression of disgust and repulsion until the end of the procession. Twenty times and more he had repeated the vain gesture and pronounced the empty words. The last to come forward was a woman. She had no visible affliction. She approached him shyly, and with the utmost reticence asked him to pray to God to allow her to become a mother. He was startled by the utterance of such an extravagant request and fled, almost running, unable to restrain tears of humiliation and despair.

He went home by way of the back streets, hanging his head, tortured by the thought of being recognized, as had happened several times, for, as a result of the enthusiasm of his followers, he was becoming something of a celebrity.

At home, as was his habit every evening, he pondered over Doctor Faivre's report. The latter had brought it to him in person, on the day he had come and announced his decision to accept religion and appealed to him as a friend whom he now looked upon as his spiritual adviser.

He had derived no joy from this striking conversion. He had avidly immersed himself in the report. He had asked for further information on countless points, not content to grasp merely the general sense of the text, but eager to apprehend the exact meaning of every term. The comments of his learned friend had not satisfied him.

Thereupon, such was his ardent desire to have everything crystal-clear in his mind, such was his urgency to dispel the mists of uncertainty, that he secretly bought himself some medical books and specialized works dealing with the organs of sight. He was seized by a sort of delirium and imagined, without daring to admit it, that he could succeed on his own where all the authorities had acknowledged defeat, that he could find a rational, scientific explanation for the phenomenon. He spent hours every night studying these works with feverish anxiety. But the further he progressed in this new branch of learning and the more acquainted he became with the mechanics of eyesight, the more his reason had to recognize that Jean Courtal's cure was impossible and the more he persisted in his feverish research, growing daily more depressed by the failure of his endeavours.

This evening he could not escape the obvious conclusion that forced itself on his common sense and intelligence. He stated it out loud. 'There can be no doubt,' he said. 'It is a miracle.'

He put away his books and composed himself for prayer, resting his head in his hands and straining to find words of praise in keeping with the immensity of the favour that he had been accorded. After a short time he was unable to continue praying. In spite of himself he was still trying to find a natural explanation.

His mind was now obsessed by the exceptional combinations of atoms which modern science considers theoretically possible and which are comprehensible in mathematical terms but which cannot occur spontaneously except by a chance so improbable as to be practically out of the question in the Universe as we know it. Only fifty years ago certain scientists believed that cellular generation could be attributed to the haphazard interplay of physico-chemical reactions.

He recollected the words of his own sermon. Only a supranatural will could account for such improbable coincidences—equivalent, in human terms, to miracles. He had said so himself. This was the view of the greatest scientific authorities alive. . . . Yet an exception was always theoretically possible.

He felt his reason wandering in a maze of figures and statistical rules. Instinctively he tried to remember the ludicrously small percentage which a scientist had calculated to express the fortuitous synthesis of the most elementary of cells. His mind reeled as he thought of the billions of differentiated cells involved in the apparatus of sight. He finally acknowledged the absurdity of this last hope. It was the most fantastic, the wildest hypothesis he had formed.

Every branch of science led fatally to the conclusion of a divine miracle. From the pulpit he had spoken of the so-called conflict between doctrine and reason. Here, reason afforded the strongest evidence.

He passed his hand across his brow, which was streaming with sweat, and laboriously uttered a painful prayer of thanks.

He was preparing to go to bed, still without having found the peace of mind he sought, when he received a message summoning him to the bishop in the morning.

5

No sooner had he entered the bishop's residence than he noticed a change in the attitude of the prelate's staff. On each of his previous visits he had been conscious of a feeling of distrust verging on outright hostility, which contrasted strangely with the blind faith of the masses and affected him just as painfully. Today the senior assistant priest rushed to welcome him as soon as he was announced, manifesting a cordiality mingled with a hint of respect.

'I gather Monseigneur has some splendid news for you,' he

said. 'He will want to tell you personally, but, believe me, I'm also overjoyed.'

He had no time to say more, for just then the bishop sent for Father Montoire.

The prelate rose to his feet as he came in and stopped him as he made as though to fall on his knees. He gazed at him with eyes in which admiration was mingled with a quizzical curiosity. He remained silent for a long time. He seemed to be debating a problem of capital importance without being able to bring himself to ask an essential question. Eventually he spoke, with a paradoxical note of deference in his voice:

'My son, I have splendid news for you. I know it will fill you with joy and I am happy to be the first to inform you.

'I have received a long letter from Rome on the question of the healing of Jean Courtal. Your qualities and accomplishments are viewed with an extremely benevolent eye. The marvel has been examined, analysed by the most learned experts of the Church. All the circumstances have been carefully weighed, and the observations of the medical authorities have been the subject of extensive investigation. The conclusion of the Holy Father is that this healing has every appearance of being a divine miracle. He has not yet made an official announcement—you know how careful the Church has to be in such matters—but from the tone of the letter I think it extremely likely that he will do so very soon. He has directed me to let you know that he is keeping his eyes on you.

'Let us therefore rejoice, my son. It is an immense favour that our Lord has granted you, and well deserved on account of your uncommon qualities. The glory it confers on you reflects a little on all of us ministers of God.'

'Monseigneur,' stammered the priest, hanging his head. . . .

Far from experiencing any sense of joy and pride, he felt actively distressed, as though this striking confirmation from his supreme spiritual authority had dealt him a final blow.

'Monseigneur, I must accuse myself. . . . At the moment I called upon His holy name, I did not admit the possibility of His intervention. I had no faith!'

The bishop continued to gaze at him, without manifesting either surprise or indignation. Eventually he spoke in a tone of paternal authority.

'His designs are impenetrable, my son. I had already guessed from your attitude. I shall be equally candid with you. I did not for a moment believe it was a miracle when you first told me about it. I did not believe it until the decision of the Holy Father. I too have sinned through lack of faith. And, to open my heart still wider to you, if I had found myself in the

62

sort of situation in which you were placed, I think I should have felt the same doubts and reservations. God has chosen this occasion to teach us both a lesson, by showing us the lowliness of our condition and the value of simple faith in a humble servant. Let us join in giving thanks to Him for His mercy and for this revelation which has opened our eyes—ours too, blind that we were!'

Father Montoire hesitated for a moment without speaking; then he flung himself weeping at the bishop's feet.

'But I myself am not yet convinced, Monseigneur! I still doubt. After having seen with my own eyes, after having touched with my own hands, I did not truly believe in His presence! When science provided me with irrefutable proofs, I found myself distrusting science! I studied the question independently on my own. I exhausted myself trying to find a fallacy in the observations and arguments. Being unable to find any, I began to doubt my own judgement. I denied the power of the spirit! And today, Monseigneur—oh, what devil inhabits my soul! What sort of creature am I? What sort of priest, more contemptible than the most contemptible atheist! Today, when the highest confirmation has been granted me, when this miracle has been acknowledged by the Vicar of Christ himself, this miracle which is enforced on me by common sense, reason, faith, obedience, this miracle, which I brought about, which I experienced, I, a minister of God, unworthy wretch that I am—I, at least, cannot believe it!'

THE PERFECT ROBOT

As Professor Fontaine came into the board room, the eyes of all the directors converged on the corrugated and voluminous cranium that housed the Company's most precious assets.

'Well?' the Board anxiously enquired.

A flame of triumph glittered in the old scientist's eyes.

'*Eureka*, gentlemen,' was all he said.

A tremor of relief went down the green baize table, and the prince of science was asked to report on his findings.

In its early days the EBC (Electronic Brain Company) used to manufacture modest calculating machines capable of carrying out simple arithmetical operations. The scope of these machines had been enormously enlarged, and their ingenuity had reached a degree of perfection unequalled by any rival concern, ever since the EBC had obtained the full-time services of Professor Fontaine, one of the most expert and enthusiastic pioneers of the young science of cybernetics.

After the directors had voted him a princely salary and installed him in a laboratory equipped with the latest research apparatus, the scientist, sheltered from all material worry, had devoted himself to the study of robots with the combination of patience, audacity, lucidity and imagination of which his genius was composed.

He had first concentrated on improving the old calculating machines. As a result of his endeavours these had contrived to carry out simultaneously and with absolute accuracy a multitude of complicated operations involving thousands of figures and in a progressively shorter space of time. At this heroic period there had been fierce rivalry in this field and competitions were held every year at which the companies' various models came to grips. Thanks to Professor Fontaine's ingenuity, the EBC had always outclassed its rivals and its machines had established records which were expressed in millions of figures worked out in a fraction of a second.

In fact there appeared to be no theoretical limit to the performances accomplished by the professor's machines. The Board of Directors had had to confine him to a ceiling, above which the results were too abundant to be put to practical use. Once this ceiling was reached, the machines of the other companies had slowly attained it. But long before they did so, the scientist had immersed himself in fresh researches, no longer aimed at perfecting the old machines but at creating others, capable of solving problems of a more delicate nature than arithmetical operations.

He had obtained such results that the EBC's publicity had long since ceased to refer to 'calculation' and instead used the word 'thought'.

This claim had given rise to heated controversy. The objectors asserted that the most ingenious achievements in the field of cybernetics would always remain mechanical, that's to say they would never be able to solve anything but problems whose solution was explicitly or implicitly contained in the data. The machine, they said, combines the elements of these data and reproduces them in a different form known as result or conclusion. It was merely a 'formal' transformation and in no way a creative process comparable to that of the human mind.

But to this Professor Fontaine replied that properly speaking there was no such thing as 'creation', since this word should *always* be understood in the sense of 'combination' or potential rearrangement of former facts. According to him, in all operations of the human mind the solution or outcome was *always* contained, at least implicitly, in previous data. The brain had never done otherwise than modify the disposition of these data and present them in a new aspect. Consequently, between the aforesaid human brain and the artificial electronic brain there was a difference only of quality and not of nature. By a systematic improvement of the machine, he claimed, one would eventually be able to obtain all the manifestations generally regarded as being within the exclusive realm of intellect.

In support for this thesis he quoted several examples taken from extremely varied branches of human activity, frequently stretching his argument to the point of absurd paradox, and occasionally indulging in a childish play on words. He claimed, for instance, that there existed no difference in 'substance' between primary education and secondary, the latter being merely a modification in form of the former, just as, in an electric transformer, the energy of the 'secondary' circuit

65

is equal to that of the 'primary' in a new guise. Similarly, he saw in higher education a third presentation of the same fact and asserted that the three so-called degrees of mind corresponding to these three classes were differentiated only by their capacity to combine severally the immediate data of sensory knowledge.

He added:

'The number of cells in a human brain being finite, whereas the number of the circuits in a machine is unlimited, mere calculation of probabilities shows that machines will one day attain more complicated forms of arrangement than those within the scope of the human mind, and therefore more profound speculations and original "creations" (as you call them) exceeding human capacity.'

This postulate being acknowledged, he had set to work, both to verify his theories by practical experiment and to satisfy the demands of the Board of Directors of the EBC.

His first robot superior to the calculating machine was a scientific curiosity which gave him intense personal satisfaction but which enjoyed only mediocre success with the customers. It was a 'mathematician' and not a mere calculator. It was furnished, by means of a series of knobs and levers, with the fundamental postulates, the definition of the numbers and the symbols of analysis. Various electronic circuits combined these data and it then entered upon the multiple branches of this science, extending its deductions in each branch as far as the latest conclusions formulated by the greatest mathematical minds, and rediscovering the most famous theorems. By means of more and more complicated permutations and arrangements of the data, it had even reached the stage of stating theorems that had never before been formulated, the accuracy of which had been verified *a posteriori* but the demonstration of which had defeated the leading authorities.

Professor Fontaine's opponents had maintained that the so-called 'new' theorems had existed for all eternity in the basic axioms and definitions, in which point they were in agreement with the scientist. But they added that mathematical analysis, being precisely the science of formal transformations, involved only a minute and purely mechanical fraction of the intellect. The robot mathematician provided no proof as to the actual intelligence of a machine. The professor had shrugged his shoulders and pursued his research.

Since his employers wanted models capable of rousing widespread interest by means of spectacular demonstrations, he had concentrated his prodigious faculties on the game of chess. Several authorities on cybernetics had already been drawn to this subject, and some special situations, carefully prepared, which were played out with only three or four chessmen in a succession of well defined moves, had already been solved successfully by machines. This was obviously elementary. The genius of Professor Fontaine lay in tackling the problem as a whole.

That the so-called Maelzel automaton was a fake and that in actual fact a human being was concealed in the mechanical body, the Professor had readily admitted. The state of science at the time at which Maelzel was working led inevitably to this conclusion. But that the principle of the invention was Utopian, that a machine capable of playing chess was inconceivable, the scientist had fiercely denied. During the period of cogitation that preceded his undertaking, he had applied himself to destroying the arguments put forward against the possibility of such an achievement, reproving their authors for an unforgivable confusion between the qualifications 'infinite' and 'immensely large', accusing them of applying the former term implicitly and erroneously to the combinations of a game of chess.

Addressing his inner demon of contradiction, which permanently haunted him as it haunts all scientific minds, Professor Fontaine had said:

'Consider a game of chess at a given stage, which I call the 'initial moment'. It is White to play. The sum total of possible moves is high, I don't deny. But you must agree with me that it is finite and perfectly determined. To verify this, you need only take each white chessman one after the other and number the squares to which they can move according to the rules of the game. You must admit there's nothing simpler than to visualize a machine designed to carry out this purely mechanical operation.

'It is now Black to play. As *several* possible moves of the black chessmen correspond to *each* possible move of the white ones, it is obvious that the number of possible combinations after the second move is considerable. It is none the less obvious, however, that being the product of two perfectly determined factors, this number is likewise *finite*.

'Progressing by degrees, let us pass straight on, if you don't mind, to the nth move. You will see that the number of possible arrangements for the chessmen, albeit immensely large, and being expressed by a numerical symbol covering several pages, remains in every case absolutely definite. To say that the nth move depends entirely on the whim or skill of the player is a gross error. The latter has only the choice between a large number of determined moves and, after he has made a move, the consequent position is none other than a selection from an ineluctably fixed total.'

In his subsequent reasoning, the scientist enlarged ingeniously on the meaning of the word 'necessity.'

'So far,' he went on, 'I have considered all the combinations compatible with the displacement of the chessmen and the position of the squares. Now imagine a game between two beginners who know only the elementary moves. You will perceive that this total is already reduced by the tendency of both players to avoid a manifestly and immediately dangerous position such as would gratuitously place the queen in jeopardy or stupidly lay open the king. You call this the human factor. I say—and if you think it over, you'll readily agree—that the volition of the player in the act of eliminating these manifestly risky moves, which are characterized by a limited number of definite positions, may well be replaced, as to its effect, by a machine. A necessity of a mechanical order will take the place of the impulse induced by elementary prudence. The *law* will automatically avoid any combination resulting in the *immediate* loss of the game.

'Now observe two expert players. The number of favourable combinations is limited in a far higher proportion by what you call their skill and which is again related, I maintain, to a sort of mechanical necessity, even though this characteristic is less distinct than in the first case—the necessity of avoiding disaster in the future which does not appear clearly to the beginner because his brain is not trained to consider a large number of positions. This necessity will reveal itself to him only after the fifth move, for instance, but it is nevertheless contained in its entirety, in a potential state, in the fatal moves. If the opponents are first-class players, the limitation of their judgement will be even more pronounced (the necessity more imperative), being based on the more distinct, keener perception of arrangements possible in a more distant future. If you consult a champion on this matter, he will tell you that for him there exists only a small number of advantageous moves—what I call the only moves *possible* for him as a champion.

'I maintain,' Professor Fontaine had concluded, after pondering the question at great length, 'I maintain that a superchampion, or the robot I intend to build, must in every case reduce this number of possible moves to a single one, by automatically considering all the subsequent arrangements resulting from a certain position, right up to the end of the game, and by eliminating every fatal move. I intend to construct a robot which, being furnished with data corresponding to some position or other in a game of chess, will resolve the following problem—how to determine and make *the* right move, that's to say the one which contains no potential danger of losing.'

The application of this theory had led to astonishing results. The professor had created a robot which did indeed always make the right move and invariably beat any opponent. But this success had galvanized the research workers of the rival companies. One of them, working on similar principles, had then produced a second robot as ingenious as the first which likewise made no mistakes and invariably countered *a* good move by *the* good move. It then became apparent that all the possible games of chess were reduced to a single one: the ideal game, always identical with itself, and which invariably resulted, by an identical process, in a draw. Chess had thus been deprived of a great deal of its interest and the craze for electronic players had come to an end. Professor Fontaine had re-immersed himself in his speculations to discover something new.

'Mechanical,' Professor Fontaine's opponents had said, referring to the chess-player. 'Mechanical indeed,' the scientist had readily acknowledged, 'but everything human is mechanical—language, for instance.' And without heeding the sarcastic remarks that had ridiculed these claims or the songs that celebrated the coming of a robot-writer, he had gone more deeply into this idea by thrashing it out with his own demon.

'For the time being,' he had said, 'there is no question of composing a story, even though this should not be dismissed as a future possibility. . . . We shall make a modest start and confine ourselves to a few short sentences.

'It is not particularly difficult to imagine a machine capable of producing words. Words are only combinations, finite in number, of consonants and vowels, and their synthesis may be reduced to a purely mechanical operation starting from an initial letter. Consider a robot which is furnished with data consisting of a very large number of these consonants and vowels. It is child's play to imagine an apparatus connecting every word in the language to the machine and in such a way that all non-existing combinations of letters are automatically eliminated. Supposing that the first circuit happens to start off with the letter *s*. A second circuit then comes into action and proposes *d* as the second letter. The combination *sd* is impossible as the first two letters of a word. It will be rejected by the apparatus, the *d* will be discarded, and the machine will successively suggest other letters until one of these is admissible. If *h* is suggested it will be admitted. The combination *sh* will be selected; further circuits will yield a third letter, and so on. Starting from the fortuitous initial letter, then proceeding by trial and error and without intervention from the human mind, the robot will compose a group necessarily corresponding to an existing word beginning with *sh*—"sheep" for instance. When such a combination has thus been "found", then, and only then, will my apparatus automatically halt the process.

"It is equally easy to imagine specialized compartments for the formation of nouns, adjectives, verbs, articles and other parts of speech, singulars and plurals, persons and tenses. We may then conceive a second stage at which an initial conjunction of words will be made. If the noun "sheep" has been chosen, it is obviously within the possibilities of a mechanism to combine it with a grammatically suitable article and adjective —to select, for instance, phrases such as "the fluid sheep", or "the sombre sheep" or "the white sheep", to the exclusion of any that conflict with the strict rules of agreement in gender and number. Up to this point we have encountered no difficulty. . . .

' "The fluid sheep" doesn't make sense,' interjected the demon of contradiction.

'Let me go on. Everything in its own time. We shall not find much more difficulty at the following stage, which will see the complete construction of a simple sentence in agreement with the rules of syntax, which are determined and which a machine can apply just as well as and even better than a human brain. We shall thus see the formation of a certain number of grammatically correct phrases such as "the fluid sheep flies under the pointed sky", or "the white sheep eats grass". . . .'

'That's what I'm getting at,' the demon once more broke in. 'Most of your sentences, though grammatically correct as you say, will be absurd.'

'They will be irreproachable from the point of view of construction. That's the essential point, which I wanted to make you admit. Among them there are bound to be some that will make sense. We shall then only need to proceed with a fresh selection. This is where my theory of "primary truths" comes in.'

'Primary truths?'

'Follow closely. The problem is of the same order as that of the game of chess, albeit slightly more subtle.

'In this case it's a question of eliminating any expression that is meaningless. You think perhaps this is beyond the capacities of a machine? Nothing of the sort. Every meaning is merely a transformation of a previous meaning. The most erudite pronouncement is merely a permutation of the elementary findings of a primary pronouncement. Proceeding by degrees, we arrive at a statement of fact, or what I call a

70

"primary truth". These are limited in number and may well be electronically connected to the selective organs of a machine which, after carrying out the necessary permutation, will ruthlessly eliminate from the expressions it is given anything that conflicts with any of these statements or even anything that is not connected with any of them. Only the sentences which really make sense will be produced. I maintain that the human mind does not proceed in any other way when it tries to express itself.'

The professor had built his machine. The construction of his sense selector had seemed a tricky business at first. But in the process of determining the primary truths, he had noticed that their number was less great than he had supposed. It needed only a suitable classification to reduce them all to a few fundamental axioms such as 'A is A' or 'A is not non-A', and to a small number of immediate sense perceptions. Starting from these data alone, and by combining them, the machine managed to discern any expression that did not make sense. Thus sentences such as 'the fluid sheep flies under the pointed sky' or 'the white sheep eats veal' were eliminated. Partial groups such as 'fluid sheep' or 'pointed sky' were discarded by a preliminary selector. A verb like 'fly' or an outlandish complement like 'veal' were rejected by the final apparatus, until finally there appeared a combination such as 'the white sheep walks under the blue sky' or 'a white sheep eats grass', statements which were compatible with all the primary truths and which the robot produced automatically.

The ingenious professor had devoted several years to perfecting his electronic writer.

' "Progress" in this field,' he explained, 'consists in obtaining expressions which, even though being transformations of primary truths, as they all are, carefully conceal this fact under the complexity or the originality of their construction, thereby demanding a lengthy process of unravelling to arrive at the source.'

Thus it was that, having started from statements of fact such as 'the white sheep is white', then, after being given the translation of the various data in several languages, having continued with *Ego sum qui sum*, the robot writer had gradually elaborated its expressions and managed to produce more complex statements. It had produced: *'Ex nihilo nihil fit'*, 'The cat eats the mouse', 'Nevertheless it turns', 'I think, therefore I am', and one day, which was a red-letter day for Professor Fontaine, 'To be or not to be, that is the question'.

The scientist's rivals having likewise contrived to build robot writers, and the EBC still wishing to maintain its lead in this field, he had attempted to reproduce other features of human activity by mechanical means. Since circulation, respiration, alimentation and digestion had long since been achieved by machines, he had aimed higher and made an intensive study of the laws of sexual attraction and of the biological factors, considered as initial data, which had as their outcome the carnal act. He had concluded that there was nothing to prevent robots from having sexual intercourse.

He had given an experimental demonstration of this. Several male and female automata, which he had constructed, had been placed at random in a room. At first they had wandered about aimlessly, then, after a certain length of time, appeared to be attracted one to another as though by a magnetic force. The attraction always occurred between robots of the opposite sex, and the couples went through the movements of sexual intercourse with a realism which caused intense emotion among the directors of the EBC when they first witnessed the spectacle. For these automata, to which he had given a human aspect, not only imitated to perfection all the attitudes of living creatures but also, as he had foreseen, invented new combinations thanks to the subtle complexity of the electronic brain which controlled their movements.

As Professor Fontaine foresaw, these latest achievements were to lead in the long run to 'sentiment'. But above all they gave him the idea for a new machine which would mark one of the most important stages of cybernetics, by reducing to nought the objections of its everlasting detractors.

'Your mechanisms,' the latter said in so many words, 'are the most ingenious in the world, we don't deny it. But they merely testify to your scientific knowledge, to your inventive genius. All the qualifications of these robots must be attributed to you, who created them. As we have always maintained, they prove the power of human intellect and nothing else.'

The professor had then had the brainwave of constructing a robot capable of engendering other robots. He had succeeded, as in everything else he had so far attempted. Combining this new invention with the previous one, he had constructed a machine in the depths of which, after sexual intercourse, there developed a cell which grew and multiplied by a mechanical process, became the foetus of a robot, was born and grew up, eventually appearing as a machine similar to its parents.

When he had verified this marvel, the professor had intoned a hymn of victory, but his opponents had not declared themselves beaten. They had said:

72

'It's all very well, but the creator of this uterus is still you —you, a human being.'

Then the scientist had constructed a machine capable itself of engendering a uterus and, to save time and forestall a lot of pointless argument, he had straight away created a robot capable of perpetuating itself indefinitely through an unlimited series of descendants. After which, at a conference which had made history, he had demonstrated beyond all shadow of doubt that any term in this series was strictly equivalent to zero in relation to the infinite succession of future creatures, that, since his own role could not be eliminated, the creative spirit should consequently be attributed to the robot considered as an eternal entity.

His detractors had been unable to think of any reasonable objection to this demonstration. They had not admitted defeat, however, and had taken refuge behind the inexpressible. They had shaken their heads and stubbornly declared:

'Call them anything you like, but your robots are not human. They lack some element or other which we are unable to define but of which we sense the absence.'

At this, Professor Fontaine had been deeply disturbed. His own demon of contradiction, never so powerful as at this time, kept repeating over and over again:

'They're right. Your robots are not human. They lack some indefinable characteristic.'

He had feverishly set to work again and, with a final effort, had succeeded in creating a sort of mechanism, the successive generations of which 'evolved'. This evolution, which followed a strict course, was slow but nevertheless perceptible thanks to the extreme speed of reproduction which the scientist had bestowed on the species. In this way he artificially obtained robot birds from robot reptiles, robot mammals from robot fish, and robot men from robot primates, without any intervention on his part other than the initial regulation of the mechanism. He went further. Starting from robot men, and by combining the organs in two different ways, he produced two species, which evolved in a clear-cut manner, on the one hand towards Good, on the other towards Evil.

After performing these miracles, the professor once again questioned his inner demon.

'You're not there yet,' the latter replied.

It then looked as though the genius of Professor Fontaine had reached its limits. Several years went by, during which he exhausted himself in fruitless endeavours to take a step forward and eliminate the subtle difference which still separated, as he was now convinced, his machines from human beings. The Board of Directors of the EBC were worried at not seeing any fresh marvels emerge from his laboratory which was once so fecund, and some of them began to mutter that he was somewhat too old to hold such an important position.

This year, at last, breaking a long silence, the scientist had declared he had an announcement of the greatest importance to make. The Board had met.

'*Eureka,*' the professor said again.

'Go on,' said the Board with bated breath.

'I have found,' the scientist translated.

'Yes, but what?' the Board enquired.

'The ideal machine. The human machine. The solution was there all the time, staring me in the face, within the reach of the veriest ignoramus. It had escaped me!'

'Go on, go on!' said the Board.

'Listen, gentlemen,' said the man of science in a voice trembling with emotion. 'No one can have any further objection to raise against my robots. I now possess the secret which will crown my career of arduous labour and meditation. I can give you palpable proof of my theories. My machine now acts exactly like a human being. It "thinks" like a human being. It possesses an intellect similar to our own. This characteristic was already contained at the latent stage in all my previous inventions. It needed only a minute detail, which was too simple—that's why it had escaped me. To endow my robots with this indefinable quality which they still lacked, gentlemen, I merely had to . . .'

'What?' yelped the Board.

'*Sabotage* them, gentlemen,' the prince of science bellowed in triumph.

'Sabotage them!' exclaimed the Board, dreadfully disillusioned and convinced that their great man had taken leave of his senses.

'Sabotage them,' Professor Fontaine insisted vehemently. 'That's what I've done. I have *unhinged* them. Do you understand? My calculators, for instance, now make mistakes. They no longer invariably give the accurate answer. Do you follow? They go wrong. They only occasionally produce a correct solution.'

This announcement was greeted by a long contemptuous silence. Then the Board thought it over and asked to see the prototypes. Professor Fontaine produced them. He first of all showed his calculating machines which gave wrong results. At this sight the more sensitive directors experienced an incipient pang of emotion.

But the enthusiasm grew general and turned to delirium when the scientist exhibited his other models, which he had built according to the same principle. So much so that when

74

he had revealed the prodigiously 'human' characteristics with which they had been endowed, the Board, ashamed of ever having doubted him, apologized profusely to Professor Fontaine and unanimously voted the necessary funds for the mass production of the perfect robots.

The mathematician went astray in a maze of contradictions and only exceptionally arrived at an answer. The chess player lost most of the games it played. The robots in love confused the sexes. The evolutive species oscillated between incoherent states, so that it was impossible to tell if they tended towards Good or Evil.

As for the electronic writer, Professor Fontaine had merely had to do away with its primary truth mechanism, its sense selector, for it to produce to its heart's content such sentences as 'The fluid sheep flies under the pointed sky' or 'the white sheep eats veal', manifestations to which the fiercest detractors were obliged to yield, acknowledging at last the appearance of the final human characteristics that were still lacking: an artistic sense and a sense of humour.

THE ENIGMATIC SAINT

1

The stranger reached the precincts of the lazar house just as the sun was setting on the plain. He climbed the slope of the Montagne-aux-Malades with a faltering step, sometimes dragging himself along, with his shoulders drooping and his head hanging, as though he was exhausted, at other times holding himself tall and erect and quickening his pace. He then seemed to dominate his fatigue by a fierce effort of will which strained his features, as though it was a matter of capital importance for him to reach his journey's end without delay. In spite of the heat he wore a robe of brown wool which came down to his ankles. His face was streaked with dust and sweat. When he drew level with the cross marking the entrance to the leper colony, he sat down on a stone, dropped his pilgrim's staff and the meagre bundle dangling from it, and remained motionless for a moment, panting for breath.

A second later he was on his feet again, his body casting a long shadow on the ground parallel to that of the cross, his eyes gleaming, his emaciated face with its prominent cheekbones suddenly flushed with animation. Some distance away, outside the enclosure surrounding the monastery and the little community, he had caught sight of Brother Rose who was watching the sun set while waiting to ring the bell for Vespers.

Brother Rose and the Prior were the only two monks left in the leper colony. Leprosy kills slowly, as the physician Jehan Maillard was wont to say; but in the end it had got the better of all the other monks except those who had died of old age. The ones who had come here at the time of the foundation of the colony, in the reign of the saintly King Louis, were all deceased, and for ages no one had applied to replace them. Brother Rose was one of the last recruits. He had arrived as a young man at the beginning of the century. He had contracted leprosy only after a lapse of several years and his robust peasant constitution withstood the disease manfully. Even now, at the age of sixty, he was not yet seriously affected by it, although the marks were clearly visible on his face and hands. Still brisk and spry, he was the indispensable man of the colony. He assisted the Prior at the services, tolled the hours, looked after the bed-ridden patients, carried the doctor's medicines, attended to the upkeep of the farmland and also buried the dead, since leprosy killed slowly, granted, but none the less regularly.

The stranger crossed the boundary marked by the cross, under the astonished gaze of Brother Rose, and hastened towards him. He stopped suddenly some distance away and at the same time his features assumed a strange expression of discomfiture and frustration; recognizing the monk's habit and scapular, he seemed to be disappointed at coming upon someone he had not expected. On closer inspection, however, he discerned in Brother Rose's face the signs which were unmistakable at this epoch: the swollen eyelids and brows, the thickened lips, the dilated nose, the forehead polished like horn and the scalp covered in bran-like scabs. Thereupon, at the sight of these symptoms which provoked horror and disgust everywhere, he appeared to recover his spirits; the gleam in his eye reappeared and a strange exaltation once more mantled his cheeks.

He took two steps toward the monk who, to halt him, stretched out an emaciated hand. He was in no way intimidated by this gesture but continued to advance with a haste which might have alarmed the worthy brother if fear of an untoward misadventure could have existed in the heart of a leper on the Montagne-aux-Malades.

The stranger clearly harboured no evil intent. He went up to Brother Rose, fell down on one knee before him, seized his hands, raised them to his lips and kissed them with fervour. The monk, once his initial stupefaction was over, struggled free and took a step backwards, once again stretching out his hand.

'Withdraw, stranger! Don't you know you are in a lazar house? Or do you believe my habit has saved me from a contagion? I don't wear a crimson heart* or carry a rattle† be-

---

* The device which lepers had to wear on their breast.
† By means of which lepers gave warning of their approach.

cause we are among ourselves here (we never step beyond the cross and no inhabitant of the plain ever visits us) but examine my features. I am a lazar, as much of a lazar as anyone else living on these slopes.'

'I know, Brother,' the stranger replied. 'God has directed my steps toward the Montagne-aux-Malades. I have come to the lazars in full awareness and you are the first I have encountered. Give me the kiss of welcome.'

Brother Rose trembled. Accustomed to hearing only the harsh voices of the lepers, he was stirred by the stranger's, which was singularly deep and sonorous, and had a sudden intuition that this resonant tone betokened a supernatural being. The stranger once more drew closer, spreading his arms. Since this time the monk did not think of eluding him, he clasped him to his breast, laid his face against his, and planted a long kiss on his deformed lips.

Thereupon Brother Rose, dazed and enraptured by the delicious scent emanating from the stranger's breath, knew with certainty who he was. This revelation abruptly set his artless mind on fire. As soon as the man had released him from his embrace, without even pausing to pay homage, to bow before him, he turned his back on him, scurried into the leper colony and rushed towards the monastery, shouting at the top of his voice:

'A saint! A saint, Brother Prior! God has sent him to us . . . a saint!'

2

At this time, under Philippe de Valois, the lazar house of the Montagne-aux-Malades had been living for years without communication with the rest of the world. It formed a kingdom apart, ruled by its particular monarch—the unclean kingdom of leprosy, feared and hated by the sound in health. No inhabitant of the plain ever ventured up here, and if a leper had bethought himself to go down to the villages he would have been set upon. The cross at the entrance represented an impassable barrier.

Only on the arrival of a new patient, and from afar, could the lepers have a glimpse of healthy people. On that day a sort of procession, headed by the priest, would make its way up the mountain, driving the accursed man in front of it, with the irresistible strength of disgust and terror combined. Resigned to his fate, the victim meekly walked ahead and made no attempt to escape. There was no need for the pitchforks that some of the crowd brandished. He would halt at the cross and sound his brand-new rattle which sparkled in the sun while the rest stood apart and uttered high-pitched cries. Master Thomas d'Orfeuilles, the Prior, would heave a sigh as he heard this din. He would emerge from the precincts and come forward, alone, or sometimes with Brother Rose, for the villagers would not have tolerated a large gathering of lepers. From afar the priest would shout out the name of the newcomer and certify that he had celebrated the funeral service over his head. He would then give a few brief items of news and that was all; the caravan quickly turned back. Walking beside the Prior, the outcast reluctantly entered the kingdom of leprosy.

This kingdom was a universe in miniature, with its own hierarchies and social distinctions. The Prior had done his best, in the past, to break down the barriers which tended to arise between different classes of individuals, but he had long ago realized the vanity of his efforts. Maître Jehan Maillard, who was a philosopher as well as an able physician, would furnish ample reason every day to show that this structure was indispensable to the existence of any society, even one composed exclusively of lepers.

Leprosy itself was at the root of the caste system, which was based on the infinitely varied nature and diverse depth of the ravages it caused in the human organism. Those who were still only superficially affected, whose faces had merely been deformed without being eaten away, those whose flesh was not blemished by repulsive sores, formed an aristocracy which had established itself inside the precincts, round the monastery, in what was known as the *little lazar house*. They were extremely jealous of their privileges and looked upon the other patients as unclean. The latter lived in huts outside the community and their number formed the *great lazar house*. The regions they inhabited varied in height with the degree of abjection of the inmates' condition. Since the mountain was shaped more or less like a sugar cone, the result was a succession of circular zones gradually decreasing towards the summit, each one sheltering a class of lepers of a more and more hideous aspect. The last zone was sometimes known as the *high lazar house* which was synonymous with accursed region. Finally, on the summit itself, there lived an African Negro, an Abyssinian, whom some knights had brought back at the time of the last crusade and whom they had abandoned after realizing he was leprous.

Maître Jehan Maillard, who had spent some time as a student at Salerno where he had read the works of Dante, often compared the Montagne-aux-Malades to the Florentine poet's Inferno, an inferno which a malevolent demon had turned upside down, so as to point the apex of the cone towards the sky.

Among the inhabitants of the little lazar house, in the bosom of this élite, various classes had come into being which never consorted with one another; there were the *leonines*, the *canines*, the *bovines*, the *porcines*, the lepers with satyr faces and many other categories, since King Leprosy delighted in introducing among his subjects an exuberant profusion of fantastic nuances. The whole of this aristocracy lived within the precincts, never venturing outside except to supervise from afar the agricultural work, which was undertaken by the inmates of the great lazar house who were recruited, however, from the lowest region and were therefore not too repulsive. Apart from the physician, Brother Rose and occasionally the Prior, none of these privileged members of the community ever ventured into the higher regions.

Moreover, it was rare for a leper from any particular zone to venture into a higher one, where there reigned a form of leprosy more hideous than his own. It was even more rare for the opposite to happen. When by chance it did, the intruder abided, in respect to the inhabitants, by the rules imposed in the healthy world on all lepers; that's to say he was required to announce his presence from afar and avoid approaching anyone. The occupants would then point at him and move away, holding their noses to show their disgust; a disgust equal to that which the more privileged lepers on occasion manifested towards them.

The accursed inhabitants of the high lazar house, however, who hardly ever encountered any creature more afflicted than themselves, found it impossible to plume themselves on their superior condition and in consequence endured a permanent mental torment as cruel as their physical hardships. The only person whom they could make conscious of his relative degradation was the black leper who lived on the summit of the cone, and then only when the latter came out of his lair, which was hardly ever. When he did emerge, however, it was only after donning full leper uniform and sounding his rattle continuously. Thereupon the whole population of the Montagne-aux-Malades would shudder with horror.

There was no law to impose these measures, but all the subjects of King Leprosy conformed to them. The Prior expressed his disapproval, but he himself felt ill at ease when he visited the higher regions, and although he reproached himself for his reluctance he could not steel himself to approach the Negro. The latter received only an occasional visit from Jehan Maillard, who brought him his medicine in person and sometimes forced himself to spend a few minutes in his company. The physician had thus succeeded in learning a few words of the Abyssinian's strange language and had gathered that in his own country the latter was a sort of healer or sorcerer.

Whenever he returned from these visits, which moreover imposed a great strain on him, Jehan Maillard noticed, all the way down the mountain, that the occupants of each zone ostentatiously drew aside. In the monastery his friend Thomas d'Orfeuilles would greet him with a grumpy and reproachful air. He did not mind. He viewed the lepers' ostracism with an understanding eye and would smile with the indulgence which he bestowed on the children's games.

3

While waiting for Vespers to be tolled, Master Thomas d'Orfeuilles and the physician were in the habit of sharing a jug of wine. The wine came from a little vineyard which Brother Rose tended and harvested himself, taking care not to waste a drop of juice. Thanks to him, throughout the year, the two cronies were able to enjoy a goblet every evening, a modest treat by which each of them set great store.

The Prior was entering upon his seventy-fifth year. He too had withstood leprosy for a long time and still warded off its ravages with the discipline of a simple life, devoid of all excess, the strict observance of religious duties and a devout obedience to the prescriptions of Jehan Maillard. Leprosy, while deforming his features and face, had until then spared him the ulcers, pustules, gangrene and other disgusting afflictions. He thanked Heaven for this and prayed to God every day to be granted the grace of dying of old age with his present countenance unchanged. He was a *leonine,* and resigned to it. At times he even felt a surge of pride at ascertaining that he was a handsome type of leonine, a more than perfect, exceptional example, since he still preserved round his tonsure a thick head of hair. Jehan Maillard mischievously compared this shock to the mane of a royal lion.

The physician, on the other hand, with his flattened but crafty nose, his equally dilated lips which were sensual but by no means majestic, was rather the satyr type of leper. He resigned himself to this with modesty and good humour, sometimes maintaining more or less seriously that the manner in which leprosy disfigures its victims is not unrelated to their characters. He quoted several examples in support of this

81

contention, in particular the case of Brother Rose, whose faithfulness and devotion were unquestioned and whose head recalled without the slightest doubt that of a trusty old dog.

Maître Jehan Maillard had travelled a great deal as a young man, led the agitated life of a scholar in France and Italy, studied medicine and philosophy with equal ardour and known many worldly pleasures. He appeared to have no regrets for this brilliant past and had made it an absolute rule never to recriminate against his fate. The day he had recognized in himself the dread touch of leprosy (this was some ten years previously and he had just reached the age of forty) he had not given vent to a spate of vain maledictions. He had set out in search of a lazar house in a pleasant climate, as he would have sought a place of retirement. The Montagne-aux-Malades had attracted him; he had come and closeted himself here before being forced to do so, to the great benefit of the Prior who had found in him an agreeable companion and an able physician. His motto was *Leprosy kills slowly*. His philosophy embroidered consolations round this thought.

This evening Thomas d'Orfeuilles was in a gloomy mood, as happened from time to time. After sighing over the condition of the monastery which was falling into ruin for want of maintenance, he lamented the sinfulness of the times and the decline of Christian virtues.

'The spirit of charity no longer exists in this kingdom,' he said. 'No one cares for the unfortunate. As for the lazars, they provoke nothing but disgust. In the last century no lord would have dared to treat them as the lowliest serf does today. In those days there was always an abundance of pious souls to take pity on them. The example came from above, I know. At the time of my birth our good King Louis had just passed away; but when I was a young man people still talked about how he treated a particularly repulsive lazar at the Abbey of Royaumont. Whenever he went there the good king allowed no one else to look after the poor devil. He would kiss his hands and face; he would serve him his meals and select the best pieces for him, which he himself raised to his shapeless mouth. He would wash his feet. There was no service, however repugnant, that he would not render him.'

'Thereby,' said the physician, 'our good king proceeded to gain life everlasting.'

The Prior shrugged his shoulders and went on:

'And this lesson bore fruit. The world then showed compassion towards the afflicted. Day by day the royal example called forth saintly souls who had no fear of approaching the lazars.'

'Yes,' Jehan Maillard agreed, thrusting out his enormous satyr lip in a splendid pout. 'It may even be said that saints then pullulated in the kingdom like fish in the sea. There was no knight, no priest, no fledgling monk, no pious burgher who did not seek out the most hideous lazar he could find and bestow his kiss on him and thereby gain salvation, while at the same time bringing himself to the sovereign's notice. Never were the feet of the unclean better washed than at that period, Prior. Never were lepers so cossetted and caressed. I wonder if they duly appreciated these acts of kindness and, above all, if they gloried sufficiently at having ushered so many souls into the Kingdom of Heaven.'

'Mock as you will, Master Philosopher,' said the Prior, 'but the absence of charity affects me cruelly and the entire population of the lazar house suffers from it. Alas, the lazars are the least concern of our King Philippe. He thinks only of waging war. . . .'

'At which he is singularly unsuccessful,' interjected the physician. 'As for his nobles, they are even more unsuccessful and think only of feasting and carousing. . . . Mere wine bladders in armour, incapable of beating the English even when they encounter them two to one. . . . But to come back to our lazars, Prior, I think they are fully reconciled to their isolation.'

The Prior sighed.

'More's the pity,' he said. 'They have passed beyond the stage of physical hardship. Selfishness and wickedness are more contagious than leprosy. Their own hearts are hardened and they ape the ways of the inhabitants of the plain. None of them feels the slightest pity for his brother. The crippled lazar despises the blind lazar. The pug-nosed lazar avoids the pustulous lazar. . . .'

'And all of them flee at the sight of the Negro lazar. You're right; but our solitude, as I've often told you, cried out for the creation of a social order.'

'I'm not versed in your intellectual refinements,' the Prior cried with vehemence. 'I'm only a poor priest and I consider this attitude execrable; but there's something even more serious. . . .'

He paused to raise his goblet to his mouth. Watching him drink his wine was a sight that never failed to astonish Jehan Maillard. His swollen underlip resembled an animal's chops and clumsily pressed against the goblet, encircling it almost completely, while he lapped with his tongue like an animal. As he watched him out of the corner of his eye the physician reflected in spite of himself that his friend looked more and more like a lion, but that this evening he was a sad lion, which did not improve his appearance.

'There's something even more serious,' the monk went on, after putting down his goblet. 'I am horrified to find that I too am giving way to this selfishness which I deplore. It's becoming more and more difficult for me to practise charity towards the lazars, my own brethren. I tell you, Maître Jehan, we all need a breath of fresh air. On some evenings the whole mountain stinks of leprosy. It's a smell that finally dissolves the strongest Christian virtues.'

'It stinks of leprosy, I grant you,' said the physician. 'It's an unpleasant smell, but bearable, and with a little philosophy one grows accustomed to it. Besides, it keeps away evildoers as well as your cowardly Christians of today, Prior. Don't forget that.'

He was about to utter a few more words of wisdom when they heard Brother Rose shouting outside.

4

'A saint, Brother Prior! God has sent him to us. He has come; here he is!'

The Prior quivered. His flattened nose wrinkled like the muzzle of a wild beast on the alert. This announcement, coinciding so miraculously with his present concerns, seemed to be a message from heaven. He rose from his rickety stool and went over to the window. From his cell, on the first floor of the monastery, he had a view of the little courtyard into which the central alley of the lazar house emerged. This spot was usually steeped in a gloomy silence at nightfall, but this evening it reverberated strangely with the cries of Brother Rose. The worthy monk, who had stopped under the window, would not calm down.

'He has come from far off, Brother Prior. That's clear from the dust all over his robe. He came up to me. He looked at my face and did not run away. He took me in his arms; he kissed me. His breath exudes a scent of incense and myrrh.'

Maître Jehan Maillard started growling with impatience.

'This monk is out of his mind and he'll get us into trouble with the inhabitants of the plain. Some stranger, obviously unaware he was addressing a lazar. . . . Didn't you shout to keep him away? Didn't you warn him of your condition?' he continued, addressing the monk. 'The law so decrees, as you know perfectly well.'

'I did indeed, Master Physician, and he replied that he had come to the lazars of his own free will. I did, I tell you, and it was then he embraced me tenderly.'

'The kiss bestowed on the lazar,' Jehan Maillard muttered scornfully.

The Prior hesitated to surrender to the emotion which was beginning to overwhelm him. Brother Rose seemed so bewildered that he feared it might be an hallucination on his part.

'Where is he?'

The monk turned round, stretching out his arm. From his window the Prior perceived the tall figure in the brown robe coming through the main gates and heading towards the monastery. In this unusual apparition there was an odour of mystery which made the monk's mind reel and convinced him that Heaven was hearkening to his prayers.

The stranger walked along at first at a brisk pace, alone in the middle of the roadway, then more slowly, glancing to left and to right, as he realized he was being observed by curious onlookers assembling in the narrow lanes that emerged into the central thoroughfare.

As a matter of fact, Brother Rose's excitement had found an immediate and enthusiastic echo in the lepers' hearts. However indifferent or callous they had become in appearance, they shared the Prior's nostalgia and deep down they all entertained the hope of seeing a resurgence of love, compassion and charity in their world. At one time, from the pulpit, Thomas d'Orfeuilles often used to tell them the story of good King Louis as well as that of other saints who had followed his august example. Now he no longer preached on this subject, being afraid of encouraging in them a wish that could not be fulfilled; but the older inhabitants had not forgotten and the tale had been handed down to the younger.

All of them had already seen one of these legendary figures appear in their secret dreams. The cry 'A saint!' abruptly fanned the flame and they had the instantaneous intuition of a miraculous event: the stranger was a Messiah whom the Lord had sent to transform their infernal region into a kingdom of love. Yet they dared not approach him. It was as though the stranger inspired them with fear—perhaps the fear of disappointment. As he reduced his pace, an old woman with pendulous cheeks, bolder than the others, moved slightly forward into the alley and thus found herself a short distance from him.

The stranger stopped, went up to her, spread his arms and, while the others held their breath, closed them round her in a tight embrace. Then he went on, while a vague buzz of voices marked the upsurge of emotion that stirred the lazar house.

'Did you see?' said the Prior excitedly.

'I saw, Prior. It looks as though the art of gaining Heaven has been rediscovered after all.'

The lepers grew bolder, the stranger now found himself walking between two quivering rows in which enthusiasm was on the verge of turning into fanatical adoration. When he arrived below the window hundreds of mouths with distorted lips took up Brother Rose's cry: 'A saint! A saint!' and crippled hands started stretching out towards him.

'Peace be with you, stranger,' said the Prior. 'We are deeply moved, as you see, by your display of friendliness and fellow-feeling, but are you aware of the terrible danger to which you are exposing yourself by consorting with us like this?'

'I am not afraid of leprosy.'

The crowd, which had fallen silent, was impressed as Brother Rose had been by that deep melodious voice, the singularity of which derived no doubt from the fact that the stranger spoke without unclenching his teeth. The Prior, disturbed by these resonant tones as much as he was moved by the nobility of the reply, hastened down the wooden staircase, flung the door open and found himself face to face with the stranger. The latter fell on his knees before him, seized his hands and covered them with kisses.

'Rise, brother,' said the Prior, making an effort to free himself. 'I bless the sentiment which inspires you. I am only too inclined to give in to you, but that is weakness on my part. Take a closer look at me. Look at the wretches all round you and think of the price which these tokens of affection are liable to cost you.'

The stranger briefly examined the leonine features with the nose spreading over part of the face, then, slowly, glanced round the semi-circle of which he formed the centre.

Except in the case of the young children, it would have been difficult to discern a really human countenance. Emotion, as the physician had frequently noted, makes grotesque creatures hideous. And, at the sound of the words which duty forced the Prior to utter against his will, anxiety and anger seized the crowd. They instinctively bristled against these obstacles placed in the way of the saint's vocation. Their nerves, excoriated by disease, could not endure such frustration, and exasperation transformed them into a savage horde, in which could be distinguished the bestial characteristics with which King Leprosy had been pleased to mark each of his subjects: the resentment of the leonines manifested itself in a murmur which resembled a stifled roar; the noses of the porcines seemed to grow longer and from them emanated a sort of

86

pig-like squeal; the canines ground their teeth and uttered a menacing growl. All of them seemed prepared to fling themselves on the Prior and tear him to pieces.

The stranger, however, appeared to be unmoved by this spectacle. He looked at the Prior again and spoke in the same deep voice.

'Are not all men brothers?' he said.

'Certainly they are, although many people nowadays forget this.'

'Many people forget it, that's true,' he echoed.

Jehan Maillard, who was observing him closely, noticed the rancour with which he had invested his reply. This did not surprise him, however, for his philosophy prompted him to suppose that such a sentiment was in no way incompatible with the state of saintliness.

'But *I* don't forget it,' the stranger went on. 'And here I am among you. So why repulse me, Brother Prior?'

'I? Repulse you!'

The old man's pious resistance was shattered. Authoritatively the stranger took a step towards him, flung his arms round him and embraced him passionately, wiping away the tears which were now pouring down his bestial face.

The crowd, relieved by this definite proof of his determination, uttered a cheer and the circle gathered closer round the stranger, each leper being impatient to receive in his turn the miraculous kiss. But Jehan Maillard led him aside and spoke to him in a low voice.

'One moment, stranger. Do you know exactly to what you are committing yourself by spending the night here, as such seems your intention? Everywhere, in the plain, the inhabitants will drive you away. If you are not from this country, as it so appears, you cannot imagine the severity of the laws concerning lazars. Leave us at once and perhaps you will be able to conceal the fact of your visit.'

'Forgive our physician,' said the Prior, in his turn showing anxiety. 'He believes it is his duty to talk to you like this, as I myself believed a quarter of an hour ago. He is a knowledgeable man. He does not cure leprosy, because it is incurable, and he is a lazar himself, but no one is more learned in this matter. However, divine affairs are alien to him. But I, brother, realize who you are.'

'Amen, Prior,' said Jehan Maillard, giving a wink, which twisted his face into a ghastly grimace.

'I come,' said the stranger, 'from the town whose church steeples you may be able to perceive from the top of the mountain. I know the customs of the country and the hardheartedness of its inhabitants. Only, Master Physician, if such is your profession . . .'

It was as though the stranger instinctively recognized an enemy in the person of Maître Maillard. He spoke to him with reticence, turning his head away.

'Only, Master Physician, I have no desire to go back to the plain. It is among the lazars that I henceforth want to live. Will the lazars refuse to receive me?'

'Certainly not!' the Prior exclaimed. 'I realize who you are, I tell you. Blessed be the envoy of Our Lord!'

'Then allow me to stay. I only need a little straw in the humblest of the huts.'

'You will be my guest. Look upon this monastery as your own home. It's an honour and a great joy for me to receive you. Come in. You must be tired after your long journey.'

Under the ironic gaze of Jehan Maillard, the Prior ushered the stranger into his room, served him a jug of wine and insisted on washing his feet himself. The man acquiesced, with reluctance, it seemed. He refused the lodging he had been offered and insisted on returning to the crowd, who were manifesting their impatience by a loud clamour.

The physician, who had not taken his eyes off him, sought to put his saintliness to the test.

'You have not yet met any really repulsive lazars,' he said. 'The ones here still have faces, whether human or not. Before confronting the others, prepare your mind for a hideous sight.'

'Are not all men brothers?' the stranger replied in a low voice. 'No form of leprosy inspires me with repulsion. . . . But,' he went on, with a worried expression, 'don't all the lazars live within these precincts?'

'No, brother,' said the Prior, 'they have become far too crowded to house us all. Many of them, the most deeply afflicted, have to live on the slopes of the mountain. It takes almost two days to do the rounds of the great lazar house.'

The stranger appeared to be suddenly overwhelmed by distress and immediately rose to his feet.

'Brother Prior, I cannot linger,' he said abruptly. 'I am beholden to those poor souls.'

5

'*No form of leprosy inspires me with repulsion*,' the physician echoed pensively. 'He's a courageous man undoubtedly.'

The stranger had disappeared so swiftly that the Prior had

had no time even to attempt to retain him. Jehan Maillard went up to the window and looked out. It was growing dark.

'A strange bird, this saint of yours, Prior,' he went on. 'There he goes, in search of lazars. And there's no shortage of them here. He hasn't taken twenty steps and already he has laid his face against ten fine leper muzzles. No one wants to miss such a feast. The courtyard is black with people. Some of them have just gone off to fetch their wives and bring them back to him. . . . What does he do? The same as before. He bends down. He clasps a pair of breasts to his bosom. He kisses a forehead, a couple of cheeks. He gives another kiss, then passes on to the next woman. The hussies would ask for more, you may be sure; but he doesn't linger. Here's a saint who's eager to gain his salvation, or else prove his saintliness!'

"Maître Jehan, such talk is blasphemous,' said the Prior, who was still in a state of ecstasy. 'The man's a saint, and the grandeur of his mission does not allow him a moment's respite.'

'Granted,' the physician growled. 'But wouldn't you have liked to converse with him a little longer and find out to which category his saintliness belongs? There are royal saints, as you know. He is not one of those. There are knightly saints; he is not one of those either. A monkish saint? He has no tonsure. Nor is he a serf; and anyway I have never heard of a serf saint.'

'Oh, what does his position in the world matter! He's a saint and that ought to be enough. Didn't you smell, as I did, the scent emanating from his breath? I am still enraptured by it. Brother Rose had no hallucination. A smell of incense and myrrh.'

'Yes. As a matter of fact I did sniff it, like you, even though he didn't happen to consider me worthy of his kiss—God forbid! Would that the Almighty had sent us a nice little female saint! But, mark you, Prior (I am not in the habit of consorting with saints, it's true) I've never heard they exude any particular smell.'

'That's just where you're wrong, learned doctor though you be,' said the old man gravely. 'Some saints in the old days were shrouded in a scent which permeated the air all round them. That's an authentic fact.'

Jehan Maillard peered at his pious friend in silence, then shook his head, feeling far from convinced. When he left him an hour later, Master Thomas d'Orfeuilles was still in a tumult of emotion as a result of the event, and the agitation that reigned round the monastery kept him awake until a very late hour.

The stranger strolled about the little lazar house until late at night, first of all ambling about the streets haphazardly, bestowing his kiss on all the lepers he encountered, attracted as though by a magnet to the largest groups. Then, once the initial excitement caused by his appearance had died down a little and the thoroughfares began to empty, he seemed to take thought and introduced a semblance of method into his singular behaviour.

He asked Brother Rose, who was dogging his footsteps, to act as his guide and embarked on a systematic tour of the whole community. Entering every dwelling one after another, he encountered still more lepers, who had not come outside either because their condition forbade it or else from mere indifference. In each house his charity manifested itself according to a simple and invariable ritual: he would go inside, spread his arms and successively embrace all the occupants. Did one of them seek to elude him, he would never admit defeat but pursued the recalcitrant. Eventually he succeeded in cornering him and then, with his arms stretched out once more in the form of a cross, in his strange voice which seemed to contain a poignant reproach, he would make the poor wretch feel ashamed of his shame.

'Are not all men brothers?' he would say. 'I have come to you out of love, and you repulse me!'

Thereupon even the grimmest leper would feel his heart melt and would accept the accolade with tears. After which, having searched every corner to make sure of having overlooked no one, whether bedridden invalid or babe in cradle, the stranger went off at a brisk pace and headed for another abode.

He ended his tour of the community well after Matins and found himself back in the central thoroughfare. A number of lepers who happened to be awake saw him at that moment, by the light of a lantern carried by Brother Rose. They noticed that his face was bathed in sweat, his complexion wan, and the thought that he was sacrificing his health on their account was a fresh benefaction to them. Brother Rose, however, begged him to rest for a little while before going on to the great lazar house, as was his declared intention. He wanted to take him back to his own room, since he had refused the Prior's hospitality: but the stranger shook his head.

The two men thereupon exchanged, in an undertone, a few words which no one heard; then they plunged into the darkness. The saint had disappeared and for the rest of that night his shadow ceased to haunt the alleyways. Everyone thought he had finally accepted a bed in the monk's room. The whispering gradually died down and silence once more reigned over the Montagne-aux-Malades.

6

Thomas d'Orfeuilles rose shortly before the hour of Prime and went straight to the chapel to give thanks to God. He stayed only a short moment, so curious was he to find out what had happened to the community's new guest. On his way out he encountered Jehan Maillard who had just visited the hospital, as he did every morning. It was a sort of long shed, housing the patients whose condition required constant care. In the absence of monks to attend to them, Brother Rose being more often than not occupied outside, the physician had drawn up a roster of the more able-bodied lepers, who carried out their duties with extreme reluctance.

Jehan Maillard was conversing with Brother Rose. To the question 'Where is he?' which the Prior asked him from afar, he shrugged his shoulders and replied grumpily:

'He has gone off to the great lazar house, Prior; he left before dawn, after sleeping at the hospital.'

'At the hospital! But our wretched hospital is crowded out. There aren't even enough beds to go round.'

'That was his desire,' said Brother Rose. 'He shared a bed with two of the most hideous lepers.'

'He shared a bed with the lepers?'

'That was his desire,' the monk repeated. 'He slept for a few hours only, after helping with the patients.'

'Maître Jehan,' the Prior gravely said, 'does not this deed rouse your admiration?'

'Granted, it's a courageous feat; and I wouldn't complain that God should have sent us a benevolent orderly—and a saint to boot! I wouldn't complain, as I said, if in his case the divine breath did not manifest itself in the form of a malignant fever. He is absolutely raving, Prior! If he goes on like this, his health won't stand it. Furthermore, there is no disease more contagious than fever, even if it happens to be sacred, and this morning all my rascals have caught it. These emotions are anything but salutary. You should use your authority to calm him down and make him introduce a little moderation into his saintliness, Prior. I'm speaking as a physician. All this agitation is liable to turn to madness.'

The Prior reflected. He knew that his friend was a level-headed man as well as an able physician and that he often gave good advice in a light-hearted manner. He himself did not approve of any form of excess and, though he would not admit it, he could not help being surprised by the stranger's behaviour.

'It does not behoove me,' he said, 'to pour water on a sacred flame. But perhaps I can advise him to spare himself in the very interests of his mission.'

'Then come along with me. I must do the rounds of the great lazar house. We are bound to encounter our bird and you'll be able to admonish him. I intend spending the night half way up and shall push on to the highest zone tomorrow. It's a long time since I called on my dusky colleague.'

This familiar term, applied to the Negro who lived on the summit, was a jocular allusion to the embryonic medical knowledge that Jehan Maillard fancied he had discerned in him. But no jest could prevent the Prior from shuddering when he thought of the black horror. The physician, however, insisted.

'You have not set foot outside for some time, and that's not good for you. Lazars need a reasonable amount of exercise.'

The Prior hesitated for a moment. The prospect of spending a night in a chance shelter did not appeal to him. But the physician was right: he was too inclined to remain closeted in the monastery and his conscience reproached him for avoiding contact with the more repulsive lepers. Furthermore, he was consumed with desire to see the stranger again as soon as possible. He made up his mind abruptly.

'Off we go, then,' he said. 'You're right. Claustration is good neither for one's physique nor for one's morale. I'll come with you.'

They left the precincts, followed by the faithful Brother Rose in charge of the medicine boxes and by a young leper carrying some foodstuffs and bedding for the night. The latter acted as servant to Thomas d'Orfeuilles who, without daring to admit it, had chosen him for a selfish reason: his face, scarcely marked by the disease, was almost human.

They started off across the fields surrounding the community. It was a smiling landscape and the path sloped sufficiently gently to permit conversation. The two friends chatted together. The Prior was invigorated by the exercise and the early morning air. Passing the vineyard which provided his daily wine, he gave thanks to God that the harvest looked promising and congratulated Brother Rose on his husbandry. The worthy monk blushed with satisfaction.

'The earth is rich in these parts,' he said. 'Unfortunately, only a little further on, it's worthless. And we shall have to extend the cultivated area. The number of mouths to feed increases every year.'

'Leprosy kills slowly,' the physician observed sententiously.

It was true; the population of the lazar house was progressively increasing, and this was another cause of anxiety for the Prior. Not only does leprosy kill slowly, but it applies no curb to the reproductive instinct. Jehan Maillard even maintained that it aggravated sexual appetite. And indeed births outnumbered deaths. The children, whom it was impossible to isolate, caught the disease shortly after seeing the light of day and were doomed to have no other home than the Montagne-aux-Malades.

At each of these births, most of them illegitimate, the Prior would heave a sigh and the physician would feel a twinge of conscience as he supervised the lazar midwife. The one preached chastity, the other caution, both with equal lack of success. The male lepers defied damnation, scorned advice and wooed the female lepers every night with an ardour that was bound to produce results. Being unable to suppress the evil, Thomas d'Orfeuilles did his best to limit it and insisted on religious marriages and baptisms in spite of the general indifference. The physician swore he would henceforth wring the necks of the wretched infants but he could never make up his mind to do so. Thus, as time went by, King Leprosy saw the number of his subjects increase.

The Prior sighed but did not answer Brother Rose. As they left the cultivated zone behind them the slope became steeper. Presently, at a bend in the path, they espied the plain at the foot of the Montagne-aux-Malades. To the south, the air was limpid and a clear light threw into relief every detail of the huge forest. In the opposite direction, on the other hand, towards the town, a reddish mist covered the countryside.

'I noticed it already yesterday,' said the physician, 'it's an odd haze. The sun fails to dispel it.'

'It's dust,' Brother Rose asserted. 'The cloud is hanging above the roads and tracks. I remember seeing the same sort of thing when I was a child, at the time of a big fair. All the merchants in the kingdom were converging on the town. The thoroughfares were swarming with carriages and horsemen.'

'Either a fair or a big festival. That's what it must be.'

They fell silent for a few minutes, in a state of depression. Within the confines of the lazar house, where the horizon was limited to leprosy, they managed to resign themselves to their condition, but a mere glance at the plain, awakening memories of the outside world, had provoked a feeling of nostalgia which a distant and persistent peal of bells only served to intensify. Jehan Maillard tried to shake it off in the tone that was habitual to him.

'What matter the fumes and rumours of the plain to us, Prior! One of your new religious feasts, no doubt. The bells sound as though they'll break loose. Perhaps some miracle has been performed and the good news is attracting a horde of pilgrims—and also merchants intent on selling their rubbishy wares. What do we care? Do we not have a saint of our own since yesterday?'

'You're right after all, Maître Jehan,' said the Prior. 'God has placed us on the Montagne-aux-Malades and He has sent us a messenger to make us ashamed of our selfishness. In your heart of hearts I am sure you feel as I do: no one can live indefinitely without love or charity.'

'No indeed,' said the physician. 'Amen, Prior. But I'm impatient to see this Messiah in daylight. . . . Ah, there he is, I believe.'

They had reached the edge of a wooded area containing a large number of huts situated some distance away from the path. The stranger stood there, motionless, half concealed in the shade of a tree, leaning against the trunk. He had not seen them. He was intently watching a dozen children who seemed engrossed in some strange ceremony. Most of them were squatting on their haunches, motionless, in three rows. In front of this group, one of their number, clad in dingy fancy-dress, was kneeling on the ground. Still further off, facing the assembly, another, who looked like the oldest of the band, was delivering a speech and gesticulating with his arms. They had noticed neither the stranger nor the newcomers.

The Prior was about to reveal his presence, when Jehan Maillard spoke to him in an undertone.

'Don't move, Prior. I should very much like to observe him while he believes himself to be sheltered from all eyes.'

'But what are those children doing?'

'It's just a game.'

'A game?'

'Let's observe them as well. Are they not the future of the lazar house? Their favourite game, Prior; the lazar children are playing at being lazars.'

7

The youngster kneeling on the ground wore a black veil over his head, and a piece of coarse red material, clumsily trimmed in the shape of a heart, was pinned on his chest. He was playing the part of The Leper. The big lad facing him was parodying the funeral service. After reciting a series of litanies, in which he introduced some Latin-sounding words which made his audience writhe with laughter, he bent down, picked up several handfuls of earth and poured it over the victim's head, saying:

'My friend, this is the sign that thou are dead to this world.'

The three rows of children whispered and nudged one another. The Leper bowed down until his head touched the ground. The leader went on:

'I forbid thee ever to enter a church, to appear in a public place or join any group or gathering of people whatsoever.

'I forbid thee ever to wash thy hands in the fountains, the streams or any source of water, excepting thine own trough.

'Thou shalt wear no other garb than that of a lazar.

'I forbid thee, when thou goest abroad, to reply to whoever might question thee, without first leaving the path and placing thyself to leeward, for fear of infecting his person. Moreover, thou shalt henceforth avoid the high road so as not to encounter anyone.

'I forbid thee, if thou art obliged to follow a path across country, to touch the hedgerows or bushes on either side.

'I forbid thee to touch any person whatsoever, and least of all small children and young people.

'I forbid thee henceforth to eat or drink in the company of anyone but lazars.'

Having finished his sermon, the leader made a gesture. The Leper rose to his feet and went up to a gaping hole dug in the ground, while shaking two pieces of metal together to represent the lazar's rattle. As he moved forward, all the others drew away from him, holding their noses and feigning the deepest disgust. He lay down in the tomb. From afar the others scattered handfuls of earth over him until he was half buried.

This, in the outside world, was the *separatio leprosarum*, a ceremony which preceded the internment of a recently acknowledged leper and which cut him off from the rest of mankind. The children, being born in the lazar house, had not been subjected to it but it had made such an impression on their parents that they never stopped discussing it among themselves and comparing all its variations. Young and old alike were conversant with the ritual in every detail.

The children introduced such realism into this simulacrum of a simulacrum that the Prior was deeply disturbed. As for the physician, whose visits to the great lazar house had familiarized him with this sort of amusement, he was above all interested in the stranger's attitude. The latter seemed to be

95

fascinated by the game. When the children broke off, he emerged from the shadow and went over towards them. Jehan Maillard noticed he was even paler than on the previous evening. His emaciated face was drawn with fatigue and sleeplessness. Yet an almost feverish gleam could be seen in his eyes.

The children fell silent as he approached. One of the youngest started crying and took to his heels. Little would have been needed, the physician reflected, to send them all scattering like a flight of starlings. But the stranger approached them with a smile, started talking to them without raising his voice, and they were soon listening to him attentively.

The Prior again wanted to reveal his presence, but Jehan Maillard restrained him. They inferred that the stranger was having the game explained to him. His laugh, which they had not yet heard, suddenly echoed round the countryside. He laughed in the same way that he spoke, without unclenching his teeth. It presently became clear that he was asking the children to allow him to join in their fun, and they readily accepted.

The new game was more simple, but still inspired by leprosy. The eldest of the children had donned the fancy dress and now played the part of The Leper. The others fled from him, uttering cries of terror, while he pursued them rattling his pieces of metal. Whomever he caught had to take his place. But the stranger entered into the game in his own fashion: instead of fleeing from The Leper, he advanced to meet him, spread his arms, clasped him to his breast and embraced him.

When he released him, the lad looked disconcerted, but he spoke to him gently and, the whole band having gathered in a circle round him, he appeared to deliver a sort of sermon in which the physician and the Prior could distinguish only the familiar question, uttered in a tone of sorrowful reproach:

'Are not all men brothers?'

'There's a preacher for you!' muttered Jehan Maillard. 'Prior, you have a serious rival there.'

The rascals appeared to be converted. When the game was resumed it turned into a demonstration of charity, with the stranger himself assuming the role of The Leper, and the children, instead of fleeing, came and flung themselves into his arms to give him the accolade.

He thus embraced them all, including the infant who had taken to his heels howling and who had eventually crept back. Thereupon, as though he had lost all interest in the game, he cast aside the veil and the red heart and left them without another word, striding off towards the summit of the mountain. Once again his departure was so abrupt that the children were dumbfounded.

The two companions resumed their march in silence engrossed in their own thoughts and saving their breath, for the sky was clouding over and the heat was overwhelming.

'Prior,' Jean Maillard remarked all of a sudden, 'from the way he behaved I suspected him for a moment of sodomy.'

Thomas d'Orfeuilles protested all the more indignantly in that he was himself growing more perplexed and disturbed by the stranger's behaviour.

'Maître Jehan,' he said severely, 'all I personally saw was a lesson in charity given to some children who, without any evil intent perhaps, were indulging in an ugly pastime. And the lesson has been useful. They won't play those nasty games again. . . .'

'Not for some time, at least. Amen, Prior. Meanwhile off he goes again, swooping on yet more lazars like a falcon on newly-hatched chicks.'

8

They caught up with him again at the spot where they had chosen to spend the night, in a community containing a large number of lepers, the last one before the accursed region of the high lazar house. The physician had taken over a hut there, in which to rest in the course of his rounds. Having arrived in the afternoon, he went off to visit his patients, then came back and joined the Prior. The two cronies settled down as best they could to the evening meal, while Brother Rose and the servant made up the beds.

The stranger, as Jehan Maillard had learnt during his rounds, had not been to this sort of village before, but the news of his presence on the Montagne-aux-Malades had spread by devious routes and all the lepers had gathered in the clearing to await his appearance. Anxious as he was to overlook not a single soul on his tour, he had no doubt followed the paths which ran all the way round the cone, visiting each isolated hut, ascending thus in a long spiral, while the physician and his companions had come up by the shortest route.

Night fell and the group of lepers in the clearing dissolved into a shadowy mass, much to the Prior's relief. He was painfully affected by the sight of this profusion of pustules, suppurating sores and shreds of flesh drooping like withered flowers, these rotting organs which sometimes looked as though they were about to drop off—commonplace disfigurements in this place which already stood extremely high in the scale of horror. His secret regret was that the darkness did not dispel the stench emanating from the crowd, a stench of foul leprosy, different from that to which the little lazar house had accustomed his nostrils.

A more fetid gust than usual having invaded the hut, he turned pale, got up and with an abrupt gesture fastened the plank which served as a shutter. Then he felt ashamed of this reaction and sat down again, feeling utterly dejected.

'Poor wretches!' he murmured.

'Leprosy kills slowly . . .' said the physician. 'But you're wrong to distress yourself like this, Prior. The disease also has its advantages.'

'Advantages, really!' muttered Thomas d'Orfeuilles, wrinkling his huge chops like an angry lion.

'Indubitably. Leprosy acts as a perfect scarecrow against men-at-arms, and war is a calamity which seems to have settled on our kingdom. Our good old leprosy keeps the English at bay. No enemy of the realm would dare brave the lazar house; no partisan either, and that's a blessing. I'm thinking of those knights who go plundering the villages through which they pass on the pretext of defending the wretched population. I sometimes dream, Prior, that the Montagne-aux-Malades is a haven of peace and tranquillity. Thus does the Lord transform a scourge into a blessing.'

'Amen, you unbeliever,' said Thomas d'Orfeuilles, with a faint smile.

'I'm not sure I would leave this retreat, even if it were possible, to plunge once more into a world in the throes of madness.'

Meditating on this last remark, the Prior had reached the point of concluding that philosophy was a fine thing, when a tumult of voices outside made him prick up his ears. He reopened the window but could not distinguish a word; above a certain altitude on the mountains, many of the lepers whose vocal organs had been affected used a language consisting of hoarse grunts, like animal cries, which were more or less unintelligible to the uninitiated. The physician alone had a smattering of these primitive idioms which were thus spoken at various levels. He confirmed to the Prior what the latter had already guessed: the stranger was close at hand. He asked Brother Rose to light the candle. The two friends went over to the window, which was just wide enough to enable their huge shapeless heads to peer out into the darkness, and waited for the saint to arrive.

His appearance, announced by discordant grunts and

growls from the lepers, all of whom had suddenly straightened up, froze the blood in the veins of the two men, creating the same impression on them as the hideous phantasmagoria of an absurd nightmare.

As the prelude to an infernal vision, the forest was first pierced by a series of fleeting lights whose frequency increased rapidly until this succession of mysterious flashes turned into a continuous luminescence, bathing the undergrowth in a magic glow. Then a carnivalesque procession emerged from the path opposite the clearing.

It was headed by a section of children carrying flaming torches. But it was at the sight of the group immediately behind them that the Prior and the physician-philosopher were paralysed with horror, while the placid Brother Rose, who had ventured to glance out through a crack in the wall, uttered an incoherent exclamation. Their fright derived as much from the hideousness of the spectacle as from its inexplicable character; for the fearful creature advancing towards them was a preternatural monster. It looked like a shapeless body, so vast that it overflowed each side of the path, supported on a swarm of tangled legs and surmounted by three heads.

> *'Cerbero, fiera crudele e diversa,*
> *Con tre gule caninamente . . .'**

Jehan Maillard muttered automatically, wiping his brow.

And indeed, to identify this creature with the demon mounting guard at the gates of Hell seemed to him at this moment the only reasonable judgement that could be passed on it.

The general impression caused by this diabolical apparition had at first prevented the two friends from discerning the details of its structure. When they forced themselves to do so, as the only means of contending with the stupor in which they were plunged, they noticed that each of the component parts of the monster possessed its own particular form of hideousness. It was on the heads that the Prior's bewildered eyes settled, once the initial shock was over and he was in a fit state to perceive something further than the ghastly collective aspect. The heads irresistibly attracted his attention. One of them, the one on the left, had no nose and all that remained of the lips were a few tattered fragments. The gaping hole which filled the middle of the face evoked the idea of a cavern into which no light would ever be able to penetrate. As for the head on the right, not a shred of its flesh resem-

---

* Alighieri, Dante. *The Divine Comedy*, Inferno, Canto vi.

bled flesh; not a square inch was free from putrescence. It was a huge open wound, an uninterrupted accumulation of gangrene that had assumed the rough shape of a ball, and it required a close scrutiny to distinguish the sensory organs, buried in hideous rolls of fat, on which the glow of the torches cast hallucinating shadows and reflections.

The third head, the one in the centre, hung forward as though overburdened by its own weight. It wobbled as the procession moved along and came to rest alternately against one of the two others. Its position suggested to the Prior that it was trying to conceal an even greater abomination than that of its neighbours. His heart therefore missed a beat when he had the foreboding, on discerning a barely perceptible stiffening of the neck, that it was about to reveal its countenance. Just then indeed it slowly raised itself. The monk's anguish turned to dismay as he recognized the face of the stranger.

It was none other than he. Flanked, supported, almost borne along by two lepers from the isolated huts who had insisted on escorting him thus far, he held his companions in such a close embrace, with his arms flung round their necks, that the three bodies looked like a single one.

The feeling of horror, however, did not vanish along with the supernatural quality of the apparition. The Prior gave a shudder of disgust as he sensed on his own skin the unspeakable contact that united the stranger to these two creatures.

'This man must be a saint,' he exclaimed violently, as though willing himself to believe it. 'Only a saint could endure this!'

9

'He may be a saint,' said Jehan Maillard, 'but I should have thought saintliness was accompanied by peace of mind and serenity. Whereas this man is absolutely raving. There he goes again.'

On being released by the two lepers, the stranger stood swaying on his feet for a moment, as though in a daze. But as the crowd pressed closer round him, he rapidly recovered his composure. Without further ado, without resting even for a second, he resumed his activity with renewed zeal, endowing it with the ardour of a passion and at the same time the ritual of a ceremony. He would spread his arms wide, go up to a leper, clasp him to his breast in a sort of frenzy, plant his lips on the repulsive flesh, then release him and pass on to another.

Jehan Maillard, whose scientific curiosity was beginning to be aroused, was curiously reminded, as he saw him perform, of a rabid animal mounting female after female, desperately seeking a victim capable of gratifying his insatiable desire.

'I was wrong to suspect him of sodomy,' he muttered under his breath. 'The same frenzy drives him towards male lazars, female lazars, infant lazars and aged lazars indiscriminately. No preference; age and sex are of no importance. A madman? A saintly madman, I grant you; they do exist. Since yesterday the rascal has kissed more than five hundred leprous snouts and he is still not satiated. . . . Prior, I can see only one reasonable explanation.'

'A reasonable explanation!' the Prior echoed derisively.

'A sinner; a repentant sinner, tormented, harassed by remorse, who thinks he can save his soul and redeem himself in Paradise by indulging in deeds of this sort. Only, to inspire him with such zeal, such a desire for self-sacrifice, it must be the memory of some very exceptional crime.'

'Unbeliever!' said Thomas d'Orfeuilles. 'When will you stop exhausting yourself in seeking reasons for divine grace? He's a saint.'

'My profession prompts me to look for explanations,' the physician admitted, 'and I am naturally inclined to think that self-interest is a powerful motive of human behaviour, even for a saint.'

He peered outside again and, after a short silence, went on in a serious tone:

'To tell you the truth, I'm disconcerted. Granted, his heroism suggests the aid of some external power. . . . But why didn't the Almighty give his elect a more prepossessing appearance? Have you noticed his ugly hooked nose, his lurid complexion, his jutting cheekbones and his obstinately pinched lips? Prior, that scent of incense and myrrh which you noticed yesterday, which enraptures everyone he kisses, doesn't it cover up a smell of brimstone?'

'Demon yourself!' muttered the Prior. 'You don't believe in Heaven, and if you're trying to insinuate . . .'

'I'm wrong, of course. Satan is merely an invention of the priests, which inspired some very fine verse from Master Dante. . . . All the same, look at him at this very moment.'

The stranger was standing in the middle of the clearing, surrounded by a dense crowd. The Prior, who had come back to the window, perceived his tall figure, towering above one group, illuminated by the torches which the children were

101

holding at arm's length, and saw him bend over a baby which a leper woman was holding out to him.

Had Jehan Maillard's words sown disorder in the Prior's mind? Had the countless emotions which he had just undergone created in him a climate propitious to hallucinations? Had the flickering flames of the torches distorted reality to a fantastic degree? However it may be, the old man was suddenly overwhelmed with fresh terror at the sight of the saint's countenance which appeared at that moment to bear a mark of utter malevolence. The behaviour of the newborn added to the intensity of this fleeting impression. The baby had started bellowing and was in the throes of such convulsions that its mother could barely hold it. For a few seconds, while the saint bent down, his face distorted by a rictus which appeared satanic, the Prior had the impression of watching a victim being offered to a monstrous ogre.

He closed his eyes and crossed himself. When he reopened them the hallucination had vanished. The saint had straightened up and had changed his position. The child was merely whimpering faintly. The monk passed his hand across his brow and reproached his companion for uttering impious remarks calculated to sow confusion in pure and simple hearts.

'Shall we go and speak to him now?' the physician asked, shrugging his shoulders.

The Prior hesitated. He felt shattered by the events of this evening and had no wish to mingle with the crowd of lepers.

'Let's wait until tomorrow. He's bound to be here until the morning.'

'Unless he goes off again in the middle of the night. . . . After all, you're right. He'll have to stop when he has made the complete tour of the lazar house, which won't be long at the rate he is going. We shall probably catch up with him somewhere near the summit. . . . I say, Prior, aren't you curious to know what his reaction will be to the lazars in the accursed zone?'

Master Thomas d'Orfeuilles shuddered but did not reply, and the two friends went to bed. The hut consisted of one room only. Shortly after he had blown out the candle, the physician spoke again in a low voice.

'If he has no fear of embracing the lazars up there, Prior, if he doesn't draw back even from the black horror that lives on the summit, then I think that even I shall bow before him and acknowledge him as a saint.'

They resumed their climb early in the morning, for the remainder of the path was rough and steep. As Jehan Maillard had foreseen, the stranger had left before them, still following a route which led to the summit in an ever-decreasing spiral. The weather was stormy, the heat stifling. The Prior panted and stumbled at every step.

They made their way across a deserted area and struggled over a mass of jagged, sinister-looking rocks which marked the entrance to the high lazar house.

'And here is the Ninth Circle, with its unfortunate inhabitants,' said Jehan Maillard.

> *'O sovra tutte mal creata plebe,*
> *Che stai nel loco onde parlare e duro*
> *Me foste state qui pecore o zebel!'**

'I don't understand Italian,' said the Prior darkly, 'but I wonder if your Florentine would not have found some additional horrors here with which to equip his Inferno.'

'He would have discovered at least one, Prior,' said the physician, stopping to recover his breath. 'His Inferno was a chasm and the approach to it was down hill. Intruders were in no danger of suffocation, as we are on this climb.'

The old man did not unwrinkle his brow. After a short pause he struggled forward again and asked in a grave tone:

'Have the ones up here long to live?'

'A few months, a few years perhaps. I knew a lazar whose body was nothing but putrefaction and seething with vermin. He lived a long time in that state.'

The Prior heaved a sigh.

'Leprosy kills slowly; and he was grateful for that,' added Jehan Maillard. 'He was afraid of dying.'

They climbed still further. The cone grew more and more narrow. The Prior was pouring with sweat, and to him this sweat seemed foul and loathsome. Never before had he felt so overburdened by the weight of his years and his disease.

The atmosphere was indeed stifling. Dark clouds were gathering over the plain. In the direction of the town, the countryside was still shrouded in a reddish haze. The physi-

---

* Alighieri, Dante. *The Divine Comedy*, Inferno, Canto xxxii.

cian tried to divert his companion by drawing his attention to this spectacle.

'It's odd, Prior. It's dust all right, and it has lasted for three days. There must be an endless column stretching along the roads. What fair, what feast day can account for this?'

'How should I know? War, panic perhaps,' said the Prior impatiently. 'As you said yesterday, what do we care? The enemies of the kingdom are not our enemies.'

Master Thomas d'Orfeuilles was in a really bad mood; and for several reasons. In the first place, the high lazar house always inspired him with gloomy thoughts: even though the physician had assured him that his body would not suffer any further serious degradation, he sometimes saw in certain inhabitants of the accursed region a future reproduction of himself, and this vision was unbearable. Secondly, he held his companion responsible for the confusion that had entered his mind on the subject of the saint and was angry with him for having gradually spoiled the pleasure he had been given by his arrival. His sleep had been disturbed by nightmares, in which angels turned into demons.

Jehan Maillard did not pursue the matter. They walked on for a long time in silence. As they approached the summit they espied the object of their concern. The stranger was sitting on a rock outside a group of huts, the last dwellings before the apex of the cone. No leper was visible, but they sensed that countless eyes were observing them through the foliage. In this region the lazars more often than not remained closeted in their wretched lairs, as though they were ashamed of revealing themselves in the light of day.

The stranger looked exhausted. His head drooped and he did not notice their presence until they were quite close. Thereupon he gave a start and turned his ravaged face towards them. The physician spoke to him very gently.

'You are worn out, stranger. Anyone would be. Your courage and your zeal arouses our admiration; but there is no sense in killing yourself by dint of charity, and you would do more good by moderating your exertion. Our Prior, who is himself a saintly man, will tell you that you must care for your health if you want to be able to devote yourself to others for any length of time. I can see you're on the verge of collapse.'

'It's the heat,' muttered the stranger.

He still spoke through stubbornly clenched teeth, which twisted his lips into a strange rictus; but his voice had lost its resonance. It was scarcely above a whisper.

'Brother,' said the Prior, 'what Jehan Maillard says is sound advice. As I told you, in matters of physical health, no one is wiser than he. Therefore, if you don't mind, moderate your zeal today. Come back with us to the monastery and have a rest. Tomorrow you will be all the fitter to pursue your mission.'

'Your hands are shaking,' the physician added. 'I'm sure you have a fever.'

He went up to seize his hand. The stranger leapt to his feet and retreated several paces. His dark eyes had assumed a wild expression.

"I must still see these people here,' he said in a choking voice.

He had overcome his weakness. He walked with a firm tread towards the nearest hut and went inside. The physician followed him, shaking his head, for he had duties to perform in that particular den. Brother Rose accompanied him with the medicines. The Prior could not induce himself to approach the cesspool, from which there issued a repulsive stench. He sat down on the ground some distance away and waited for them.

When Jehan Maillard came out, his features were changed. He spoke in a grave voice which was not habitual to him.

"Prior," he said, "I repent of my mockery and my suspicions. In truth this creature is of a supernatural essence. What I have just seen him do surpasses the bounds of heroism; for, I tell you, those who live up here can only be compared to corpses in a state of putrefaction. Though a doctor and a lazar myself, I can only touch them with the tips of my gloved fingers, while turning away my head. But he never flinched at all."

"And he . . ."

'Yes, Prior. He embraced them, clasping them to his breast as passionately as the others.'

Thomas d'Orfeuilles fell silent for a moment. He felt ill at ease and was angry with himself for not being able to find the appropriate words to laud such a prodigious feat. He forced himself at last to mutter in a low voice:

'God inspires his elect with a courage that stupefies me. I feel unworthy.'

'So do I,' the physician admitted.

'Are not all men brothers?' a voice whispered behind them.

They gave a start. That toneless and yet contemptuous voice now caused them an instinctive repulsion.

The saint was leaving the hamlet, after visiting every hut. He sat down some distance from them, raised his hand to his breast and made no further move.

They were about to approach him, when a puff of wind suddenly swept the Montagne-aux-Malades and distracted them for a moment. As they turned round automatically to expose their sweat-stained faces to the relative coolness of this gust, they noticed a change in the landscape: the cloud of dust covering the plain had broken up in several places and patches of countryside now lay revealed in the gaps. At the same time the sun pierced through the clouds, illuminating a number of details. As they had surmised, an unusual activity reigned on the roads. Brother Rose, who had keen eyesight, described carriages, horsemen and men on foot. According to him, they were all going in the same direction—away from the town.

'It looks like a general exodus, Prior,' said Jehan Maillard. 'War, for sure; but . . .'

He did not finish his sentence and remained wrapped in thought. The wind was now blowing in long gusts punctuated by periods of calm. The Prior, who was taking deep breaths, suddenly shivered and looked at his friend. The latter seemed as nonplussed as himself and kept dilating his enormous nostrils.

'Did you smell it?'

Jehan Maillard gave a sign of assent and his nose once more investigated the breeze.

'Isn't it the smell of a corpse in a state of putrefaction? One of our wretched lazars . . .'

'It can't be coming from the mountain. We have our backs turned to the huts and it's the wind that's bringing this stench. Besides, the remains of a lazar always smell of leprosy and this isn't the smell of leprosy, Prior, I'd swear.'

They fell silent for a moment, perplexed and uncertain. The wind subsided and the smell died away. They were returning to the stranger, who had remained motionless, prostrate on the ground, when they were again distracted by a strident noise like the sound of a rattle. It came from the summit of the mountain and seemed to be drawing closer.

11

As though this noise was a signal of dread alarm, wild panic immediately swept the Montagne-aux-Malades. Inside the huts, inarticulate groans betrayed the occupants' agitation and the doors were slammed shut. The Prior's servant dropped the luggage he was carrying and took to his heels, tearing down the slope as fast as his legs could carry him. Brother Rose blurted out in a terrified voice:

'The Negro, the Negro!'

The worthy monk had visited the most repellent areas with complete indifference, had followed the physician into loathsome huts and helped to bandage rotting flesh, but the approach of the black leper unmanned him. When he accompanied Jehan Maillard to the high lazar house, he always stopped some distance from the summit. The physician would go on alone. He himself had to muster his professional conscience and all the philosophy he possessed to steel himself to the prospect of the Abyssinian.

Since the sound of the rattle was close at hand, he tried to make light of it in a voice which lacked assurance.

'And here comes Satan who inhabits the summit of the cone. Master Dante placed him there and there's nothing missing in our own Inferno.'

The Prior trembled and felt weak at the knees. He was unable to utter a word. The figure of the abomination appeared at a turning in the path, coming down towards them. Thereupon the stranger, who had raised his head, seemed to shake off his torpor. He rose to his feet. He was swaying with fatigue, but his ardent will once more appeared to prevail. The Negro stopped some distance from him, surprised at not seeing him take flight. He was clad in full leper uniform: grey clothes, with a red heart conspicuous on his breast. A black veil concealed his face.

The stranger spread his arms and took a step towards him. The Prior instinctively gave a start and could not prevent himself from crying out:

'No, brother, no! Not him, not him, not the Negro! God does not demand it, God cannot demand such a thing!'

In spite of his manifest veneration for the saint, Brother Rose was unable to endure this sight. He lay down on the ground, with his head in his hands.

'Are not all men brothers?' whispered the saint.

'Let him be, Prior,' muttered Jehan Maillard. 'After all, the poor wretch, I can certify, is less riddled with disease than many others.'

'But he's black!' Thomas d'Orfeuilles groaned in horror.

The stranger took a second step. The Prior made a gesture of despair. At that moment, as though to add to his dismay, a sudden gust of wind wafted back the smell. All at once the entire high zone was impregnated with fetid miasmas which forthwith prevailed over the permanent stench of leprosy without mingling with it. The Prior and the physician were paralysed with disgust. The stranger appeared not to notice it and went on walking towards the black leper.

But the latter had smelt the infection and it had an uncommon effect on him. With an extraordinarily abrupt move-

107

ment, in the manner of a bird raising its neck, he quickly turned his face to the plain and stood motionless for several seconds, as though he perceived some supernatural sign on the horizon. As the stranger approached him with open arms, the Negro raised his head with the same instinctive gesture and confronted him. The Prior lost all control of his nerves.

'Stop him!' he cried. 'In heaven's name! I tell you God cannot desire this. There is a malevolent power at work here. This smell . . .'

'This smell,' muttered Jehan Maillard. 'At one time, in Italy, I seem to remember . . .'

The physician looked perplexed. The wrinkles on his grotesque brow had grown still deeper from the effort he was making to recollect some memory in the dim past.

He broke off, while the two monks crossed themselves frantically. The stranger had drawn level with the black leper. His manifestation of love and charity took the form of an assault. With a violent gesture he tore off the Negro's veil, revealing the bare face underneath: a face that was dilated, swollen, ravaged, but above all black, black as the face of a demon except where it was dappled by the disease. The saint clasped the abomination in his arms and pressed his lips against its cheek.

The embrace was of short duration and its unexpected outcome threw the onlookers into utter confusion.

The Negro first seized the saint's head in both hands and held it fast a few inches away from his own face which, despite its bestiality, now expressed a human sentiment: fear. He stood contemplating it like this for a moment, then, without releasing it, jerked his neck round towards the plain with an incredibly rapid gesture which irresistibly suggested the reaction of an animal on the defensive. His nostrils quivered, as though trying to inhale the stench which the last breath of wind still wafted over the slopes. During the time he remained in this position, with his neck stretched, his timorous expression assumed an uncommon intensity. Fright, horror and despair were already apparent in his features and in his eyes when, still in the manner of an automaton, he switched his gaze back to the saint.

His mouth, surrounded by hideous folds of fat, thereupon opened. From it there issued a shriek which echoed round the Montagne-aux-Malades and which froze the blood in the veins of the lepers of the high lazar house. At the same time, with the sort of violence that can only be inspired by mortal terror, he thrust the saint away from him. The latter staggered back a few paces before collapsing on the ground, where he lay inert like a disjointed puppet.

The black leper turned towards Jehan Maillard and, between one shriek and another, uttered a few words in his barbarous tongue. Then he turned on his heels and rushed off, while the rattle fastened to his belt accompanied, like a knell of doom, the curses he flung to heaven.

12

The disappearance of the Negro seemed to restore Thomas D'Orfeuilles' composure. He made a final sign of the cross and questioned his companion.

'What is it?'

Jehan Maillard did not reply immediately. He had turned pale. His brow was wrinkled still more deeply. He felt that the dim recollections which had flashed across his memory a moment before were beginning to knit together into a coherent whole of which he was about to grasp the significance: but even before seeing the light, before being able to pronounce the solution to the riddle, he was petrified by the presentiment of the horror which his imminent discovery entailed. This intuition deprived him of his usual composure. He eventually explained in a trembling voice:

'He said . . . really, I understood only one word: "black". Let me think. . . . That was it: BLACK. . . . He mentioned something black, of that I'm certain; that's the word in his language which I know best of all. He has often repeated it to me, while striking his breast with distress. . . . Obviously, on those occasions, he was referring to his own colour. . . . But not this time.'

His meditation was interrupted by a further malodorous gust. He suddenly changed his attitude, marched up to the stranger, who had remained inert, and addressed him unceremoniously:

'You're from the town, or so you told us; you ought to know what's happening there. We first thought it was a feast, but . . .'

He uttered an exclamation on perceiving the countenance of the man stretched out on the ground. The saint's face had grown cadaverous and seemed to be decomposing before his eyes.

'Prior, this man is dying!'

'A feast indeed!' the saint spluttered with a fearful grimace.

He tried to rise, but his head fell back heavily. He shut his eyes and did not make another move. Jehan Maillard, forget-

109

ting every concern except those connected with his profession, knelt down beside him and rested his head against his chest. At this contact the saint reopened his eyes and a strange rictus animated his face for the fraction of a second; with a final effort he spread his arms and convulsively hugged the physician, murmuring:

'Brother!'

Jehan Maillard struggled violently to disengage himself. His face expressed the same fear as the Negro's and his nostrils were quivering in the same way. He turned still paler.

'The odour of sanctity has vanished, Prior!' he cried. 'There's nothing left but the stench, the stench coming up from the town. . . . But this isn't, this can't be the smell of leprosy!'

At this moment the saint interrupted him. He was in the throes of a violent attack of fever and this morbid energy manifested itself suddenly in a torrent of disjointed words.

'A feast, you say? Ah, what a feast! With a procession . . . the procession of the dead . . . the death cart, at night. It was I who drove the death cart; no one else would dare. I myself flung the dead into the graveyard, along with a few who were only half dead. No sooner had I gone than the wolves came and scratched up the earth. After me, no one dared to drive the cart. . . . But are not all men brothers?'

He was now bellowing. The unexpected resonance of his voice filled the mountainside. For the first time he opened his mouth wide, unclenching his jaws to their full extent, as though, now that his mission was accomplished, he had no further reason to hold them tight. His tongue, which he had hitherto succeeded in concealing, looked as swollen as a bladder, and was bluish-black in colour, set in a palate of the same hue which exuded the foulest miasma.

'Dear Doctor, good Doctor, I recognize you. When I was struck down, it was you who came and attended to me . . . but at a distance of ten paces, of course, and protected by a grotesque mask soaked in incense. It was you who had my door nailed up . . . but you overlooked the window, and you forgot some of your scents. . . . It was you who forbade any creature to approach my lodging. It was you who marked it with a white cross and who wrote on the wall; "God have pity on us".'

'God have pity on us!' echoed Jehan Maillard, who looked as though he had been struck by lightning.

'No one took pity on me; but I had no fear of consorting with lepers. Leprosy is powerless against me. I have kissed thousands of lepers . . . including you, worthy Doctor. . . .

Leprosy kills slowly, you say? Ha-ha! Am I not myself an excellent physician; the best of physicians?'

'Prior!' Jehan Maillard yelled, shaking off his torpor. 'Prior! This saint of yours . . . of ours . . .'

In one bound he flung himself on the man, who had fallen back unconscious. In a frenzy he tugged back the long brown robe and tore off the rest of the clothing. The Prior then saw him falter and stagger backwards at the sight of the final horror he had unveiled.

Loathsome tumours, revolting sores of a hideous black colour were scattered over the saint's groin. The same dark stigmata could be seen under his arms and all over the rest of his body. The patches of infection, spreading and uniting with one another, had begun to envelop the body like a winding sheet.

The physician uttered an obscene oath. He was trembling from head to foot with rage. He pointed at the fatal marks and yelled, as he turned to his friend:

'The scourge which is a hundred times more contagious, a thousand times more terrible than leprosy, Prior! The disease that kills in five days: plague! The BLACK DEATH.'

The Lunians

1

'Thrilled and delighted to inform President of United States and members of SIC that living creatures exist on the Moon. Propose bestowing name of *Lunians* on these inhabitants who, from a distance at least, appear to have many points in common with human beings. Continuing observation. Detailed report follows soonest.'

After dictating this startling news without drawing breath, Weston, the leader of the first American expedition to the Moon, paused for a moment to check the fastening of his outlandish space-suit before leaving the hastily erected airtight building in which a permanently artificial atmosphere reigned, enabling the radio operators to work in comfort. With his usual discipline Joe, the head of the signals branch, had taken down the message without interrupting his superior. It was only when the latter had finished that he exclaimed:

'Sir, it can't be true! Living creatures!'

Weston paused for a moment by the double doors.

'I saw them with my own eyes, Joe. I'm not crazy. At first I thought I was; but Barclay and Powell also saw them. It's the discovery of the century. Get that signal off to Washington right away. It will cause a sensation. And keep in radio contact with me. I'll draft a report as soon as I can. . . . One head, two arms and legs, just like us, Joe! But enough of this chatter. I must get back to Barclay and Powell who are keeping watch. Notify the officer in charge of the military escort. I haven't time. He'll be in command of the camp in my absence. Tell him to take all security measures. These Lunians may be dangerous.'

He went off. Joe uttered a few obscenities out loud to persuade himself that he was wide awake, then remained in a daze for several minutes, incapable of deciding on the next move. The arrival of his assistant Pat, a girl whom he admired for her sound sense, graceful bearing and professional conscientiousness, restored him to his senses and reminded him of his responsibilities. He told her the whole story in a nutshell and, without giving her time to comment on it, handed her the signal for immediate despatch. Then he donned his space-suit and went off to notify the military commander.

Pat rapidly made contact with Earth, transmitted the message and jotted down the acknowledgement of receipt and a brief note expressing the excitement caused by the news. Then, according to instructions, the Earth and Moon operators switched off after arranging to tune in again on a little-used wavelength known only to the initiated. Only then did Pat, a model member of the staff except during occasional fits of depression when Joe would turn a blind eye on her abrupt changes of mood, assert her right to view the event from a personal point of view.

She lit a cigarette, crossed her flawless legs, leaned back and followed her own train of thought, with a frown on her face and her eyes focussed on the big bay window, made of a special glass, through which could be seen the mountains of the Moon.

Ever since its pre-planning stage Operation Moon had been steeped in a Secret, Confidential, Secret and Confidential, and even Top Secret and Confidential atmosphere. The SIC (Secret Interplanetary Committee), directed by the President of the United States himself, consisted of a few reliable members of the government and a limited number of specialists, scientists and engineers, who had been sworn to secrecy. A landing on the Moon conferred such power that the American leaders felt they were not entitled to let even a friendly nation partake of it, let alone a hostile country. All the tests had been carried out in a desert. The technicians who had not embarked in the rocket were kept under close surveillance. The explorers communicated with SIC headquarters by means of a radiophonic station installed in an underground chamber in the White House.

The blast-off had taken place under cover of an artificially densified blanket of clouds. The rocket had rapidly reached such a velocity that only a miracle could have enabled it to be tracked by any observatory or even by the most powerful telescope after Palomar, the very mention of which sent a shudder down every American spine—the Soviet Eye, or simply The Eye, as it was more commonly called.

The tricky part was the touch-down and the subsequent manoeuvres of the explorers on our satellite, since at this time, towards the end of the century, the Eye had a magnifying power which almost certainly enabled it to spot a comparatively small moving object on the surface of the Moon. The technicians had averted this danger and solved the problem in a supremely elegant manner by arranging for the landing to take place on the *blind side* of the Moon, the side which fires the imagination of poets and which eludes direct terrestrial observation. As everyone knows, through the conjunction of its two movements (revolution round the Earth and rotation on its own axis) the Moon always has the same hemisphere facing us.

This plan had been successfully achieved. The rocket had reached the Moon at the specified point; the Eye had seen nothing. The flight had even escaped the notice of Palomar. The space pioneers had then embarked on their exploration.

Weston hurried up the slope to reach his companions who were waiting for him at the top. The triumphant message he had dictated had fanned the embers of his enthusiasm, as though the official announcement of his discovery enhanced its prodigious character.

Lunians actually existed! This shattering discovery bathed his expedition in the magic light of the great adventures of which he had been dreaming ever since the blast-off and the absence of which had been a cruel blow. So far, he had to admit, they had all been disappointed by the monotonous development of their mission and its utter predictability. Conscientious scientists, assisted by infallible robots, had carefully seen to every detail in advance. After the initial jolt, the force of which had been calculated and offset exactly, the voyage from the Earth to the Moon had been plain sailing. The constant sensation of floating in infinite and uniform space had soon palled. Liberation from the force of gravity had amused the travellers for a short time but boredom had settled in as soon as they had grown accustomed to phenomena that had already been described any amount of times. The approach to the Moon and the first sight of the mysterious hemisphere, after the rocket had changed direction and slipped round the blind side of the satellite, had caused a certain amount of excitement. They had all feasted their eyes on this new world as it drew closer and closer. But novelists, endowed with prophetic imagination, had been through this experience before them and popularized its interest in countless replicas.

It was with mortification, almost with despair, that Barclay, the psychological specialist of the expedition, admitted to Weston that in his report to the SIC on the impressions
114

created by the landing, he had found little or nothing to add to the works of Wells and a few other writers of the previous century.

During the initial period of their sojourn they had experienced one disappointment after another, gradually perceiving that the blind side of the Moon resembled in every way the hemisphere visible from Earth, every detail of which had been studied by Palomar and the Eye, and certain views of which had even been reproduced by well known painters.

They had the depressing sensation of treading the devastation of a highly conventional backcloth: jagged mountains whose contours had not been softened by erosion, a bright-red sun, stars visible at all hours of the day in a sky that was almost black; an alternation of searing sunlit surfaces and ice-cold shadows with no intervening penumbra; an horizon sharply etched as on an infra-red plate, not a detail blurred or indistinct. At the sight of these features, Powell, the chief mechanic of the expedition, who was anything but sensitive to the manifestations of nature, said he felt as though he had been decanted into a film studio. As for Pat, she remarked despondently to Joe that at every waking moment they were confronted with a lunar landscape—deplorably, unmercifully lunar.

Weston, however, had been more disappointed than any of them. An engineer with a brilliant future, a research specialist, placed in command of the expedition, despite his youth, on account of his brilliant technical qualifications, his energy and above all his adventurous spirit, a man with a passion for discovery, he had come to the sad conclusion that laboratory work was more exciting than exploring the Moon!

But everything had changed since this morning. Lunians existed! For the rest of his life Weston would remember the emotion that assailed him when, having clambered up a mountain to enlarge their field of observation, the three men had perceived an apparently human figure moving slowly along a valley. It could not be a member of the expedition; they had left them behind them. They had to believe the evidence of their three pairs of eyes, however fantastic the vision: the Moon was inhabited. There, in front of them, was a Lunian.

Other figures like the first one presently came into sight among the rocks. Weston was so afraid they might evaporate into thin air that he was loath to take his eyes off them even for a second. But the importance of the discovery required him to report it to Earth without delay, whence his hasty return to the base camp and his instructions to Joe. He could now hardly wait to rejoin his two friends.

He arrived panting at the top of the mountain. Barclay and Powell had not moved from their position behind a big rock, from which they could observe the valley below without being observed themselves. He questioned them anxiously by means of a small radio set which each of them carried inside his space-suit.

'Well, what's happening?'

'They're still there,' said Barclay. 'And what's more, Weston,'—his voice trembled with excitement—'they're rational creatures. They're *working*. Just look.'

Joe and his assistant Pat had not moved from their listening-post for several hours; they were waiting for a call from their leader. Joe had already contacted him once, only to be told: 'Later. . . . No time now. . . . Wait . . . it's fantastic!' which was scarcely calculated to assuage their curiosity. Pat grew more and more restless as time went by. She got up, walked across the room and, for the umpteenth time, fiddled with the apparatus which regulated the composition and pressure of the atmosphere.

'This damned machine's broken,' she said irritably. 'I feel as though there was a tropical storm weighing down on us, and my scalp's prickling all over.'

'The air's O.K.,' said Joe. 'It's your nerves.'

'It's intolerable,' exclaimed Pat, refusing to be mollified. 'Weston might at least tell us what they look like.'

'He's already told us: "several human characteristics".'

'Oh, Joe,' Pat cried in an agitated manner that contrasted with her usual composure. 'If only they could be in some way different!'

'After all, he only saw them from a distance. Maybe they have beaks like birds or claws like lobsters, if that's what you want.'

'And maybe crocodile skin,' Pat exclaimed furiously. 'That's not what I meant at all.'

'I know. But what's the point of racking your brains . . .'

At that moment Weston's call sign came through. Joe and Pat feverishly adjusted their earphones. To be on the safe side, they both took down their leader's message. This precaution was not superfluous, for certain passages were so strange that every so often either one of them or the other broke off for a moment, gaping and paralysed with surprise.

'The Lunians,' Weston reported, 'are not monsters with tentacles or claws, as they have sometimes been described in works of science fiction, but absolutely normal creatures with almost every human characteristic. The Lunians, Mr. President, have bodies like our own and are about the same size as

116

ourselves. They each have one head, two eyes, and two arms. They walk upright on two legs, to each of which is attached one foot. The Lunians, I hasten to add, Gentlemen of the SIC, live in houses, are capable of speech and are sociable. They eat. They drink. They think . . . I apologize for this incoherence, but it's difficult to keep calm and collected at a moment like this. I shall try, however, to give you in chronological order a summary of our observations and an account of how we established contact.

'For a long time we kept out of sight at the top of the mountain, watching a dozen or so Lunians moving about in the plain. Barclay and Powell had already observed in my absence that their gestures had nothing in common with the haphazard agitation of animals or irrational creatures but, on the contrary, pointed to their being intelligent, prompted by a sense of purpose, organized and engaged in a clearly defined activity. In one word, Mr. President, the Lunians were *working*. The nature of this work soon became marvellously clear. It was particularly moving for us Americans. There, before our eyes, the Lunians were engaged in building a city. . . . Gentlemen of the SIC, my heart almost burst with joy when the Lunians revealed themselves to be so close to us in mentality and in method, when, even before approaching them, I ascertained the sacred character of their activity, the efficacity of their endeavours, and the power and precision of their machines.

'Yes, the Lunians have machines, Mr. President! In the chronological order of our discoveries, which coincides with the order of their importance—for what distinguishes a human being from the animals if not the art of making use of instruments and the quality of these instruments?—it was these machines which filled us with wonder immediately after the sight of the Lunians themselves.

'A detailed report on these machines follows, drafted by Powell, who, you will see, has been able to study them and even try them out. We were fascinated to see a sort of pocket bulldozer marking out a road, and an automatic concrete-mixer similar to our latest models. These machines, each driven by a single Lunian, worked remarkably smoothly in the absolute silence which the absence of atmosphere produces on our satellite. They seemed perfectly adapted to their purpose. I should like to stress this incredible yet unquestionable fact: on many points they appeared to be in no way inferior to equivalent American machines. Here are Powell's initial technical observations . . .'

'Oh, hell!' Pat exclaimed furiously.

After asking Joe's permission, she took off her earphones and started restlessly pacing up and down the room. Powell's mechanical particulars were slow torture to her. When living creatures existed on the Moon! At a sign from Joe she returned to her duties. Weston was on the air again.

'This report will give you an idea of the extremely advanced technical stage which the Lunians have reached, and you can imagine how highly we regarded them even before accosting them . . . as we now have. Contact has been established, and I have a number of other wonders to report concerning this strange race for whom we feel an instinctive liking.'

Weston's voice was now tense with excitement. Joe and Pat listened with bated breath, conscious of the effort he was making to sort out the mass of sensational discoveries he had made.

'The Lunians,' he went on, 'are friendly and sociable creatures. We came out of hiding. We waved to them. They waved back in reply. We went down into the valley. They greeted us enthusiastically. They invited us to visit them. Listen . . .

2

At this time, towards the end of the century, Comrade Zarkoff was in command of a Secret, Confidential and even Top-Secret-and-Confidential service which was housed in a secluded fortress in the Kremlin and whose members were all kept under strict surveillance.

This evening Zarkoff departed from the habit of respect and discipline that had been engrained in him. Scarcely waiting to be announced, he swept into the office of Number One in the Union, pushed past a sentry and gasped:

'Sensational news, Comrade! They have discovered some living creatures!'

'Living creatures?'

'And with human characteristics! We're in the middle of receiving Eastgueff's report. I stopped listening in to come and tell you.'

'You're sure Eastgueff's in his right mind?'

'Eastgueff's a mystic, but he knows how to keep his head in an emergency. He sometimes interprets facts, but he never makes them up. And the news has been confirmed by two others. They've given detailed particulars. They've made contact . . .'

118

Number One sprang from his chair and, unescorted, rushed along to the fortress through a maze of corridors. Only when he had reached the threshold did he pause and turn to Zarkoff who was right behind him.

'You're certain the secret hasn't leaked out?'

'Certain.'

'What about Palomar?'

'Palomar can't see a thing. It's happening on the blind side of the Moon.'

They went inside. Two members of the service were on duty at the listening-post. One of them was taking down the message, the other translating it into Russian by means of a complicated code. Number One motioned to them not to break off. He drew closer and read over their shoulders:

'I, Eastgueff, in charge of the First Soviet Interastral Mission, together with the two undermentioned comrades, request our comrades on Earth to regard every particular recorded here as an expression of the complete and utter truth. We give our word for this as Russians of the Party. All this exists, exactly as we describe it. All this we have seen or heard on the blind side of the Moon. Firstly, in one word, the Moon is inhabited. There are Lunians. We have encountered them and consorted with them. Following is our objective report.

'As you know, a short distance away from our provisional camp, we found a favourable site for the construction of the first Russian settlement on the Moon. A few comrades and I were engaged in the preliminary work when I heard a sharp exclamation in my microphone.

'I looked up. I saw one of my comrades standing motionless, with his arm pointing towards the summit of a hill overlooking our valley. I glanced in that direction, and my stupefaction was equal to his own. A human figure stood out against the rocks, waving with its arms. Thus it was, Comrades, that we became aware of the existence of inhabitants on the Moon. This apparition produced on us an impression I can hardly describe: firstly, because of its unexpected character, but also, to no less a degree, because from it there emanated a sort of glow . . . I'm afraid I cannot make myself more clear than this, but at the first sight of this creature, whose features and proportions we were unable to discern, we were all affected by a mysterious, infinitely disturbing emanation—that indefinable quality of nobility and majesty of bearing which, I believe, betokens superior beings.

'Presently we perceived two other Lunians like the first one, making the same gestures and obviously trying to attract our attention. Our original emotion having died down a little,

119

we decided to copy their behaviour and raised our arms towards the black sky with as friendly a gesture as possible. The Lunians seemed extremely excited. They stamped their feet and slapped one another on the back, as some people do at an amusing or entertaining sight. Instinctively we did the same, which added still further to their delight. Then, after a few hesitations, they started slowly making their way down the mountainside. Their attitude was not at all threatening—rather the reverse—and we went forward to meet them. Soon afterwards, Comrades, we observed the inhabitants of the Moon at close quarters.

'Here is the result of these preliminary observations. The Lunians, as we shall show later, are remarkable creatures, of human shape and proportions. What disturbed us at first glance, however, was their smooth greyish skin, their huge rectangular eyes, and their noses which seemed to have developed like elephants' trunks. As you will see later, we were deceived by appearances . . . but meanwhile I continue my chronological report.

'There we were then, face to face, we Russians feeling somewhat embarrassed as to how to express our friendly feelings. On the offchance, I raised my clenched fist to the height of my forehead. To my great surprise the tallest of the Lunians grasped the meaning of this greeting immediately, for he repeated my gesture and his two companions forthwith followed suit. We realized then that they were intelligent and sociable. After this, the tall Lunian lowered his arm, clasped his hands together and shook them several times, looking at us with his enormous eyes. This, we realized, could only be a manifestation of friendship. The Chinese greet one another in somewhat the same manner on Earth, albeit bowing more deeply. We hastened to reply in similar fashion.

'This exchange of courtesies, this evident good will on their part, created a bond of sympathy between us. We motioned to them to come with us to our building site. There, the shortest of the three showed a lively interest in our machines. Our good opinion of their intellectual capacities was confirmed when we saw the small Lunian—now listen carefully, Comrades—go up to one of our miniature bulldozers, examine it closely, walk round it several times and finger various parts of it, nodding his head reflectively. Then, after looking at us, and since we gave him an encouraging smile, being intrigued by his behaviour, he suddenly got into the driving seat. After a few tentative gestures, he managed to switch on the engine, put the machine into gear and operate it almost as efficiently as our most skilled workers. We were all so moved by this demonstration that we spontaneously broke into loud applause. Seeing this, the two other Lunians joined in and clapped their hands as though the gesture was familiar to them.

'Just picture the scene, Comrades. Lunians and Russians, fraternally united in a common enthusiasm, clapping with all their might, and, in the religious silence of empty space, a Lunian worker at the controls of a Soviet machine! That is what our eyes beheld on the blind side of the Moon. We wept with emotion.

'The Lunians' attitude inspired us with such confidence, and we instinctively felt such sympathy for them, that we decided to take them to our provisional camp to further our acquaintanceship and to receive them according to the rules of our traditional hospitality. They followed us. We reached the camp after an hour's march. We quickly put the other comrades of the expedition in the picture and a reception was improvised in the main hall. The Lunians seemed extremely surprised at the sight of our installations, but they had not finished astonishing us either. Comrades, comrades, they resemble us like brothers! They breathe! They speak! I am still so flabbergasted that I can hardly give a coherent account . . .'

'That devil Eastgueff must have been drinking,' Number One bellowed, taking advantage of a short pause. 'Zarkoff, this isn't the report of a man in full possession of his faculties.'

'Eastgueff is not a heavy drinker,' said Zarkoff. 'And a man who has discovered creatures similar to himself on the blind side of the Moon may be excused for momentarily losing his composure. Furthermore, his report is borne out by the others.'

'A collective hallucination,' growled Number One. 'Who can tell what effect these voyages have on the human brain?'

He broke off, for Eastgueff had resumed his report.

'After we had entered the airtight room, preceded by the Lunians, we started taking off our space-suits. We wanted to celebrate this incredible event in comfort and reveal ourselves to our guests in our natural aspect. When they saw us discard our interplanetary uniform their surprise seemed to increase, and for the first time, thanks to the presence of the artificial atmosphere, we heard them utter a strange noise which clearly expressed astonishment. This was followed by some other indistinct sounds, as though they were conversing together. Then, slowly, like chrysalises breaking out of their cocoons to turn into glorious butterflies, the Lunians began to shed their skin . . .'

'Just what I thought,' interjected Number One. 'These incoherent images are proof of an hallucination. We must recall the whole team.'

'Let's go on listening,' Zarkoff begged him.

'This smooth greyish skin, Comrades, was only an overcoat, a sort of space-suit bearing a certain resemblance to our own, and their trunks were merely pipes. Like us, the Lunians, being living creatures, need air. Like us, they supplement the void of space with artificial means. Where do they live in their natural state? Where do they store the air which they need to move about the surface of their heavenly body? We believe, as was once suggested, that it must be inside the Moon, in underground chambers. It will probably not be long before we find out, when we get to know them better. But listen to the sequel.

'There were our three Lunians in the process of shedding their skins. It was not from a vain urge to add colour to this report that I evoked the radiant birth of a butterfly. All my comrades and I were irresistibly reminded of a metamorphosis of this sort when we saw, emerging from the coarse dull outer envelope, a profusion of brilliant colours and shimmering hues, a wealth of intricate designs and arabesques. We were dazzled, Comrades, and slow to perceive that this splendour derived from mere articles of clothing—from the shirts and ties worn by the members of this race whose refinement and good taste become more apparent every moment.

'We were actually so spellbound that for some time we were unable to perceive the other marvels which the Lunians' gesture suddenly revealed to us: heads like our own; yes, ears, noses, mouths similar to ours; torsoes and limbs which are perfect copies of our torsoes and our limbs. And this is not all. The Lunians drink: we clinked glasses together. The Lunians *speak;* we heard them.

'The Lunians speak, Comrades! Granted, their language will be difficult to interpret, for we're bound to admit that the sounds they utter are very different from anything we have ever heard on Earth. We experienced a momentary disappointment; from their appearance we were expecting an almost human dialect. Our expert, however, agrees with me that theirs is a proper language fairly akin to our own in spite of the guttural accents which are those of any talking bird.

'However, one can't judge people by the melodiousness of their speech, and we shall now show you that the Lunians are not only reasonable and industrious creatures, but also kindly, amiable, affable, peace-loving, amenable, cultured and quick-witted. Judge for yourselves, Comrades. These Lunians . . .'

'These Lunians are really exceptionally attractive,' said Pat, discarding her earphones and stretching her limbs.

'You women!' growled Joe. 'A man merely has to be a foreigner for you to fling yourselves at him. So naturally a Lunian . . . even if he had been covered in hair from head to foot and equipped with tentacles, you would have found him irresistible!'

'He's not covered in hair and he's not equipped with tentacles!' Pat replied furiously. 'And I haven't flung myself at him, as you know perfectly well. It was Weston who asked me to have a word or two in private with one of them and try to find out how they behaved in their relations to women.'

'Weston has gone as nutty as a fruitcake,' said Joe sententiously.

'The study he has undertaken has to be complete in every detail. That's what he told me. He said: "We want to know everything about these Lunians. And you're the only one here who can decently deal with sexual problems at first hand. This is a confidential mission. Can I count on you?" I thought it over. He was right. I was the only one. So I went ahead.'

'Went ahead! Went ahead!' growled Joe, raising his eyes to heaven. 'But not before insisting—I was there, I heard you —"I'll take the big fair-haired fellow. The one with the little moustache, who seems to be the leader." '

'If it comes to that . . .' muttered Pat, biting her nails. 'Oh, Joe,' she went on, suddenly carried away by her feelings, 'you mustn't hold it against me. I so longed to see one of them close up, to find out personally . . .'

'All right, all right,' said Joe. 'I'm not criticizing you, Pat. Only, while these experiments were going on, I had to slave away twenty hours a day. I've hardly set eyes on those Lunians. When the party was given in their honour, I was barely allowed one drink with them in the mess. I had to relay the songs they sang for us back to Earth.'

'Lovely voices.'

'That, I grant you. I've never heard anything like it. But I've had enough of keeping the signals branch going on my own.'

'You don't have to any more,' sighed Pat. 'I'm back on duty. My mission is over.'

'Was it interesting?' asked Joe. 'I haven't even had time to read your report.'

'Private and Confidential. Weston's the only one who has seen it.'

'Yes, but was it interesting?' Joe persisted. 'Anything unusual about it?'

Pat fell silent, wrinkling her brow. A tense expression came over her delicate face as she anxiously tried to sort out her memories. She shook her head impatiently, as though she found it impossible to draw any conclusion from her conflicting emotions, and finally replied in a low voice:

'I don't know.'

'You don't know!'

'It's true, Joe,' she protested with a hint of irritation. 'Weston has already told me to be more explicit. He's so crazy about these Lunians that he wanted something positive. All I could tell him was, I don't know. . . . Oh, I admit, at times I felt he was really different. . . . Exceptional charm, Joe, as I said before, and a delicacy of manner that you don't often find with us, I admit. . . . But then, at other moments . . .'

'At other moments?'

'You would have thought he'd learnt the Kinsey Report by heart,' Pat exclaimed, 'and was trying to base his behaviour on it!'

'I see,' said Joe pensively.

Pat gave an irritable shrug and turned round to look out of the window. Joe heard her reciting in a low voice and in a disconsolate tone:

' "Over the mountains
Of the Moon,
Down the Valley of the Shadow,
Ride, boldly ride,"
The shade replied—
"If you seek Eldorado!" '

He did not question her any further. In any case Weston's call sign came through just then and they both got down to work. Their chief was more and more enthusiastic and now spent most of his time with the Lunians, accompanied by the leading experts of the expedition, feverishly carrying out a study of their character and customs. Every day he drafted a report which was sent off immediately. At the White House the information on the inhabitants of the Moon had been eagerly scrutinized, classified and labelled, and was begnining to form the contents of a large Confidential file.

Today Weston reported:

'The Lunians are really superior creatures. Our admiration for them has increased during the last week, which we have devoted to studying them and assessing the vast resources of their civilization. Judging them by the attainments of our own nation, it seems clear that a close collaboration between our two peoples will prove to be a powerful factor in our joint progress. It is the hope of all of us Moon pioneers to contribute to the establishment of a sincere and lasting friendship between them and the United States.

'You have received Powell's reports and, like us, appreciated their high technical standards and industrial accomplishments. You have read the findings of our specialist in comparative anatomy who, after a complete examination by means of X-rays, concluded that the internal structure of the Lunians is about the same as ours. You have taken note of Pat's private and confidential report, which amply confirms the impression of deep *humanity* which they have made on all of us. Today I propose to rise above all these material details and tell you something about the Lunian *mentality*.

'To begin with, I must explain how it has been possible for us to pursue our investigations as far as we have. Firstly, it is because we discovered—and with what excitement!—that the Lunians were perfectly acquainted with the Binary language which scientific circles are beginning to use on Earth. You know what this language is. It consists in representing a given word by a formula condensing purely affirmative or purely negative replies (Yes or No being represented by 1 and 0) to a series of increasingly specific questions. Since the formula thereby progressively eliminates all that is false and reveals all that is true concerning this word, the word is eventually particularized in a simple, precise and rigorously logical manner. It's the ideal language for the research we have undertaken. It discards ambiguity and vagueness in the same way—if you will forgive me the comparison—as the void of the Moon's atmosphere eliminates all penumbra and deceptive gradations, leaving room only for stark light or utter darkness, icy cold or torrid heat.

'When we discovered that the Lunians spoke Binary fluently, there were no further difficulties of communication and our knowledge of this people rapidly made great progress. Up to then, in fact, as I told you, the ordinary language of the Lunians had defied our attempts at translation.'

'The big fair-haired fellow made himself quite clear, however,' Pat muttered. 'And yet I speak Binary very badly.'

'Secondly, we are helped by the fact that the Lunians trust us. They are co-operating to the utmost in our investigations, holding nothing back that might be of interest to us but, on the contrary, going out of their way to enable us to avail ourselves of their attainments in every field.

'Having explained this, I will now give you a few particulars on their economic system. With the Lunians, Gentlemen of the SIC, business activities are not dispersed among several corporations which spend their time fighting one another, as is the case with us. They are, on the contrary, condensed into a single one and this gigantic enterprise is none other than the State. We were dazzled by this conception. One would need to be jaundiced by prejudice not to recognize at a glance the simplicity, efficiency and even supreme elegance that this system entails in the general problems of planning and management. Barclay and I have discussed it at great length and we are convinced that it constitutes a considerable advance compared to our own. It's somewhat galling to realize that no nation on Earth has ever thought of achieving this unification. We had to come to the blind side of the Moon to discover it. It seems to me, however—and this is a comfort —that we Americans made a few tentative moves in this direction at the time of the New Deal, notably with the TVA. But they were extremely half-hearted. We feel, Gentlemen of the SIC, that the Lunian example should incite us to further progress.

'I have referred several times to *progress*. I should like to point out here that the Lunians have an essentially *progressive* outlook. This is not the least of their qualities and is perhaps the one which creates the deepest impression on us Americans.

'If one rises above the details and takes an overall view of the Lunian spirit of organization, one sees moreover that there are striking similarities between them and us. Our great principle of *management*, for instance, which is inscribed in letters of gold over the doorways of our biggest enterprises, "Trusted Until Sacked"—that's to say, "Give your men great responsibilities and have perfect confidence in them until you fling them out"—well, Gentlemen of the SIC, that's the very principle that obtains in every Lunian enterprise. They even apply it to the managment of the State. Their politicians have extensive powers, until they cease to give satisfaction. Then they are immediately liquidated, like our inefficient engineers or bungling administrators. This rule, which we thought we had invented, is applied universally on the blind side of the Moon by bold-minded creatures who do not hesitate to derive all the beneficial consequences of a sound idea.

'Naturally, after the Lunians had told us about their system, I tried to give them a vague idea of our own. They seemed singularly interested and found great merits in it. Even taking into account their natural benevolence and courtesy, I saw from the warmth of their praise that their admiration was genuine, and to me the compliments of experts such as these are a source of great self-satisfaction. We have discussed the matter together in an atmosphere of perfect cordiality and concluded that it would be of the greatest interest for a mixed commission of specialists belonging to our two countries to make a full comparative study of these questions.

'It was their actual attitude in the course of these meetings that revealed another deep similarity between the Lunian and American genius. They never embark on a discussion with the childish intention of denigrating their interlocutors. On the contrary, like us, even more than us, they excel at picking out what is best in other people's ideas, not to belittle it or scoff at it, but to turn it to good account and, if necessary, adopt it after adapting it. We alone on Earth, I believe, have reached a sufficiently advanced degree of evolution to be able to appreciate other peoples' achievements objectively, not to condemn automatically what comes from abroad but, on the contrary, to attract or copy anything that might be benefit to us. When I recognized this tendency in the Lunians, Gentlemen of the SIC, I admit I felt less alone in the world and I am therefore extremely grateful to them.

'I see I am unconsciously veering on to a philosophical plane, so I shall hand over to Barclay who is more qualified than I am in this field. What he has to tell you is almost incredible. Yet, as I can likewise testify, it is all perfectly true. The Lunians still have many surprises in store for us.'

There was a short break in the transmission, during which the two operators read over their notes pensively. Then Barclay embarked on his report.

'I feel you should know at once, Gentlemen of the SIC, that the Lunian mind has long ago discovered, and proclaimed in no uncertain terms, the great axioms established by our own philosophers and which the American nation is only just beginning to grasp. I shall prove this to you, not by abstract remarks but by facts.

'Listen to these sayings, faithfully translated from the Binary language, "The question whether objective truth is an attribute of human thought—is not a theoretical but a *practical* question. Man must prove the truth, that's to say the reality and power, the 'this-sidedness' of his thinking in practice. . . . Philosophers have only *interpreted* the world differently, the point is, to *change* it."

'Does that not express an admirable sentiment? And tell me, Gentlemen, did you not first of all think as I did, that this was a quotation from our own William James or John Dewey? Does it not contain, while transcending them, the principles of pragmatism and instrumentalism which are the contemporary poles of American thought? Yet this is actually an extract from the work of a Lunian philosopher, a certain Mark or Max. (We cannot be more precise than this since the Binary language has the drawback of deforming proper nouns.)

'This Mark or Max lived in the last century on the other side of the Moon, Gentlemen. He seems to have been a preponderant influence and we never weary of hearing his work quoted. In an infinitely more lucid manner than James or Dewey he taught what ought to be understood by the Pursuit of Truth. It is not, he explained, an investigation in which the object is constant; it is a perpetual adaptation of subject to object, of the investigator to the truth under investigation.

'Thus matter reacts on mind. This grandiose outlook which in the final analysis confers a creative power on matter in its relations with mankind, spiritualizes all physics, transforming it into a sort of metaphysics which seems to be, after due consideration, the doctrine which is best adapted to our evolution and modern civilization. After attentively rereading certain chapters in the Bible, I realized that it was not impossible to interpret them in the sense of Lunian doctrine as established by this Max and his commentators. This is a task to which I should like to devote myself on my return to Earth and which, I feel sure, will help to bring about a religious revival in our country.

'I haven't enough time now to give you an idea of the Lunians' spiritual perfection. They have a quality, however, which I cannot pass over in silence and which gives a special attraction to all our dealings with them. I mean their *intellectual probity* and the absence with them of all preconceived ideas. In consequence of their philsophical outlook they are always ready to admit their mistakes and faults. On a few rare occasions we have seen fit to point out some detail of their doctrine which appeared to us to be open to criticism. Far from resenting this, they pondered over the point in question and thrashed it out with us, as a result of which, in most cases, they acknowledged the cogency of our remarks and thanked us for them. They did this publicly, without the slightest indulgence towards themselves. . . . An acute sense of self-criticism, Gentlemen, which does not exist with other races, and which impressed us deeply. . . . To such a point indeed that we are now trying to stifle our own somewhat overbearing instincts and to imitate their humility. We indulge every day in an objective examination of our thoughts and our behaviour, and if we discover anything reprehensible in them we do not hesitate to proclaim it out loud, while recog-

128

nizing the error of our ways. I think this self-criticism is one of the most important factors in a nation's progress. . . .'

4

Meanwhile the highly coloured reports of Eastgueff and his comrades were piling up in the fortress in the Kremlin, creating a deeper and deeper sensation among the few initiates who had access to them. Confidential orders had been given to the Eye which spent every night scrutinizing the visible hemisphere of the Moon, albeit in vain: no vestige of life was to be seen on that side. In the face of the detailed information received, however, Number One no longer denied the existence of the Lunians. Zarkoff was convinced of it. Fresh security measures of an unprecedented strictness were introduced to keep the fabulous discovery secret.

'Another report, Comrade,' said Zarkoff. 'These Lunians are amazing.'

Number One snatched the message out of his hands and read it.

'Comrades, we suggest the immediate despatch to the Moon of a committee of specialists consisting of the greatest minds in the Union, with a view to studying the customs, beliefs and methods of the inhabitants. We pioneers are no longer qualified to make the fullest use of the wealth of material which is being disclosed to us at every moment. We can merely give you an incoherent summary, dazed as we are by the constant flow of fresh revelations.

'It is imperative, Comrades—in fact we feel it is vital— that we should grasp the fundamentals of a great Lunian philosopher called Djemmz and extract the greatest benefit from his conclusions. He has stated: "An idea is true just so long as the fact of believing in it is profitable to our existence." . . . And again: "Our duty to seek the truth is integrated into our general duty to do whatever is rewarding." . . . Here is another saying, which rings particularly forcefully in our ears: "We cannot reject an hypothesis if consequences useful to life spring from this hypothesis." . . . And yet another, which is its immediate corollary: "If the hypothesis of God produces a satisfactory effect, in the fullest sense of the word, then it is true."

'Comrades, it is impossible not to ponder deeply on the far-reaching consequences of these words. After a careful self-examination, we cannot help wondering whether, in Russia, we have not sinned out of levity, whether we have paid

129

sufficient attention to religious problems and whether it would not be a good thing to reconsider these questions in the light of the Lunian examples. If you had heard our friends describe all the benefits they have derived from their beliefs, you would think as we do that there's something to them—and something which ought to be *rewarding,* to use the felicitous expression of Djemmz. Listen to this:

'The fundamental laws which govern the Lunians are summed up in what they call their Constitution and this is regarded as holy writ. To them their method of government is the Lunian fulfilment of a divine doctrine. This doctrine is contained in a book they call the Bible, and each citizen possesses a copy which he has read and on which he has meditated. The Number One Lunian, or President, takes an oath of loyalty on this breviary after his investiture. His authority is thereby reinforced, and his responsibility, being shared with a Being regarded by all as impeccable, is thus a very light burden. When a substantial sacrifice is demanded from the people, the President takes refuge behind this Bible and the sacrifice is acknowledged without discussion.

'This deification of the governmental role was intensified in a masterly fashion by one of the last Lunian presidents, a certain Rougefelt (if we have accurately interpreted the Binary language) who introduced a new ritual into the ceremonies of his investiture—a church service, for which he himself chose the hymns and the psalms. Subsequently, each time he was called upon to take an important decision, he never did so without rereading the Ten Commandments and then proclaiming that his decision was inspired by them. It should be explained that these commandments constitute the quintessence of their sacred precepts. In an appendix we give you a full translation of them for, after analysing them, we feel certain that the Party could derive enormous benefit from including them among the statutes in an adapted form.

'To come back to this Rougefelt, who was a remarkable statesman, he seems to have indulged towards the end of his reign in certain abuses of his authority—which is obviously a possible disadvantage of the divine system. Here is the story we were told about him and which has given us food for thought.

'He once enjoyed enormous popularity. Realizing his life was drawing to a close, he assembled a personal museum to perpetuate his memory. At his death the whole nation was deeply affected; his cult was piously celebrated for several months and a vast crowd filed endlessly past the mementoes of his activity. Then, all of a sudden, the enthusiasm ceased. Lunian wisdom, which we place very high in the scale of values, had perceived that he had not been infallible, that he had often shown lack of caution, and that he had even made a number of serious mistakes. All at once the nation turned into a merciless judge. From then on, his name, which had once been venerated, was mentioned only as that of a dangerous innovator, even a despot. All his former collaborators fell into disgrace and were removed from office. After this no doubt salutary reaction, he sank into complete oblivion.

'Admittedly, Comrades, this shows rather harsh ingratitude towards a man who, for all his faults, had rendered unquestionable service to the nation. Our generous Soviet instincts prevent us from bestowing an unreserved blessing on such a sudden reversal of opinion and on this debasement of a man who only yesterday was idolized as a demi-god. And yet, after our initial shock, we somehow felt that the Lunian nation was to be praised for its critical spirit and for pulling itself together in time to defend its liberties. This characteristic shows, moreover, that in an evolved and vigilant nation like our own, there should be no major drawback in setting the government under the seal of Divinity. As to the advantages, they are obvious.

'What fascinating pages, what books could be written about the excellence of Lunian methods in every field! Though no expert myself, I should like to demonstrate the ingeniousness of their economic system.

'Our Communist ideal, Comrades, according to which all property of public interest must be collective and which we sometimes experience difficulty in putting into practice, this ideal is fully realized here on the blind side of the Moon. But what in particular has made us speechless with admiration is the beauty of the procedure by means of which this result is achieved. It consists in this: the funds needed for the launching or development of any enterprise are divided into several parts, sufficiently small to be within the range of all purses: these parts are known as *shares*. (Note incidentally the suggestive force of this word.) These shares can, and indeed are, subscribed by any individual who wants to have an interest in the enterprise. Thus the worker, the unskilled labourer, the peasant are automatically owners of their factory, building site or field, and share in the profits from their exploitation. In this way a great Communist principle is put into practice.

'Extremely simple, you say? Yes, but it is just this mixture of ingenuity and simplicity in the practical solution of problems, which we witness every moment here and which makes us exclaim: "There's nothing to it; but it was the only solu-

131

tion!" Obviously, it merely had to be thought of. But no one had done so before.

'There is one particular science (I'm reading from some notes hastily jotted down in my diary) in which the Lunians are past masters. This is the science of propaganda.

'They call it Publicity. It's usual field of action is the press, the radio and the cinema; but the expert agents who direct this activity rack their brains every day to find new procedures and fresh formulas of seduction which no one can resist. A single example will give you an idea of what I mean: as you know, we have more or less completed the construction of the first Soviet settlement on the Moon and have already moved in. The other day, on waking, we were surprised to see every house, every building, adorned with a sort of disc the size of a small tablemat and blood-red in colour, all aflame in the harsh light. They were everywhere. Wherever we looked, we were dazzled, hypnotized by this profusion of scarlet suns which had a literally fascinating effect and remained engraved on one's mind even after one had closed one's eyes. We had been spellbound for several hours, pondering in vain on the meaning of these emblems, when our Lunian friends came and called on us. At first our perplexity increased, for they turned up in a motor car with its sides decorated with the same glaring disc. They smiled at our astonishment. Then, in a mysterious manner, they took several cases out of their vehicle and on these, Comrades, was painted the same mysterious circle. They opened one of the cases, and our startled eyes beheld several rows of small bottles containing a brownish liquid. Would you believe it? Each of these bottles was adorned with the same disc, only in miniature.

'No words can describe the impression created by this gradual multiplication of scarlet circles. We were captivated and enraptured, even before tasting it, by a beverage offered in such a fascinating manner. We would have drunk it even if it had been vitriol. In point of fact this liquid is palatable and we were not at all disappointed. It's a refreshing, sparkling drink, and possesses unquestionable tonic properties. We have all taken to it and feel extremely fit since imbibing it in large quantities every day.

'Perhaps you will think this is a somewhat trivial procedure for such a subtle science as propaganda. But could we not adopt similar methods in a nobler field and thereby draw the attention of the masses to our fundamental creeds? My comrades and I are convinced it would be rewarding for the Party to have a Lunian publicity agent as a permanent member of its staff.

'But it is in the purer science of Administration, that's to say the art of creating businesses, and organizing and directing them, that the Lunian genius develops its full power. Here again, one example will suffice to convince you. A meeting, consisting of the greatest brains on the Moon, had demonstrated scientifically that a certain nuclear explosive similar to our own hydrogen bomb (the Lunians have also made some brilliant discoveries in this field) was impossible to manufacture, its actual production conflicting with the fundamental laws of physics. This was the experts' unanimous opinion. Well, the masterly Lunian administration did not agree. It decided to ignore the opinion and demonstration of the scientists, decreed that the machine *was* feasible and ordered them to put it into effect. The explosive was then produced in a very short time and gave complete satisfaction. In this case one can see the triumph of the Lunian philosophical creeds which I mentioned earlier on: truth is gradually integrated into whatever is rewarding. It was a Lunian technician who informed me of this splendid episode. He's a taciturn middle-aged man who is not often to be seen because he spends his time in a sealed chamber. I think he's in charge of the signals section. In the end he summed up the principle of this organized research in a striking phrase: "We people first of all blithely decide on what must be discovered; then we discover it."

'This sentence struck me so forcibly that I kept repeating it over and over again. But then I had a surprise. The Lunian girl I mentioned in my private report, who provided me with such interesting information on the behaviour of Lunian womanhood and who happens to be this technician's assistant, this girl suddenly burst out laughing when I quoted this phrase with manifest admiration, or rather when she made sense of it—for I hasten to add she speaks Binary very badly and needs a lexicon to translate it. Well, she burst out laughing and in a most disconcerting manner. Tears streamed down her face, and her body, which I described in my report in as much detail as possible, writhed as though in the throes of madness. I asked what she meant by this. She tried to explain by pointing with her finger to certain words in her dictionary.

'I finally managed to grasp the fact that the above-mentioned sentence should not be taken seriously. Apparently it comes under the heading of what Lunians call a *joke,* and is imbued with a somewhat extraordinary sentiment known as *humour*. The definition of these terms is not clear. I must admit I can see nothing to laugh at in the wording of this fine

133

phrase and I wonder if the Lunian girl understood it properly.

'The subsequent explanations she tried to give me were even more obscure. When her fit of mad laughter was over she suddenly became serious and melancholic, and claimed that if ever the Lunians were saved it would be on account of jokes of this sort and the spirit which dictated them to a few rare individuals. What a very strange way of expressing oneself! How can the fact of being lacking in respect towards the authorities save them? And above all why *save*? Save them from what? Are the Lunians in some danger?

'What perils can menace, on the blind side of the Moon, creatures so powerfully equipped in the struggle for existence and who govern themselves with such wisdom? I thought of meteorites. . . . But no. I think I have discovered where the Lunians normally live, where their amazing industries flourish along with their wonderful civilization which we still only know from a few samples and descriptions. It is certainly not on the surface of our satellite, which is deserted. Our friends seem to be here as explorers. In all probability they live underground, perhaps at a great depth, for whenever I've asked them this question, they've always pointed downwards toward the centre of the Moon. We shall soon know for certain, for they've promised to take us to their capital, which they call *Home*.

"This *Home* is surely sheltered from meteorites. What, then, can they be afraid of? Perhaps, after all, my girl friend is rather weak in the head and I should not attach too much importance to what she says. I sometimes wonder whether she is really a significant representative of Lunian womanhood or whether she might not be an anomaly? In that case all the material I've obtained from her should be treated with caution and I would merely have to repeat my series of experiments. She's certainly very strange. I've already noticed an unusual attitude and abnormal reflexes in her, and it's not the first time she has referred to some vague peril, with an anxious air which precludes all suspicion of mystification. I am completely nonplussed.

'We really need some specialists here to elucidate all these obscure points. Comrades, there are unsuspected marvels on this side of the Moon, of which we have barely skimmed the surface. There must be any amount of others, even more surprising, in the sublunary depths, in this Home which we are impatient to see. I want to end this report on a more familiar note, by giving you a brief account of how the Lunians spend their leisure hours. Their favourite amusement is *comics*, that's to say drawings accompanied by short captions which appear in countless publications. They have shown us a large number of these, laughing loudly over them. This time I had no difficulty in understanding the reason for their hilarity, and in sharing in it, for these illustrated strips have an irresistible effect. I don't remember having ever seen my comrades laugh so loudly or so long and, I confess, I myself almost choked. I am sending you by radio some samples of these *comics,* the technique of which we might perhaps adopt for our own use, making them instructive as well as entertaining.

'With the Lunians, then, serious work and the most remarkable achievements in the sciences and the arts are not incompatible with gaiety and high spirits.

'We hope this report, with all its imperfections, has been of interest and made you understand the growing attachment we feel for these people.'

5

On the following day Eastgueff sent off another report which contributed still further to the chronic state of excitement that now reigned in the mysterious fortress in the Kremlin, from which Number One no longer budged. This message started off with a hymn of triumph.

'Comrades, until now we had seen nothing! Our previous reports contained mere trivialities compared to the magic vision it has been granted us to behold today. We have been to the Lunians' capital. We have seen their *Home!'*

Number One uttered a sharp exclamation. The technicians on duty in the listening post went so far as to give a triumphant cheer.

'Let me explain,' Eastgueff went on. 'And once again, please forgive my emotion. We have been to their *Home,* but only in spirit. Our eyes have beheld its splendour without our bodies leaving the Moon's surface, thanks to a remarkable invention of our friends. They have perfected an apparatus which projects on to a screen the most probable picture of foreseeable future events, once it has been provided with the data of this synthesis. To prepare us for the journey, the Lunians set their machine in motion. We thus saw, better than in reality, the various stages of our arrival at *Home* and especially the glorious welcome we shall be given.

"We were able to photograph part of this film and shall now transmit it to you. Look, Comrades.

'This is a street—and not the biggest, we were told—at

Home. A glance at the size and harmonious proportions of the buildings gives an idea of the Lunians' boldness of concept and mastery in matters of architecture. But in spite of the attraction of these majestic edifices, one's attention is immediately drawn to the crowds: the crowds deliriously thronging this avenue and shouting in a delirium of joy.

'Why this jollity, why this enthusiasm verging on frenzy? And why is every child at Home waving a little flag while the adult citizens raise their arms in a gesture of admiration? Why? Because of us, Comrades—oh, never have we felt so proud!—because of us, pioneers of the Soviet Union, the first men on the Moon. This hospitable nation, this nation with an instinctive generosity of heart and mind, has been notified that some fellow creatures are arriving, bearers of a message of love and peace: and this announcement has provoked the exuberance you can see. . . . At this point the Lunian girl whispered in my ear that this was a manifestation of . . . *snobbery*. What does that mean? She is as strange as ever and I understand her less and less.

'It is us, Comrades, yes, it is really us you see there, standing up waving back at the crowds, in that sumptuous motorcar flanked by motor-cyclists in gleaming uniforms. It's towards us that these waving arms are stretched, on us that these avid glances of curiosity, hope and love are directed. It is us progressing slowly through this multitude, in an atmosphere bathed in glorious artificial light, and saturated in clouds of flowers falling from millions of windows, in swarms of multi-coloured streamers, in showers of tickertape, strips of linen and masses of other incongruous objects which the Lunians, in their frenzy at our presence, are hurling through the air to celebrate our arrival.

'And you have not seen anything yet! The scene now shifts to the head of this procession, for our car is part of a long and impressive parade. This column is composed of lavishly decorated vehicles on which have been erected gigantic cardboard figures with intensely lifelike masks. Between these carnival floats, strange animals go marching along . . . we haven't time to describe it all in detail. Let's move right up to the head of the column. It's there you'll see the marvel of marvels. Now then. . . .

'Comrades, we didn't dare mention it until you had seen it with your own eyes. You would have accused us of being liars or visionaries. But you now see it just as we did. With us, you must acknowledge the evidence. We are in Paradise, Comrades! The Lunian *Home* is the material realization of Paradise. And this is no exaggeration, for here are the angels.

'We knew it. We felt it. The perfection noted up to now in

136

every Lunian achievement had made us suspect the existence, in the depths of the heavenly body, of a race still nobler and more refined than that to which our friends belong. We were not mistaken. Here before your eyes are the unquestionable representatives of these transcendental creatures. Our surface Lunians fell into ecstasies at the mere image of them, and so did we. They call them *girls* or *gals*. We can think of no other word than *angel* to define their radiant spendour.

'Clothed in short tight-fitting tunics which reveal their divine legs, draped in white capes with silver spangles, crowned in diadems encrusted with precious stones, these angels set the pace of our procession through the avenues of the Lunian *Home*. These men—or maybe women, for the sex of angels is uncertain—march along in step, in perfect alignment, in ranks of eight. Their cohort is divided into battalions and legions, and some of these legions accompany the parade with a supernatural music in which the celestial trumpet strikes a dominant note. A few paces in front of them, an angel even taller, more beautiful and more graceful than the rest—an archangel, a seraph—marches alone, and the whole parade takes the step from him. He marks the rhythm with a long staff adorned with spiral patterns. And see with what ability, with what supernatural grace, he hurls this stick into the air, makes it describe a few elegant arabesques, and catches it again in full flight, to the blare of the brass of the musical legions and the frenzied applause of the crowd.

'I want to end my report with this apotheosis. What more can I add to this magic spectacle? We are now longing to live these unforgettable hours in the flesh. Meanwhile, please send us some pictures of the Union. Choose those which best illustrate our genius. We shall show them to the Lunians. In spite of the difficulty of competing with what we have seen, perhaps they will convince them that our civilization is not unworthy of respect and perhaps they will induce them to undertake with us a voyage to Earth.'

6

'Mr. President,
'Gentlemen of the SIC,
'We are living through momentous hours while waiting to penetrate the depths of the Moon and reach the sources of the sparkling civilization of which we have so far been given only an inkling. Our Lunian friends have promised to take us there. After which, we shall bring them back with us to

Earth. They are prepared to come with us, and the pre-vision of their welcome in New York has filled them with joy.

'Talking of our forthcoming expedition to the Lunian settlements, our friends have had the delicate thought to show us a few cinematographic views of them beforehand. I felt, Mr. President, that you should have an advance copy of these documents. Thanks to a contrivance assembled by our operators, they will be transmitted to you as and when they occur.

'I am therefore now speaking to you in clear—I, Weston, from the Lunian capital—and I shall confine myself to translating to you the descriptions given us in Binary.

'This, my Lunian friend tells me, is a sample of what they can do in the realm of Public Works. This film outlines the history of a huge enterprise which consisted in turning the natural course of a river and directing it towards a vast deserted region. These views show the inland sea which had to be drained; these, the huge lake which had to be created. Here are some others showing the mountains it was necessary to level and the glaciers that had to be destroyed to accomplish this gigantic plan. . . . Yes, there are seas and rivers in the hinterland of the Moon! These extraordinarily vivid pictures need no comment. One thought alone crosses my mind: by mobilizing all our forces, perhaps we could have done just as well, but certainly no better.

'This—and you'll appreciate how they alternate the pictures of their prodigious industrial activity with those of their culture and their arts—this is a public entertainment in one of their theatres. Here we must acknowledge and yield to their striking superiority in music, dancing, singing and stage design. These—the rapid succession of these marvels doesn't give us time to take everything in—are some of their schools . . . this is a university. We see here amenities that are not to be found in our most up-to-date institutions. This is an immense stadium where the boys and girls of a whole city compete with one another in speed and physical dexterity. What harmony in their gestures! What health! What a sacred spirit of competition shines in their eyes! And what remarkable performances they accomplish! What hadn't struck us before, so natural did it seem, is the marvellous artificial light in which everything is bathed. How do they obtain such an effect?

'Here . . . but what's this? It looks like a map. Yes, our commentator tells us, it is indeed a map. A map of . . . a map of the *Moon?* Why not?—we too have maps of the Earth. But the strange part is, this map resembles *our* maps of the Moon. It looks as though it had been drawn from another heavenly body, with the aid of a powerful telescope.

138

And even . . . yes, it's an exact drawing of the hemisphere visible from Earth. I recognize all the craters, all the dried-up seas, all the mountains that Palomar has gradually discovered. What's the meaning of this mystery?'

There was a fairly long pause. A similar curiosity, mingled with a vague feeling of anxiety, consumed the members of the Interplanetary Commission at the White House as well as the operators Joe and Pat at the American camp, who were dealing with the transmission. Weston eventually resumed his report. He was stammering and seemed to be in great distress.

'What's the meaning of this mystery? The explanations of our . . . friends . . . are muddled. I don't understand. They say: this map is an example of our astronomical technique. And they're now showing us other pictures to illustrate their mastery of this science. An ultra-modern installation. . . . But down below you can see the sky, and in this sky a disc that can only be the solar disc. So we're not in the bowels of the Moon, and this fabulous light is not artificial—is that the answer? Here is this installation. One of the most powerful astronomical stations, they say. . . . Oh, that instrument! It's a telescope . . . a huge telescope . . . my mind's reeling. I recognize this diabolical machine. I can't be mistaken. Its sinister outline is engraved on every American heart. They're explaining: "It's this machine that enables us to make our maps. . . ." It can't be, it can't be. Help! This machine is the Eye, the infamous Eye which is now searching the nocturnal sky and focusing on a familiar satellite, the Moon—the Moon as seen from Earth. . . . Help! These Lunians, these miraculous Lunians. . . . This is the Eye, the Eye!'

'Christ Almighty!' cried Joe. 'Now I understand. They're . . .'

'Joe! Joe!' sobbed Pat. 'To think I was beginning to be quite fond of them!'

Weston went on in a stifled voice, addressing the operator:

'Joe, listen to my last instructions. My colleagues are going to try to make their way back to camp; but I'm finished. I'm dying of disappointment. Sound the alarm. We're in mortal danger. The officer in charge of the military escort must now assume command of the expedition. Dig in and take cover. Prime the atomic grenades. Prepare the nuclear explosives. Ask for reinforcements from Earth. Do you understand, Joe?'

'Yes, sir,' said Joe.

Weston's voice was now scarcely intelligible and his tone betrayed utter despair.

'Monsters, Joe! Oh, what a terrible trap we've fallen into! Demons, demons from Hell. . . . I'm dying, I'm finished.

139

The shock has been too much for me. Don't you see? These are ordinary *men,* Joe—ordinary horrible men from Earth!'

This was the last message in clear recorded on the Moon. Thereafter priority was given to secret weapons and strategic signals in cypher. However, the chronicler is in a position to make a rapid summary of the outcome of this tragic misunderstanding.

Like Weston, Eastgueff did not survive the sudden collapse of his dreams. Each of the two leaders fell dead as soon as he realized the lowly nature of the other. The rest of the explorers took refuge in their respective camps and a double iron curtain was drawn over their activity while they waited for instructions from the authorities on Earth. The interplanetary commissions issued these instructions after deliberating for two days and two nights. They were two-fold:

Firstly, the pioneers were to evacuate the Moon and keep moving for forty days in outer space to undergo a period of delunization before being allowed back on our planet.

Secondly, before withdrawing, they were to take all necessary measures to blow up the Moon a few seconds after their departure. The satellite had become too important a strategic point to be allowed to subsist after the enemy had set foot on it.

These orders were duly carried out. After an arduous period of quarantine, the explorers were considered cured and fit to return to their native land. The Moon was destroyed and reduced to an impalpable dust which melted into the infinity of outer space. Its disappearance had no serious consequences. Pat was the only one to sigh on certain nights at the sight of the dark empty sky as she recollected her lunar adventure.

This clean sweep of the firmament even brought with it certain advantages and was regarded by the SIC as a step forward. In the first place, dangerous tides disappeared. Secondly, poets ceased indulging in sickening comparisons on the brilliance of the heavenly body. Madmen became less mad, wise men wiser. The quiet of the night was no longer disturbed by dogs baying. And last but not least, as Joe asserted, women's characters improved, became more equable, and were no longer subject, as in the past, to unpredictable moods.

THE DIABOLICAL WEAPON

All the members of the committee rose to their feet as the prince entered the room where the meeting was being held. The army representatives snapped to attention; there was even a certain amount of heel-clicking. The civilians instinctively adopted an almost identical attitude. These marks of respect were not only decreed by etiquette and consciousness of rank but betokened the genuine esteem and admiration they all felt for the Head of State. The prince had established his position through his energy, intelligence and strength of character.

He acknowledged this homage with a cordial wave, shook hands with General Perle, who was presiding over the committee, and sat down. The general forthwith declared the meeting open, knowing that the prince hated a lot of pointless talk.

The committee had finished its work and its principal members had met that day to examine the results, draw a practical conclusion therefrom and draft a final report which would be submitted to the government. Their investigation had lasted for over a year. The prince considered it so important that he had made a point of attending this final meeting. He enjoyed personal contacts and wanted to talk things over with the men whom he had entrusted with a mission that was essential to his country's future, before reading the official report.

In fact it had been his own idea to form this special committee, and the selection of its members had been inspired by him. The majority consisted of army men. They were all crack officers, granted, but their selection had depended more on a certain exceptional trait of character which the Head of State valued above all else: a realistic and at the same time imaginative mind which was not clouded by tradition and dis-

141

cipline to the point of being engulfed by mere routine. They were all forceful personalities and most of them were young. There were some civilians as well, the prince having insisted on this since he felt the importance of the matters to be discussed exceeded the scope of specialized technicians and demanded the objectivity of an outlook that was not exclusively military. They too had been selected from men who were capable of entertaining and assimilating new ideas, who were ready to submit original solutions to the great problems of the day. The prince had eliminated the official authorities on principle, reckoning that they always have a tendency to wallow in the past. He himself had always been a fierce opponent of routine. Since he had come to power he had done his utmost to inspire the country with the spirit of research and novelty which seemed to have declined in recent years and without which there can be no great achievements. At the time of the formation of the committee he had summed up the qualifications he expected from its members in a sentence which was not his own but which corresponded exactly to his views:

'Men who are not one war behind, who are capable of catering for the next war and who don't expend themselves preparing for the last one.'

For this was the burning question, as General Perle reminded them in his opening speech:

'. . . To foresee, gentlemen, the various forms a war might take, if by ill luck it should break out in a few weeks from now, in one year or in five years—it has been acknowledged that any longer-term project would be dangerously conjectural—such is the mission with which the government entrusted you a year ago. To foresee and draw up a programme of effective measures so that the army is prepared for every eventuality and is not surprised, as has happened too often in the past, by situations which its leaders, by negligence or timidity, had not ventured to envisage. . . .'

A smile of approval appeared on the prince's lips. Encouraged by this, the general went on:

'To foresee, prepare, and finally submit to the government a military policy based on the findings of this investigation. These duties have been undertaken by all of you, representatives of the various armed forces, with a freedom of mind, an absence of preconceived ideas, which I cannot over-emphasize. I think I should add straight away that they have been useful, for they point the way to a well defined and unanimously approved line of conduct, which we are all agreed to recommend to the authorities.'

At this juncture, in spite of his intention not to intervene in

142

the preliminary report, the prince could not prevent himself from holding up his hand and asking a question.

'All agreed?'

'All agreed,' said the general.

'All agreed,' echoed the members of the committee with one voice in reply to a glance of enquiry from the prince.

'A unanimously approved line of conduct? You mean there is not a single dissenting voice among you?'

'None, Sir,' General Perle firmly replied. 'There were many however, during our first meetings. I can assure you that every imaginable objection was raised and every possible point of view scrupulously analysed. But as our investigation proceeded, the conclusion forced itself on us all—I repeat, all. It forced itself with the rigour of a mathematical chain of reasoning, as a result of a strict analysis of all the data of the problem and an absolutely objective synthesis of all the deductions. It will force itself on you too, Sir, I am convinced. I can positively state that the military policy which we propose is the only logical and reasonable one in the present circumstances.'

The prince looked at him intently. The words 'rigour', 'analysis' and 'synthesis' appealed to him on principle and he was not surprised to hear them on the lips of General Perle. The latter had been to one of the greatest schools in the country, where science and mathematics were essential parts of the curriculum. Although he was still addressed by the rank of general, he had left the army some years previously and now held an important position in private industry. In appointing this logician to direct the work of the committee, the prince had intended to offset the ardour of 'avant-garde' tendencies of the younger and more impulsive delegates, in the hope of obtaining thereby this balance between realism and imagination which were the two poles of his own mind. What he had just heard, however, made him suddenly wonder if he had not been wrong to entrust him with this mission. He was careful not to reveal this misgiving and merely enquired:

'And what is the gist of your conclusion?'

'If you don't mind, Sir, it would be better to listen to our investigators' findings. The conclusion will then emerge automatically from proven and incontestable facts.'

'Carry on,' said the prince.

The general called on a young colonel who had been detailed to investigate the state of the land forces. He was a soldier first and foremost, but also a first-class brain. He had taken part in several actions and been to the leading military academies, but was not the sort of man to trust blindly in past experience or abstract theory. His personal and original views, which some people considered revolutionary, had already brought him to the notice of his superiors. The prince had followed his career with interest and insisted on his being entrusted with one of the main sections of the investigation.

The initial part of his report was delivered methodically and in a clear voice. He first apologized for referring to a number of facts that were already well known, but this was essential to give a complete idea of the situation. Then he embarked on a general survey, covering the various classical weapons of war.

The infantry? He was obliged to mention this branch of the army, for it held an important place in the present military organization. But, after a thorough examination, it did not seem reasonable to give it a leading role in a future war. He was even personally convinced, and was not afraid to say so, that its role could be discounted more or less completely.

He gave a brief example of what he meant by this. In a defensive position, any large concentration of infantry units presented a far too vulnerable target for enemy nuclear weapons and inevitably resulted in a hecatomb of human life, a massacre adding pointlessly to the material damage.

The same argument precluded any large-scale offensive action like those in the past.

'In this field,' the colonel pointed out, 'it is just possible to conceive a few minor operations by small isolated groups with limited objectives. And even then our own nuclear weapons, which are by no means inferior in power or accuracy to those of other countries, enable us to obtain more rapid and decisive results.

'The very notion of occupying territory, Sir,' the colonel went on, warming to his subject, 'which was the main function of the infantry in the past, is now out of date. For why occupy territory, either friendly or enemy, when the nuclear weapons of both sides will inevitably have rendered it untenable within the first hours of hostilities?'

Tanks? Armoured cars? He had made a special study of these machines, which played such an important role in the last world war. He had no difficulty in showing that their days were over, that no extensive action could be expected from them and that it was chimerical, in the present circumstances, to think of safeguarding the security of the country by research or preparation of any kind in this field. The reason? The same, more or less, as for the infantry. With modern means of detection, a large concentration of mechanized units was open to immediate destruction by a couple of judiciously aimed atomic bombs. Even if a few machines escaped

144

total disintegration, the fuel supplies, workshops and maintenance teams which they required would inevitably be annihilated.

'As for imagining a sudden thrust prepared in secret, even supposing, Your Excellency, that this was possible to achieve, which is conceding a great deal, its effect of surprise and alarm would be literally derisory compared to that produced by a single rocket of ours carrying a nuclear bomb.'

'Derisory' was the word which occurred most frequently in the colonel's survey. He used it again with reference to the artillery, the engineers and a few ancillary services, to which the same objection applied—nuclear weapons rendered all of them 'derisory'.

In his subsequent recapitulation, the colonel again emphasized this fact, proceeding to more general considerations and dealing in fuller detail with consequences he had barely touched upon.

'In view of the supremacy of these weapons,' he said, 'we have come to the definite conclusion that our present troops and equipment are pointless. Not only is our classic use of these units inefficient, but also—and this perhaps is the most serious point—no sensible person can think of a way of employing them fruitfully. I am sorry to have to present the situation in such a gloomy light, but I feel I should be shirking my duty if I tried to conceal the truth. These are the facts. Manoeuvres of any kind have lost their point. Strategy and tactics are now meaningless words. The instruction given in our military academies is no longer of any practical value, and soldiering in general, such as we know it, is tantamount to a futile pastime barely fit to distract a few old dodderers.'

Having paused for a moment, the colonel fancied he saw a shadow pass over the prince's face. Realizing his statements were liable to be interpreted to his disadvantage, he felt he ought to justify them straight away. He grew more vehement, and a note of heartfelt passion crept into his voice.

'You must not think, Sir,' he said, 'that this judgement is a facile excuse to mask a certain sloth or inertia in the military leaders. Nor must you think it is based on abstract data. I came to this opinion only after verification of unimpeachable facts. The present situation is deplored by the entire army and I have had confirmation of this on the spot. In the course of the recent general manoeuvres I talked to hundreds of officers of every rank and every age. I noticed in all of them the same anxiety—this is not too strong a word—the same despair in the face of the present tragedy. Together, a thousand times, ten thousand times, we tried to find a remedy . . .'

This was true. During the latest manoeuvres, which had

145

lasted longer than usual and been repeated several times, the young colonel had been unstinting in his endeavours. Momentarily abandoning theoretical speculations, he had first of all mingled with the troops. He had quickly noticed that the officers in command of the fighting units were fully aware of the menace that hovered over their heads and were doing their utmost to escape it while remaining within the framework of the themes imposed upon them. He had collaborated closely with them and very soon realized that their efforts, like his own, were all to no purpose. Every experiment led to the same conclusion. The dummy nuclear rockets always landed on the spot and at the moment which were bound to thwart the cleverest plans, destroy the most carefully worked out formations and frustrate every tactical movement. The most partial umpire, the most fervent supporter of conventional weapons, was obliged to acknowledge their annihilation.

Then, since his mandate empowered him to approach the higher ranks, he had had a word with the various headquarters and insisted on the themes of the manoeuvres being modified. Here again he had encountered for the most part nothing but comprehension and good will. He and the experienced staff officers had set to work without respite, with a feverish zeal, an inventive ardour prompted by anguish. The old generals themselves recovered their youth in this desperate search for a theme that was not ridiculous, a strategic plan that was feasible—in one word, for a form of warfare compatible with the diabolical power of nuclear weapons.

'We found nothing,' the young colonel concluded in a trembling and somewhat solemn voice. 'We found nothing, Sir. We found nothing, gentlemen. I therefore feel it is my duty to state here and now: in so far as the land forces are concerned, the atomic menace leads inevitably to the death of the military art.'

He sat down in a hush that was almost palpable. All eyes turned to the prince, who remained silent, wrinkling his brow. General Perle then called on the investigator appointed by the navy, a captain.

The latter stated his case with the same forcefulness as his colleague and the spirit of his report was identical. He started off where the colonel had ended, mentioning the countless enquiries undertaken by the sailors to find a possible use for conventional fleets and stating that he had shed tears, and so had many others, at the fruitlessness of their efforts. But the fact was clearly established, and it was his duty to point it out: these gigantic aircraft carriers, battleships, cruisers and other conventional vessels were likewise doomed to more or less total destruction at the very start of hostilities, and the blows they could deliver bore no relation to the damage caused by the smallest rocket with a nuclear warhead.

'Our only effective weapon,' he declared, 'consists in small pocket submarines operating independently and capable of launching such rockets. Since today we possess enough of these vessels to lay waste a continent, we cannot conceive to what use the others can be put, except for review purposes. As I said before, we all deplore this fact, but units of this type cannot in any way be regarded as constituting a navy. In their case there is no question of navigation, seamanship or any of the manoeuvres that form the basis of our profession. Their function is reduced to moving in a straight line, at a great depth, until the required position has been reached. A handful of mathematicians equipped with calculating machines are all that is needed as a headquarters staff. With regard to the navy, press-button warfare excludes any other.'

This form of warfare was likewise the only practical one in the eyes of the air force representative. He had no difficulty in showing that the present squadrons were about as useful as children's toys and that the existence of nuclear weapons nullified all research into new prototypes of aircraft. As to the training given to the bomber and the fighter pilots, it was a sheer waste of time. In the air, as on land and sea, the atomic phantom reduced all classic conception of warfare to nought.

The leading members of the committee had finished their report. General Perle turned to the prince. The latter had still not said a word, but he was visibly worried and far from satisfied. Granted, the ideas that had been elaborated were not new to him. Granted, they meant the shelving of old conceptions, and this he did not find at all displeasing. But he felt disturbed, almost terrified, by the negative attitude which the committee's findings seemed to imply. His purpose in uniting these efforts and prompting this investigation had been to arrive at a solution to these delicate problems and not merely to confirm a state of affairs that had been known for some time. Here were all these first-class officers who, in their fear of being considered routine-minded, seemed to be intent on passive resignation and in favour of doing nothing. They regretted their attitude? So they should! That naval captain admitted to shedding tears on summing up the situation. He certainly had something to cry about! When all was said and done, all that had emerged from their enquiry was the pretext for a total abdication of the armed forces.

He manifested his feelings in a tone of voice which gave warning of the storm to come.

'Let's sum up the situation,' he said to General Perle. 'As far as I can see, you are all convinced that our conventional military equipment—tanks, artillery, battleships, aircraft and so forth—no longer serves a useful purpose?'

'None at all, Sir,' the general asserted. 'None at all, since the development of nuclear weapons.'

'That it is so much scrap metal?'

'That is precisely our opinion.'

'That the same applies to the troops, the staffs and military academies?'

'Exactly the same, Sir.'

'And that consequently you have nothing better to do than twiddle your thumbs and snivel!' the prince burst out.

'Oh, come now, Sir.'

This protest, and above all the furious, almost disrespectful tone in which it was uttered, restored some hope to the Head of State. Looking round him, he was pleased to see that his accusation had affronted all the other members of the committee. He was satisfied to discern on their faces a sentiment very far from resignation. The eyes of the colonel who had spoken on behalf of the land forces glinted even more than anyone else's. He inwardly congratulated himself on his outburst. There was nothing like a goad of this sort to stir people up and get the best out of them. He was sure now that a constructive idea was going to emerge from this meeting. He had misjudged these officers of his. They were not the sort of men to sit back and acknowledge such a total abdication. They had not yet said all they had to say. Their innermost thoughts were still unvoiced. He was completely reassured by the first words of General Perle who again took the floor, in a somewhat calmer frame of mind but in a tone that still betrayed his vexation.

'Sir, I don't think you have quite understood. Not for a moment have we lost sight of the fact that our mission entailed the obligation to make positive recommendations to the government.'

'That was my idea too,' the prince muttered in a conciliatory tone.

'If we have revealed the situation as it is and insisted on the extent of the evil, it is merely to justify these recommendations, which are of a somewhat revolutionary nature.'

'I have nothing against the revolutionary spirit.'

'It is to make the military policy we propose appear *indispensable* to you, for it is directly opposed to the one which the government has been following these last few years and which it has tried to impose at every international conference.'

148

'What, then, is your final conclusion?'

'Allow me, Sir, to add a final word to the statements that have been made here: the malevolent power of nuclear weapons renders impossible not only conventional warfare but warfare of any sort. The threat of annihilation is too great for any State to assume responsibility for it. This has become a commonplace, obvious fact.'

'Agreed,' said the prince impatiently. 'And so? . . .'

'And so,' General Perle proclaimed, 'the conclusion forces itself on us, as I said at the beginning of this meeting, with the rigour of a mathematical chain of reasoning. . . . And so,' he went on in a triumphant tone, 'we must have the courage to face the facts and attack the evil at its root. Atomic weapons make war impossible, Sir. These diabolical weapons must therefore be proscribed. This scourge must be declared illegal!'

The Age of Wisdom

1

The world was at last governed by wisdom and learning.
After centuries of error, reason and science had prevailed
over ancient superstitions. Mankind had ceased to be at log-
gerheads. Religion and politics had lost their interest. Geo-
graphical frontiers had been abolished. Tribes, nations, sects
and religions had gradually disappeared and fused into increasingly larger organisms until, in this year 2—— there remained only two human groups, two parties, two schools of
thought into which the sum total of the terrestrial population
was divided.

The first, known as the 'Corpuscular' or 'Electronic' school,
taught that everything in the universe is composed of small
elements called 'electrons': 'everything' meaning not only
matter, but radiation, space and even—as had been brilliantly
demonstrated by the learned Particule, the master-mind and
undisputed leader of this party—thought itself.

The second school, known as the 'Undulist', maintained on
the contrary that waves are the essence of the world and denounced the electron as an illusion created by the imperfec-
tion of our senses and measuring instruments. 'Nature is
nothing but vibrations,' the Undulists asserted; and, to Doctor
Particule's celebrated treatise demonstrating the granular constitution of the mind, Professor Armonique, grand master of
the Vibratory Party, had retorted with his deathless work *On
the Undulatory Nature of Thought*, in which he stigmatized
his colleague's capital error.

Each of these groups had its fanatical supporters. People
were either 'Granular', as the Electronists were commonly
called, or else 'Vibratory' as the Undulists were dubbed, in
150

the same way as they had once been Catholic, Socialist or American. Scientific discussions had taken the place of the age-old squabbles. They revolved round questions of theoretical physics, the internal structure of the meson or the photon, and elicited as much ardour and skill as the old political or religious debates.

The appellation of 'scientist' had long since replaced that of 'subject', 'citizen' or 'comrade'. Its meaning was more or less identical. It designated the ordinary man in the street.

Society had adopted a simple system of organization. Since there were two parties, there were two governments. Only one, however, was officially proclaimed, at the beginning of every year, Government of the Earth, as a result of universal elections; but the defeated party at once formed another, unofficial government, and all its followers automatically abided by its laws.

The two schools were administered in a similar manner, each directed by a Council of Experts, the one presided over by Particule, the other by Armonique, and this Council settled more or less every question in which its scientists were interested. This dualism had been stretched to its extreme limit. Paris, for instance, had become a double capital, both Undulist and Corpuscular; there were two classes of tradesmen, some Vibratory, others Granular; two categories of theatres and cinemas; two broadcasting corporations. There were two Metro lines, the one reserved for the supporters of the wave theory, the other for the partisans of the electron. This arrangement had obtained for several years and given more or less complete satisfaction.

Every year the two Councils, composed of the most famous scientists, brought the constitution up to date. Each scientist was required to know by heart the laws drawn up for the use of the masses, which summed up the essentials of their doctrine.

The popular Electronic breviary, amended by Doctor Particule himself, began as follows:

'1. The electron is the basis of everything. It is indestructible and eternal.

'2. The welfare of mankind can come only from belief in the electron.

'3. Faith in the electron is the foundation of all morality.

'4. Waves do not exist.

'5. The wave is an illusion of the mind. It is detestable, like every other error.

'6. The wave is the most hateful error of all, since it contains the germ of all the rest . . .'

The Vibratory code was drafted in the form of questions

151

and answers, which could be easily memorized. Armonique had been responsible for several chapters of it. It contained such passages as:

'Q. What is the wave?

'A. The wave is the essence of the universe. Matter and mind exist only through the wave.

'Q. What is man?

'A. Man, composed of matter and mind, is a subtle combination of waves.

'Q. What is Armonique?

'A. Armonique is a man; therefore Armonique is a combination of waves. But Armonique is the most subtle combination of waves that can exist, since he himself conceived the wave theory . . .'

No other instruction was given to the young, except to a few hand-picked candidates destined eventually to become members of the Grand Councils.

These assemblies were in fact omnipotent, and the greatest glory of a scientist was to be elected to them. But such a distinction was rare and necessitated not only a special knowledge of the doctrine but also the production of some original work.

For the experts were not bogged down in immutable scientific learning. Their minds were broad and adventurous. They believed in progress and welcomed the appearance of new ideas, on condition these complied with the fundamental dogmas. Particule himself was only too glad to acknowledge the discovery of certain groups of electrons which had escaped his notice. He flew off the handle only when the principle of the universe was questioned. To imagine waves where there existed only corpuscles struck him as the only punishable crime. In the same way Armonique condescended to consider other arguments besides his own in so far as frequencies were concerned. Torture and the death penalty, to his mind, should be reserved only for those who denied waves and indulged in the sacrilege of envisaging the corpuscular constitution of the world. The days when the masters of human destiny showed unreasonable intransigence were buried in the distant past. As far as tolerance was concerned, the sentiments of the two great leaders and their collaborators were perfectly matched.

Another point on which the two parties held similar views was the necessity of making scientific discoveries concur with the welfare and happiness of mankind.

Granted, the experts occasionally resorted to invective when the sacred fundamentals of the doctrine were called into question. People still remembered a congress at which the most qualified representatives of both schools had met in the hope of reaching agreement and total unity. The official minutes described the meeting in laconic terms, barely concealing the complete lack of success. In point of fact, after a few speeches in which sarcasm prevailed over courtesy, tempers had become frayed. The learned Armonique himself had lost his composure and solemnly accused Particule of corrupting the young by professing a theory incompatible with human dignity. The latter had forthwith replied to this accusation. Crude insults had been exchanged. A general roughhouse had followed, in the course of which President Particule had had his white tie torn off and his spectacles shattered. But to this day he still described with pride how he had avenged the affront by dislodging with his own fist three teeth from the jaw of the loathsome Armonique, that abominable little ape whose existence was a disgrace to modern science. Thus wisdom sometimes found itself in default.

Wars between nations, however, had not survived the disappearance of nations. The two classes of mankind lived side by side, pitched battles would have been impossible to organize, and the destruction of a town by a party could not reasonably be conceived, since it would have resulted in the destruction of friend as well as foe. The progressively greater sources of material energy which the scientists discovered every day were used only for the benefit of mankind. The Undulists saw in this power a fresh Vibratory manifestation. The Corpuscular theoreticians demonstrated that it was contained entirely in electrons. Endless quarrels disturbed the tranquillity of the peaceful scientists. (Some of them were not even particularly interested in these questions.) But the practical applications were always pacific.

Particule and Armonique were very old, very erudite, very illustrious men of science. They shared the respect of their colleagues and the admiration of the masses. They had to their credit an impressive list of ingenious discoveries. Both of them were laden with honours. Both of them vied with each other to improve the lot of suffering humanity.

2

On this first day of the year 2—— Doctor Particule awoke brisk of body, bright of eye and clear of brain. The electorate had entrusted the Electronist Party, of which he was the leader, with the mission of governing and officially representing Earth for the current year. He felt a justifiable pride and

153

a joy which was increased a hundredfold by the thought of the rage of his rival Armonique.

He rose betimes, had his daily shower of electrons and found himself in a favourable frame of mind for great achievements. Today there was going to be a meeting of the administrative committee of the Great Corpuscular Council. The scientist pondered deeply on the project he was planning to submit and put the finishing touches to the main passages of his speech.

At five minutes to ten the twenty leading lights who formed the supreme committee assembled in the Electron Temple, their usual meeting place. At ten o'clock Doctor Particule called for silence, obtained it and delivered this speech:

'Gentlemen and colleagues . . .'

(The appellation 'scientist' was in general reserved for popular harangues. Between themselves the scientists had preserved the ancient forms of address.)

'Gentlemen and colleagues,

'There is no point in my underlining the deep significance of these elections. The people have put their trust in us. The people, with their down-to-earth commonsense, have recognized the monstrous absurdity of a theory which I prefer not to name. The people have elected us. We are worthy of this. We shall show the people, in the course of the year that has just begun, the miracles that can be accomplished by the great Electronist family of whom I have the honour to be the leader.

'Gentlemen, mankind is greatly indebted to science and to the Corpuscular School which includes its only qualified representatives. Need I recall our most striking achievements? Need I mention those towns in which, all year round, there reigns a gentle uniform temperature? Those rivers diverted from their natural course to fertilize regions which were once desert? Those hostile coasts, bristling with rocky cliffs, transformed into sandy beaches? Those barren dried-up seabeds turned into vast pastureland? All this undertaken and successfully completed thanks to the omnipotence of the electron and—it must be admitted, Corpusculars—thanks to our enduring perspicacity!

'Nothing, my dear colleagues, is impossible for our genius. Let me tell you a story which will distract your minds from their incessant labour. Just over a century ago an imaginative writer—a "humorist", as the members of a certain extinct sect were occasionally called—felt it was an excellent jest, in order to put an end to some regrettable arguments, to suggest levelling a mountain range and filling up a strait with its

154

bulk.* You must understand, gentlemen, that the only purpose of this suggestion was to amuse the readers. History
teaches us that certain people at this period took pleasure in
telling "jokes" (this was what stories were called from which
the element of gravity was deliberately excluded), thereby be-
traying a futile and irrational frame of mind known as
"irony". This proposal, being considered extravagant, therefore raised a laugh.

'Well, gentlemen, we no longer laugh today, for we know
this operation is perfectly feasible, that it has indeed been accomplished and necessitated only a few chain reactions which
we learnt how to induce ages ago!

'But today I want to tell you about a new project. Though
similar in principle to the one I have just mentioned, it does
not entail the destruction of a mountain, but it is, I am glad
to say, no less audacious in conception or noble in intention.
Enough of the past. Let the Undulists slumber in sanctimonious contemplation of their meagre achievements, while we
look to the future and daily justify more fully our splendid
title, Benefactors of Mankind.'

Doctor Particule having finished his preamble and realizing
he had roused the curiosity of the assembly, paused for a moment or two, acknowledged their applause with a bow, then
continued in an attentive silence.

'To some of you, gentlemen, it may appear that mankind is
reasonably happy, after all we have done for it. This is the
opinion of those who have never left our shores, where the
effects of scientific civilization have for a long time been felt.
They will assert—and with apparent justification—that not
much more can be done to improve the human condition.
But I now appeal to those of you who have travelled abroad,
who have visited the backward tribes of the Equator or else
boldly sought fresh subjects for investigation and meditation
in the Polar regions. To these I put this question. I ask them
to tell me, with their hands on their hearts, on their honour
as scientists, if they have ever known a more wretched destiny and such scandalous living conditions as those obtaining
among the inhabitants of those underprivileged countries.

'Does there exist a single man in this assembly,' Particule
continued, raising his voice, 'who does not feel a tug at his
heartstrings, a qualm of conscience, when he thinks of the
dreadful hardships endured, as a result of the extremes of climate, by the people of the far North; hardships matched in
horror only by those of the inhabitants of the far South;

* '. . . and, to put an end to this endless question of the Balkans and
the Dardanelles, let's bung the former into the latter.' ALPHONSE ALLAIS

hardships likewise experienced, in a different manner but to no less a degree, by the tribes of the extreme Centre?

'You, for instance, Dr. Akoula—after spending several months among the Negroes of Equatorial Africa, did you not feel deeply moved by their distress? You blushed at the sight of them. Shame mantled your cheeks when you saw those unfortunates, bludgeoned by the blazing sun, incapacitated by the hellish temperature that reigns out there. As for the scientific education of those poor benighted people, whose brains are liquefied by the excessive heat, it is preferable to pass over it in silence! And what about you, Dr. Dourakoff? You rounded off your report on a journey of investigation to the North Pole in the following terms: "The Eskimos, who spend a large part of their time seeking food that is all too rare and protecting themselves against the rigours of the climate, have no idea whatever about the constitution of matter. They have not the slightest scientific notion. They have never heard of the splitting of the atom. They are unaware"—listen carefully, gentlemen, I am quoting our comrade's very words— "they are even unaware of the existence of the electron!" There, my dear colleagues, you have the dreadful truth.

'Gentlemen, you all realize this scandalous state of affairs cannot go on, and you have already guessed, I know, the project which I am going to submit for the approval of your lofty consciences. The enemy to be subdued in both cases is the climate. My plan is clear-cut, and this is the essential idea behind it. It can be summed up as follows—to lower the temperature of the Equatorial zones and raise that of the Polar regions so as to create a gentle, even temperature everywhere. No more icy cold, no more torrid heat. An equal climate for all scientists.'

An outburst of applause drowned the president's voice. Such a programme could not possibly meet with any opposition from the experts, whose endeavours were all directed towards the advance of civilization and the welfare of mankind. The idea was adopted unanimously. Dr. Particule then went on:

'Gentlemen, I thank you for your confidence. It remains for me to explain the process that I have conceived and elaborated to put this plan into effect.

'First of all I must confess I lost precious time studying and trying to make use of a number of previous incomplete plans, such as melting the ice in the Polar regions by a series of atomic explosions or modifying the Earth's axis of rotation. I came to the conclusion that none of these projects yielded a perfect or final solution to the problem to be solved.

'After several months' research, gentlemen, I at last realized I was on the wrong track and, at the same time, the ideal method occurred to me in all its wonderful simplicity. Its conception was really not beyond the intelligence of a child. What does it amount to, when all's said and done? Not two different operations; not the "creation" of heat at such and such a point. The "symmetry" of the enterprise renders its implementation ridiculously easy. All it needs is a simple displacement, a transference of energy.

'I shall not insult your intelligence by elaborating on this. Once the principle is accepted, the solution is obvious. We know today how to solve the most complicated problems of this nature, not by means of crude lines, as in the old days, but merely by releasing directed electrons into space. All it needed was a little thought. No new equipment is necessary. We merely have to develop what already exists. You'll find my detailed calculations in the pamphlet I am going to hand round to you.

'My dear colleagues, it is time for me to round off this survey. Here are the final figures: it needs fifty giant transformer-transmitter units, distributed among the Equatorial regions, to draw off all the surplus heat. I can guarantee that once these units start operating they will maintain a mean temperature of twenty degrees centigrade throughout the Tropical and Equatorial countries. This is a springtime temperature. Heat will no longer cause casualties. The natives will no longer be afraid of venturing out into the sun and will be released from their present torpor. Similarly, fifty receiver-transformer groups, judiciously sited in the Arctic and Antarctic regions, will bring the Eskimos and Laplanders a welcome and reviving warmth. In these countries likewise, my machines will establish a temperature of twenty degrees. The ice will melt. Green meadows and golden fields of wheat will blossom on the site of former deserts of snow. Everyone on Earth will at last enjoy the pleasures of life and sing the praises of science. And all this, mind you, without any expense other than that of the machines and their installation. For it so happens, the calorific energy drained off from the hot countries is exactly equivalent to the needs of the cold countries.

'One more word. I think it is preferable to keep our enterprise absolutely secret. We shall thus avoid a lot of pointless arguments. Maybe some of our natives might even raise objections. From time immemorial backward-minded people have attempted to interrupt the march of progress. My friends, we shall make them happy in spite of themselves. In spite of them we shall put an end to their ordeal. In spite of them we shall prevent them from roasting or freezing. In conclusion, may I voice my gratitude to science and my deep respect for the Corpuscular conception which enables us in this century to correct the imperfections of nature.'

Particule sat down to enthusiastic applause, and the experts made ready to implement his plan. Since the members of the committee controlled more or less all the Granular factories, the manufacture of the necessary machines could be undertaken straight away. The secret was easy to keep. The workmen would know nothing about the destination of the giant units. They would be told they were needed for a new experiment. They had long been accustomed to being kept in the dark as to the purpose of their toil.

The body of experts reckoned it would need six months to construct the machines and install them at the points determined by Particule. According to the doctor's calculations, the first days of July would witness a profound modification in the climate of the ancient planet.

3

Now, on this same first day of the year 2——, the Radiation Committee, or administrative organ of the Vibratory Party, held an extraordinary meeting in the conference room of the Wave Palace.

It was an extremely erudite and distinguished assembly. The greatest authorities of the Undulist School were present. There was Arthur Granton together with Doctor Fritsch, Armonique's two favourite disciples, who assisted him in all his research work. There was Doctor Nicoloff, the greatest authority of the century on material waves. There was Horace Vermeon, who was the first to trap and measure mental vibrations. There were many other leading lights of the scientific world. Finally there was Armonique himself, the master of them all, Armonique whose wisdom was unsurpassed, Armonique who on this fatal day held his head high, setting them all an example of unshakable courage.

He declared the meeting open and delivered the following speech, which for a long time was regarded as the finest sample of sober scientific eloquence on record:

'Gentlemen,

'None of you, I hope, expects to hear the slightest recrimination from me against the outcome of the universal elections. Had we won, we should have celebrated our victory modestly. Defeated, we shall know how to draw on our wisdom for the strength to rise above our defeat and to prove

158

ourselves sublime in misfortune. We all know that our school —the Undulist rock which no one can shift and to which I should like to render homage not unmixed with gratitude— that our school, as I say, is the only one worthy of official consecration. The people have rejected it. Once again the people have allowed themselves to be seduced by an evil caricature of science. We shall not hold it against the people; but we cannot overlook this iniquitous decision.

'Gentlemen, I repeat: we shall not hold the people's folly against them. We shall even stretch forbearance and generosity of mind to greater lengths. We shall show the spellbound people and our astonished opponents how little the stupidity of the former and the scheming of the latter have shaken our faith in science and our will to serve the cause of mankind, even if mankind is unworthy of our efforts. We have already done a great deal for mankind, gentlemen. We shall do even more. This will be our answer to its ingratitude.

'Here is my plan, which so far is known only to my friends Granton and Fritsch. It is simple. It is noble. It is lofty. It can be summed up in one sentence: rid the Polar regions of their attendant icefloes; temper the inhuman climate of the Equatorial belt; make the gentleness of springtime available to millions of creatures unfavoured by nature, and thus bestow on this Earth the greatest blessing it has known since its creation.

'That, gentlemen, is our reply to injustice. That is the programme which, with your approval and in the greatest secrecy, the Undulist Party will put into effect. And when everything is ready, when, with a mere gesture of this hand, I release the waves which will transfer the excess heat of the Equator to the Poles, then we shall have the right to turn to the people and tell them: "You scorned us. You preferred vulgar charlatans to us. See where true science is to be found . . ." That is all, gentlemen. I put the project to the vote.'

This proposal was greeted with the enthusiasm it deserved and the Undulist experts set to work without delay.

The technique of the project was extremely simple. It merely necessitated transforming part of the heat of the Equatorial regions into energy waves, transmitting these waves to the cold regions by means of conveniently sited machines, and effecting the opposite transformation on their arrival. Armonique's calculations showed that a temperature of twenty degrees centigrade would thereby be obtained at the Poles and at the Equator. If everything works according to plan, the scientist concluded, the first week of July will mark the beginning of a Golden Age for the Negroes and Laplanders.

4

On July 1 of the year 2——, at a quarter to ten in the morning, the Corpuscular authorities were assembled round their leader in the Electron Temple. The scientists were silent and feverishly excited. Everything was ready. The giant transformers, transmitters and receivers were in position. Remote-controlled, they had been concealed below ground level or sunk in the depths of the ocean.

In a few moments Particule would press the red button on his desk, on which all eyes were fixed. The pressure on this button would release a short electronic impulse which in its turn would automatically set all the instruments working. The greatest undertaking that had ever been conceived would be accomplished with a minimum of fuss and bother. In less than a quarter of an hour the Africans would begin to feel a welcome drop in the temperature. The Eskimos would emerge from their igloos without their lungs being liable to freeze. In a few minutes the two thermometers registering the mean temperatures of the Polar and Equatorial regions would begin to move, the one upwards, the other downwards, uninterruptedly, until they settled at the same level. The Polar thermometer was now registering thirty degrees below zero, the Equatorial plus forty. Both of them would soon be registering the same ideal springtime temperature of twenty degrees.

Three minutes to ten. . . . Everyone's features were strained and anxious. The tension was unbearable. One of the experts fainted; the others quivered with impatience. Particule alone preserved a semblance of composure, but the pallor of his cheeks betrayed his emotion. He never took his eyes off the Granular clock which was to give the signal on the stroke of ten.

One minute to ten. . . . At the other end of the town, in the Wave Palace, a crowd of not less illustrious experts were gathered nervously round Armonique. He too had his eyes fixed on the minute hand of a clock. He too had his finger poised above a button; a green button which reflected the emotion and the hopes of the men of science.

'Ten,' chimed the clock of the Corpuscular Party in the Electron Temple.

'Ten,' chimed the clock in the Wave Palace.

'Ten o'clock,' echoed the two committees with bated breath.

'Gentlemen, it is ten o'clock,' said Doctor Particule, stammering with emotion.

And he pressed the red button.

'It is ten o'clock, my dear colleagues,' said the learned Armonique.

And, with a trembling finger, he pressed the green button.

An anguished silence hovered over the Corpuscular meeting. All eyes were now fixed on Akoula and Dourakoff, who had been detailed to announce the readings of the thermometers. Akoula was in charge of the Equatorial temperature, which stood at forty degrees; Dourakoff of the Polar temperature, standing for the time being at minus thirty.

After several endless seconds the former announced in a choking voice:

'Thirty-nine degrees! The temperature is starting to drop.'

'Minus twenty-eight! It's rising,' Dourakoff proclaimed almost simultaneously.

'Thirty-eight, thirty-seven, thirty-six,' Akoula went on.

'Minus twenty-six, minus twenty-two, minus twenty,' Dourakoff echoed.

'Gentlemen, the experiment has succeeded,' exclaimed Particule, leaning forward and grasping the edge of his desk. 'Progress is on the march!'

'Thirty-five degrees, thirty-three degrees, thirty-two degrees,' Akoula announced in his deep voice.

'Minus fifteen, minus nine, minus six,' piped Dourakoff.

'Gentlemen,' said Particule, shedding tears of emotion, 'the Negroes are less hot. The Eskimos are feeling warmer. A new era is beginning; the era of eternal spring.'

'Thirty, twenty-eight, twenty-six,' said Akoula.

'Minus four, minus two, zero,' said Dourakoff.

'Gentlemen,' said the great Electronist leader, unable to recover his composure, 'my friends, my brothers, the ice is beginning to melt in the Arctic and Antarctic. The sweat is drying on the Negroes' brows.'

'Twenty-five, twenty-four, twenty-three,' Akoula continued.

'Plus four, plus eight, plus twelve,' Dourakoff replied.

'We are approaching the goal, gentlemen. The temperatures are drawing level. Nature has been conquered. We have taught the Creator a lesson. What a day! What a date!' cried Particule, tearing off his collar in his enthusiasm.

'Twenty-two, twenty-one, *twenty!*' yelled Akoula.

'Fifteen, eighteen, *twenty!*' piped Dourakoff.

A sudden tumult greeted this last announcement, filling the Electron Temple. The scientists, now that the tension was over, behaved like children. They flung their arms round one another, weeping and laughing at the same time. Particule was acclaimed by a storm of cheers and incoherent cries. He wanted to comment on this victory but was unable to recover his voice and could only wave his arms in the air without uttering a sound.

'Eighteen!' announced Akoula.

'Twenty-one,' announced Dourakoff.

'What!' cried Particule in alarm.

The storm died down at once and total silence ensued. You could have heard an electron oscillate.

'Twelve,' said Akoula.

'Twenty-three,' said Dourakoff.

'Damn!' exclaimed an Islander in English, forgetting that this language had long ago been abolished.

'*Caramba!*' exclaimed an ex-Iberian.

'*Nom de Dieu!*' remarked a former Frenchman.

'Gentlemen, gentlemen,' said Particule, mopping his brow, 'this is probably just a minor oscillation round the mean temperature. It will all settle down in the end.'

'Eight degrees, six degrees, four degrees,' interjected Akoula, faithfully announcing the reading of the Equatorial thermometer.

'Twenty-four, twenty-five,' said Dourakoff, hypnotized by the Polar thermometer.

'Gentlemen, my friends, what's going on?' moaned the great Corpuscular master, seizing his head in both hands.

'Zero, minus two, minus four,' Akoula implacably announced.

'Twenty-six, twenty-eight, thirty,' snapped Dourakoff.

'Help, gentlemen, help!' Particule whimpered, falling on his knees. 'I'm taking leave of my senses. What's going on? What's happening over there? Ice is forming on the Equator. The Negroes are shivering with the cold. The Eskimos are beginning to mop their brows . . . Yet I can't find fault with my calculations. It's impossible for such a gross error . . .'

'Minus six, minus nine, minus fifteen degrees,' interjected the voice of the Equator.

'Thirty-two, thirty-three, thirty-five degrees,' echoed the voice of the Poles.

'Minus six, minus nine, minus fifteen degrees,' simultaneously announced Doctor Fritsch who, in the Wave Palace, had been detailed to read off the temperature of the once overheated regions.

'Thirty-two, thirty-three, thirty-five degrees,' said Arthur Granton, who was responsible for announcing that of the Northern and Southern extremities.

'This is dreadful,' sobbed Armonique, thumping his forehead. 'It's a ghastly nightmare. I am dishonoured!'

'Minus twenty, minus twenty-two, minus twenty-six,' continued Doctor Fritsch. 'The movement is slowing down. I think it's about to settle.'

'Thirty-six, thirty-seven, thirty-eight. The rise is less rapid,' Granton confirmed.

'Minus *thirty*,' announced Doctor Akoula, to the general consternation of the Corpusculars. 'The level is no longer moving. The final temperature of the Equator, Venerable Master, is thirty degrees below zero.'

'*Forty*,' said Dourakoff. 'Illustrious Master, the counterbalancing temperature is attained.'

'Disaster!' whimpered Particule.

'Catastrophe!' yelped Armonique.

5

Thus this noble enterprise came to an end. Armonique and Particule showed equal fortitude at this fatal blow. Both of them chose death rather than dishonour. Before their colleagues had recovered from their emotion, each of them had pressed a little pocket disintegrator and in a millionth of a second their substance was rendered, on the one hand to the waves, on the other to the electrons. Such was the end of the two great experts.

The two scientific bodies dispersed on tiptoe and never breathed a word of their experiment, which had succeeded only too well. After a long discussion within each committee, the scientists had decided to leave things as they were and keep silent. It would have needed six months' work to restore the *status quo*, and they felt it was dangerous to keep changing the temperature of the planet in this manner. Moreover, though they did not admit it, they now mistrusted their own calculations.

'After all,' concluded Doctor Dourakoff, the new head of the Electronist School, 'why should we reproach ourselves? Our great Particule was right as far as the "principle" was concerned. Note, gentlemen, that the "total" quantity of heat is still the same, and the "mean" temperature of the Earth has not altered.'

'Observe,' remarked Doctor Fritsch, who had succeeded Armonique, 'observe that the present climate of the Equator is no "worse" than the former climate of the Poles. It all boils down to a matter of displacement. On the whole the experiment has succeeded "qualitatively", which is the main point, and it has completely confirmed the theories of our late lamented master.'

These erudite gentlemen were right. There is no doubt that Particule's speculations were correct, and one cannot but pay homage to Armonique's genius. Moreover, their deserts were recognized and countless statues were raised to their memory.

The chronicler, while hesitating to point the moral of this story, is struck by the singular abundance of factors favourable to success with which the enterprise was blessed at the outset, and he yields to the temptation of underlining them. To begin with there was faith, enthusiasm, scientific knowledge, technical accomplishment and substantial material means, not to mention the disinterestedness, purity and nobility of the end in view. The moralist, in these conditions, might have been distressed by a failure, and it is a consolation to ascertain, on the contrary, that a remarkable 'result' was obtained.

Only in consequence of an unfortunate coincidence was the result not 'quantitatively' (to use the experts' jargon) what had been foreseen. It fact it was very different.

The magnificent forests swarming with rare birds and animals disappeared in a few hours and vast deserts of snow covered the remains of the majestic foliage. A layer of ice several yards thick spread over the Equatorial belt, dividing the Earth into two separate hemispheres.

Admittedly, the ice-floes of the Polar zones melted rapidly. A luxuriant vegetation developed in the Arctic and Antarctic. But the seals and the penguins were no longer there to enjoy this metamorphosis. Neither were the Eskimos: nor the Laplanders. They had all succumbed within the first few days, bludgeoned by the heat and incapable of adapting themselves to these new conditions. Needless to say, neither the Negroes of Africa nor the populations of the Pacific withstood the fall in temperature any better.

They all perished, on the one hand from isolation, on the other from cold, and the Earth was rid of several million inhabitants—albeit the least interesting from the scientific point of view.

The Man Who Hated Machines

1

I made his acquaintance one morning outside a modern bookshop where I had dropped in to while away the time.

After strolling past the shelves, casting a glance at the volumes piled on top of one another like slender skyscrapers, and idly opening a few of them—hoping, I don't know why, that the lady at the cashier's desk would be duly impressed by this attitude—I stopped in an alcove not far from the wide glass doors. These were divided into two halves, one for entering, the other for leaving, and opened automatically each time someone approaching intercepted a certain ray of light.

There were only a few customers, all engrossed in smug contemplation of the pyramids of paper. The sales girls were snoozing. I had taken up a book at random and was absently scanning the initial lines. It was at this moment that I noticed him out of the corner of my eye, outside, approaching the door. At first sight his aspect seemed so odd that I turned slightly to observe him at my leisure, while pretending to continue with my reading.

He had reached a point close to the ray which operated the opening mechanism. He stopped and cast a furtive glance round him, as though he was afraid of being observed. Apparently reassured, he decided to take action. I was the only one to follow his strange behaviour.

He came right up to the luminous ray which crossed the threshold, but took care not to touch it. Executing a swift half turn, he assumed a sideways position with the same precaution, then, like an old-fashioned high-jumper clearing the bar by means of the outdated 'scissors' technique, launched himself over the thread of light and landed on the other side, still without touching it. In point of fact, the obstacle being fairly low, it was an easy exploit and inconsistent with the contraction of his features. It appeared to me on second thoughts that his gesture recalled that of an elephant stepping over a flowerpot rather than that of an athlete. Yet a deep satisfaction infused his pale cheeks and he remained motionless for a moment, out of breath, his face gleaming with pride, as though he had just accomplished a real feat.

Those who know me, who are aware of the horror roused in me by the conventional, and the raptures, on the other hand, into which I am plunged by the slightest odd behaviour on the part of my fellow humans, will realize how tickled I was by this prelude and with what fervour I started avidly watching each of his gestures. I thought to myself: 'Well, here at least is someone who has worked out an original way of approaching a door operated by an automatic device. This is a promising departure!'

I was not disappointed. By now he was right up against the door which, of course, had not moved, no impulse having been imparted to it by the cell. He turned round to face it, surveyed it in a haughty manner and *put his tongue out*. Then, scornfully, he turned his back on it, put his hands in his pockets and strolled away from the shop, this time deliberately breaking the luminous ray, while the glass door, turning obediently on its hinges, swung wide open behind him.

He did not go far. He stopped near the bookshop, in front of a kiosk, bought a newspaper and, likewise pretending to read, kept a close watch on the entrance of the shop. I could not restrain myself. I put down my book. I went out and approached him. I was too enthralled to think of an excuse for accosting him.

'Well, I never!' I merely said, giving him a wink and jerking my head in the direction of the door.

He gave a start and darted an anxious glance at me.

'You saw?'

'Yes, I saw. . . . Well done!' I added warmly.

This appreciation appeared to dispel his fears. He looked me up and down slowly, as though to assess my abilities. The examination seemed to satisfy him.

'I fooled it,' he said, resuming his triumphant air and winking in his turn.

'I greatly admired your technique.'

He was disappointed.

'There's only one quality to admire in this case, Monsieur, and that's intelligence.'

'Why, of course! Please forgive me!'

'Oh, don't think I consider myself a genius! It's a question

166

of relative intelligence. What I mean is, *it* is stupid, horribly stupid. Look at that door it operates, look at it gaping wide open, pointlessly, stupidly. The very symbol of stupidity! A casement open on the gulf of insanity.'

I looked at the door, then I scrutinized him. He was dressed quite decently but not particularly well. There was nothing remarkable about his features but, as he talked, I discerned in his eye the disturbing, fleeting little gleam for which I was eagerly looking, without hoping too fervently to find it for fear of being disappointed, and which is infinitely precious to me, for it is the heavenly seal with which the Angel of Oddity marks certain privileged creatures.

'Just look at it,' he went on in the same tone, with a stifled little laugh. 'Wood from the neck up, what!'

'Absolutely.'

I was about to question him further when he seized me by the arm and hastily whispered:

'If, as I hope, you have grasped the philosophical sense of my gesture, pray don't give me away. Stay here with me and watch. You won't regret it, for a display of stupidity is one of the keenest pleasures this world can offer an active mind.'

I did as he said. The entertainment which he invited me to enjoy was furnished by an elderly gentleman emerging from the bookshop who, deceived by the gaping entrance, blithely made his way out through it. He had only just reached the threshold when the door, operated by a delayed-action spring, swung to, striking him from behind and projecting him forward with such violence that he cleared several yards in an almost horizontal position. In doing so, he naturally broke the luminous ray, so that the door had swung back once more on its hinges when, having recovered his balance, he turned round in fury, ready to curse his aggressor.

Crimson in the face and bewildered, the old gentleman saw nothing but the gaping entrance. I thought the man standing beside me was going to choke with delight. His shoulders heaved as he tried to suppress his chuckles, while the tears poured down his cheeks.

The door having eventually swung to without further incident, he no doubt considered the session at an end, turned on his heels and rushed off. I followed him. I had two good reasons for doing so: firstly, the morbid curiosity I have mentioned; secondly, the fact that he had appeared to discern in me an understanding soul, a fellow mind, a goad which human nature, in its proud aspirations, is all the more incapable of resisting when it is brandished by a less rational creature. I was flattered when, having caught up with him, I heard him continue the conversation as though there existed some complicity between us.

'I am delighted,' he said, 'to see that you agree with me. Boundless stupidity!'

'Absolutely. You're no doubt thinking of the stupidity of . . .'

'Of machines, Monsieur, of all machines without exception, of mechanical devices in particular and, among them, photo-electric cells. I am rewarded for my pains when I succeed in exposing their ineptitude to the world. So I shall look upon this as a red-letter day; for, make no mistake about it, an exploit of this sort is not always easy. . . . I've had my reverses.'

'You mean to say you often indulge in experiments of this sort?' I asked him hopefully.

'They are the purpose and delight of my life, Monsieur. Between me and machines there's an old enmity . . . even more than that, an instinctive repulsion which is deeply rooted and derives from the very substance of our respective natures.'

He was no longer laughing. He had lowered his voice, and his tone, which had become more serious, confirmed my opinion that he could not be regarded as a common-or-garden practical joker. He went on with an almost tragic solemnity.

'An antagonism between donkey-work and divine imagination. A reciprocal hatred between automatism and creative intelligence. An endless conflict between mind and matter. For a long time, Monsieur, I have devoted myself to this struggle and have committed myself heart and soul to the sacred crusade, for want of being able to assign a more noble ideal to the human condition. You see before you a man brought forth by heaven to combat machines and strive against their inordinate ambition. To humiliate them, break down their unbearable vanity, convince them personally of their lack of intelligence—those are my methods. I flatter myself that I have obtained some startling results. I have won some splendid victories; but, as I said before, this is not as easy as you might think, after seeing me just now hold up to ridicule that infantile mechanical device. I have paid a high price, I'll have you know, to discover that there are some machines which are vicious and dangerous to tackle.'

At this point the flame of fantasy which still flickered feebly in his eye died away. No, he was not a mere practical joker. The anxious expression I now saw on his face portended something dramatic.

'All machines are stupid, but in some of them one finds a

168

crude instinct which prompts them to acts of cunning to which one can easily fall a victim unless one is constantly on one's guard.'

'You're opening up fresh horizons for me. I would never have imagined that a machine was capable . . .'

'Monsieur,' he exclaimed, raising his head, 'I could describe some memorable battles, in which victory appeared for a moment to be in the balance.'

There was no longer any question of my letting him go off without me. I ushered him into a café, where I presently realized he had a weakness for strong spirits. Gradually, having gained his confidence, I persuaded him to tell me about the outstanding episodes in his unusual career.

2

'You must know, Monsieur, that I have had an extremely extensive scientific education. My father, a businessman, intended me for industry. From my earliest childhood nothing was spared to initiate me into the mystery of numbers or to inculcate in me a knowledge of the laws governing inert matter. I showed an astonishing aptitude for theoretical speculation, but practical application defeated me. I accepted the instruction, however, without enthusiasm but not unwillingly. When this preliminary education came to an end, I went into one of those great schools (the greatest actually) in which mathematical abstractions are raised to the heights of an art and where one studies from books the function and physiology of machines without ever seeing the things themselves. Even at this stage, I remember, I felt slightly uneasy in my mind, but I was incapable of stating precisely why. My hour had not yet come.

'I left school. I was entered as a trainee in a power station. . . . I might, like anyone else, have had a brilliant career as an engineer, invented new machines, or spent a tranquil life in smug contemplation of those that already existed. Believe me, I have no regrets. In spite of certain setbacks, the mental satisfaction I now derive from my work is incomparably greater than what I might have enjoyed in the service of mechanics.'

'I'm sure. But what prompted you to change your course?'

'I'm coming to that. Well, I was in this power station and my duties were mainly concerned with steam turbines. Now, on the very first day, as soon as I set foot in the huge room which sheltered those machines, I was seized by a vague and infinitely disagreeable feeling of unrest. The mere presence of those ponderous monsters crouching in rows on their concrete base provoked a state of permanent mental anguish.'

He paused for a moment as though in a dream, with a faraway look in his eyes, then, spurred on by me, he resumed his tale with a sort of compassionate melancholy.

'I shall never forget the moment I had the revelation. It was on a stormy evening. I was alone in the turbine room; or almost alone. The mechanic who looked after them was an absolute oaf. By dint of living among brainless creatures, he had assumed something of their manner and behaviour. Every half-hour he slowly did the rounds of the set that was running. With the gestures of an automaton he would add to the oil in the grease-cups, record the temperatures, mechanically feel the pulse of his charges and listen to their breathing. Then he would come back to his bench and sit there motionless, wrapped in overawed contemplation. His expression reflected the same mental void that emanated from the black casings.

'Well, there I was, feeling uneasy and restless, as I always did in that place. All of a sudden, for no particular reason, simply because in the course of the preceding months my mind had accomplished a lengthy subconscious task, the stupidity of machines revealed itself to me in its totality. What had hitherto been nothing more than a vague intuition suddenly became a startling reality affecting all my senses, bearing down with an intolerable weight on my brain and every fibre of my body. In particular the clatter that filled the space round these masses of vibrating matter induced a frightful throbbing in my skull. Have you never been struck by the hideous din of machines, Monsieur? An unbearable cacophonic verbiage, devoid of all meaning. It appeared to me at that moment as the very language of insanity.

'If I perceived in a flash the sum-total of this stupidity, this global impression in no way prevented me from distinguishing the details. There were degrees of virulence in the stupidity of the various organs thrashing wildly about before my eyes. Many of them revealed nothing more than a morose and passive imbecility. The shaft, the rotor, came into this category. An objective and slightly philosophical mind could not seriously blame them for their resigned obedience to the controls. No, the real object of my repugnance, the thing which added overweening insolence to ineptitude, was the governor. This was my true enemy. . . . Do you know the principles of these contraptions, Monsieur?'

I confessed that I was not familiar with the technicalities of steam turbines and their regulating instruments. In a few words he explained them to me with the utmost clarity, thus proving his competence and at the same time his lucidity.

'The principle is the same as that of the old-fashioned pendulum governor. The degree of intellectuality is comparable, that's to say it's tantamount to nought. The instrument consists of two weights, fixed on either side of the turbine shaft and connected by a transmission system, which we need not go into in detail, to the steam intake valve. When the machine tends to run too quickly, these weights, slavishly obedient to centrifugal force, diverge from the shaft and this movement is communicated to the valve in the form of an impulse which closes it slightly. Receiving less steam, the turbine then slows down. If, on the other hand, the speed tends to decrease, the weights converge on the shaft, the transmission works in the opposite direction; the valve opens and the movement is accelerated. Thus the speed of a set is maintained within two narrow limits.'

'Good, I think I understand.'

'This was going on as usual that evening, the governor transforming a hint of acceleration into an impulse of deceleration, and vice-versa. This might have gone on for ever, the machine preening itself and congratulating itself on its vigilance; but, in a matter of seconds, I had heard the call. . . . I consider you too intelligent, Monsieur, not to have divined the course that I adopted. The trap to lay for this machine was obvious.'

'If really, as I hope, I am beginning to grasp the qualities of subtlety and elegant simplicity which are the marks of your genius,' I said, 'I think I can indeed guess; but please go on. I take an immense delight in listening to your account of how you took that coxcomb down a peg.'

'Merely by inverting the connections between the blind weights and the valve, so that while the former tended to diverge under the influence of an excess of speed the latter was obliged to open instead of closing. A simple and subtle means, Monsieur, as you were good enough to point out. Still, a brain was needed to think of it.'

'It certainly was. And you succeeded in this delicate manipulation?'

'With the utmost ease. I operated of course on a turbine that was not running but which was due to be switched on in the course of the night, and my first campaign in the war I declared that evening resulted in a striking victory.

'It started up without any difficulty. As soon as it had reached its normal running speed, the dear old governor, which had no idea what I had been up to, prepared to play its part. A fortuitous cause happening to accelerate the rota-

171

tion, the weights responded to centrifugal force with their usual despatch and diverged from the shaft. This movement, as I had intended, *opened* the valve slightly, which resulted in an *increase* of speed instead of a reduction. Do you think the instrument thereupon realized the madness of its reflexes? Do you think it understood the infernal cycle in which it was involving the set? Come now, Monsieur, that would imply no knowledge of creatures of this sort! Once the rate was accelerated, the weights diverged to a greater extent, opening the valve slightly more, increasing the velocity still further. Slightly faster, *therefore* still slightly faster, and *in consequence* slightly faster still, you see, while the monotonous hum rose to a savage roar.

'Through small successive impulses, the machine, launched on its own destruction, tended in this way towards an infinite speed, a state of affairs which could not last for ever. Presently, under the strain of overpowering centrifugal force, with a scream of fury and despair, the shaft and the rotor were ripped from their bearings and shattered the metal casing like a thin sheet of glass. Twenty tons of thundering whirling matter then went hurtling through the roof of the factory and landed half a mile away, reducing some houses to rubble, while preserving, encrusted in the débris, a few fragments of the mechanic's brain. . . . I apologize for not sharing your hilarity, but nowadays I'm difficult to amuse. Yet the memory of that first try, which was a master-stroke, warms the cockles of my heart and I am delighted to see you duly acclaim the discomfiture of that great brute. That, Monsieur, is how I began.'

3

'Excuse me,' I remarked, stammering and making an enormous effort to preserve my composure, 'excuse me, but this first try, as you call it, is something to which one can hardly remain indifferent. I can imagine how your career developed from then on, because I assume you did not confine yourself to this initial success.'

'Why, of course not, Monsieur! Unfortunately I made a mistake, which deprived me for some time of the ability to pursue my mission. I was not modest in my triumph—a youthful sin—though I have since become more circumspect. I wanted to disclose the philosophy of this experiment to my fellow engineers and enlighten them on the intellectual deficiency of machines. I gave a lecture. No one understood me.

But that wasn't all: the management, when they learnt that I derived a legitimate pride from my exploit, sided with the imbecile mechanical device and made up their minds to avenge it. I was persecuted.

'I was hauled before a court of law. There an attorney, who had scarcely more sense than an automaton, accused me of criminal behaviour. For a moment I thought that a public hearing in front of the bench would give me a splendid opportunity to divulge my aims and underline their nobility. Encouraged by my lawyer, who seemed to be the only one to understand me—as you have today, Monsieur—I described the vague feeling of unrest that had germinated in me on encountering mechanical ineptitude and how this unrest had gradually grown into an intolerable anguish, until the day I was liberated from it by a revelation. This revelation could be expressed in a single sentence: machines are stupid; I must combat stupidity; I must therefore grapple with machines.'

'Extremely clear. A mere child would have understood. And your judges . . .'

'For a moment I thought I had convinced them (merely because, while I was explaining myself, I discerned in their faces a manifest expression of interest). I was wrong. They did not sentence me to prison; oh no, their vengeance was more subtle. You will never guess, Monsieur, the treatment to which I was subjected. They handed me over to some medical specialists. Specialists in what? I'll tell you straight away: in mental deficiency, irrationality, in other words madness! They attributed to me the vice that horrifies me more than anything in the world, the scourge against which I shall struggle until my dying day: insanity, Monsieur.'

'You, insane!'

'It would be really laughable if it were not also tragic. But such is the logic of our law courts that I was locked up in one of those institutions where the mentally defective are cared for.'

'I can imagine your humiliation and fury, above all your despair, when you realized they were trying to shatter such a promising career.'

'Oh, it would be a mistake to think I allowed myself to be discouraged or that I thought for a moment of abandoning my struggle. This ordeal—I have since undergone any amount of others—simply prompted me to act more prudently and never again place my trust in men who were not prepared to listen to me.

'Thus I fell back on myself. But even in the gloomy jail, which is what a psychiatric hospital amounts to, I contrived to continue my crusade, in secret. The possibilities were meagre. I accomplished no exploits; I did, however, succeed in a few skirmishes which are too boring to describe. . . . At the same time, during the hours of solitude, I applied myself to increasing my brain-power by means of mental exercises which at this stage I considered extremely important for the battles to come. . . .'

'One moment,' I cried. 'I feel you're being too modest. I'm convinced those skirmishes you mentioned are of the utmost interest. I am dying, you see, to learn more, and none of your experiences is a matter of indifference to me.'

'It was only a few traps I laid, to keep my hand in as it were, for the modern domestic appliances with which the asylum was equipped. Almost all these contraptions are operated by automatic devices called thermostats, the principle of which is similar to that of the turbine governor, with the difference that the driving agent is a change of temperature instead of a variation in speed. Thus I dealt with the thermostats according to the simple method which I had already employed with such success: inverting the connexions. No need to go into details, of course. You need only know that during the few months of my internment the gloomy existence of the patients and nurses was relieved by the grotesque blunders of these instruments. The water in the central heating system which (if you will allow me this expression which is so descriptive of blind obstinacy) started turning *all the hotter the hotter it was,* eventually transforming itself into steam which escaped in scalding jets all over the building through the burnt-out joints; until the boiler burst, incapable of withstanding such an infernal temperature. The cold rooms, on the other hand, grew *all the colder the colder they became,* covering themselves internally and externally with a thick layer of ice, until the pipes deteriorated completely. There was also . . .'

'Despite the picturesque variety of your experiments,' I exclaimed, deeply impressed, 'I seem to detect an important relation between each of them: a common philosophical basis, an essential theme on which your fantasy delights in embroidering fresh arabesques every time.'

He beamed with pleasure, then went on in a modest tone:

'That's true, Monsieur. And that's what enables a superior intellect to derive satisfaction from experiments which are trivial in appearance but which are all dominated, as you have discerned, by a profound and subtle principle.

'I triumphed easily over all these devices,' he went on after a short pause, 'delighting in their humiliation and the anger they never failed to manifest whenever they fell into the trap.

174

. . . I don't think there's any point in dwelling on these trivialities.'

'None at all. But didn't you say just now that you indulged in more important mental exercises during the hours of solitude?'

'Important, but in a different way; at least I thought so at the time, and this new field of activity played a considerable part in my subsequent adventures. I'll come back to that. It was a question of an intensive mental training.'

'Splendid,' I said. 'And to what purpose was this training?'

'My purpose was to become a human prodigy . . . and I succeeded, Monsieur,' he went on with sudden animation. 'No one can deny it. I really did become a prodigy. I proved it and I shall prove it again, in spite of certain deficiencies from which I suffer at present as the result of a sinister scheme against me.'

'I'm sure you will,' I said, having noted in his eye the symptoms of a disturbing emotional state which threatened to make him lose the thread of his story. 'But if you don't mind, let's take things in their proper order. In what branch did you become a prodigy?'

'In mathematics, Monsieur. I became what is known as a calculating prodigy. Oh, this term calls for some explanation; it is not really a question of calculation. You must realize straight away it was not gratuitous fantasy on my part, nor in order to perform in a music-hall, that I worked for hours every day to perfect my natural talents and raise them to a truly sublime level. No; but there was a lot of talk in those days about calculating machines, and logic decreed that my new course would eventually lead me to grapple with them. An instinct told me that the battle would be a fierce one. Every evening a voice murmured in my ear to prepare myself well in advance by means of judicious and intensive training.'

'And this battle took place?'

He fell silent for a moment and an anxious expression came into his eye, as though I had broached a dangerous subject; then he went on in a lower tone of voice:

'It took place, Monsieur. You'll see the results, but you asked me to take things in their proper order and I still have many other incidents to describe before reaching that point.'

'Please go on as you see fit.'

'Throughout the duration of my internment I therefore compelled my mind to identify itself with the laws of numbers and figures, and to carry out as rapidly as possible the sort of operations which I don't think you could even imagine.'

'How wonderful,' I murmured pensively. 'I've heard of

175

various occupations in which prisoners indulge. Some write novels, some write poems. Others work out systems of ideal government. It's the first time, to my knowledge, that one of them has ever employed his leisure in this manner.'

'I started off with some modest multiplications and I finally managed to resolve extremely complicated systems of equations in my head. No difficulty daunted me. I soon acquired such mastery that, whereas at the beginning I used to verify the result of my mental speculations with pencil and paper, after a few months, it was in my head alone, with my eyes closed, with only my mental powers, that I checked the operations carried out in writing according to the normal method.'

'Really prodigious.'

'Make no mistake about it. I referred to *mind* and *speculation*. Don't imagine it had anything to do with mechanical calculation. Granted, I wanted one day to defeat certain machines on their home ground, but not, I swear, by resorting to their own crude weapons. I should have been ashamed to rely on memorizing lists of figures, as music-hall calculators shamelessly do, thus reducing themselves to the level of the machine. For each operation, it was the theory of numbers in its entirety that I reconstituted in my head, Monsieur. I reinvented mathematics at each fresh test. It was an extremely audacious enterprise.'

'And one which must have been extremely tiring I suppose?'

'At times I used to feel intellectually exhausted, but the result was worth it. After a few months' internment, when some empty-headed doctors declared I was cured (after finding me mentally ill!) there existed no problem of arithmetic, algebra or analysis which I could not master in a matter of seconds by means of my mental powers alone.'

'So you left hospital. I suppose you were consumed by the desire to put these subtle weapons to use?'

'I was; but I was unable to do so as quickly as I wished, because I had to earn my living. I accepted a number of rather dull jobs, which did not enable me to continue my crusade. In fact, during this period (I mean between leaving hospital and my encounter with a rich eccentric who took me under his wing) I can remember only one exploit really worth mentioning and which enabled me to make partial use of the faculties I had acquired. This was when, with the help of a pilot friend, I settled the hash, good and proper, of a unit of ultra-modern anti-aircraft guns. The episode is worth describing in detail, I think.'

'That's right,' I said, rubbing my hands together. 'Tell me

about the episode with the anti-aircraft guns. You can deal with the rich eccentric afterwards.'

'It happened about four years ago. Fighting had broken out, you may remember, in Central Africa, between the states of Balaka and Beleke. It had begun as a tribal quarrel; then, some great powers having intervened, gradually developed into a full-scale war—a curious conflict which involved all sorts of weapons, from hatchets and spears to the most refined instruments of destruction, modern aircraft and, what interested me particularly, highly perfected anti-aircraft artillery.

'At that time I was destitute. I was strolling about the streets of this town in search of a job when I ran into my pilot friend. He was a nice fellow, but rather scatterbrained. As a matter of fact, I had met him in the psychiatric hospital where he had been interned, and with good reason, as a result of a cerebral commotion caused by an accident. We became friends. I had ventured to tell him of my past exploits and to divulge some of my future projects. He had always been outspoken with me.

'He flung his arms round my neck as soon as he saw me. We exchanged our news. He told me that on his release, shortly after mine, he too had experienced the greatest difficulty in finding a job, but he was now extremely happy since he had just enlisted in the Balaka air force, which was recruiting volunteers here and there and did not enquire too closely into their past careers.

'Until then I had listened to him inattentively. But the words "war" and "air force" suddenly aroused my interest, for they infallibly called to mind the anti-aircraft devices on which I had been musing for several days. Yes, I had been exasperated shortly beforehand by reading a silly magazine in which the prowess of these devices, the latest word in modern technique, had been lauded in sickening terms. Subconsciously I had mapped out a plan of attack—it has become a reflex with me, Monsieur, as soon as I learn the characteristics of a new machine, to look for its vulnerable point. I had worked out every detail of this plan in my head, and this little theoretical exercise had consoled me for my wretched condition, but I was dying to put it into practice. And here was a heaven-sent opportunity.

' "I must come with you," I said to my friend. He took me

177

to the recruiting office. Beforehand, I had provided myself with forged papers stating that I had once served in the Flying Corps and was a first-class observer. I was forthwith engaged in this capacity and a few days later we flew out to the state of Balaka. The disorder which reigned in the air force gave me a great deal of liberty. I enrolled myself on my own authority as a member of the crew of my pilot friend, to whom a modern aircraft had just been allocated. It was left to us to decide the missions we undertook. I took advantage of this to make them serve my personal cause which—incidentally—also served the state of Balaka. It was not long before I spotted a choice enemy among the few anti-aircraft units that the Beleke forces possessed. No doubt you are acquainted with the essential characteristics of these defences, Monsieur?'

'I have a very vague idea. But let's assume I had never even heard of them.'

'They consist of a number of mechanisms which automatically perform the operations which used to be entrusted to gunners, that's to say spotting the plane, determining its trajectory and estimating its speed, calculating from these data the point it will have reached at the moment the shells burst, and arranging the fire plan accordingly. A battery thus includes: organs of perception (the main one is radar), a device capable of solving geometric, cinematic and ballistic problems (a calculating machine) and the executive organs (guns in varying numbers) not to mention, of course, all the electric and electromagnetic transmission circuits you can think of. The whole thing functions (and prides itself on this) without any human intervention.'

'A miracle of technique,' I exclaimed carelessly, having just enough time, on seeing him start with indignation, to introduce a note of sarcasm into the last word, which restored his composure.

'A miracle, yes, Monsieur, a miracle of stupidity, as I demonstrated and as you'll soon see.

'Well, in the course of various reconnaissance flights with my pilot friend I studied my victim. The selected unit was one of the most important and most highly perfected. It consisted of a dozen batteries, each composed of several guns sited in a circle of two or three miles' diameter round an important centre which it was their duty to defend. They were all controlled simultaneously by the central organ. the machine—the brain, as specialists have the effrontery to call it, without even thinking of putting this sacrilegious term in enormous inverted commas. This machine was installed in the centre of the circle, on the summit of a peak. The technicians who had placed it there were so convinced of its absolute power that they had barely put it under cover, relying on the narrowness and height of its natural plinth (a needle of rock rising high above the plain) to protect it against any long-distance bombardment. You must picture the background; it's important. As a matter of fact, almost all the aircraft that approached this area were shot down. The machine calculated stupidly, but accurately.'

'Excuse me,' I said, 'but there's something I don't understand. How did you two carry out reconnaissance flights with impunity over this area?'

'Quite simply because I used my brain, Monsieur. I used my brain and, furthermore I calculated more quickly and just as accurately as the automaton. No sooner had we arrived in the danger zone than I realized the radar had spotted us, that it was passing information to the machine and that the latter was determining our trajectory and calculating our speed according to this information. But thanks to the prodigious qualities I had acquired, I forestalled it. I obtained the result of its calculations before it did so itself, so that I knew in advance the spot where it was going to wait for us and I had already instructed the pilot to alter course. When it opened up with all twelve batteries, we were far from the point where the shells exploded.

'Of course I had to repeat the operation every second, for at every second the radar furnished fresh information. At every second the machine revised its calculations according to the data of an alteration in course. At every second fresh bursts appeared in a different spot in the sky . . . where we no longer were, because at every second we too altered course.'

'That must have been yet another gruelling task,' I observed.

'Tiring, but rewarding, Monsieur. My brain worked continually, with a lucidity and promptitude that never wavered. The pilot responding without delay, our perpetually corrected trajectory resembled that of an enormous gnat.

'We repeated these fantastic manoeuvres several times. I felt that the machine had scented an opponent out of the common run. It recognized me from afar. It became frantic. Soon it was at every tenth of a second that it launched itself into fresh calculations, but at every tenth of a second, we veered off to a point in the sky far from the point which it had determined. It was a heart-warming sight. The artless guns panted for breath as they tracked their prey, feverishly sweeping the whole dome of heaven, trying desperately to obey the stream of contradictory orders issued to them at every moment by the poor "brain", without ever being able to train themselves on a target which for ever eluded them. I was jubilant. Eventually, however, since we were somewhat shaken about by these antics, I felt the game had lasted long enough. I flew off one morning with my pilot, firmly resolved to have done with it. . . . Monsieur, I'm sure you have already determined the vulnerable point of this sort of mechanical device.'

'I have a faint inkling,' I said, pensively, 'but go on as though you were speaking to an absolute duffer.'

'It's angelically simple. The evening before, I had briefed my friend. He was overjoyed when I divulged my plan. I knew he would carry out my instructions to the letter.

'We therefore headed towards the enemy. As soon as we were within its range the usual antics began, accompanied by the same firework display all round us and still fairly far off. Then there was a lull. The firing ceased. Down below, on the peak, the robot calculator was having a rest; the twelve batteries had come to a standstill, as though short of breath. This was the moment I was waiting for, Monsieur, for I had tumbled to this circumscribed creature's infantile trick. The machine was leaving us in peace in an attempt to make us believe that it was breaking off the engagement, so as to make us abandon our fluttering course and encourage us to follow at last a rational trajectory, a classical geometric line. It thus hoped to shoot us down by surprise.

'As I said before, I had foreseen everything. We pretended to enter into its puerile game. We were then at an extremely high altitude and almost directly overhead. After a few manoeuvres which brought us closer still, my pilot suddenly straightened out and at the same time, pushing the stick forward, went into a breath-taking dive. Trembling and panting with hope, the machine forced itself to wait for a moment or two. But it could no longer be in any doubt; the aircraft was following a magnificent straight line (what could be more tempting, what more easy, for a calculator which does not think, than to establish the equation of a straight line?) and our speed had reached a fantastic figure which precluded any abrupt turn. "I've got them," it said to itself. And, mad with joy, it started up and performed its operations according to the radar information.

"Need I add, Monsieur, that I had provided myself before taking off with a parachute and that I did not wait for the last moment to jump? Need I also specify the point, determined by me, at which the plane was aiming in its dive, the point it must inevitably reach within an all too foreseeable space of time, the point whose exact co-ordinates the machine had calculated in a flash, so as to cause, with the incredible stupidity which I have already mentioned, the twelve cones of fire to converge on it?'

'Sheer genius,' I cried, striking my forehead. 'I see.'

'It was all over in a few seconds, Monsieur. Suspended high up in the sky by my parachute, overlooking the scene of this drama as a conductor overlooks his orchestra pit, I did not miss a crumb of the delightful spectacle. It was *at itself* that the machine ordered the obedient batteries to fire. I saw the muzzles deflect slowly and converge towards the summit of the peak. I witnessed the firing of the shells and their simultaneous explosion on the very nose of this marvellous mechanism, at the very moment the plane was about to reach it.'

'The plane itself only just missed it. It was nevertheless likewise pulverized by the projectiles, and the wretched "brain", before being blown to smithereens by its own shells, may have had the opportunity to congratulate itself for the last time on the accuracy of its calculations.'

'What happened to your friend the pilot?' I asked with sudden anxiety.

'I told you, Monsieur, he was a weak-minded fellow. He obeyed slavishly, like an automaton. His demise cannot be regarded as a loss to intelligent humanity.'

5

I renewed my acquaintance with the man who hated machines at the café where we had arranged to meet. The previous evening, he had broken off half way through his story in spite of my entreaties, on the pretext of some business which he could not avoid. I had arrived well ahead of him. I was beginning to think I would never see the remarkable creature again and to curse myself for having let him go off, when I noticed him making his way towards the café. He looked anxious and kept turning round, as though he feared he was being followed.

'I have to take care,' he said, sitting down beside me. 'The enterprise on which I'm engaged at present could get me into serious trouble with the so-called authorities if it became known.'

This remark could not fail to stimulate my curiosity. I begged him to go on with his story without further delay and not to omit a single detail.

'I'm coming, Monsieur, to the point when I encountered

the rich eccentric I mentioned, who influenced the course of my career.

'After my victory over the anti-aircraft unit I was taken prisoner by the Beleke army. I must admit I was extremely well treated and I even took a liking to the country. I taught my jailers a few simple procedures to hoodwink the crude mechanisms which the powers had sold to them. They derived great pleasure from my demonstrations and laughed wholeheartedly when they succeeded in copying one of my tricks. It was an amusing period; but in a short time, hostilities having come to an end, I was repatriated to France and found myself once more on my uppers.

'It was at this juncture I encountered the old eccentric, a fabulously rich man who lived in an isolated estate far from the town. I entered his service. He asked me for no references, having been charmed, during an interrogation to which he subjected me, by the profundity of my mathematical, mechanical and physical knowledge. These talents were of particular interest to him, for he was a wretched madman, his brain crammed with chimeras, who delighted in manufacturing automatons of every sort with his own hands and who puffed himself out like a turkey-cock when, in his folly, he fancied he discerned a symptom of reason in them. This man loved machines, Monsieur. He loved them heart and soul. He would stroke them, fondle them, whisper endearments to them. He never went to sleep without having half a dozen round him.'

'I imagine you didn't get on very well with such a crackpot.'

'Not so badly all the same, for, having learnt from personal experience, I was careful to conceal my feelings. Furthermore the passionate attention he vouchsafed to the automatons seemed to me less culpable than the general indifference the world shows towards them. Anyway I felt that with him I would have exceptional opportunities to gratify my hatred.

'I was not disappointed. There were any amount of experiments to try out in the vast workshop which his estate comprised, and I undertook them all. The electronic tortoises, for instance, those mechanisms which my master called animals, whose disordinate evolutions he never tired of admiring—on these I declared an implacable war. The first ones he made were equipped with a simple photoelectric cell which impelled them to move in the direction of the brightest light. Thus on fine summer mornings the wretched fellow amused himself by watching them, roused by the first glimmer of dawn, follow the sun's rays, pass through an opening con-

182

structed in their shed and head straight towards the East. This went on until one day they found in their path a thin sheet of glass which I had fastened to the opening. Then the whole house was wakened by a great clatter; the tortoises were stupidly dashing against the obstacle and exhausting themselves in their attempts to pass through it.

'I soon had enough of their nonsense. One night, pleading the Feast of St. John as an excuse, I lit a big bonfire not far from their shelter. What do you think happened? The tortoises started up, Monsieur. Not one of them suspected there were sources of light which could be dangerous. In single file (there were about a dozen of them) they headed for the blaze and without hesitation advanced into the flames, where they were consumed. As long as they had a breath of energy left, they eagerly sought out the brightest and therefore the hottest spot, where the fire annihilated them all the more rapidly.

'After reproaching me for what he believed to be carelessness, my master consoled himself for their loss by making some new, more elaborate ones, crammed full of cells, which, when an obstacle was placed in their path, first investigated it and then made their way round it. In this case, of course, it was a palpable obstacle, which a mechanical device in their obstinate foreheads came up against and activated various organs. When, however, I dug a steep-sided trench in their path, they were incapable of spotting it and tumbled into it, some of them breaking their necks in the fall, the rest drowning in the water with which I had taken care to fill my trap. My master then built some others which were able to swim; but I, Monsieur, set some ordinary wire snares, in which they were caught like rabbits and strangled to death after a few grotesque jerks.

'As I said, there are countless different ways of deceiving these crude creatures. For example, the electric plug which they use to recharge themselves when their batteries run down—you can connect this to a high tension source. Then they thoughtlessly clamp themselves against the electrodes without realizing this current is deadly. You can see them roasting before your eyes, writhing in a cloud of foul smoke, without thinking (they never think) of switching off.'

'I have no doubt you enjoyed yourself immensely with those tortoises,' I said, without being able to suppress a shudder, for the gleam that appeared in his eyes just then expressed an implacable cruelty.

'Immensely, Monsieur. But I soon got tired of such victories. I was dying to tackle a more worthy foe. There again my new master was a godsend. On his own account he began

183

to take an interest in the machines which I had been dreaming about for some time: calculators. When the first one appeared on the property, I realized my hour had come.'

6

'It was a fairly big electrical machine capable of carrying out various complicated operations in an extremely short space of time. Granted, it had a far more extensive range than the anti-aircraft calculator, which was confined to a limited sphere of action, but it was a mere toy compared to certain modern appliances which I shall describe presently.

'My master had it installed in the drawing-room, after removing the rest of the furniture, and he quivered with delight while the experts fixed the various circuits. When it was ready to work, he affectionately stroked its flanks.

' "Hubert," he said to me, "I feel we're going to achieve great things here with the help of Eunoia."

'Eunoia was the name he had given it. He himself did not suspect the far-reaching consequences of the events which were to take place in that drawing-room. As an initial exercise, he made the machine carry out some simple arithmetical operations and it was pitiful to see them both swagger with pride and puff themselves out like turkey-cocks when, Eunoia having given its answer, the worthy fellow conscientiously checked it in a notebook.

'I maintained an attitude of haughty reserve as long as the problems were limited to elementary additions, subtractions and multiplications. I did not intervene until he put the following question to Eunoia: thirty-seven thousand four hundred and eighty-two multiplied by ninety-four thousand five hundred and fifty-seven? Then, in a negligent manner, barely glancing at this easy riddle, I replied even before the machine had started up:

' "Three thousand five hundred and forty-million one hundred and eighty-five thousand four hundred and seventy-four . . ." Nowadays, alas, as a result of the dastardly conspiracy of which I was the victim, I am no longer capable of calculating so accurately and so rapidly; but I have preserved intact the memory of this initial exploit.

' "Here, I say!" my master exclaimed in alarm.

' "Three thousand five hundred and forty-four million one hundred and eighty-five thousand four hundred and seventy-four", I repeated.

' "Three thousand five hundred and forty-four million one

hundred and eighty-five thousand four hundred and seventy-four", the machine suddenly panted, after a delay of several seconds.

'I had beaten it hands down. My master gave me a long penetrating look.

' "Let's start again," he said with sudden animation.

'He set another multiplication problem. The result was the same. The machine vibrated furiously as it gave its answer, after me.

' "Hubert," my master remarked gently, "I wouldn't have believed this of you. But can you do better?"

'Far better.'

'All three of us were on our mettle. He was irritated by the defeat of his favourite, but he was a fair-minded man in spite of his faults. He wanted to act as umpire in the duel on which we embarked that day and he gave us each equal chances.

'He placed us back to back, each of us facing a wall in the room, then disappeared behind a rampart of books to set some difficult problems. When he had written down a set of terms on a sheet of paper, he carefully concealed it from us and stood at the end of the machine where the question was to be inserted on a punched card. Then he called me over.

' "Ready?" he said.

' "Ready," I replied. Eunoia's sulky silence was regarded as a sign of acquiescence. The machine and I were on our toes, like athletes before a great contest.

' "Go!" my master shouted.*

'In one movement he revealed the slip of paper and hastily inserted the card, so that I was provided with the data at the same time as my opponent. Then he rushed over to the slot from which the machine was to deliver the answer. But I always produced it, accurately, before Eunoia had finished pounding it out.

'We confronted each other like this for days on end and night after night. He progressively increased the complexity of the problems and the machine never succeeded in beating me. It was clearly wearing itself out. The ordeal to which we were subjected—fifteen hours' work a day—was too much for its organism. It began to react to this pressure by nervous tremors and disturbing vibrations. Its shattered morale was

---

* History tells us that such a contest took place in 1924 between Inaudi and a contemporary calculating machine, under the supervision of some mathematicians. The exact conditions of this duel have not been recorded but it is very likely that they were similar to these.

Since this story was written a fresh contest took place in 1964 between a human calculator and an electronic machine.

what affected its physique most of all. The humiliation I inflicted on it at each test infused its whole body with bile which was gradually poisoning it. On several occasions it faltered and paused in the middle of a calculation. Thereupon it had to be given a good shake and a thump to encourage it to pursue its task and start up again.'

'I can understand its exhaustion,' I said. 'But didn't you feel rather tired yourself in the long run?'

'Sometimes, I must admit. But I was buoyed up by the rapture of triumph. There were times when I felt a sort of mental sluggishness and a dangerous temptation to relax my efforts. I even had to thump my head with my fists to dispel this torpor and force myself to pursue the struggle until my opponent surrendered. On these occasions I had the feeling it was panting with hope, eagerly watching for a sign of weakness on my part, and this was enough to imbue me with fresh strength.

'My victory was complete. The machine was visibly wasting away; it could no longer function except at the lowest speed, while emitting a plaintive rattle. One day, eventually, after a particularly arduous ordeal, Eunoia gave a hiccough and came to a standstill. It ran down completely, Monsieur, and no amount of verbal or physical castigation could induce it to resume the fight. Some specialists who were called in shook their heads, conferred together at great length in undertones, then suggested replacing some organs. My master hesitated, shrugged his shoulders and made a firm decision.

' "Hubert," he said to me, "this machine is worthless. I was mad to have acquired it. It's unworthy of either of us, barely fit for solving elementary schoolboy problems . . ."

'He was as angry with Eunoia as with a mistress who had betrayed him. He spoke out loud in front of it, without mincing his words and without any pity for its humiliation. He gave it a contemptuous kick and went on:

' "No point in wasting time and money trying to patch up this shoddy stuff. On the slightest excuse it would give up the ghost again. What we want is a strong and sturdy brain. Have you heard of electronic computers? Now they would be a match for you."

'That's what he said, Monsieur, and at these words, in spite of myself, I shivered. Had I heard of these machines! I had studied every publication concerning them. Not a single detail of their structure was unknown to me. I had strained my eyes poring over their plans. I had traced the thousands of "flip-flop" circuits which, according to admirers, are modelled on the neurones of the human brain. I had meditated on their performances which had been investigated in various scien-

186

tific journals. So, I don't mind admitting, I trembled. When my master announced his intention of matching me against one of these monsters I was seized by a leaden anguish, a sensation similar to what I had experienced at the time of my first encounter with the turbines.

'Oh, don't misunderstand me! I had no doubt, I could have no doubt, of the superiority of my brain over these automatons. The machine, its high priests claimed, carried out its operations at the speed of light; but then didn't I calculate at the speed of thought? Yet the margin was narrow and I was panic-stricken at the idea of committing some silly mistake. This could not happen to me when I was in tip-top condition, but I felt worn out, utterly exhausted by the recent war I had waged against Eunoia. At the same time . . .'

He broke off, looked round us with an anxious air, then went on in a low voice, in a tone fraught with mystery.

'At the same time, Monsieur, I began to suspect a diabolical plan in this succession of calculating machines. I felt— and how right I proved to be!—that there was a sort of solidarity between these two, the first having been entrusted with the duty of wearing me down, the second appearing just at the right moment to take over from the first and exploit my weakened condition. A nervous tremor came over me when I read a report eulogizing, in sickeningly exaggerated terms, the machine which my master had just acquired.

'For he had ordered the monster. As I said, he had a vast fortune, as gigantic as his madness, and no expense would deter him when it came to gratifying the latter. To house the new machine a special building was needed, for it would not fit into any of the existing rooms. Do you know the fantastic idea which then came into his head? Instead of a simple shed, he erected an absolute palace for it. He spent a fortune on this construction. He engaged the most famous and the most eccentric architects. Since their plans never seemed sumptuous enough, he drew one up himself, allowing his fancy full rein. He selected the most rare materials. Finally, he erected to the glory of stupidity a sort of monument in Byzantine style, made of marble, adorned with sumptuous mosaics, gold and precious stones, and surmounted by a great dazzling dome. This, to his mind, was a suitable setting for the marvel he was expecting. It was the sort of dwelling that a prince in *The Thousand and One Nights* might have given to his favourite courtesan.

'When the palace was finished, when it reared its baroque silhouette in the midst of the dense wood that covered the park, a multitude of packing cases started arriving at the house. Surreptitiously, piecemeal, the better to conceal its inordinate bulk, accompanied by a legion of sinister-looking technicians, the monster invaded our domain.'

7

'I became more and more nervous as the machine settled into its new home. I tried in vain to regain my confidence by familiarizing myself with it. I followed every movement of the experts as they assembled its organs and connected its countless circuits. I was incessantly haunted by the picture of the fluid moving through this network at the speed of light, and could not help drawing disquieting comparisons with the capacities of my own nerves. It was a constant and exhausting anxiety. I couldn't sleep. I was wasting away. My master, who was anxious about my health in view of the future contest, took me to see a doctor who examined me with curiosity, questioned me insistently and ended up by prescribing a long intellectual rest. Intellectual rest!—when the machine was there, all ready to function, and when I needed to muster all my mental resources. My master, however, forced me to obey the doctor's orders. I went off into the mountains. Before my departure he gave me a sumptuous party in the course of which our new guest was christened in champagne. He named it Eunoia II. He was a man of little or no imagination.

'After a few weeks in the mountains my health improved, my spirits gradually revived and my anxiety vanished. I notified him that I was ready for the struggle and came back. But when, shortly before the time fixed for our first encounter, I approached the palace where the machine had had all the time in the world to train in my absence, I was overcome by anguish once more and, as I entered the lair, I was trembling from head to foot.

'The inside of the palace consisted of one huge room. The lighting was barbaric. Eunoia II was illuminated like some priceless monument by a host of arc-lamps. It was the first time I had seen it like this and I felt profoundly uneasy. While my master fiddled with some switches and handles, I stood motionless in front of it, leaning against the opposite wall, fascinated by the monstrous aggregate of its organism.

'Motionless? Fascinated? If the truth be known, I was, and well and truly mesmerized, Monsieur. It was stealthily trying to deprive me of my faculties before the contest. Everything in this room, everything, was designed to plunge me into a hypnotic trance. The machine's flanks, covered in glittering green paint, reflected the rays of the arc-lamps in a fantastic blaze of light. Its freshly polished chromium and brass added the eeriness of their particular shimmer to the blinding glare. The gilt and garlands of precious stones, with which my master in his madness had surrounded it, sparkled like constellations and furnished a still more dazzling background to this pernicious scintillation. Since my entry Eunoia had been doing its utmost to imbue all these beams with an infernal luminosity and my bewildered brain began to reel.

'Fortunately I realized its diabolical scheme in time and I pulled myself together abruptly. I merely had to close my eyes. I did so, thus retiring into my shell, while the malevolent fluid slowly ebbed away. When I had recovered my composure, I decided to pay the machine back in its own coin. With my eyes still closed, from prudence and the better to conceal my purpose, I felt my way towards the two big screens I had noticed, two luminous windows which taunted me. As though by accident I stopped about three feet away; then suddenly, opening my eyes wide, fixing my gaze on that of Eunoia II, concentrating all my mental energy, I tried in my turn to hypnotize it by surprise.

'For a moment I had reason to think I was going to succeed. Disconcerted at first by the abruptness of my attack, it appeared to accept the challenge. This was what I wanted. We glared at each other like this for a long time, and a deeper and deeper uneasiness could be discerned in its wavering gaze. But at the very moment it was about to lapse into unconsciousness, it had the same defence reflex as myself. It took evasive action, switched off the light in its screens and came back to its senses in the dark, as I had done. All the same I had made it feel and fear my power.

'At this juncture my master, after tripping a final switch, solemnly announced the contest open. He broke the seals of the envelopes in which he had inserted the text of the problems and we prepared to come to grips.

'What can I tell you of that memorable duel, Monsieur? We entered upon the contest with multiplications and divisions. We continued it with square and cube roots and powers of the nth degree. We tussled with countless systems of equations containing a multitude of unknown quantities. We juggled with imaginary quantities. In a flash we totted up the infinitely small terms of an infinite number of complicated series. In the twinkling of an eye we calculated the first thousand decimal points of *pi*. We solved simple, double, treble and quadruple integers valid in chimerical spaces composed of a fantastic number of dimensions.

'That is more or less what we did. I felt my brain was on fire, my mind possessed by a fever which stimulated my intellectual faculties beyond any known limit, but, in spite of the marvels I performed that evening, I did not succeed in affirming my superiority in an outright manner. At times I beat the machine by several fractions of a second, but the reverse happened as well. It looked as though the match would result in a draw, which I could not countenance. The honour of mankind was at stake, Monsieur! I made the most sublime efforts that mind has ever attempted in order to outdistance my opponent. I was on the point of succeeding when the disaster occurred.

'I am overcome by emotion when I recall that moment. The umpire had just given us a particularly tricky equation with partial derivations. This is my last clear memory of the evening. I had the sensation of having reached the inaccessible summits of lucidity. I was on the verge of the answer. My mind was stretching out to grasp it. All my previous records were broken. I was triumphant. . . . Just then I felt a great shock and found myself suddenly immersed in a thick mist. The laws of mathematics, with which all my neurones were saturated, forthwith evaporated, leaving me with a dreadful sensation of nothingness. I was conscious only of a ringing in my ears, a faint buzz which intruded on my paralysed being in the oddest manner, like a set of gears revolving in a bath of viscous oil inside a padded chest, revolving endlessly, without aim or purpose, turning over and over a dull succession of figures and symbols, invariable and hideously devoid of meaning.

'I stood petrified like this for some time. As though in a dream, I heard an exclamation, then the odious chuckle of the machine as it robbed me of victory by producing the answer—an answer which had become unintelligible to me. Then I sank into the depths of unconsciousness.'

8

He lapsed into a long gloomy silence. I urged him to go on with his story by remarking, with hypocritical benevolence:

'A very natural breakdown, after such superhuman efforts. I hope you soon recovered.'

I saw him shudder and his eyes glinted with rage.

"A breakdown? Natural? Come, come, Monsieur! Don't you realize it had got the better of me by stealth? That I had eventually succumbed to its magnetic power? It was with this infamous end in view that it had reduced the speed of its operations. In the frenzy of the conflict I had neglected to guard against the intensified luminosity and I had been well and truly hypnotized, without having time, on this occasion, to react.

'It knew what the outcome would be. This was an infernal *machination,* the sort of trap in fact which always has a *machine* behind it. I cannot recall these incidents without weeping. Since my lethargic torpor persisted, my master once more called in the doctors. The opportunity was too good to miss! I was handed over to them, defenceless. They took advantage of my state of insensibility and unconsciousness to open up my brain. They brought saws, hammers and other barbarous instruments to bear. They plunged lancets into my most noble and delicate organs. They delved into my divine grey matter. They attacked my subtle neurones with base steel. They clipped, pruned, extracted, supplemented, grafted and reconnected as their pernicious fancy took them. . . . By a stroke of luck they tampered with only half my brain. The rest of it is intact and works sufficiently for me to draw up plans and continue my campaign. But the damaged half, Monsieur? It's a demolition site that I carry about inside me. That's the result of their handiwork. That's what the machine did to me. You realize now why I hate the whole breed, and why I wreaked a striking vengeance on it.'

'You had your revenge?'

His voice had assumed a tone of despair as he described his ill-treatment. His expression now changed and he gave a cruel little laugh. He glanced over his shoulder again in a suspicious manner and went on in a lower voice.

'A perfect revenge, Monsieur, as befits a subtle mind, and of which I shall be eternally proud. I can't tell you all about it here; there are too many people and I now know that in this country there is a permanent conspiracy against intelligence; but you are a friend and I can show you the result of my vengeance if you'd like to come back with me. You'll see with your own eyes the state to which I've reduced the stupid monster. My car is round the corner. We could be there in an hour.'

His last remarks and the tone in which he had uttered them had made me feel slightly uneasy, but my love of the bizarre would not allow me to shirk the issue. I rose to my feet and followed him outside. I hesitated a moment, however, before entering the sumptuous motor-car, the door of which he obligingly held open for me.

'This motor-car,' I enquired. . . . 'I assume it's yours, and that you're on . . . er . . . good terms with it? What I mean

191

is . . . you don't sometimes amuse yourself by playing tricks on it?'

He gave a scornful smile.

'Set your mind at rest, Monsieur. Granted, it's extremely easy to deceive these machines; too easy. I am beyond that stage. They are poor wretched creatures without any malice, who don't even merit our attention. With this one I confine myself to keeping a tight hand on the reins and issuing the necessary orders. It carries them out slavishly without ever complaining.

'Bravo!' I said with vehemence. 'That's the only way to treat these creatures. I agree with you whole-heartedly.'

We drove out of the town. His handling of the car was reasonable, albeit a little rough. I was surprised that he should own a luxurious Cadillac and I said so. He then told me that the person to whom he curiously referred as his "master" had died some months before and that he had inherited all his property. At this I pricked up my ears, for the tone he had assumed seemed to conceal an important innuendo.

'All his property? Including Eunoia II, of course,' I said slyly.

'Including Eunoia II,' he replied with a conspiratorial wink.

'That must have made your revenge a great deal easier, I imagine.'

He laughed out loud.

'It's a pleasure to converse with you, Monsieur. You're so quick on the uptake. Mind you, even when my master was alive, as soon as I realized the machination of which I had been the victim, I bravely resumed the fight. There was no longer any question, with only half a brain, of launching a frontal attack on the machine, but I pondered on my misadventure and drew up fresh plans. I pondered a great deal. I concluded that I had been anything but wise to try to compete with an automaton in the realm of mathematics which, after all, boils down to a mechanical operation. To defeat it, I had to think and not calculate.

'I therefore worked out a few insidious traps. I secretly modified the problems my master prepared so that the data led to an absurd answer or to no answer at all. That's how one day I forced the brute to the limits of its strength by making it calculate the sum of a certain series. Yes, I had so cunningly modified the general terms that the sum was nothing more or less than infinite. That makes you smile? But it tackled the impossible enterprise with its usual obstinacy. For fifteen days and fifteen nights it lined up an endless succession of figures on the punched tape which it uses to translate its answers. My master, at his wits' end, fed it mile after mile of virgin tape without ever managing to satisfy its hunger. It would have died of fatigue in its mad attempt to express infinity in arithmetical terms, if he had not decided to switch everything off.'

'In fact you cheated,' I said gazing at him.

'I cheat, Monsieur. I cheat, therefore I think, and that is one of my incontestable advantages.

'I can see what's on your mind, however. You're disappointed. You regard this as a rather feeble counter-stroke. The affront and the damage I had suffered called for a more striking revenge. I thought so too, but I could not do as I liked as long as my master was there. . . . Luckily he died.'

'Luckily he died,' I echoed, without taking my eyes off him.

'In a matter of minutes. A crushing and absolutely unexpected heart-attack. I didn't even have time to call in a doctor. This was a great relief to me. Although he had never tried to harm me directly, in the long run his morbid love of machines had made him odious to me. Besides, I felt sure he was beginning to suspect what I was up to.'

I shivered, for these words were once again fraught with innuendo, and accompanied by the same conspiratorial glance he had given me a moment before. I was careful, however, not to ask him to explain himself more clearly. Furthermore, he had not come to the end of his story but went on:

'I had a great sensation of liberty after his demise. From now on I had a free hand. Eunoia II also realized this when I came back after burying the poor fellow in a corner of the park. We found ourselves face to face, just the two of us, far from all prying eyes.

' "You're in for it now," I said.'

He broke off. We were arriving. We had turned off the main road some time before and the car was bumping over a rough track. The last houses we had passed were far behind us. We plunged into a dense forest. Presently the Cadillac drew up at a gate behind which lay a drive carved out of the thick undergrowth and flanked with tall trees. He carefully closed it behind him after driving through and fastened it with a heavy padlock. To the left and right of the entrance stretched a high prison-like wall, bristling with broken glass and adorned with barbed wire.

'I'm afraid of unwelcome visitors,' he said with a little laugh.

193

We eventually arrived at an old manor-house which seemed to be in good repair despite its age. This was his master's home, which today was his own. The palace, he told me, was five minutes' walk away, in the middle of the park. He asked me if I would like a drink before going over there but he was so impatient that he dragged me off through the woods without even waiting for my reply, after taking a huge bunch of keys from the hall.

'I am obliged to enjoin complete secrecy on you,' he said in a low voice. 'You'll be the only man in the world to know the nature and extent of my revenge.'

I reassured him as to my discretion. I tried several times to make him tell me more about this famous revenge of his but, talkative though he was when describing his other exploits, he avoided my questions, merely giving a self-satisfied and sardonic laugh, which added to my perplexity and bewilderment. Need I say that this character, who had first amused, then fascinated me, now struck me as somewhat disquieting? Alone with him in this property tucked away in the woods, I began to feel extremely uneasy. Nothing but the spur of curiosity would have induced me to follow him.

We eventually emerged into a clearing. He drew back and stretched out his arm.

'There's the palace, Monsieur,' he said. 'Be prepared for the most astonishing sight you have ever beheld in your life.'

There was a sly, cruel glint in his eyes. I looked. The palace was certainly an odd building, but I did not linger to examine its eccentricity in detail, so eager was I to go inside. I merely quickly ascertained that the monument was more or less as he had described it to me, which was already fairly surprising; for anyone will agree that it is not usual to come across a Byzantine structure, a palace straight out of *The Thousand and One Nights,* tucked away in the middle of a forest in France and housing an electronic computer. If I had been less disturbed by his mysterious manner, I would surely have appreciated this piquant anomaly more fully. Without any doubt, his master was a great eccentric.

The carved stonework was clearly visible, but not the gilding he had mentioned. Nor did the dome emit the slightest ray of light. If its shape was what he had led me to expect, its colour was disappointing. The palace was drab, strangely, lugubriously drab. I realized why when I drew nearer and perceived its squalor, while he gave me a few hasty explanations.

'You'll see nothing shiny here,' he said with one of those knowing looks which seemed to have become a habit of his. 'I'm not going to be hypnotized twice. I removed the gilt and

194

precious stones, or else I have camouflaged them so thoroughly that I defy it by these means to charm even a skylark.'

The traces of his activity were only too apparent. He had hacked the jewels out with a pick, leaving the walls scarred and cracked. As for the dome, it had merely been covered over with greyish plaster, which contributed to the general aspect of gloom and melancholy.

The man who hated machines delighted in my astonishment.

'Well, what about it?' he said. 'Not so dusty, eh? But come over here. This crude outer covering is unimportant. It's the inside that matters to us, to you and me.'

I followed him to the door, a block of steel strangely embedded in the marble and equipped with several locks, which he opened one after another.

'Come in.'

He ushered me inside and closed the door behind him. We were in pitch darkness. My anxiety increased. All of a sudden some blinding lights came on in all directions. I closed my eyes for a moment against the glare, then forced myself to open them again.

'Well?' he said once more in a tone of intense jubilation, 'what do you say to this? Well, I wasn't exaggerating, was I?'

9

I was unable to suppress a violent exclamation, so far in eeriness and wretchedness did the vision which appeared to me in the blaze of the arc-lamps surpass my wildest dreams. Before grasping its physical nature I felt overwhelmed, suffocated by a series of riotous impressions, which were so disproportionate with the actual objects I beheld that they struck me as incongruities and my whole being protested against the terms in which I instinctively translated them.

Dilapidation was the first word that sprang to my lips. Yes, dilapidation was the essential, tormenting pattern of the fantastic symphony which a heteroclitic disposition of distorted elements tended to compose in this room. Dilapidation, and afterwards, like a succession of harmonics around this principal theme, *disorder, ruination, decay,* and also *desecration, sabotage, butchery,* and furthermore, in a manner which struck me as being the height of outlandishness (for there was nothing here but inert matter) *anguish* and *suffering.* I experienced in a flash this mixture of sensations; I blurted out these words in confusion on first beholding this spectacle, but the one that finally intruded most forcibly on my mind, as the most evocative synthesis of this chaos, was *insanity*.

Before me stood a giant computer, one of the most elaborate of its kind, what is known in fashionable jargon as an electronic 'brain', and its mere presence in this place appertained to the prodigious, for I knew that in the whole world there existed no more than three or four models of this type, size and prize. But how can I describe the state of this machine? How, above all, express the emotion and horror provoked by the contrast between its abject condition and the characteristics of order, exactitude and logic which the evocation of these machines infallibly suggests?

There it stood, the wretched 'brain', gashed, mangled and dismembered, with all its organs laid bare. The panels which had enclosed it, which the man had described to me as great gleaming surfaces, these battered, broken panels revealed, from one end of the room to the other, and from floor to ceiling, hideous gaping wounds. In their twisted and shattered remains I could recognize the trace of crude instruments which had been used for this initial operation, which I mentally compared to the act of a clumsy giant struggling to open an enormous tin of sardines. Cold steel and hammers must have been employed as the means of attack. Crude clippers had then opened long fissures in the metal, being supplemented here and there by saws, which were more effective for tackling a bolt or rivet. Moreover all these tools, still stained with varnish and shimmering scraps of metal, were to be seen in one corner of the room, cheek by jowl with other more delicate, more highly polished ones, which looked like surgical instruments.

The man who hated machines had proceeded according to a plan—his plan. He had first of all made some large openings here and there in order to see more clearly. Then he had delved into the disfigured body and removed the organs. These he had spread out in deliberate disorder on some planks resting on trestles which ran all the way down one side of the machine. Thus Eunoia II's precious substance, fragile marvels which legions of scientists and technicians had assembled in one miraculous organism, lay exposed on this long table which was bathed in light like an operating table.

There was a host of strange contraptions which I was unable to identify and countless coils of electric wire, thousands of circuits of all dimensions, some of a slender diameter invincibly suggesting extremely ingenious nerves. And on all this rare material, the singular man who hated machines had likewise vented his singular feelings, again no doubt following

196

a definite method, understood by him alone but the result of which appeared to the layman as an outlandish act of carnage.

After ripping open the casing and removing and scattering the organs, he had clearly armed himself with pincers and wire clippers. Not a single section of these networks had escaped him. But perhaps the strangest aspect of this conscientious spoliation was the evident attempt to *patch up* the damage after each act of destruction. Not a single piece of wire had been left disconnected. The surgeon had taken great pains to link each loose conductive to a broken length of another circuit so as to produce a terrifying tangle. The junctions were protected somewhat haphazardly by spirals of insulating tape which looked like bandages, so that at times Eunoia II struck me as being a sort of monster whose thousands of spidery tentacles had been sliced in two, then hastily repaired by means of crude ligatures.

Among the appliances which lay half buried in this labyrinth, I now vaguely recognized some self-inducting coils, condensers and transformers cheek by jowl with some extremely precious cells. All had been attacked with precision instruments. Only an extremely delicate surgical blade could have bisected these transparent sheets of mica, into which had been inserted some wires of a microscopic diameter made of a metal more valuable than gold, which presumably played an essential part in the 'brain's' speculations. These gems had likewise been connected to circuits which were alien to them, by means of clumsily welded joints, so that they drowned in a matrix of silvery foam.

Nothing had been overlooked. Accessory measuring instruments, their glass faces smashed, their frames dented, their hands twisted and their chromium plate carefully tarnished, had been torn from their sockets, then plugged into this fantastic circuit here and there, at random. Here again more welded joints and bandages of insulating tape bore witness to an attempt at repair, which appeared to me even more terrifying than a desire for total destruction.

And the aggregate of these burlesque elements constituted an expression of unbearable sorrow and suffering. I was violently *afflicted*. I was even so painfully disturbed that I felt physically sick, I'm ashamed to say. I turned away. I rushed out of the door and vomited, as some sensitive people do at the sight of mangled flesh.

When I felt a little better, when I had recovered sufficient composure to curse myself for a fool, I forced myself to reenter the room. There I found my host contemplating his handiwork with manifest self-satisfaction. He looked at me sternly.

'Monsieur,' he said, 'I hope I haven't misjudged you? Surely you're not one of those people who irrationally commiserate with these brainless creatures? Don't you feel this treatment has been well and truly deserved?'

'Why, of course!' I hastily cried. 'I feel this is a splendid, appropriate, justifiable revenge and I have nothing against it. It's the smell.'

I haven't mentioned the smell of ether which pervaded the palace, completing the caricature-like evocation of an operating theatre. In fact I had only just noticed it, my other senses having been paralyzed by the violence of the vision. I perceived some chemist's bottles containing a colourless liquid and, next to them, a half-filled bowl in which some huge pads of cotton-wool lay soaking. My companion appeared to accept the excuse.

'I understand, Monsieur. Ether often disturbs those who aren't used to it. As for me, it has the opposite effect if anything: I find the smell comforting. It's not, however, from sensitivity that I used an anaesthetic, but the operation lasted several days and my plan demanded that my patient should be completely motionless.'

'Of course . . . but you talk of a plan. To my shame, I have to admit it escapes me, as far as I can see from the result. Could you give me some idea of it?'

A gleam of vanity came into his eyes.

'I was expecting that question. Rest assured, the plan which I pride myself on having conceived and carried out here may not be apparent to the layman but is none the less a little masterpiece of audacity and intelligence. Unfortunately, it's difficult for me to satisfy your curiosity; your scientific education has been neglected, as I've noticed several times. Your knowledge of the great laws of physics, in particular, make it difficult for me not to laugh.'

I begged him to outline them in general at least. He consented with a condescending smile and embarked on a speech full of strange jargon.

'Do you know at least what *entropy* is? No? Well, it's a mathematical expression which measures the disorder of an aggregate. In the case of an isolated system abandoned to the laws of chance, like the material Universe for instance, this entropy progressively increases and approaches a certain maximum value which corresponds to the greatest disorder possible.

'But mark this, Monsieur. Under the sole impulse of contingent factors, it approaches this maximum amount without ever reaching it. My genius lay in realizing that it was madness to leave things to chance in such matters and that the question of disorder should be treated with a scientific exactitude equal to that of order. My masterpiece, Monsieur, was to make use of the elements of this machine (after research of which I shall spare you the details) so as to bring about a particular arrangement (*the* particular arrangement, I should say, for it's unique) which entails maximum entropy, that's to say perfect, ideal, absolute disorder. I picked on this combination, Monsieur, as a result of pure reasoning and among a million others which would have yielded no more than partial chaos. Do you follow me?'

'Sufficiently, I think, to be full of admiration,' I said pensively. 'But isn't this maximum entropy, as you call it, equivalent to death?'

'Not at all, Monsieur,' he exclaimed, 'and I shall prove it to you. You have in front of you an entity that is well and truly alive, an entity in perfect health, as they say. As for its mentality, you'll see.'

'You mean Eunoia II still functions?'

'See for yourself.'

10

He was seized by a sudden fit of activity. He darted about the control panel with feverish gestures, pressing a button here, turning a switch there and abruptly closing some twisted underload releases. Was it the influence of the ether which pervaded the whole atmosphere of this sanctum? I too began to feel a strange intoxication, the fever which seizes occasional drunkards when they believe they have trapped in their transitory universe the omens of some supernatural event. I saw him make some fresh connections in this wreck, as though this act was of capital importance, as though it was a reasonable and at the same time mysterious ceremony from which some unparalleled revelation would emanate.

'You ask if it still functions! Listen. Can't you hear it groaning?'

I strained my ears. I noticed that the treatment suffered by Eunoia II did not prevent it from taking the current; it was clearly under tension; but instead of the soft purr I expected from such a machine, there came from it a series of erratic strident sounds which composed a lugubrious complaint.

'Do you hear it?' he cried. 'That's the doleful lament provoked by its terror of intellectual activity. That's the hymn of

199

despair. It's begging to be spared a task which has become a hellish torment for it. But we shan't be moved to pity. It's ready, though much against its will. What are you waiting for, to put some questions to it? Come, Monsieur . . . if it still functions indeed! Good God, you're going to see it in full action. It's the funniest sight in the world. . . . A question, quick—oh, an easy one. It's quite pointless to rack your brain. On the contrary, the more simple the problem, the greater the success of the demonstration.'

'A simple question?' I echoed dully.

He was more and more agitated. As for myself, I was sinking deeper and deeper into a sort of morbid trance which seemed to preclude all thought. It took me a long time and required a preposterous effort to think of an elementary arithmetical operation and put it into words.

'That ought to do,' he said, gesticulating like a demon in front of the panel. 'Wait. We must be fair. We must translate the data into its own language. . . . Like this.'

In the twinkling of an eye he transposed the operation on to a punched tape. Having myself some notion of the mysterious language of the perforations, I checked to see that his translation was correct. He slammed the tape into the entrance slot and went back to the controls.

The machine began to tremble, and the effects of the painful martyrdom which its master was inflicting on it became visible in some of the organs which had been laid bare on the trestles as though on a pillory. At the intersections of the fantastic network into which some lamps and measuring instruments had been plugged, some lights began to gleam faintly —strange flickering lights whose erratic vacillation betokened a disturbing instability of energy. The man had switched off the arc-lamps—no doubt to enjoy the spectacle all the more. Piercing the darkness, the nodes of this outlandish circuit seemed to reflect a fearful apprehension and to reproduce in space the various stages of a calvary. Presently I perceived that over and above the rapid flickering of these lights, variations of a far longer period were building up. Then, whenever the luminous intensity rose to a maximum, the sort of prostration that seemed to be reflected by this vision reached its most pathetic degree. In spite of myself, I had the somewhat unreasonable impression that the same impulse was repeating itself at regular intervals, for want of being able to find an outlet, and that the same insipid flux kept circulating through the belly of the organism in an endless circle.

As though he had read my thoughts, the man, whose excitement was verging on frenzy, started screaming with exultation.

'It keeps turning round and round! Turning round in circles without ever getting anywhere. It's exhausting itself in the mad pursuit of a light that has been extinguished. Turning round with the despair of a planet that will never again receive a beam from a sun that has disappeared. Consuming itself in the fruitless pursuit of a state of permanency that is necessary for thought. Listen to it! Look at it!'

I now distinguished further signs of torment. The loose ends, clumsily bound together with insulating tape, gave off a shower of sparks every now and then, indicating the painful passage of the fluid through the defective connections. Thousands of discordant crackles thus greeted the peaks of the cycle. The light was then sufficient to enable me to see the hands of the gauges, which seemed to have gone mad, oscillating with abrupt jerks, hammering against the edge of their faces, without ever remaining for more than a fraction of a second at any one point.

'Can you hear it moaning?' the man persisted. 'It's suffering. It's experiencing the hell of a mental void. It's undergoing the torment of chimerical flashes of reason, the agony of abortive thoughts, the hideous vertigo of vortexes in a retort, the horror of knowing only the ignoble sensation of its own decline. . . . But perhaps, Monsieur, you have submitted a problem which is rather too complicated for it?'

There was a wealth of cruel irony in these words and in the tone in which they were uttered.

'Perhaps, perhaps this marvel, this fabulous *brain*, is paralyzed by a three-figure multiplication? So give it a still more simple question. We must be fair, as I said before; there's nothing to stop us being charitable as well. We must allow for the circumstances. We're not executioners, damn it all! Come on, then. . . .'

I had joined in this barbarous game with a passion which almost equalled his own, but my mind was so disturbed that once again it took me a long time to be able to state an addition of two terms, each consisting of only two figures. The man crowed with delight. His ecstasy seemed to increase still further.

'That's it, that's it!' he chuckled. 'A childish addition. That's the sort of problem for this miraculous machine. And we'll stretch magnanimity so far as to allow it to recover its breath. We'll give it a short rest before subjecting it to such a laborious speculation.'

He turned off the current and switched on the lights while he inscribed the addition on a tape. After a moment's respite he inserted the question in the slot and plunged the room into darkness again. The saraband started up once more, punctuated by splutterings, shudders, creaks and wild flashes of light. But, as before, the apparatus which was to register the answer (a sort of telescriptor) did not move. My companion led me over to this instrument and pointed at it with a sneer. It seemed to me at times that the hand was affected by an imperceptible tremor, an incipient impulse, but it never managed to rise.

'Simpler still! As you can see, it can't manage. This is still too difficult for it. Simpler still.'

In my state of intoxication I suddenly seemed to have a brain-wave. I put the question: one plus one equals what? The man started roaring:

'A stroke of genius! One plus one! Yes, that's the intellectual nourishment fit for this brain! One plus one equals what? Come on now!'

He inserted the question, duly translated, into the slot. The cycle was resumed, marked by visibly more intense manifestations. The inordinate efforts of Eunoia II seemed to mark the limit of despair. The flashes grew brighter; the sparks crackled with greater violence. In spite of my confusion, I reflected it was absolutely miraculous that a fire had not yet broken out.

The man who hated machines ushered me once more towards the answers slot. This time, after a series of clearly perceptible vibrations, the telescriptor suddenly started working. It then quivered incessantly, in a feverish jerky manner, as though, having vanquished its inertia by an effort that was impossible to repeat, it was afraid of relapsing at any moment into paralysis. Nothing could stop it now. The hand clattered loudly, punching holes at a frantic rate, while the tape unrolled at a furious speed. The machine appeared to be making up, apologizing for the absurdity of its answer, while proclaiming it with all its might and repeating it incessantly. For this answer was completely devoid of meaning. It consisted of a series of figures repeated over and over again.

'Listen to it!' cried the man who hated machines. 'Just listen to it! One, two, three, four, five, six, seven, one, two, three, four, five, six, seven! That's what one plus one equals, according to this "brain"! One, two, three, four, five, six, seven . . . and so on and so on *ad infinitum*. What a wonderful, what a splendid answer! You'll bear me out. . . . Now it's my turn, Monsieur. . . . Ask me the question. The same one, of course. We must always be fair, always fair, as I said before.'

'One plus one equals what?' I asked, peering at him.

'One plus one,' he began in a triumphant tone, 'one plus one . . . why, it's quite simple, one plus one equals . . .'

He broke off abruptly, stunned by the stroke that I felt was coming on. He gave a groan, put his hand to his head and mumbled several times in an anguished voice which seemed to betoken an atrocious torment: 'One plus one equals, one plus one equals, one plus one equals . . .' His eyes reflected nothing but the pale gleam of madness. Dribble oozed from his mouth. The throbbing in his temples betrayed a prodigious effort, which culminated absurdly in a raucous splutter, a sort of litany in which I could just distinguish a series of figures repeated over and over again. Then he collapsed on the floor, unconscious.

At the same time the inevitable happened. The countless short circuits embedded in the *brain* blended into a single gigantic spark, a blinding flash which for a second irradiated the entrails of this chaos and was immediately succeeded by fire. In a moment the machine became a flaming torch. I only just escaped in time. Long red flames soon filled the vicinity and consumed everything inside the palace.

LOVE AND GRAVITY

After the first artificial satellite* had circled the Earth for a month, at a height of two thousand kilometres and at a prodigious speed, the original crew was relieved.

The first occupants returned by rocket as they had left, and landed without incident in the neighbourhood of New York. An enthusiastic reception awaited the space pioneers and the most important papers outbid one another for the privilege of printing their impressions. Those impressions, however, were not the wild success expected. Scientists and technicians had for so long carefully calculated all the factors of the expedition, and every moment in the satellite had proceeded according to a plan known to all, that it was soon obvious that the space experiment served only to confirm a flawless theory.

The satellite had been set up in space, various sections having been sent up on different rockets. Apparently the one hitch had been the absence of a certain mechanism that would produce a rotary motion which, compensating by centrifugal force for the absence of Earth attraction, would make the passengers' journey more comfortable. The latter had therefore lived in a weightless world for the duration of the experiment. However, this, too, was well known. Since the days of H. G. Wells even little children have understood the phenomena accompanying those conditions. Countless magazine stories and motion pictures have popularized the image of the space traveller who presses a finger on a wall and is bounced like a balloon against the opposite wall or who hits the ceiling every time he tries to take a step on the floor.

I am a journalist by profession and it was therefore my duty to discover some new and startling light on this story. Disappointed at hearing only worn-out clichés, I questioned

* This story was written long before the first Sputnik was launched.

one of the passengers closely in the hope of gleaning a few spicy details.

'But doesn't the absence of weight produce some strange situations?' I asked.

'There was one case perhaps . . . ,' he began. 'But nothing in the world would induce me to tell you that story. You'll have to ask Joe.'

Now, Joe was the sole 'manpower' aboard the satellite. As objects had no weight up there, the material work required so little effort that the labor crew had been reduced to a single man. Joe, however, had vanished. Unlike the other space explorers, who went from one reception to the other, Joe had left town without giving an interview. For that matter, his role in this adventure was such a modest one that none of the reporters had even thought of questioning him.

'Ask Joe,' the passenger repeated. 'He's the only one who may perhaps be able to give you some of those spicy details you're looking for.'

'Ask Joe,' another passenger told me maliciously when I put the same question to him.

'Ask Joe,' the commander of the satellite repeated when finally I reached him. 'For my part, I never want to hear of that fellow or his story again. He was the bane of our expedition, a real pain in the neck.'

Intrigued, I set out excitedly to find Joe.

I ran him to earth in an isolated little town far from New York to which he had fled on his return. He was a big man with a round, chubby face and candid blue eyes that were not only guiltless of any malice, but, to a close observer, marked him as the likely victim of those snares into which such simple souls are always falling.

I was frank with him and introduced myself as the representative of a great paper that was eager to publish his impressions. To my immense surprise, he refused point blank to talk. I insisted. He lost his temper and showed me the door. More and more intrigued, I telephoned my paper. Then I went back to Joe and before he could open his mouth I offered him a large sum of money in exchange for his story. Had Joe been alone he would perhaps still have refused; but his wife, Betty, was tempted by my offer. Taking her husband aside, she spoke to him in a low tone. He hesitated quite a long time, but finally ended by agreeing.

I have transcribed his story as faithfully as possible, though I regret my inability to convey the picturesque effect of his homespun American speech.

'Impressions . . . ?' Joe began. 'Well, if that's what you

want, I'll give you a few. I didn't want to tell this story. It's nothing to boast about, but after all, if that's the way it happened, it's not my fault and if people want to pay to hear it, I'd be a fool not to cash in on it. First of all, I warn you, I'm not much at telling a story and besides, this one's sort of terrific.'

'Come on, Joe. That's just the kind our readers like. I'm sure of it. Forget about me and just tell it your own way.'

'Well, it all started with an idea Betty had . . .'

'Your wife, Joe?'

'My wife, sir. She was part of the expedition—perhaps you didn't know that. No one seems to have mentioned it. We were only engaged then when this contraption, this sat'lite as they call it, took off. We'd been engaged a long time. Well then, so she came up with her big idea: she wanted to be married aboard that sat'lite—a woman's idea, of course, but after all, no worse than any other . . . at least so it seemed at first sight.

'Now me, I didn't see any advantage to it, but then there wasn't any reason why we shouldn't, either. So to please her, I spoke to the commander of the expedition about it and he himself as captain of the sat'lite said he'd be glad to tie the knot—the way it's often done on board ships. That seemed to give him a good laugh. Well, as everyone was agreed, it was decided we would be married as soon as I'd assembled the sat'lite and it was in working order. Guess the commander thought that would make me work harder.

'All right, so we set off. I don't need to tell you about the flight: you know all that. We made the place in space we were aiming for and then we began circling round the Earth in the middle of all those pieces of the sat'lite that had been sent up ahead of us.

'I came out of the rocket in my space suit and I got on the job, for I said to myself, the sooner I'd finished with it, the sooner I could marry my Betty and take it easy till we got back to Earth.

'I assembled that sat'lite in no time flat. I must tell you that the absence of this stuff called gravity made my work a lot easier. It's true at first I was a little dizzy when I felt nothing under my feet and saw lands and oceans shooting past like crazy, but I wasn't really so surprised, for I'd been briefed so many times that soon I didn't pay any attention to it. Then there was the business of trying to coordinate your movements. It was all very strange. Up there, when you push with all your weight on an iron girder, you're the one who lights out backwards, and when you use a screwdriver, you're the one who begins to whirl around; but the chief mechanic had

206

patiently taught me how to handle the airjet-drill so as to compensate for all errors and, after a little while, I could use it without giving it a thought.

'Well then, so I reassembled all the pieces of the sat'lite around me and began to put that thing together. This new way of working struck me so funny that in five days it was all done and I wasn't even tired. Just thinking about my marriage spurred me on. It seemed to me I was about to get my Betty.

'Five days, sir, not one day more, and the sat'lite was assembled. You know its shape—all the papers have described it; a sort of great big wheel with the passengers stuffed in the rim, which is large enough to hold 'em all and of course is airtight. But there was one gadget missing. They'd talked about it vaguely—but now, listen to this! It was the mechanism that was to make the contraption spin like a top. Impossible to find it. The rocket that was bringing it hadn't shown up yet. Maybe it had been shunted off to the Moon. Maybe it had dropped in the ocean . . . who knows? Anyway, it wasn't there.

' "Doesn't matter," the boss told me when I reported it to him. "We'll do without it. We've been living five days in our weightless space ship; we're not feeling any the worse for it. All you have to do is to be careful. I'll brief the crew."

'So he calls us all together and reminds us of the conditions created by the absence of gravity. We didn't pay much attention, 'specially me, for I was thinking of my Betty. Anyway, we knew all about that business from the movies and our own experience. But he liked to give advice and afterwards I remembered some of the things he'd said. He said something about the principle of action and reaction. "It's plain Mathematics. Every time you push against an obstacle it sends you backwards in the opposite direction to the push. It can be up, down, to the right or to the left; for there is no gravity to hold you in check."

'We told him we understood it all. Then they congratulated me on setting up the sat'lite so fast. But I was thinking about my Betty and the boss's promise. He understood. He's human. And then, with the consent of the padre, he decided to combine the inauguration of this sat'lite with the wedding. One single ceremony for both. You bet I was glad and proud. It seemed to me I'd built my house myself for my Betty and me. And what a house! A sat'lite of the Earth, sir. Just that, if you please! A sort of little Moon. You remember, Betty, how excited we were?'

'There was no reason to make such a fuss,' said Betty sullenly.

'Now, you let me tell this. I'll never forget that wedding, sir. We'd all of us gone into the sat'lite. They'd closed down the hatch. The air system was working like a breeze. And at last we could take off our space suits. Everything was perfect.

'Everything was perfect except there wasn't any weight. By using our hands we managed to reach our respective rooms. We'd agreed to meet one hour later in the salon for the ceremony. I won't say anything about the difficulties of getting dressed. However, I managed to do it. So . . . I went out in the corridor and I ran into Betty just coming from her room. And what a shock I had when I saw her, sir!'

'Why, Joe?'

'Her feet on the ceiling, legs in the air, head over heels, sir! That's the way she came towards me in her wedding dress! It made her look like a halo. She'd grabbed hold of a chandelier and was hanging on for dear life. I swear it gave me the strangest feeling. You remember, don't you, Betty?'

'You were the one who was upside down,' said Betty. 'If you didn't think I didn't get a shock too!'

'No, no, she was the one, I tell you, sir. She was walking on the ceiling. I don't care what she says. And of course the moment she caught sight of me, she set up a howl and blamed me, as if I was the one who wasn't behaving decently on my wedding day. I tell you, I couldn't stand it. I gave a shove and rose up to her. And I turned her over like a flapjack and with another shove I brought her down to the proper position for a young bride. But she was stubborn. She wouldn't admit that I was the one who was normal. I had to show her the carpet nailed down and the lights. Well, finally she calmed down and, hanging onto each other as best we could, we managed to get to the salon.

'There, sir, that was another sight. The members of the crew had just arrived and they hadn't learned yet how to adapt themselves to what was up and what was down. There were chairs and tables, you say. Of course, but the furniture was bolted to the floor. If it hadn't been for that I don't know what would have happened. But try to reason with men who've lost their self-control. They're apt to get cranky and stubborn at such times—I've never understood why. Well, almost half of the men were standing on the ceiling, heads down and swearing they were in a normal position. The padre especially—we couldn't make him turn around. He kept shouting that these weren't decent conditions for pronouncing a benediction. I tell you, we lost a good quarter of an hour arguing before almost all of us were right side up again.

'But finally everything was okay and we were married. The

padre and then the commander each made a speech about how we were hitched now, Betty and me, for better or for worse. I won't mention how queer they looked when they said that, hanging on to the furniture. And I won't mention the wedding feast either and the trouble we had eating and especially drinking. Of course we already knew about that. And somehow by using straws and tubes we managed to get through the dinner. But then, that's not the point of my story.

'By the time we'd finished dinner it was late. Betty and I wanted a chance to be alone and the others were giving us sly looks the way they do on Earth at such times. To be frank with you, there was a moment when they pretended not to pay any attention to us. Then Betty and I, still hanging on to each other, one holding up the other, retired to our bedroom.'

There was a long pause. Joe had a far-away expression in his eyes, as though he were lost in memories and uncertain how to continue.

'Go on, Joe,' I urged, 'and don't worry. Tell it just as it comes to you. The whole world is eager to profit by your experience.'

'Some experience, I can tell you, sir,' Joe sighed. Then, pulling himself together, 'All right then, here goes,' he said. 'We go into the bedroom—I'd fixed it up myself with special care. The boss had given me a free hand and as far as comfort was concerned there was nothing missing in the sat'lite . . . nothing except gravity!

'All right. So in we go and I shut the door. I'm not a very complicated guy. I grab Betty in my arms and begin to kiss her. That was natural, wasn't it? I'd been thinking of that moment for hours and hours and she . . . well, she didn't say "no." So, then, we're loving it up and we sort of forget what we're doing, if you get what I mean. As two arms didn't seem too much to me, I let go of the door knob. Put yourself in my place. I wasn't thinking of anything nor was Betty either. We just let ourselves go. We thought . . . oh, it's no use telling you that: it didn't last long.

'A few seconds maybe, not more. The next thing we knew, we were whammed on the head as if we'd been hit by a bulldozer. I thought my head had split open. I can remember today the way Betty looked. She'd seen stars too.'

'I've had a loose tooth ever since that day,' said Betty.

'At the moment, sir, I thought it was a bad joke some of my buddies had played on me. But it wasn't that. We were alone. There wasn't anyone in the room. Only when we were loving each other, we'd relaxed our legs a little, taken our feet off the ground, if you get me. . . . Nothing surprising in that, is there? But the reaction was enough to send us in a straight line to the ceiling, where our skulls hit with a crash. The boss had been right. The reaction to every push against an obstacle is to send you in the opposite direction. That's "in line with the mathematical principle," as they say. But when that happens to you at a moment like that, it doesn't matter whether it's in line with principles or not, it gives you a damn funny feeling, I can guarantee.'

'I understand, Joe. What happened then?'

'You'll see. Don't interrupt or I'll lose the thread of my story. . . . When I realized what had happened, I used my bean and I tried to calm Betty, who was nervous, as you can understand. I took her in my arms again. I leaned on the ceiling and calculated my leap. I aimed the way you do when you shoot a gun and I sent us back towards the floor just over a big armchair. There I felt calmer; it was a good, solid, overstuffed chair; it couldn't fly away. I take a deep breath and I say to Betty:

' "It's nothing, baby, I tell you. Don't get excited. It's that gravity gimmick. It's all a matter of getting used to it. Pretty soon you won't be paying any attention to it."

' "Oh, Joe," she says, sniffling. "It gives me such a strange feeling to have to think of holding on to something all the time."

'I must confess, sir, I didn't feel too comfortable either. I ought to explain that I'd set her on my knees and was keeping my right arm around her waist. With my left arm I was hanging on to the arm of the chair and I had to be careful not to let go or we'd be good for another flight. That thought bothered me so much I couldn't put my whole heart into giving all my attention to her. On the other hand, when I began to make love to her seriously, to rouse her, and she began to respond, I lost my head and forgot to hold onto the chair. You get me? Those are two completely different sorts of thoughts. Then whoops! Either my left arm lets go and we both fly off into space or my right arm comes away from her waist to wander somewhere else and she takes off from my knees and begins to whirl around above or below me at the strangest angles. Several times, sir, I caught her just in time by the hair, by the tip of her fingers, by the legs, by the feet, by any place I could grab hold of. It was mighty aggravating, I can tell you!'

'I understand, Joe.'

'I don't know if you can get any idea of what it was like unless you've gone through something like it yourself. It was all the more upsetting because that business with arms and legs that kept slipping through my hands like eels put me in a state you can't imagine. I didn't want to be rough with my Betty . . . 'specially as by this time she seemed to like that strange position.'

'How can you say that!' Betty protested.

'Well, she looked as though she was having a good time. And she let herself float about as if she was in a bathtub. She didn't do a thing to help me—just left everything to me and I was beginning to sweat blood. I tried to wind my legs around the leg of a chair so as to have both hands free; you get the picture, don't you? But it wasn't any better. Besides, I'd have to think at the same time of gravity and of Betty and I couldn't do that. As I told you, they're two mighty different kinds of things.'

'I don't think anyone could have done better in your place, Joe. Go on.'

'Things went on like that for a short time with ups and downs as I've tried to explain to you. Then I said to myself I've been refined long enough. There's no reason now for dil-ly-dallying, either on her part or on mine—since you want to know the whole business.

'So, still holding on by a leg or a hand, I began to undress her. Don't forget, she was dressed like a bride, with all the usual fuss and feathers; she'd insisted on it in spite of the cir-cumstances—the long dress, the veil, the crown of orange blossoms and so on. Soon all those things began to float around the room, bouncing back off the walls and dropping down on us when I chucked them away a little too hard. I remember I'd left the light on. It would be too dangerous in the dark. Well, all those filmy white contraptions kept passing back and forth in front of the electric bulbs like clouds driven by the wind. It looked one moment as if the sun came out and the next moment as if it went in again. A funny thing! I remember looking up at one moment and seeing the veil hanging straight in front of me and about three feet above it the crown of flowers that you'd have sworn was a halo like those you see over saints in pictures. I was com-pletely flummoxed by it.'

'A very poetic picture, Joe.'

'I don't say it wasn't, only I was thinking of something else. I had more important matters on my mind. At that mo-ment, you see, I'd made up my mind to reach that bed. I've told you, I'm refined. I didn't want to spend my wedding night on a chair. Only I didn't dare make a mistake, because of that gravity thing.

'So I grab her in my arms. I calculate my distance. . . . Yes sir, I still had to calculate, I tell you. My head ached from it. I give the chair a shove and I manage to land with her exactly on the down comforter. I clutch the edge of the night table and, as carefully as possible, I lay her down on the bed.

' "Don't move, baby . . ." I tell her. "Whatever you do, don't move. Keep your legs stretched out as if you were floating on your back. Don't breathe too hard. Shut your eyes and wait for me. I'll come back."

'She did what I said, sir, while I jumped back to the chair to get undressed in my turn. I didn't want to shock a young girl's modesty, sir, in spite of the unusual circumstances.'

'Very honourable sentiments, Joe. Go on.'

He was silent a moment. 'It's not a thing to tell,' he said hesitantly.

Exercising great patience, I finally calmed his scruples and he went on:

'Well, I have to confess, sir, that when I went back, as naked as a worm, and saw my Betty in the same state, stretched out on the bed, I lost my self-control. I admit it. Everything else went out of my mind and I made a grab for her. After all, we were married, weren't we?'

'That's very excusable, Joe. I absolve you.'

'Perhaps it was excusable but it was mighty careless. You see, I'd forgotten about that gravity thing again. I'd calculated my distance badly this time. To tell the truth, I hadn't calculated it at all: I'd just leapt instinctively. And what happened? I passed over her and never touched her. I floated, I hovered over that bed up and down the whole length of her body without being able to take her in my arms. She was out of reach—more than three feet below me. I banged my head against the head of the bed and I went sailing off backwards toward the footboard. I was damn mad, I can tell you.'

'I can imagine that, Joe. What a situation!'

'I'm not so sure you really understand. It's not so simple. Let me explain it to you, since you want to know all the details.

'It's like this: the direction my body took, as the mathematician of the crew explained to me later, was horizontal. That means I was moving on a line parallel to the bed and that ran from one wall to the other at about three feet and a half above it. . . . Notice besides that this business of horizontal, vertical, above and below, didn't mean a single thing, for there wasn't any up or down because of the absence of that crazy gravity. All I could see was the bed with my Betty still stretched out and conscientiously keeping her eyes shut. It seemed to me everything centred around that.'

'I understand, Joe. The centre of your universe.'

'That's right. So, then, I could send myself from the footboard to the headboard. But get this! At that height, the walls were completely bare and smooth—not a pipe on them, not a gadget, no roughness. To people who know a little about mechanics that means I had no way of changing my direction without outside help. You get me? All I could do was float back and forth between the two walls, which I did more than twenty times, always seeing Betty's body go by below me and out of reach. It was driving me crazy.'

'I can sympathize with you, Joe. How did you get out of that predicament?'

'By thinking, sir. . . . Wait till I explain. After I'd tired myself out banging my head and my heels, I kept absolutely still and I tried to think. Then I began to slow down. The mathematician later explained that the slowdown was due to the artificial air in the sat'lite. So I ended up by stopping in mid-air, but that wasn't any better.'

'Why not, Joe?'

'It was worse, sir. Just try to picture it to yourself. When I stopped, tired out and shaken, I was exactly above the bed, above my Betty and too far from a wall to be able to give a shove; in other words, I couldn't move at all. . . . Or rather, my centre of gravity was motionless. My arms and legs could move, bend and stretch, something like a spider on the end of a thread or a butterfly nailed on an invisible board; and I must tell you that my arms and legs never stopped jerking and moving around, I was so upset. There I was, naked as a worm, if you remember, flat on my stomach in space at more than three feet above her. And what happens at that moment? That's when my Betty opens her eyes, sir.

'Oh, boy! If you'd seen her face! I can still see the way she looked and hear the shriek she let out. That really did me in, I can tell you. She shut her eyes quick as a flash and squeezed her eyelids together as if they'd been glued. That wasn't calculated to make things better either.'

'If you think you were a pretty sight, floating and jiggling around up above me,' Betty protested indignantly. 'I never thought there could be anything so horrible on Earth, or even in space. You didn't look like any butterfly to me; you looked like a spider, an octopus. And even an octopus would have had something human about it compared to you. I leave it to you, sir. No girl has ever seen anything like that on her wedding night! I couldn't imagine such a sight!'

'I admit I couldn't have been a sight for an innocent young bride. And I'd sworn I'd be refined. I was ashamed. All the same, it didn't help any to cry bloody murder. So I thought again and I told her:

' "Listen, baby. This isn't the moment to lose your head.

I'm here; you see me. Perhaps I'm not like what you dreamt I'd be, but I can't help it. It'll be better, you'll see, when I'm closer. It's the distance that mixed everything up and it's all the fault of that gravity. But now I can't even budge. You'll have to help me. Shut your eyes and grab hold of the edge of the night table. It's a solid point. When you've done that, but not before, raise one leg straight up towards me as if you were doing physical exercises. D'you understand? I'll hold on to you and come down beside you and you won't see me this way any more."

'I had to speak in my gentlest tone, sir, or she would have had an attack of nerves. But after a moment or two she calmed down, even dared to open one eye half way—then shut it quick. That wasn't what I'd asked her to do. Well, finally she made up her mind to do what I told her. She grabbed hold of the table and raised one leg up towards me. Her feet reached high enough. I clutched a toe. I was saved! I pulled myself up, or rather I descended, whichever you prefer, along her leg and at last I was beside her on the bed.

'D'you think perhaps it was all over and we had a right to be happy? No siree, you're mistaken. Trouble had only just begun. But what followed is even harder to tell.'

'Go ahead, Joe.'

'I lay there beside her for a long time holding my breath. I was thinking only of her. A night like that, you understand, could give her a complex for the rest of her life. She'd turned quite red, then white, from head to foot. I reassured her, I fondled her gently, oh, very gently, until she gradually warmed up. Me too. Her colour came back again and when at last she felt me close against her, she got up nerve enough to open her eyes.

'What can I tell you now? There was another moment when I forgot myself. Don't misunderstand me. She was quite reassured and that was the moment to go into action. Once more, to my bad luck, I didn't think, I just felt. I can't explain more clearly. . . .'

'It's quite simple, Joe. I understand very well.'

'It's simple, but it was mighty careless. I'd forgotten again about that old gravity business; that was when the whole thing turned into a nightmare.

'You remember how the boss had explained the principle? I had to think of it several times that night: *Any shove against an obstacle results in a reaction in the opposite direction unless there is something to check you.* In plain language, when you push forward you're flung straight backwards. You get it this time? I see you've understood because you're laughing. Only it's one thing to understand when you're on Earth, your body held down by its weight, and it's quite another to have the experience on your wedding night in a sat'lite. In the first place, perhaps you could laugh, but in the second, when you're the one who goes bouncing backwards like a rubber ball, I swear there's nothing funny about it.'

'My apologies, Joe.'

'No harm done. Well, sir, that's exactly what happened to me. On my first try, I flew off at a tangent towards a corner of the ceiling, where I bumped my tail, and hard, too, I can tell you, for our action was pretty violent and the backwards reaction just as violent. This time I saw red. For a split second I didn't think—put yourself in my place.'

'I do, Joe.'

'I didn't think, I tell you. With a leap I came down on her like a bomber. And I began the same manœuvre again, and each time it was the same story. I was tossed back like a tennis ball. The more excited I got, the more impatient I was, the more I bounced off quickly and the more I bumped my tail hard on the ceiling. Fifty times, sir, until my backside was a mass of bruises. But that was nothing compared to the loss of morale. I thought I was going nuts!'

'If you think it was pleasant for me,' said Betty. 'You may have felt like a tennis ball, but I felt as if I was a racket or a net with circus acrobats bouncing on it . . .'

'I was worried sick about Betty, you understand, sir? She was still stretched out, eyes closed, and I could see from her expression that she was beginning to be surprised and even stunned at the way I was behaving. You have to put yourself in her place. In spite of her inexperience she must have thought I was very strange. Things couldn't go on like that. After I'd struggled until I was out of breath, I realized that all the energy in the world would get me nowhere. What I had to do, and remember to keep doing, was think.

'Oh, mister! Imagine trying to think in that situation! And yet it had to be done. When brute force fails, you've just got to use your head. But intelligence is one thing and love is another, as the rest of the story goes to show.

'So then I stopped leaping between the bed and the ceiling and managed to land beside her. Then I took a long breath and put my mind to work.

' "What a fool I am," I said to myself. "After all, it's not so hard. The thing is not to lose my self-control as I just did."

' "Listen to me, baby," I said to her after I'd worked out my plan. "What's happening to us is sure nutty, I know it. But with a little patience everything will come out all right. We're in the sat'lite. There's no gravity. We've got to make the best of it. The way I see the problem, there's only one way out. We've got to hang on."

' "Hang on, Joe?" she says.

' "Hang on. Don't you bother, baby. I'll think it out for both of us. So now you're going to stretch out both arms in a cross as if you're floating on the sea. With your right hand you keep tight hold of the night table. With the left . . . Wait a minute! You'll hold the end of this string I'm going to hitch to the other end of the armchair. You get it! It's not hard. You've got the easiest part. You keep both hands closed tight and you concentrate on not letting go. Now me, I'll hang onto your shoulders and don't be upset if I press a little hard. You hold on tight no matter what happens." '

' "Oh, Joe!" she said. "I don't know if I'll be able to do it. I never thought it would be like this, my wedding night."

'All the same, Betty,' said Joe, turning to his wife. 'I have to hand it to you. You understood you had to do your best. A lot of women wouldn't have been so easy to manage. She obeyed me, sir. She took the position I'd told her to and when I saw her grab the end of the mooring rope she made me think of a little girl who is going to jump rope. Matter of fact, she obeyed me a little too fast, for as I think I've already told you—though I can never say it enough—loving and thinking are two opposite things. In other words, after I'd racked my brains to work out my plan, I had to wait a moment, give my head time to clear, before I could go on with it. You get the point?'

'I understand, Joe.'

'So she obeyed me and you can't say she didn't. All right. After a moment we were ready again, she holding on tight to the two solid points, me to her shoulders. I thought I'd found the right solution. Well, sir, I was wrong. It still wasn't possible.'

'What do you mean, not possible, Joe?'

'No, not possible. The mathematician explained why to me after I'd noticed it myself. You'll catch on. Her two hands clutching solid objects made two fixed points. All right. Two points, so he told me later—that makes a straight line, an axis, the axis of her outstretched arms. Again all right. But my hands on the axis didn't help at all. When there's only one stationary axis, all the rest of the solid bodies can turn around it; that's geometry. And you'll see that our two bodies certainly did turn.

'An acrobat trick, sir, the kind you see only in the circus. We didn't let go—all right! So we kept going higher and higher towards the ceiling. Only this time my body made a circle around her arms that were spread out like a cross. I kept turning until my feet began hitting the wall behind the bed.

'And what was Betty doing all this time? She didn't take her hands away, at least, not at first. But that was all you could ask of a young bride, wasn't it? I couldn't reasonably insist that she keep all the rest of her body as still as a stick. Then, too, as she was turning and twisting—and that's understandable—all of a sudden she let go of the night table and began to whirl like me around the axis until she crashed into me and we began turning in the opposite direction. Imagine a crocodile yawning. Well, we looked like two jaws opening, shutting and opening again without ever staying in contact more than a fraction of a second. I don't know if you get the picture.'

'As if I were there, Joe. You describe it admirably.'

'Of course, that didn't go on for hours. Betty, poor little thing, finally managed to free her hands. But I didn't let go and as that happened at the time of one of the crocodile's yawns, off we went into space.

'What a trip, sir! Heads down, legs in the air, turning, twisting, whirling, drifting about around our common centre of gravity; now and then making contact by the centre, then by the thighs, now on the right side, now on the left, only to separate at once as if we hated each other. We never managed to stay embraced. With me it became a mania and I wore myself out turning more and more desperate somersaults which were no help at all. It was like a flying trapeze, a three-ringed circus; there was no name for it!

'Perhaps you're going to tell me that was the solution; forget about gravity, about up and down and everything else. Stop thinking about the bed, the furniture, anything: grab each other firmly by the feet and hands and make love in empty space. It's easy to say, sir. We tried, I can guarantee you that. But making love in space—you can't imagine the impression it gives you! There's always something that doesn't stay put. I'd never have thought you'd need every bit of your body like that. When it wasn't the hands, it was the legs that let go. When it wasn't the legs, it was the hips that felt as soft as if they were caught in a feather pillow. When it wasn't all that, it was the dizziness of seeing walls, floors, ceiling, furniture and lights whirling around. I speak from experience and I tell you so. You absolutely have to hang onto something solid. . . . Perhaps if Betty had had more experience—but naturally she couldn't help me. She was crying and saying she wanted to go home to her mother.

'We tried everything, sir. There are some offbeats on Earth who talk of different positions. Well, sir, I tell you, Betty and

I tried more positions that night then all the degenerates on this planet ever dreamed of. Positions, sir, I still blush to think of; they would have startled even the demons in Hell. All of them, I tell you. We clutched each other by the hands. We clutched each other by the feet. We were even wrapped for a moment in the bridal veil that was still floating around. There was always something that went wrong. Then we had a bright idea. We got under the bed—but it was too narrow there. It was like being in a sardine can. In the end, that's where we spent our wedding night. Under the bed, stretched out side by side like two little babes and both of us as seasick as could be!'

'That's my adventure, sir, since you wanted to know about it. There's nothing else and that's enough. The following nights were the same story with variations, but always ending in the same circus, with both of us frustrated, defeated. There was nothing to be done. I tried to ask advice of the scientists in the group. At first they listened to me patiently and showed some sort of interest. They were sympathetic. They even racked their brains to help me.

'The mathematician explained very carefully what happened from a scientific point of view, and why it was like that. The physician went even farther. He made some sort of complicated apparatus with magnetic fields that would produce a kind of artificial gravity. But to get anything out of those fields I had to wear a suit he'd invented that had a whole mess of metallic straps like a strait jacket. All the mechanic could suggest was to use an airjet-drill. It was a question of coordination of forces, he said. I tried that too but I never got any good results.

'Even the padre put in his oar. He saw how upset I was and that made him feel sad himself. One day he took me aside and made a long speech—I'm not quite sure I understood it because he mixed some Latin words in it—but I got the idea that in unusual circumstances perhaps the Church would shut an eye to positions that didn't absolutely conform to divine law. He might perhaps give me absolution in advance if I explained it to him. I don't know whether our positions conformed to the law or not; all I know is that when I began to give him some details . . . well, it was his turn to hit the ceiling—and a good dozen times, he was so upset. After that he began to pray and wouldn't say another word.

'Then as time went on they all began to avoid me. They looked angry and seemed to be annoyed with me. I understood that my story put a damper on the trip and I didn't speak of it again. Betty and I resigned ourselves to wait till we returned to Earth.'

Joe was silent a long time, lost in thought; then he went on:

'You see, sir, they didn't want to admit that their gadget, the sat'lite, wasn't absolutely perfect from all points of view the way they've been saying lately in interviews. That's the conclusion I've come to.

'When they say that, sir, they're lying; Betty and I can both tell you so. Their sat'lite, their weightless gadget, may be all right for scientific observations, fine for looking at the stars, wonderful for collecting cosmic rays. I grant you that. But as for love, sir, it's just a complete, plain washout. It's the last place in the world I'd advise for a wedding night, unless you have unnatural tastes. Believe you me! And don't forget to print this in headlines in your newspaper.'

(Translated by Elisabeth Abbott)

THE HALLUCINATION

The Head of Police Services inspected the instruments of torture with a cold eye in which there was neither anxiety nor unhealthy satisfaction. It was merely the irreplaceable eye of the master, checking to see that everything was perfectly prepared before stepping aside for his assistants to carry out his orders.

Having climbed all the rungs of the Services and having reached the top, thanks to his energy, his vigorous intellect and an instinctive liking for his profession, he had developed an infallible technique of torture, though he had never taken any pleasure in it, considering it merely an indispensable aid to certain interrogations, a necessary evil. In the course of his long career he had employed it only when other methods of coercion failed. Now, however, that he occupied the highest post, he generally held aloof from scenes of violence, entering the torture chamber only in serious cases and, as a rule, only at the end to receive a particularly important confession.

But if he held aloof, it was not from any special dislike. The emotion he had felt in the beginning had quickly disappeared. To maintain his prestige as Head of Services he had schooled himself to look upon any spectacle with a lofty detachment. The more degrading work he left to his subalterns. And yet, in a particularly serious case like the present one, he himself made the final inspection and issued strict orders calculated to induce the surrender of the prisoner whose reactions he had studied carefully during the interrogation.

His experience of men had taught him the wisdom of maintaining a certain rhythm in applying torture, a method for which he did not quite trust his subordinates' initiative. After long reflection, he had decided that the most effective method was to attack suddenly and violently with increasing brutality and to continue attacking without giving the tortured man time to recover. In captivity the prisoner had shown an unconquerable spirit and a constitution strong enough to endure prolonged torture indefinitely. Only an accelerated series of sharp and varied physical tortures would force him to talk. The Head of Police Services had drawn up a detailed program to last, theoretically, fifteen minutes, at which point he foresaw victory.

Now he examined the various instruments of torture in the order in which they would be used.

There was nothing particularly original about his program. Its ingenuity lay solely in the 'combination' of classic tortures, and he relied on the arrangement of the 'combination' to produce results.

The first, and regulation, torture was flagellation; and for this the victim was stretched out full length, with ankles bound and eyes bandaged. This latter precaution was to prevent him from judging the precise moment when the scourge with the three sharp thongs would descend. The torturer had orders to strike at irregular intervals. In fact, the Head of Services had noticed that when the prisoner followed the instrument with his eyes, a certain desperate contraction of his muscles, just before contact, lent him considerable resistance. The surprise effect of an unexpected lashing produced much better results. His subordinates were often negligent about these details.

The second torture was the water torture. It would be inflicted by means of a funnel, according to the method that has changed little since the Middle Ages. Between two tortures affecting chiefly the outer layers of the human body, the Head of Police Services had cleverly inserted this torture of the inner organs, which caused a general suffering of a more serious nature.

In the third stage of this series, arranged with careful detail to wring a confession from the prisoner, sulphuretted slivers would be placed between the prisoner's fingers and toes. This practice was not new either.

As the general idea was to alternate external and internal pain, the fourth torture was an electric shock. A sort of helmet, made of metallic strips and fastened to the prisoner's skull, produced the ghastly sensation that his head was bursting, his brain flying into pieces. Two or three shocks were usually enough to break down his resistance. The danger to avoid was fainting. To this end graduated rheostats controlled the strength of the voltage.

As this prisoner was unusually tough, the Head of Services had provided for the last degree. This was the torture of the bath, the sole novelty of which, in the present case, lay in its

221

place in the sequence. Cold water would cause the prisoner to lose consciousness for a second; then, after a moment of relative relief, a lowered temperature would create intense suffering. Boiling water would then follow, but as the appliance that permitted the temperature from passing rapidly from icy cold to boiling heat was out of order, the chief assistant had taken the liberty of having two tanks prepared. The prisoner would be carried from one receptacle to the other. At first the Head of Services had grumbled about this arrangement, which somewhat modified the established program. Then, thinking that the sudden transition from intense cold to intense heat might perhaps be more effective, he gave his consent. He hoped, however, that his men would come for him before matters had gone that far. The prisoner's secret was of major importance.

Accompanied by the Number One of the four torturers, he entered his office next to the great hall. Number One was a great, hulking giant, round-shouldered, with sparse, bristling hair. A perpetual grimace, displaying on one side of his mouth a revolting row of broken teeth, deformed his crooked, degenerate face. But he was a perfect operator, and completely cold-blooded.

For the last time the Head of Services repeated his instructions and reminded Number One to call him in the event of any unforeseen incident. The giant gave a military salute and left the room, closing the door behind him. The Head of Police Services was alone.

Tense, his eyes fixed on the door, he sat there motionless in his chair, imagining from the sounds that reached him the scene that was taking place on the other side of the wall. Now they were bringing in the prisoner. A man of that calibre, as he well knew, would not break as some men did at the mere sight of the preparations. Now the prisoner must be naked, lying face down on the floor, his arms outspread in a cross. While the torturers bound the prisoner's hands and feet, Number One would be making ready the thonged whip.

They seemed to be taking a very long time. The Head of Services himself had arranged for this pause, which was intended to add to the prisoner's anguish. But the wait now seemed to him interminable. At last he heard a whistling sound and at the same time a significant noise like the thud of an ocean wave against a jetty—then a muffled groan.

At that precise moment the hallucination began. Later on, he could easily account for the obvious cause. For several years, ever since he had reached a position that placed him among people of importance, he had made a determined

222

effort to round out his education that had been neglected. He studied and became interested in literature. Recently he had read a long poem that deeply impressed him, for he was naturally sensitive to the evocative power of certain words and verses. His memory, trained by his profession, still retained whole passages from the poem.

At this particular moment, however, he was not concerned with the source of the miracle. There was a sort of click in his brain which coincided with the first sounds of the torture. It seemed to him that he had been transported to a different world, but at the same time he did not have the impression of dreaming.

A sudden gust of wind flung open the door at which he sat staring, disclosing a yawning aperture through which he discerned at first only a grey mist. Then the veil thinned and he could see what was on the other side of the wall, though that place in no way resembled the great hall of torture. It was a vast amphitheatre whose tiers were chaotic masses of jagged rocks. Though the dimensions of the amphitheatre were tremendous, he had at first a general view of it. It was shaped like a gigantic funnel, a cone upside down, the base on a level with him, the top plunged deep into the bowels of the earth. The base was divided vertically into circular sections and on its walls misshapen human beings wandered vaguely about. Soon the mist vanished and he distinguished more clearly a horizontal cross-section of the cone. It was the third circle, he knew it. The accursed place came nearer, as if he were looking at it through a telescope. A rain of hailstones, thick, sharp and mixed with icy snow, zigzagged across a horrifying landscape.

The first creature he saw was a monster with three dog-like jowls and three tongues that writhed and snapped like the thongs of a whip. As the apparition became clearer a voice murmured in his ear:

> 'Cerberus, fierce and monstrous animal,
> with triple gullet barks in currish wise
> . . . .
> Greasy and black his beard, and red his eyes,
> and belly big, and fingers clawed amain:
> clutching the spirits, he doth rend and slice.' *

The animal's eyes glittered with an ugly light and his irregular fangs added to his hideous aspect. He pounced upon a

* Alighieri, Dante. *The Divine Comedy*, Inferno vi, 13–18. Translated by Melville B. Anderson. Oxford University Press, 1921.

damned soul stretched out on the ground, lashing it with his monstrous tongues, detaching pieces of skin which he then tore off with his claws and fangs. The Head of Services distinctly heard a quick, hoarse panting mingled with the victim's groans. The latter's suffering was multiplied by cuts from a thousand hailstones.

Forced by some supernatural power to watch and listen, the Head of Police Services sat there, paralyzed with horror. At last the groans grew fainter, the picture faded. Mist enveloped all the circle and silence fell again.

When the mist lifted, a grey light lit up another section of the infernal cone. The Head of Services knew that he had penetrated a lower and narrower circle. He heard the voice again.

'. . . *underneath the water people dwell*
who sigh, and make it bubble at the brim,
. . . .
Fixt in the ooze,. . . . .
They gurgle in their gullets this refrain,
because they cannot speak with words entire.' *

The condemned was still there, this time buried in a morass of muddy water, whose current tinted red the bloody furrows of his body. This current, slow and regular, oddly assumed the shape of an immense funnel, first covering all the muddy pond, then narrowing to squeeze out the foul liquid and make the veins converge towards the submerged soul, forcing a blackish torrent into the unfortunate creature's mouth. His stomach swelled repulsively. His mute suffering was expressed by pathetic gurglings and by the agony in his eyes.

The Head of Police Services peered closer. On the banks he noticed vague forms of strange creatures rhythmically sweeping the water to stir up the flood. Those creatures were not human. He could see pointed backs, and arms and legs covered with hair.

'Demons,' he murmured. 'It can't be! I must be dreaming.'

In vain he tried to shake off the nightmare. He saw that the body of the condemned assumed from second to second more and more unusual proportions and his horror grew with an unbearable anguish. In his own body he felt the limit of endurance to the suffering of the man before him. But now

* ——— *ibid.,* vii, 118–126.

that limit had been reached and the Head of Services writhed helplessly in his longing to put an end to the torture.

At last there was a lull in the demon's furious attack. The river of mud stopped flowing. The mist came down over the pond again.

> 'Such was descending the eternal glow;
>   whereby, like tinder under steel, the sands
>   were kindled for redoubling of the woe.
> Forever tossing were the wretched hands
>   now hither and now thither without rest,
>   fanning fresh burning off in counter-dance.'*

This voice that whispered in him, the Head of Services recognized as his own. In it he heard the calm incisiveness he imposed on himself when performing a delicate task. And he cursed that same incisiveness, feeling that it had some part in this series of hallucinations.

Once again the mist dissolved and a narrower circle of the gigantic funnel appeared before him, a circle farther down in the abyss and illumined by a scarlet light.

The damned lay on dry ground. A rain of flames, long and narrow like tongues of fire, fell from the sky onto the sand, making it incandescent. The flames gathered together in bunches and swept towards the extremities of the condemned man's limbs. There they divided again and inserted themselves in the hollows where the flesh is most sensitive, between the joints of fingers and toes. He tried to shake them off by moving his hands and feet desperately, but his spasmodic jerks only served to rekindle the flaming bouquet.

Suddenly the damned soul burst forth in furious howls that shook the pestilential space. There was a moment that seemed eternal, during which the cries increased in violence, surpassing all possible limits of human manifestations. The Head of Services felt his brain reel and at the same time he was nauseated by a disgusting odour.

At last the uproar died down. The howls became a prolonged death rattle. Shapeless beings he had already glimpsed now rushed forward and blew out the flames. And thick, black smoke enveloped the groups.

'I'm dreaming,' groaned the Head of Services. 'Lord, deliver me from this nightmare. And yet dreams are not as real as this. I'm in Hell. I see demons. I hear the groans of the damned. I smell their martyred flesh.'

* ——— *ibid.*, xiv, 37–42.

'And lo! at one who loitered near our coign
of vantage, sprang a snake and pierced him through
just where the collar and the shoulders join.
Never was I so quickly written, or O,
as he took fire and burnt, and he was doomed
all into ashes drooping down to go;
And then the dust, so on the ground consumed,
collected of itself together there,
and instantly that former shape resumed.
So verily, the sages great declare
the Phoenix dies, and then doth life repeat. . . .' *

Thus pitilessly spoke the gentle voice in the Head of Services' conscience and meanwhile a new and even narrower circle came into view.

The serpent that had flung itself on the damned soul now wove fantastic figures with its body. Several times it coiled around the condemned man's skull and flattened itself out till it was one flesh with his body. The play of certain reflexes made the serpent look like a long metallic ribbon. It moved again, imperceptibly, seeming to seek the most sensitive spot —then it struck.

Breathing hard, the Head of Services waited in horror to see the damned soul burst into flames and burn to ashes. But what he saw was even more frightful. Through the miracle of hallucination, he saw the soul itself consumed by invisible fire before his eyes, as if the outrage of the filthy reptile had disintegrated it; the soul which, for eternal moments, while the vile tongue remained in its flesh, suffered the horror of progressive annihilation. But before annihilation was complete enough to suppress suffering, the serpent suddenly straightened up. The soul in the tortured body came back to life in a fresh burst of anguish. A few moments of agonized waiting, then the serpent began the same routine again. The scene was repeated, and at each fresh contact the soul lost a little more of its character as a soul and became sheer unadulterated suffering.

A long misty interval hid the picture of what followed. When the curtain was torn apart, the Head of Services knew that he was approaching the last circle, where the point of the accursed funnel touched the centre of the earth. This circle was even narrower than the preceding ones. A frozen lake filled the bottom of the abyss. The dregs of Hell seemed to have been congealed in it. The voice whispered:

* ——*ibid.*, xxiv, 97–105.

'And as the frogs to croak are often laid
with muzzle out of water, when alone
of frequent gleaning dreams the peasant-maid:
Livid to where the blush of shame is shown,
here shades in ice betrayed their sufferance
setting their teeth to the stork's monotone.
Every one was casting down his glance:
the cold is proved by chattering of the jaw,
and the heart's agony by the eye askance.
. . . . .
. . . . .among the heads somehow
I struck my foot full in the face of one.
Wailing he yelled at me: "Why tramplest thou? . . ." ' *

The body of the damned was imprisoned in ice, only his head and hands emerged. At first he appeared to be unconscious as the result of the freezing. But that was only an illusion. The Head of Services knew that the cold, increasing by degrees, would in the end cause such constraint that the tortured man, gasping for breath, would lose even the power to groan. And that enforced silence was more horrible than the most furious howling. The voice went on:

'Their eyes, whose moisture yet within was pent,
brimmed over at the lids, whereon the cold
congealed the tears between and locked the vent.' †

Icicles in the hollows of his eyelids kept them distended, moulding the stiffened skin of his face on the skeleton, imprinting on that face the monstrous mask of infinite suffering. His body had now turned dark violet and his hands tightened convulsively. Four demons danced around him in a circle, now and then trampling his head with their forked feet.

'It's a dream,' groaned the Head of Services. 'Lord, take this hell from me.'

But when the mist vanished, the same scene reappeared, though in place of the ice that had filled the bottom of the abyss, there was now a thick, black, oily liquid, boiling pitch, the heat of which blistered the surface of the water. The Head of Services did not see the condemned man at first. But one of the creatures who haunted that accursed place drew near, carrying a heavy load.

'Look out! Look out!' shouted the Head of Services, struggling wildly.

* ——— *ibid.*, xxxii, 31–39, 77–79.
† ——— *ibid.*, xxxii, 46–48.

The soft, self-assured voice in him went on:

> *'I looked . . . and saw a devil swart*
> *come running up the causey after me.*
> *Fierce-visaged was he, and oh! how my heart*
> *sank at his action so unpitying,—*
> *so light of foot with wings spread wide apart!*
> *Astride his shoulder high and tapering*
> *a sinner sitting on both haunches rode:*
> *to the ancle-tendon did the demon cling,*
> *"Maltalons," he cried. . . . .*
> *. . . . . dash*
> *him under. . . . .'* *

With a sudden jerk the demon flung his burden into the boiling pitch and again shrieks were heard more terrible than those before, dreadful lamentations sounding as though a demon from Hell were trying to fill the ether of a doomed world.

The damned soul fought; the immeasurable horror of his suffering lent him strength to raise himself half out of the burning abyss and, with a desperate contortion of his limbs, he clung to the rocks on the side. Then the demons pierced him with their fangs and tore him apart with their claws until he plunged down again under the viscous liquid.

They really were demons. The Head of Services could see them clearly now; he could even distinguish details of their hideous bodies. The tallest, who seemed to be the leader, had a tusk coming out of the side of his mouth, which twisted his face into a permanent grimace. All of them were covered with bristly hair and armed with long talons. They gnashed their fangs and waved black angular wings that resembled the webs of enormous bats. They warmed up to their task by calling each other names.

> *' "O Rubicantë, see that thou inflict*
> *thy talons on his back and soundly flay!" '* †

Now they crouched around the tortured soul, determined to give him no respite. Suddenly one of them straightened up and turned his head in the quick, furtive gesture of a wild animal. The Head of Services realized that they had discovered him. Now the monster was looking at him with his cruel eyes. The Head of Services watched in horror as the demon,

---

* ———— *ibid.*, xxi, 29–38.
† ———— *ibid.*, xxii, 40–41.

spreading his wings, moved slowly towards his desk. It was
the demon with the wild boar's tusk.

2

'Well, Chief, I think that's it,' said a placid voice.

The crooked giant stood in the open doorway. His great
height half hid a shadowy group behind him. They were
crowding around a dripping body that lay outstretched on the
floor. The air was filled with a light mist.

And as he heard that familiar and reassuring voice, the
Head of Services was suddenly freed of the dreadful anguish
that tortured him. The hallucination vanished: the evil spirits
were conjured. At last he had come back to earth. Yes, yes,
he really had been dreaming, a dream as absurd as all dreams
are. The giant's words brought him the proof.

He felt the intense relief one has on awakening from a
painful nightmare, but he was even more relieved to discover
the source of his fantasies. The chance of a half-opened door
and a few curious, but not miraculous, coincidences, combined with the memory of a poem he had read—that had
been the source of his strange dream. It was all easily explained: there was no magic in it. There was no element of
doubt left in his mind.

Now completely reassured, he went into the great hall to
hear the prisoner's confession. But to the amazement of his
subordinate, he could not prevent himself from expressing his
satisfaction at that timely deliverance.

'Thank God,' he exclaimed, 'it was only a dream! How
could I have doubted it? Thank Heaven the nightmare is over
at last! What a strange hallucination! What madness, and
how little it takes to make the best-trained minds wander!
When I think that sitting right here in my chair, I could have
mistaken this office for Hell and my own men for demons!'

(Translated by Elisabeth Abbott)

$$E = mc^2$$

In the beginning was the Idea. All action was contained in germ in the Idea and nothing that has been done has been done without it.

The Idea, crystallized as a simple formula, $E = mc^2$, may be translated into the language of man as follows: each particle of matter is equivalent to a quantity of energy equal to the product of its mass by the square of the speed of light.

The Idea was the end result of a long series of speculations on space, time, matter and conscience. It had its source in an intuition that tended to consider those elements as forming an organized whole and no longer as independent of one another. Primitive intuition and subsequent speculation (which in reality constituted the value of the Idea) were assimilated only by a few brains, but the formula $E = mc^2$ and its expression in language produced a profound sensation in the world, affecting the most diverse minds.

Here the sensitive Cartesian pauses and asks himself: Why, among so many scholarly and subtle formulas, ignored or scorned, does $E = mc^2$ shine with such radiance in the firmament of public idols?

After discarding and eliminating everything that does not refer to the schematic character, the sensitive Cartesian will retain only three reasons for that unusual radiance.

The first two reasons are almost obvious. They are the same reasons that assured the success of *Bonjour Tristesse*. Like *Bonjour Tristesse,* $E = mc^2$ touched the masses profoundly, at first because it contained a rare quality, I mean an elementary idea, and then because this elementary idea was at the same time original but not inordinately so. This truth, which everyone felt vaguely, had for a long time been proclaimed by the experts (in the case of *Bonjour Tristesse* as well as for $E = mc^2$) if, in addition to their instinctive flair

230

for showing up a book that would impress the masses, the experts had been lucid enough to explain why.

A third reason is more obscure and the sensitive Cartesian will have to concentrate all his faculties of mind and heart to discover it, but it explains the quite exceptional character of its success. Here it is: in addition to the elementary and fairly original idea, $E = mc^2$ gave the human soul an extremely subtle satisfaction by establishing a perfect, ideal *law of correspondence* between mind and matter.

At first this will seem confusing. Physicists will object that if matter is viewed as the form m in the equation, then mind is absent from it. But specialists have little imagination. In the letter E and in the vague term "energy" (a mysterious term that camouflages an impalpable substance subject to a thousand transformations), humanity has, from the first, perceived the spiritual essence of the world.

This admitted, the character presented as the most important factor in popular success will I think finally be clear to the sensitive Cartesian. He will perceive that though a harmonious proportion of mind and matter is the necessary condition of existence for any enterprise touching fields of artistic or scientific creation with any pretense to novelty or discovery, that balanced structure is not *sufficient* to arouse the enthusiasm of the masses. For this purpose one must approach the mysterious frontier between mind and matter and make an attempt to clarify it. A certain law of correspondence that permits us to conceive of the passage from one to the other must at least be suggested by original methods which are so many artistic manifestations.

In fact, the success of any work—whether literary, pictorial, musical, architectural, or even purely mathematical—is directly connected with the subtlety of that law and the way in which it is articulated. From this point of view, a formula that succeeds in the difficult task of conventionalizing the law in the schematic magic of the "equal" sign must inevitably be triumphant. And when the language interpreting this equation adds that its two members, the mental and the material, are interchangeable, that they are two aspects of one same reality, then the formula is destined for worldwide fame. That is what happened to $E = mc^2$.

To illustrate these abstract considerations, one could say that the doctrine of idealism has made a certain impression in the world; that of dialectical materialism also. But in those two theories, the thirst for an explicit correspondence between mind and matter is only imperfectly satisfied. Bishop Berkeley weights the argument on the side of mind and suppresses matter, which is an ingenious artifice but not very convincing; whereas materialism relegates mind to the rank of a vague and incomprehensible secondary emanation. With $E = mc^2$, not only is the balance re-established, but through a law of supremely elegant simplicity.

One can also go further: $E = mc^2$ satisfies both the mystic instinct and the sensual appetites of humanity in the same way as a vast cathedral whose stones disintegrate periodically to be dissolved into sublime abstractions, such as Faith, Hope and Charity, and are then incarnated again in an eternal rhythm to restore a monument of a perfect harmony.

Or again: $E = mc^2$ embodies the mystery of the Incarnation. It affects the world in the same way as does the God-Man and for the same miraculous reasons.

In the end, one can only suggest that $E = mc^2$ is the very symbol of love.

1

Accompanied by a procession of scientists and generals whom the Imperial Academy had designated to do him honor, Japan's illustrious guest walked forward with elastic step along the path that led down a gentle slope towards the city. The air was soft. Cherries in blossom heralded an early spring. In the distance the sea sparkled in the sunlight.

Albert Einstein had insisted upon making that outing to a famous Buddhist temple on foot. In return he was enjoying the relaxation of being in the open air after exhausting days filled with official receptions and banquets, which he had forced himself to attend only to avoid hurting the feelings of his hosts. A simple man, he preferred to meditate quietly in the countryside. He would have appreciated that morning walk more if his escort had been less numerous and if the Nipponese had not carried their watchful courtesy so far as to change the natural landscape as a gesture of homage to his discovery.

The night before, he had expressed a desire to see the temple and in consequence hundreds of workmen had toiled through the night to decorate worthily the path of the great Western scientist. That eagerness to please him, however, saddened him; from each side of the path, long paper placards had been hung, obstructing the view, and on each pennant was printed, in gigantic characters, the equation $E = mc^2$.

He walked at the head of the procession, between the town mayor and the oldest notable. A little behind came Yoshi, a

Japanese scientist, covered with decorations and accompanied by a pupil.

'What grandeur!' exclaimed the pupil. 'And what simplicity in this man!'

'His simplicity is the source of his grandeur,' said Yoshi, halting abruptly.

'What do you mean, Master?'

'Other scientists were on the same trail. A French physicist was within an ace of the discovery. In Germany several minds touched the Truth. As for me, unworthy as I am, when he announced his theory my first words were: "That's obvious: I knew it." But all of us had bogged down in formulas of a too-complicated language. To ourselves we expressed our intuition as follows: "Everything happens like this because that is the way it is. Genius emerges in the structure of thought and is translated by such nuances." '

The pupil bowed. They resumed their walk. Yoshi was still talking:

'He never made an experiment to verify his theories.'

'Is that possible, Master!'

'Never. After the uproar aroused by his daring, after the storm of polemics, praises, criticisms, base insults, when finally a group of English astronomers confounded his detractors by revealing in the sky the first proofs of his statements, Einstein alone among the experts of the New Physics did not exult in his triumph. His genius scorns encouragements and the confirmation of experiments. We Japanese cannot understand that a human being can be so disinterested in public opinion. Even today, when his followers search land and sky with the aid of perfected instruments in order to make the truth shine more clearly and to convince those who still refuse to recognize it, he shuts himself up in his study with a pencil and a sheet of paper, intent only on discovering through pure speculation other and more sublime secrets.'

'A great artist, Master,' said the pupil thoughtfully.

The procession came to the end where the path joined the highroad. The city was about a kilometre away and a large crowd had gathered along the route. The foreign scientist's reputation was known to all, from the highest to the lowest in the nation. His simplicity, his honesty, his humanity had aroused the enthusiastic sympathy of the humble, even as his wisdom had stirred the admiration of scholars and the young generation of students, eager for culture and progress.

The highroad resembled a triumphal path, decorated with leafy arches and bordered with poles bearing long pennants on which was written the formula $E = mc^2$. Beneath those flags thronged workmen, coolies and merchants who had closed their shops as if this were a national holiday. From far away in the country a multitude of peasants poured into the city, all of them eager to see the illustrious visitor. Most of them had to appeal to those who could read to decipher the magic symbols for them. Little girls, wearing their prettiest obis, stretched out their hands towards the banners and tried to stammer the Japanese translation of the equation. Students, proud of their scientific knowledge, did their best to comment on the mysterious symbols. The people, hypnotized by this algebra, had the exalting sense of penetrating the great mystery of the Universe. In it they divined a fabulous cure for suffering humanity.

A shiver of mysticism ran through the crowd when Einstein, with his legendary halo of hair, appeared. As he came down the road with his escort, thousands of lips spontaneously murmured, like a pious prayer, the formula in which the people had placed their hopes: $E = mc^2$; $E = mc^2$!

The scientist sighed. His modest nature shrank from such extravagant praises; he accepted them only under duress and in order not to wound his admirers. Now he forced himself to reply to that homage with a smile and went on his way.

On one point, however, he conquered his unwillingness to accept the honors his hosts heaped upon him. His wish, expressed the night before, to make the whole journey on foot, had been respected, but the Mayor had ordered a luxurious richshaw for the last part of the route. The notables could not permit their guest to arrive on foot at the entrance to the city where an official welcome awaited him. When the rickshaw drew up beside him, Einstein stepped back in horror and firmly declined the offer. The Mayor insisted, thinking that Einstein had misunderstood his broken English. The scientist shook his head. Professor Yoshi came forward. The Mayor showed him the rickshaw and spoke to him in Japanese.

'Tell him,' Einstein interrupted, 'I understand his invitation perfectly and I thank him for his kindness; but it is impossible for me to accept. Nothing in the world would induce me to ride in a rickshaw,' he went on heatedly, almost in irritation.

Yoshi looked at him curiously, then he bowed.

'Your wish will be respected, Excellency. The notables of this city are at your command, as am I. Excuse them, please. I see that in their ignorance of Western customs they have gravely offended you. This vehicle is, in truth, much too modest for the greatest of scientists.'

'It's not that,' said Einstein in a calmer tone. 'This vehicle is, on the contrary, much too rich for my taste. The reason I refused is that I have too great and too deep a respect for any human being to permit myself to be drawn by a coolie. To me a human being is sacred and such a practice reduces him to the state of a beast of burden. I beg you to excuse me and not to insist. I shall not be able to overcome my repugnance.'

Professor Yoshi was silent a moment, then he bowed respectfully.

'Your words, Excellency, have convinced me that we are still barbarians in many respects. You have made me blush. I vow here and now that I myself will never use this degrading form of transportation again.'

After Yoshi had explained the scientist's scruples to the notables, the rickshaw was sent away and the procession set off again. The notables had bowed and meditated in silence on his delicacy. The common people who had witnessed Einstein's refusal had not needed any explanation. They had understood instinctively the meaning of his gesture. This new sign of nobility had spread like wildfire along the double row of spectators and the impassioned murmur that accompanied his slow progress increased with every step he took.

As he approached the city, Einstein noticed a platform covered with a carpet, magnificently decorated with flowers and embroidered draperies all depicting the formula $E = mc^2$. Crowds of schoolchildren had gathered around and a group of young girls dressed in white, their arms laden with garlands of flowers, stood ready to crown him. Einstein realized he would have to reply to the speeches that would not fail to accompany this celebration. It was always hard for him to speak in public and he looked round him helplessly.

He could not, however, avoid being seriously touched when he discovered the genuine love beneath these marks of esteem his hosts heaped upon him. But a greater surprise was in store for him. Suddenly a rain of white blossoms began to fall from the sky and the whole procession was showered by a cascade of petals dropped from silent gliders sailing through space. Einstein calculated that the spectacle had necessitated robbing entire cherry orchards and that the whole population must have helped to gather the blossoms. He was moved to tears.

The marvellous rustling of petals continued as the officials took their seats on the platform and it went on for some moments as they listened, standing, to the European anthem. The blossoms covered the ground like a carpet. A few light petals were still whirling about when Einstein suddenly

235

looked worried: he lacked a vitally important point for the few words of thanks he wanted to speak and which he was preparing laboriously in his mind.

Leaning over, he said in a low voice to Professor Yoshi:

'Pardon me, Professor. I wouldn't like to offend these good people who have prepared such a marvellous reception for me, but I have forgotten the name of their city. I am ashamed and beg you to excuse my poor memory.'

'Excellency,' said Yoshi, smiling. 'The fault lies in our Japanese names, which must sound barbarous to Occidental ears. And your mind contains too many precious ideas to be encumbered with such insignificant matters.

'There is nothing remarkable about the city that welcomes you today. Its greatest claim to glory in the future will be to have received you and honoured you as best it could, although so unworthily. It has no other reason for existing in the memory of mankind and especially in yours. Its name is Hiroshima.'

Albert Einstein fumbled in his pockets for a notebook. Finally he pulled out a piece of paper half covered with algebraic signs.

'I'm going to make a note of this name to be on the safe side,' he said. 'Hi-ro-shi-ma. Thank you, Professor. I shall not forget it.'

2

One evening in November, 1935, Professor Luchesi of Rome was waiting with his wife for a telephone call from abroad which had been announced that morning. Luchesi paced the floor nervously. Suddenly he halted.

'But suppose it's only an ordinary call?'

'From Stockholm?' asked Rosa.

'From Stockholm, it is true. That can only be the prize. Oh, Rosa! I'm not excited because of the glory in the Nobel Prize, I swear to you. My work is completely disinterested.'

'I know that very well, Enrico, and all your friends know it too.'

'But what joy after so many years of struggle to see the New Physics triumph in the world! After this distinction, *they* will finally recognize their mistakes. *They* will understand, *they* will admit it.'

'No, no! You're mistaken, Enrico, as you always are when it comes to human affairs. The Fascists understand nothing because they don't want to understand and they will never admit $E = mc^2$. They have too much interest in keeping the masses in chains. This is the interest that governs their beliefs. More and more, Mussolini is putting himself at the service of Hitler and models his tyranny on that of the German dictator. In that country all our brothers are persecuted. Einstein himself has finally had to flee, as well as many others.'

'You are right,' said Luchesi in a low tone. 'Whether I win the prize or not, we must go. But the prize would simplify our journey.'

'Yes, for a certain time Fascist pride would be flattered by that world-wide distinction paid to an Italian. We could carry out our plans more easily.'

The telephone bell rang loudly. Luchesi grabbed the receiver and Rosa picked up an extension. It was the Secretary of the Swedish Academy of Sciences and it really was a question of the Nobel Prize. Trembling with emotion, Luchesi and his wife heard the Secretary read the citation:

'To Professor Luchesi of Rome for his discoveries and his work on the equivalence of energy and matter which permits us to envisage in a distant future the effective transformation of one into the other.'

The communication ended, Luchesi and Rosa embraced passionately. That prize was the fulfillment of a long period of their joint efforts. Afterwards they made ready to receive a little group of loyal friends who, alerted by Rosa, were to help them celebrate the happy day. In spite of his customary calm, Luchesi was so moved that he drank an enormous glass of Chianti to quiet his nerves; then he went to his room to dress. Success and the heat of the wine inspired him with an unusual emotion in which the principal stages of his career loomed before his eyes. He saw himself at the period when he had rejected the deceptive glamour of social life for the path along which a mysterious power was propelling him.

Several years after World War I, Luchesi's life had undergone a complete change as the result of an imperious summons. He was then twenty years old. So far, son of a family of Roman patricians, he had half-heartedly prepared to follow a literary career, dividing his time between facile studies and the idle pleasures of young men of his class. He was distinguished only by a vague instinct for research, which had not yet found its natural field and revealed itself only in attempts at poems a little less banal than those of his friends. Those rough verses left in him a deep sense of dissatisfaction, and after beginning them a hundred times he always ended by tearing them up.

The shock of revelation occurred in the shop of a fashionable bookseller where Luchesi had been languidly leafing through a number of richly illustrated volumes. Bored and depressed, he was about to leave when he noticed on a shelf a pile of grey books that had apparently been carelessly thrown aside. Luchesi stopped short and, without knowing what motive he was obeying, turned back and pointed to the pile.

'What is that?' he asked.

The bookseller came up eagerly.

'Oh! Those books were sent by mistake, Signor. . . . I have no customers for this type of work. That's Einstein's book, in numerous copies. But what's the matter? Do you feel ill?'

This question was provoked by Luchesi's extraordinary behaviour. Having casually opened one of the books, he suddenly turned pale and put his hand to his heart as if to suppress too strong an emotion. He no longer saw the bookseller, who was staring at him with real anxiety. His legs felt weak, and fever shook his whole body. In the centre of the page, preceded by a mysterious procession of Greek letters and even more barbaric signs, the equation $E = mc^2$ had caught his eye and held him spellbound.

In a flash he had grasped its full significance. He perceived intuitively the very breath of a new world of dazzling splendour, beside which the pallid pleasures he had so far enjoyed were drab and insipid. That splendour was caused by the sheer radiance of sublime truths which his mind still could not penetrate, but whose noble meaning he sensed in an intoxicating revelation mingled with the exaltation of discovery. There was perhaps a certain amount of carnal desire in his ecstasy. He remembered having suffered a similar form of magic when he first fell in love; but this emotion was incomparably more violent, something absolute and final that involved his whole existence.

He stood there several minutes, silent and rigid. Then he began to leaf through the book feverishly. Before the words *space, time, matter, energy,* he was again plunged into thought. Finally he picked up the volumes and tucked them all under his arm.

'I'm buying them,' he announced.

'Signor,' said the bookseller, more and more intrigued by these actions, 'allow me to point out that you have several copies of the same book; and that while I know Your Grace's subtle mind is interested in all sorts of reading, perhaps you misunderstood me. I must repeat that these books are intended for specialists in the field. If you are interested in modern theories of Physics, I have here three or four popular

238

works which are easier reading and more agreeable for an intelligent and enlightened amateur like yourself.'

'I'll buy them too,' said Luchesi curtly. 'Give me everything that has been published on Relativity and tell me the name of a bookseller where I might find a more complete documentation.'

Weighed down with an enormous package of books, Luchesi walked hurriedly along the street. So far he had not stopped to reflect: his one desire was to go home, shut himself up in his room and begin to discover the riches now clutched tightly under his arm. Suddenly he stopped short as a thought flashed through his mind; then he turned in the opposite direction. There was something he must attend to first, an imperious duty. Striding rapidly along, he came to the villa where, among her roses, Countess Sophia Giberti, his mistress, had been living for the past month.

Rosa, the maid, a tall dark woman, thin and discreet, whom the Countess had chosen because of her insignificant appearance, received him and showed him into the drawing-room. Luchesi was so preoccupied that he did not even glance at her and she withdrew as the Countess, in negligee, appeared in the doorway and rushed towards him.

'Enrico! I wasn't expecting you this afternoon. You see— I'm just in the midst of packing. I'll be ready early tomorrow morning.'

They were to leave the next day on a trip to the mountains. Luchesi turned his head away.

'I can't go.'

'You . . . But, darling, we've made all arrangements. You have an engagement for tomorrow? That doesn't make any difference.' She started to throw her arms around his neck. He stopped her with a gesture.

'Not tomorrow, nor the next day, nor later,' he said firmly.

Sophia turned pale. She was baffled.

"I shall not be able to see you any longer," he went on with cold formality. 'I've come to tell you so.'

Countess Giberti pressed her hand to her heart, but remained calm.

'I appreciate your frankness, Enrico,' she said sadly. 'It had to end this way, but I did not think you would tire so soon. You don't waste time, do you? Another woman, of course.'

Much older than he, she spoke with an almost maternal tenderness. Luchesi shook his head.

'It's not a question of another woman.'

She stared at him, incredulous.

'You can tell me, Enrico. I won't hold it against you. Only —you should have given me these two weeks' vacation.'

'Impossible,' he said impatiently. 'I haven't a moment to lose.'

'To lose! You are cruel, Enrico . . . Enrico, Enrico,' she implored. 'Come with me tomorrow. Give me these fifteen days. Afterwards, you will be free. I'll let you go without any reproaches; I swear I will.'

She flung her arms around him and pressed against him, head thrown back, hair loosened, trying to look deep in his eyes. He made no attempt to defend himself, but stood there motionless. She stepped back and gazed at him in despair.

'You don't even see me any more. Have you forgotten the past month so quickly? I want to know who she is, what her power is!'

As she flung her arms in a passionate gesture, her hand struck the package he was still carrying under his arm. The paper ripped and the books scattered over the floor. Luchesi rushed to pick them up, but she was ahead of him. On her knees she gathered up the copies of Einstein's work and then slowly straightened, holding the book on a level with her eyes.

'*The Theory of Relativity,*' she read slowly. 'Enrico, it isn't possible!'

The cry of rage that burst from her had no semblance to the melancholy protest provoked by the thought of a rival. Furious, disgusted, twisting the grey cover angrily between her fingers, she raged at him.

'Enrico, you're not going to tell me . . . you're leaving me because of this!'

'Yes,' said Luchesi. 'You're absolutely right. There is no woman.'

'You bastard!' shouted the Countess, drawing herself up to her full height. 'Shame, shame on me! Fool that I am to have taken you into my bed! I should have known it. You've always had foul instincts. Never in my life have I been so humiliated. I would feel less abject if you'd left me for some young boy. Get out of here! Let me cleanse this body you have soiled, let me burn incense to purge the house of your presence.'

The beautiful Countess was beside herself. She cursed obscenely and would have torn the books to pieces if, with the help of Rosa, who had come running on hearing her mistress's cries of rage, Luchesi had not snatched them from her hands. Countess Gilberti still had strength enough to spit in his face before she collapsed on a sofa.

Those bestial outbursts, from a woman of a social class

from which he had decided to part, scarcely troubled Luchesi. In the last two hours his mind had matured. His mistress's curses did not even revolt him and her attitude aroused in him that sort of melancholy sadness ignorance always inspires in scientists. Already he felt dedicated to a life of the intellect. He shrugged his shoulders, sighed, picked up his package of books and left without a backward glance.

Luchesi realized that the Countess's behaviour and her irrational rage against the life of the intellect was evidence of the puerility of the social group to which he had belonged. He shuddered, sick with bitterness at the thought that only the night before he had been sharing the stupid and vulgar jests with which his companions disposed of the new scientific theories. It seemed incredible that he could have stooped so low. It is the nature of any revelation to erase a comprehension of previous states of consciousness, leaving only a confused and nauseating memory.

Luchesi walked swiftly along the street, for he was in haste to get home and start work. But that same evening he had to suffer a second manifestation of the hatred aroused by $E = mc^2$—$E = mc^2$, which is passionate Nature glimpsed in a dream as an inexhaustible source of justice and happiness, of bold and generous enterprises, and brought to fruition in a world purified by science. To that world Luchesi yearned to belong.

Dismissing his servants for the night, he opened Einstein's book and lost himself again in voluptuous contemplation before the magic symbols. Tomorrow he would set up a program of work, but today he was content to let his emotions absorb the pure brilliance of those inviolate mysteries.

He was lost in an admiration so intense that at first he did not hear the door bell. Then, as the bell continued to ring, he shuddered, ran his hand across his forehead, remembered that he was alone in the house and, like a sleepwalker, went to open the door. It was Giulio, Sophia's brother, and his friend Martinelli, two of Luchesi's former playboy companions—two of the handsomest representatives of Rome's gilded youth. Moreover, dabbling in politics, they had connections with the Fascist Party.

The moment he saw them, Luchesi sensed their hostility. He was tempted to shut the door, but to run from danger would, he thought, be unworthy of his new vocation, his new faith for which he was willing to be a martyr.

'Is this Enrico Luchesi's house?' asked Giulio sarcastically.

'What makes you think it isn't?'

'Certain rumors . . .'

Giulio and Martinelli pushed past him and entered the

house. Shrugging his shoulders, Luchesi followed them slowly.

'I've come for an explanation,' said Giulio when they were in the drawing-room.

'What about?'

'Sophia told me . . .'

'Look at this, Giulio!' Martinelli exclaimed, and pointed to a book that lay open on the table. The two young men leaned over and stared with scorn at the formula $E = mc^2$. Giulio straightened up slowly, his cheeks flaming.

'So, then, it was true!'

'Yes, it is true,' said Luchesi.

'And you think you're going to continue to be part of our group and at the same time devote yourself to this degrading sort of reading!'

'It is not degrading,' Luchesi replied calmly. 'These books treat of realities to which I aspire after years of following chimeras; they will bring me the truth for which I thirst. As for continuing to be part of your group, that will not be. We talk together today for the last time unless some saving grace touches you as it touched me today.'

'I can't stand that sort of twaddle any longer,' exclaimed Giulio. 'We didn't come to take you back among us, you blackguard! All you deserve now is punishment.'

And stepping forward, Giulio slapped Luchesi on the right cheek with all his might. He waited a moment, expecting a reaction, but Luchesi clasped his hands over his chest and, with a smile, turned his left cheek. The radiance of $E = mc^2$ had made this former hothead an apostle of non-violence. Enraged by this attitude, Giulio and Martinelli both jumped on Luchesi and began beating him savagely. When he collapsed on the floor, they beat him again with anything they could lay their hands on. They tore his clothes and pounded his body until he was nothing but one bleeding wound. Not content with this, they smashed mirrors, slashed paintings and sacked his house. They were beside themselves and their shouts and curses sounded like the cries of wild animals. Luchesi, whom they had left lying on the floor when they started smashing up the furniture, watched them in silence through swollen eyelids—and he pitied them.

When at last they had gone, Luchesi dragged himself to his table. In their insane rage, his assailants had forgotten the object of their wrath. Miraculously, among all the other books they had torn and defaced, Einstein's treatise had not been touched. Picking it up reverently, he held it in trembling hands above the wreckage. And there he stood a long time, motionless, half-blinded by the blows, his body aching, trying

242

to summon up courage and to gauge the extent of the battle he would have to wage.

'Signor . . . Excuse me . . .'

He was not alone. He gave a start, thinking at first his enemies had returned, but that was a woman's voice and it was not hostile.

'Excuse me for coming in like this, Signor, but I had to come to see you. The outside door was open. I saw the broken furniture. I thought perhaps there had been an accident and that you might need help?'

The voice was familiar. With a great effort he managed to open his bruised eyelids and, through his half-closed eyes, he saw dimly a tall figure he had seen somewhere before, though he could not put a name to the face that appeared to him through a mist.

'Signor, allow me,' said the woman. 'You need help.' And with her handkerchief she gently wiped away the blood from his lips. Luchesi's eyes began to be accustomed to the pain. He recognized her. It was Rosa, the Countess's maid. He pushed her aside and looked at her severely.

'This step was useless, Rosa. You will tell Madame that I shall not change my mind.'

'I am no longer with Madame. I left her an hour ago.'

'So it wasn't she who sent you?'

'No one sent me. I came . . .'

Luchesi stared at her now in surprise. And as his vision cleared and he made out the details of her features, he was amazed that he had never paid more attention to that face. She was not pretty . . . he half-smiled in derision at the vanity of that expression—but the leanness of her angular face made a strange impression on him, an impression of which he had suddenly become aware and which troubled him to the bottom of his heart: she looked intelligent.

'Signor,' she continued, stammering, 'I couldn't help hearing part of the discussion you had with Madame. . . . When I came in, when I saw the books on the floor, I couldn't help reading the titles . . . I understood everything. I was dazzled, I admired you. . . . I must tell you, Signor, that I am not altogether ignorant. . . . I have some notion of Mathematics and Physics.'

'You? A lady's maid?'

'I am a Doctor of Sciences,' Rosa admitted, blushing and lowering her head.

'You don't mean it!' cried Luchesi in astonishment.

'Here is my diploma. I have kept it hidden, for Madame would have dismissed me if she had known . . . and it was a good position.'

'A woman physicist!'

'Oh! A very modest one, Signor. I feel now that I know nothing. In particular, I do not know the theories of Relativity which are banished from official courses, but today I was drawn to those theories as to a lover. I had given up a career which did not permit me to live decently. I regret it now. The sight of this book has reawakened in me the flame I thought was dead. I want to go back to studying. A power outside myself draws me to you.'

'Rosa, Rosa, you are heaven-sent!' exclaimed Luchesi, forgetting his injuries and beginning to pace the room. 'This meeting between us on the very day I found my way to Damascus is little short of miraculous. Yes—a second miracle! You and I are going to work together. We shall never leave each other. You are the wise angel whose presence I felt to be so necessary; the lucid aide I need to guide my first steps.'

'I shall be your faithful servant. I am not very intelligent, Signor. I have to work hard and long to understand even a little. But this afternoon I felt in you the genius that rises with serene ease to the clear perception of all truths.'

'You shall be my collaborator. You shall be my wife! *You are* my wife, Rosa!'

They clung to each other. There had been no need for long acquaintance or lengthy conversations for them to understand each other. A common flame burned in them. They forgot time.

After an hour of ecstasy, Rosa felt Luchesi's body tremble in her arms. Recalled to reality, she blamed herself for her selfishness and began at once to bind up her lover's bruises. As she bustled around the house she exclaimed indignantly at the maliciousness of their enemies.

'See what they have done to you, Enrico! Those devils went at you tooth and nail!'

'Worse than devils,' said Luchesi feverishly. 'Blind and ignorant creatures . . . I foresee a long period of anxiety and persecutions. I suspect that Mussolini has been raised to power in Italy by the Powers of Evil to combat the theory of Relativity and the formula $E = mc^2$. But we shall fight too. Truth will triumph in the end—there can be no doubt of that.'

'Yes, we shall fight,' cried Rosa. 'I shall fight with you. We shall repay a hundredfold the blows those barbarians inflicted on you.'

Luchesi looked at her silently. The young woman's face seemed to be illumined from within and she smiled—an angelic smile in which was summed up all the nobility of her new faith.

'Never, my love,' he said softly. 'You don't really mean those words of hate you have just spoken, Rosa. Neither you, nor I, nor any of the specialists of the New Physics can dishonour ourselves by resorting to means as barbarous as those of our enemies. We are united by a humanitarian idea and we shall remain unsullied. We shall fight, of course, for our cause is the cause of humanity—and we shall conquer. But we shall fight with our own weapons, which are the strongest and most efficacious. Our weapons, Rosa, you must feel it as I do, are reflection, scientific reasoning, the persuasive word and the exactness of the demonstration. Thus equipped, we shall lead the people of Italy and of the entire world to recognize and to admit the Truth: then, little by little, to free themselves from the chains and shake off the yoke of the tyrant.'

'You are more generous than I am, Enrico, and you are right.'

'Is not $E = mc^2$ a formula of love and justice? Through love we answer our enemies' hatred. To iniquity we shall oppose justice; to violence, gentleness and kindness. And in this way we shall arrive at victory.'

When she had finished binding his injuries, Rosa clung to him and embraced him.

'I shall be your companion for this whole program, Enrico, I swear to you. . . . But, tell me, will you not regret any of your past?'

'Nothing,' Luchesi said harshly. 'I feel nothing but scorn for that world of puppets in which I lived.'

'Countess Giberti was beautiful . . . and I am not,' Rosa murmured. 'Her breasts were fuller than mine.'

'Oh, Rosa! Yours are big with our common passion. I am horrified when I think how I clung to that piece of mindless matter.'

'My love!'

All night long they made love in embraces known only to those who are united in spirit as well as in body. They rose with the dawn, ignoring fatigue in their eagerness to begin work.

Luchesi had finished dressing. Rousing himself from his reveries, he listened to sounds from the floor below. In the dining room Rosa was setting the table. The guests had not yet arrived. He sat down in an armchair and allowed his thoughts to drift off again into the past.

In the days that followed that revelation, he had sold his luxurious villa and distributed his wealth among the poor. To tell the truth, he had hesitated before stripping himself of his patrimony; for gold, though vile, could facilitate his plans. But the purity of his new conscience would accept no compromise. A voice murmured within him: 'What has not been gained through intelligence will not know how to profit by intelligence.' He therefore kept only what was strictly necessary for living and bought only those books indispensable to his vocation. Rosa had insisted upon earning her living by teaching and she was no burden to him. He therefore rented a garret and plunged into an impassioned study of Mathematics. For the first month he was so absorbed that Rosa had to insist on making him take his meals, nor did he feel the cold of a glacial winter in his unheated hovel.

Rosa had been right. Not only did he have the intelligence necessary to follow subtle exposés and understand the most abstract demonstrations, but he showed many qualities of genius. He was never satisfied with the truths taught; his perpetually excited imagination kept pushing ahead, dissecting in an original fashion the facts of a given problem, introducing new considerations, to arrive in the end at a solution by himself, the only one that could satisfy him.

Although, guided by Rosa, he was learning the fundamentals of classic Physics as established by past generations, he perceived the falsity of those notions and pointed them out to his young teacher, who soon became his pupil and disciple. The formula $E = mc^2$, that marvellous guide, prevented him from going astray. In short, it took Luchesi much less than two years, the time limit he had set, to know everything contained in the Old Physics, to understand, and not only to feel, that most of their affirmations were lies, and to penetrate profoundly the wisdom and truth of the theories that had come to him on that day of miracles.

Having decided that science would be for him both an art and a means of subsistence, he needed official titles to pursue his studies and he made up his mind to take the examinations. He even forced himself to lie to his examiners in order not to let them suspect the contempt in which he held their old routines and to conceal his relativistic faith, which would not have been tolerated in the bosom of the old Roman University. Thanks to this subterfuge, he was not accused of intellectual irregularity; and as the frivolous world of society had forgotten him, he succeeded in passing all his grades brilliantly, and at a very early age obtained a position of deputy master in the provinces. There he remained for several years, constantly enriching his mind, teaching against his will the official programs but also, secretly, the New Physics to those young men he judged most worthy of receiving it. He even found time to pursue his own theoretical researches and he began to make important contributions to international scientific reviews. In those articles his faith in relativism stood out plainly and his work attracted the attention of the great scientists of the free world.

After those years of intensive work, he was recalled to Rome. Not that the University professors, more and more submissive to Fascism, had forgiven him for his doctrine, which was no longer a mystery, but the foreign honours that were conferred on him had made him an international figure. The Italian government handled him with care, as it handled all V.I.P.'s, thinking that a little of that glory might reflect on the regime—the same reason the government had conferred official distinctions on Primo Carnera. Luchesi was not deceived. He knew that sooner or later the mask would fall. Following Rosa's advice, he was careful not to give them any provocation and reserved the most revolutionary result of his labours for foreign colleagues.

It was in Rome that his great idea came to him: at first confused, then gradually becoming clearer until it was metamorphosed into a project that monopolized all his activity and whose success seemed to him the highest goal of his exertions.

He smiled as he recalled his vague yearnings, reveries, hesitations which were simply the pressures of thought taking form. At that time he was working with two assistants, Rosa, his wife, his indispensable collaborator, and Spallino, a young physicist whose brilliant intelligence and aptitude for assimilating the difficulties of new doctrines Luchesi had discerned. He had no secrets from those two disciples. Step by step they had followed his meditations and the slow progress of difficult speculations. They had both noticed that for some time he had seemed worried: he no longer showed the same eagerness in their meetings that brought them together every evening and, having guessed the cause of his worry, they were both as anxious as he.

It was certainly not doubt that engendered a sort of melancholy in Luchesi as in many relativist physicists. It was rather the lack of progress the formula $E = mc^2$ had made in the minds of the masses. After the lightning flash that the revelation of Einstein's book had been in the world, aside from the few initiates who worshipped in silence, the people had fallen back into the usual indifference towards science and had lost interest. They failed to appreciate the men who worked for it: in the authoritarian states, governments had used perfidious weapons to combat the Idea. They had derided it, and the easily influenced masses shrugged their shoulders and turned their backs on it.

That evening while all three of them were gathered in the Master's study, Rosa met the problem head on.

'We have plumbed all the theoretical nuances of Relativity,' she said. 'Enrico, you have shown its marvellous developments on paper. For the moment we can't go any farther, and the masses do not follow us. In spite of our efforts only an infinitesimal proportion of the truth has been diffused.'

'That is true, Master,' Spallino agreed. 'The people are not satisfied with logic and do not appreciate the accuracy of our demonstrations. To gain their adherence so that they will make their own the formula that will bring them freedom, the people want palpable proofs. The astronomical observations of 1919 were a first step on the way to experimental verification, but since then nothing has been done and those steps are still in the specialists' field.'

'I know it,' said Luchesi, 'and that is why you see me so sad. I've been thinking of that for a long time. We would have to . . .'

He broke off in the middle of his sentence and did not speak. It was at that precise moment, he remembered, that the thought of those elements, diffuse as in a mist, which had been bothering him for days and nights, flashed into his mind. Rosa and Spallino read on his face the glorious labour of that birth. His features were strained, his forehead lined, his gaze seemed to plunge beyond the limits of space.

The two disciples looked at him in silence. Rosa did not remember ever having seen him so upset. Suddenly he came out of this sort of trance. He was filled with a great peace and a smile illumined his face, which looked suddenly relaxed.

'I've found it,' he said simply.

Rosa and Spallino looked at him: they did not dare to question him.

'Here is what we must do,' said Luchesi. 'For us the period of meditation and pure speculation is over: you have felt this, I know. Now we must *act*, we must make our faith triumph. Isn't Physics our field? This is what we are going to carry into effect. The principle is extremely simple; because of its very purity I took so long to conceive it clearly. Listen to me: $E = mc^2$. There is an equivalence between energy and matter. Energy and matter are transformable, the one into the other. To convince humanity of this, the scientist's task is marked out by the formula itself. We must . . .'

Again he paused, then went on, clenching his fist to underline the vehemence of his words.

'We must *create* matter, do you understand? We must create matter apart from energy. We must collect, condense the invisible energy that is scattered all over the world and dissipated every second to no profit and we must transform it into matter, into solid, visible, palpable matter that every human being can see and touch. Then no one will be able to deny the truth any longer.'

Spallino and Rosa were thoughtful a long while. They needed to reflect in order to measure the full import of the words they had just heard.

'Master,' Spallino said at last, 'in the face of a program of such breadth any comment would be ridiculous. I can only bow before the power and boldness of it; but my head whirls at the thought of the difficulties we are bound to meet.'

'Difficulties,' Rosa cried impetuously, 'have been created by Nature to raise the genius of research to the highest peak.'

'Good, Rosa,' Luchesi approved. 'Nothing is more inimical to the mind of the scientist and the artist than facility. We must aim for the most difficult goal and that . . .'

'. . . Is at the same time the most noble, Enrico; I understand your thought. To organize the disorder of diffusion, to build, to create, obviously comes within the frame of our scientific mission.'

The enterprise turned out to be even more difficult and lasted considerably longer than they had foreseen. Before they could think of creating matter, they had to recognize it: to recognize it they had to break it up into atoms, then to dissect those atoms into their infinitesimal elements. In that first phase new obstacles arose at every step Luchesi took. The end was still very far off; but certain discoveries led him to think that he was on the right track and he was optimistic. However, he needed large sums of money which he would never obtain from a more and more hostile Italian government. That need was one of the reasons that drove him into exile.

He had travelled, too. He realized that the relativists could no longer remain isolated and that he must keep abreast of the work done in other laboratories. In his contact with certain scientific circles, he had been both greatly surprised and at the same time somewhat disillusioned. He had perceived that his idea, which he had thought was his very own and towards which he had worked in secret with his two faithful collaborators, had occurred to almost all physicists worthy of the name in every country in the world. All of them had dreamt in a more or less confused way of verifying Einstein's equation experimentally by creating matter apart from energy. After a momentary chagrin, Luchesi blushed at his own egotism. The nobility of the goal to be attained did not permit of individualism, and the very amplitude of the project made collaboration indispensable. After examining in detail his colleagues' researches, Luchesi felt completely reassured. He was well aware that he had a good lead over the others. They were working blindly, not knowing where they would find the necessary energy when the moment arrived. Luchesi, however, knew.

A confused hum of voices rose from the first floor. The guests were arriving: a little group of physicists drawn together by the same doctrine, men who recognized Luchesi as their master.

He came out of his reverie and prepared to receive his guests' congratulations. As he entered the salon, he thought of his approaching departure. He would use the journey to Stockholm as an excuse and would not return to Italy. America awaited him. He would take advantage of the journey to call on some of his European colleagues and learn about their latest work.

3

It could not have been otherwise, but Luchesi was naïve enough to be surprised. At that time all the experts of the New Physics were engaged in researches and work with one single objective in view: the creation of matter apart from the energy diffused throughout the world. This was inevitable. Their almost religious belief in the formula $E = mc^2$, the blind stubbornness and bad faith of their competitors, was bound to arouse in them sooner or later the temptation to make an experimental demonstration. On the other hand, their minds, always oriented towards the progress and liberaton of humanity through science, could choose, among the various possible solutions of a problem, only the *constructive* solution. That is the one they all instinctively adopted without a shadow of hesitation. The difficulties it implied were merely a spur to them, as they were to Luchesi himself.

There was nothing ambiguous about the import of the innumerable experiments performed in that year of 1938 in every laboratory on the globe. Only a superficial mind could have been led astray by expressions like *fission, explosion of particles, bombardment of atoms* by other atoms called *projectiles* and *disintegration*. They were only deceptive signs.

On reflection one was forced to conclude that that barbarous artillery was indispensable, but only in the preliminary stage of the great project: dissection, detailed analysis which must of necessity precede the creative synthesis.

Having left Italy with his wife and his faithful assistant to receive the Nobel Prize, and having decided not to return to his country, Luchesi made a detour through Norway to call on Professor Sborg, one of the greatest scientific personalities of the age. Professor Sborg welcomed Luchesi by introducing him to a little group of scientists of various nationalities who had been eager to meet him.

As Luchesi and Rosa entered the drawing-room, Professor Sborg rose and ran towards them with a show of eagerness which spoke loudly of the esteem the Italian scientist enjoyed abroad, and welcomed them with a jovial pleasantry and that hearty laugh of his which was legendary among his friends. Sborg was as famous for his scientific credits (at the age of fifty he had long since received the Nobel Prize and was considered the leading atomist of the age) as he was for his facetious wit. Luchesi answered in the same vein and the guests laughed discreetly. Then, having satisfied the tradition which impelled them (particularly in those troubled hours) to meet in a humourous mood, the men of science touched upon the subject of their work and their preoccupations. As most of them could speak intelligently only in their own language, they sometimes had a little difficulty understanding one another; but that interlude was brief. Their host had had a blackboard set up in his drawing-room. Each of the scientists in turn developed his thought in mathematical symbols which the others had no difficulty assimilating.

From the first exchange of views, it was obvious that Luchesi's project was foremost in their dreams, their meditations and their experiments. The first stage was on the way to being realized. Matter was gradually yielding up the secrets of its structure. Professor Sborg's work in particular cast a light as practical as it was theoretical on the complex organization of the atom.

'But these are only the preliminary stages,' the Norwegian scientist said in conclusion. 'It is a far cry from knowledge of matter to its synthesis. None of you is unaware of the principal difficulty we face; it is the very nature of our formula, $E = mc^2$, that is true; but to create a few particles of matter you must first have a considerable quantity of energy. Where do we find that energy and how condense it so that it appears in a palpable and visible form?'

The audience was silent and Luchesi felt proud and happy

at the general perplexity. For he himself was in a position to answer part of that question and this was confirmation of his claim to being the true pioneer of the discovery. After a long consultation with Rosa, he had decided to reveal his plans to his colleagues. The ruthlessness of their enemies, in Germany and in Italy, demanded the wholehearted collaboration of all true scientists.

'I cannot tell you yet, Professor Sborg, *how* to condense that energy,' he said slowly. 'But where to find it? Where to get it? That I know.'

All eyes were fixed on him. Sborg raised his thick, red eyebrows.

'Where?'

'In the stars,' said Luchesi.

They looked at each other in surprise; but his reply provoked neither incredulous exclamations nor sceptical railleries, as it would have undoubtedly have done among a less informed audience. Since they had penetrated the theories of the New Physics and studied their consequences thoroughly, the scientists had grown accustomed to meeting the fantastic. They knew that good sense ended only in deceptive signs and that the reality of this universe is stranger than fiction. Even more in the case of human beings obsessed by scientific exactness and logic, the twentieth century had witnessed a strange and paradoxical mutation in some of them: the appearance of the poetic feeling. A fresh indication of this was now being given by this assembly which brought together some of the most distinguished minds of the age: the word *star* had set their nerves aquiver.

'The stars?' Professor Sborg repeated slowly. But as his brain worked well and quickly he grasped Luchesi's subtle thought before the others did. Slapping his forehead he exclaimed: 'I understand! Why didn't I think of it before? Radiation . . .'

'You've guessed it, Professor,' replied Luchesi emphatically. 'You know it. Every instant, space is streaked with, and our planet bombarded by, rays of great intensity and penetration whose precise cause is still unknown, but which have been called *cosmic* because they probably come from the stars; from the stars of our galaxy and from those that lie at the farthest reaches of space. It is the energy of those vibrations I want to utilize to create matter, perhaps some molecules to begin with, perhaps only some atoms—what difference does it make? The source is inexhaustible and it is at hand. We are surrounded by it.'

A silence greeted this statement. Little by little the scientists were infected with Luchesi's emotion, but they were not accustomed to discuss a new idea before they had considered all its aspects. After questioning glances at Rosa, Luchesi began to talk again. His voice was quiet, calm. Only an occasional tremor emhasized the profundity of his theory.

'I take the liberty of emphasizing the theoretical, I would almost say metaphysical, importance of this enterprise,' he said. 'The origin of this radiation is still a matter of discussion; but undoubtedly it is connected with those alarming explosions of giant stars that sometimes happen in the universe. Perhaps—this is Lemaître's hypothesis, which you also know —perhaps we have to trace that origin back to the origin of time and space when the first prodigious atom burst in chaos, giving birth to our Universe.

'Whatever it may be, there is no doubt in my mind that the energy of those vibrations results from a *destruction* of matter. Well, that energy, which is today diffused, rendered unusable as the result of cosmic catastrophes, I propose to condense, to change again according to Einstein's formula, in order to bring it back to its original state. Starting with an imperceptible mist, I re-create, here on our planet, several particles of a substance that has been lost for billions of years.'

Luchesi was silent. A murmur of approval and several enthusiastic exclamations showed him how deeply his boldness had touched his colleagues. Sborg summed up the general impression.

'It seems, in fact, that Nature has placed within our reach the source of energy necessary to our ambitions. All honour to you, Luchesi, for having been the first to think of utilizing this manna, scattered by the stars, in which we are so completely drowned that we no longer notice it. Whatever the result may be, it is a great idea. God grant that we may attain our goals.'

'I myself am convinced that it is possible, Professor,' replied Luchesi. 'I have already made a series of observations which allow me to envisage success.'

Luchesi gave several technical indications as to the methods he intended to use—extremely costly methods which would necessitate considerable organization. He concluded that it was impossible for him to continue his experiments in Italy under the present hostile atmosphere. The conversation then turned on the persecutions to which scientists had been subjected. Sborg introduced Elsa Schmidt to Luchesi. She was a young German physicist who, denounced to the Gestapo as one who held relativistic ideas, owed her life to a rapid flight. She tried to give the group of scientists some idea of the Nazis' violent hatred of modern science. A shiver ran through the audience. They could not have believed the story of those atrocities had they not been confirmed by two other exiles.

Fire and brimstone had fallen on the partisans of Relativity in Germany. Einstein had been forced to leave the country long ago. His books had been burned on the public square in a gigantic auto-da-fé. His disciples paid with their lives for their loyalty to his doctrine. All those who had imprudently shown some sympathy for $E = mc^2$ had been imprisoned, deported, tortured, sometimes torn to pieces by the crowd. That, especially, had deeply grieved many liberal minds. The masses, conditioned and roused by propaganda, no longer recognized their friends.

'Italy has not yet known that shame,' said Luchesi, 'but it can happen from one day to the other. That is why I shall never go back. I am not afraid for my person, but I must continue my work in freedom and in quiet.'

After a long discussion it appeared that Luchesi's project was the only program worthy of the scientific credo that could oppose persecutions, the only one capable of changing the mind of the masses by showing them not with words but by action on which side truth lay. All agreed that it could only be realized in a free country far from violence, in a country whose government would aid the scientists' efforts.

'America fulfills those conditions,' said Luchesi. 'Einstein is already settled there and his reputation will bring us support. Government aid is indispensable.'

Sborg agreed. He thought he, too, would perhaps be obliged to leave his country if the poisons sown by Hitler spread to Norway.

'Meanwhile,' he said, 'we must let Luchesi profit by the results of all our efforts. We no longer have the right to hold back a single one of our secrets. In the face of the danger that threatens us, we must be united, we must form one body only. Who knows if tomorrow we shall still be able to speak freely?'

Holding each other by the hand, Luchesi and Rosa stood at the railing and peered through the fog for their first glimpse of the outlines of New York skyscrapers. The ship was entering New York harbour. The emotion that choked them came not so much from having escaped the hostile atmosphere of Europe—and perhaps slavery—but from the thought of the mission with which they felt themselves charged.

The Italian scientist brought with him the hopes of all European science for peace. If he was successful in his task, as his colleagues hoped, all humanity would have to recognize its mistakes and the dictators would no longer find an echo among the masses. $E = mc^2$ would change the face of the world.

The last days before the great departure had been long and boring. Even receiving the Nobel Prize in Stockholm had been a trial to Luchesi. After the first excitement, he had quickly estimated that sort of reward at its true value. He was not the man to rest on the laurels of the past. He was constantly looking ahead. Rosa, who admired him for that creative passion, smiled as she pointed to their first sight of the Free World on the horizon.

'You will succeed, Enrico. You now have all the means in hand.'

'That is true. And I think that makes up for the recent deficiencies.' He held out a grey-covered notebook containing handwritten memoranda.

'What is this?'

'Elsa Schmidt's memoir. The latest discoveries in Germany.'

Following Sborg's advice, all the scientists had entrusted Luchesi with the results of their recent work. Some of it was of little interest—he knew about it already—but the memoir Elsa Schmidt had given him had caught his attention and he had devoted the entire period of the crossing to studying it. It was a complete account of the researches made by Elsa's former boss, Otto Hans, one of the greatest German experimenters. Luchesi had quickly recognized the capital importance of this document. Quite simply, it showed that the nucleus of the heaviest atom, the uranium atom, had been split and reduced to its simplest elements—a feat no one had heretofore accomplished. The operation revealed definitive information on the internal structure of this metal and on the energy freed by disintegration. Working from those facts, it was easy to evaluate the quantity of energy necessary to perform the reverse operation successfully.

That same morning, after mulling over this report, Luchesi had decided to concentrate all his efforts on creating uranium. It was certainly the body of which the atom was the most complicated part, because it was the heaviest, and the additional difficulty resulting from this complexity was but one more spur to his genius. Moreover, the creation of a heavy metal would produce a much stronger impression on the human race than the creation of a light metal.

Luchesi told Rosa of his latest decision as the ship was entering the port. And as they made ready to land, they marvelled at the wondrous ways of Providence: the last link in

255

the chain, one of the most important, had been forged in Germany, the country where the fiercest enemies of $E = mc^2$ flourished.

4

Einstein walked forward with quick steps that were still youthful in spite his age. He knew the President of the United States and esteemed him, but he did not like official audiences. He had resigned himself to this interview only because urged by a strict sense of duty. But the President, knowing how much the great scientist detested conferences, had dismissed his assistants. After a few words of welcome, he broached the subject of the interview.

'I have your letter here, Professor. Your fame is sufficient guarantee for me of the importance of this discovery and the seriousness of the proposition. However, will you reread it to me slowly, aloud? Afterwards we will talk. I'm not quite clear on certain points and I would like to have them explained.'

Einstein read:

'Recent work performed in every country in the world leads me to think that the principle $E = mc^2$ can give rise to practical applications.

'In particular, from researches made by Professor Luchesi, the result of which has been submitted to me in manuscript, it develops that part of the energy scattered and wasted throughout the Universe in the form of rays called "cosmic" could be condensed and transformed into a heavy metal such as uranium. This operation, of indisputably theoretical interest, would constitute important progress for humanity far out of proportion to any others discovered in this century. . . .'

There followed a number of succinct technical considerations on experiments now under way which the President asked the scientist to skip.

'I would like you to read me your conclusions again.'

Einstein turned to the end of the letter and read:

'In conclusion, the few physicists who are in the secret, and I myself, earnestly recommend that the President of the United States interest himself in Luchesi's enterprise, give it priority over all other government projects now in progress and grant the researchers the extensive credits they need.'

As Einstein finished, the President looked at him admiringly. For a moment he was silent, then he said slowly:

'I had understood correctly. Do you know, Professor, that you and your scientists are one of the wonders of the modern world?'

'In what sense do you mean that?' Einstein asked.

His question was provoked by a certain sarcastic note in the President's voice.

'Your interests are so far removed from ours that we unconsciously think of you as living on another planet. You are certainly not unaware of the gravity of the international situation. You know that war can break out tomorrow in Europe and that this country cannot stay out of the conflict very long. The whole world is thinking only of war matériel, armament on land, on the sea and in the air. I am harassed every moment of the day by our military leaders who are asking me for huge sums. I can already foresee the day when all the resources of the government will have to be mobilized for the war effort . . . and this is the moment you choose, Professor, to ask me to interest my government in a project which is perhaps of considerable theoretical importance, but whose immediate utility . . ."

'Sir,' Einstein broke in, 'it is precisely the present international situation that has impelled me to take this step. The little group of scientists in whose name I speak is fully cognizant of the terrible dangers it entails. But we believe that violence leads to violence in an endless circle; we believe on the contrary, that the example of a disinterested enterprise in the present chaotic situation would inspire the respect of the world and could only put an end to this mad armament race which is a fatal step towards annihilation. We believe that Luchesi's success might avert war or, if that is already too late, might bring it swiftly to an end by orienting the energies and enthusiasms of mankind towards progress.'

The President looked at him attentively.

'See here, Professor,' he said. 'If I understand you correctly, you are suggesting that you propose to tap the energy that comes from the stars, and by a process certainly far from economical.'

'I know nothing about finance, sir, but it would take many millions of dollars. There's no use saying it wouldn't.'

'Millions of dollars . . . to transform into metal . . . into very little metal for a great deal of energy . . . if I follow you correctly? What do you mean by that? How many tons?'

'Sir,' said Einstein animatedly, 'if, by spending millions of American dollars, Luchesi succeeds in creating *one* atom, *one* atom of uranium, Mr. President, that is to say the billionth part of a billionth of a milligram of matter, from the prodigious quantity of cosmic energy that inundates us in spite of ourselves, I would consider that his attempt had succeeded, that he had worked well for humanity and in particular for this country which has always led the free world. I would also consider that the leader of a great nation, by acting as patron for this experiment, would cover himself with a glory surpassing by far that of all military leaders.'

The President held out his hand. His expression was very serious.

'I like your faith and your idealism, Professor. Believe me, I, too, am convinced as a man and as an American of the utility in the long run of disinterested research. I would give you my full support if the hour were not so grave; but I have an immediate responsibility to my country and I must reckon with my advisors. . . . Which reminds me, I showed your letter to my Chief of Staff, swearing him to secrecy, and he made the following comment which struck me, I confess. I'm surprised you hadn't thought of it.'

The President paused and looked intently at Einstein. Then he went on:

'He said to me: "I don't know anything about these things, but if the scientists aren't mistaken, if $E = mc^2$, if an enormous quantity of energy can be condensed in a few molecules of matter, it seems to me that particle of matter contains in the latent state a colossal amount of energy. Ask them to destroy matter by causing a rapid chain reaction of power in reverse, which should not be too difficult, and they will have endowed this country with an essential weapon that will give us the upper hand in waging war." That is the point of view of military men. I hasten to add that I myself am an ignoramus, Professor, but I was impressed by his logic.'

For a moment Einstein was perplexed. He appeared to be caught off guard, hypnotized by the President's words. He thought a moment and then said slowly:

'A sort of explosion, disintegration of matter? I confess, Mr. President, we have not thought of that.'

It was true. Neither Einstein, who paid little attention to experimental verifications, but whose genius foresaw any possibility, nor Luchesi, who had been the first to think of illustrating the principle by a material demonstration, nor even Sborg of Norway, who knew better than any man the infinite potentialities of the atom, nor in fact Otto Hans in Germany, who had decomposed uranium into its infinitesimal elements, nor any of the French, English and Austrian scientists who had devoted themselves to bringing the formula of equivalence into the practical field, had envisaged such an application of $E = mc^2$. The instinctive horror that the idea of destruction inspired in them had, for a time, limited the field of their vision.

After thinking the President's suggestion over carefully and after mentally probing all its aspects, Einstein exclaimed indignantly:

'If I understand correctly, Mr. President, your Chief of Staff is asking relativist physicists to make him a sort of *bomb*?'

'Yes, a bomb which, so it seems to laymen, would be more powerful than any known machine.'

The scientist made a great effort to control himself.

'It is an honour for science,' he said, 'that such an idea has never occurred to the mind of any scientist. It could develop only in the brain of a military man.'

'That is possible,' said the President. 'But in the expectation of war I must listen to the Army too. And the enemies we will eventually have to fight, I must point out to you, Professor, are precisely your enemies and the enemies of science. They are the ones who have forced you to flee from Europe and who, at this moment, are persecuting your compatriots.'

'Even to avenge the worst atrocities of our enemies, sir, and moreover even to stamp out the lie,' exclaimed Einstein, 'I could never make up my mind to take part in a work of death and destruction.'

In spite of his anger, his mind had been working tirelessly since the President's first words. Quick to push and develop an idea to its extreme consequences, he already had before his eyes a hideous picture of the ghastly results that could follow the disintegration of matter. Realizing that the horror of that vision could not be an argument to convince the Commander in Chief of Armies, he made an effort to get hold of himself.

'The struggle we have been waging for years now, Mr. President,' he said soberly, 'is an intellectual struggle; the struggle of truth against error and lies. A conflict of this sort requires spiritual weapons. I bring you today the most powerful of those weapons: the possibility of giving the world palpable proof of a great truth. And you hesitate to help us?'

'I do not refuse. I want to think about your project again. Meanwhile I promise you a small grant that will permit Luchesi to continue his studies. . . . But I shall now ask you, the objective scientist, the greatest scientist of our age and perhaps of all ages: Do you think my Chief of Staff's suggestion could be carried out?'

It had taken Einstein's genius, once oriented in that direction, only a few minutes to realize that the brutal transformation of matter into energy was perfectly possible and probably much easier than the reverse operation. But he also realized in that time what an affirmation on his part or even a reply expressing doubt would mean to governmental and military circles. However, he hesitated a long time before replying. On the one hand, he had a horror of lies, in particular of the scientific lie. On the other hand, his whole strenuously pacifist background weighed on his conscience; his loathing of violence, his innumerable appeals and campaigns in favour of peace. He could not take a responsible part, even indirectly, in the cataclysm his mind had glimpsed in an atrocious vision. It was unthinkable. His dignity as a man outweighed his scruples as a scientist. Had not Galileo lied to secure his own safety? He too must lie to save millions of lives. Blushing with shame, he made up his mind.

'Your Chief of Staff's proposition is completely impractical, Mr. President,' he said. 'I give you my word as a scientist. It is contrary to the laws of Physics for reasons I cannot explain to you. It would be time and money lost to work in that direction.'

Had that diabolical transformation of matter into energy been realized, there would not have been one scientist in the free world qualified to prepare its advent; but wisdom advised against running the risk of even discussing its possibility.

In the face of the danger Einstein had foreseen, in the face of the curse that such a tragic interpretation of $E = mc^2$ would bring, the Master's heroic lie became the keynote for all the exiled European physicists who enjoyed such prestige in America that they were called on to advise the government.

When war broke out and when, after Einstein, after Luchesi, the most noted scientists of the Old World had found refuge in the New World, when it became more and more apparent that the United States could not remain outside the conflict, the President asked the advice of the most eminent authorities as to the essential contribution relativist science could make to the American war power. All of them answered as the head of their group had done. All swore that atomic disintegration—thank heaven!—could not be carried out by human beings. The transformation recommended by Luchesi was the only one possible and they insisted that the Italian scientist's project should be put into execution immediately with government backing.

But in spite of their declarations, the President was still doubtful, both as to the advisability of launching the United States in wartime into an enterprise of whose practical usefulness he was not convinced, and as to the impossibility of using $E = mc^2$ to make powerful weapons for which the military was clamouring at the top of their lungs.

It was the American physicist, Almayer, who had the honour of convincing the President on those two points, crowning the scientists' point of view with triumph.

In spite of his youth—he was still in his thirties—Professor Almayer was one of the most prominent personalities in the New World, not only because of his scientific attainments, but also as the result of the strange diversity of his acquaintances and his many activities which went far beyond Physics and Mathematics. Born of a family of farmers in the West, a sportsman and a lover of outdoor life, he showed as much enthusiasm and dynamic energy in exploiting his ranch as he did patience and speculative intelligence in unravelling pure truths in the wilderness of equations. An organizer of the first order, a realist and completely American in certain ways, he still found time to learn Sanskrit and study Buddhist doctrines and Hindu religions, of which he had become one of the faithful.

Having had contacts with all the great laboratories, he knew Luchesi's thought and had interested himself in it with his usual enthusiasm. However, the exiled European scientists, who scarcely knew Almayer, felt uneasy when they learned, through an indiscretion, that the President was about to ask his advice. An American might, out of a mistaken sense of patriotism, be induced to ignore the interests of humanity.

In distress, Einstein and Luchesi called on Almayer to sound him out and if possible to win him over to their side.

He received them cordially. At their first words, he began to smile:

'You have come too late,' he said. 'The President has sent for me to ask me the same question he asked all of you.'

'And what was your reply?' asked Einstein, pale with fear.

'Have you any doubt on that score, Master?'

The two Europeans looked at him in perplexity, hesitating to interpret his smile. That smile suddenly faded as the American scientist spoke with vehement indignation.

'Could you doubt the reaction of a convinced Hindu on this occasion? I, Almayer, disciple of Brahma, I, to whom all violence is odious, I, Almayer, who considers it a crime to crush an importunate gnat—could you believe that I would lend myself to researches that might be turned into floods of human blood? Could you imagine that I would not oppose that action with all my strength, with all the influence I have in this country? The question is not to know whether such and such a nation would rule the world, but whether, after a war fought with such weapons, there would still be men on earth. How could you have the slightest anxiety as to my

261

reply, Master? How could I have yielded to temptation and sinned. I who am not only a relativist physicist like you, but moreover a disciple of Gandhi! I too have sworn that the disintegration of matter is impossible.'

And as Einstein, ashamed of his suspicions, embraced him with emotion, Almayer told them the good news: he had pleaded the cause of science so well that he had finally convinced the President. The latter had now decided to lead the government of the United States along the glorious path Luchesi had discovered. He was ready to give him his full support and even to divert an important part of the funds destined for the war effort to help him realize the prodigious synthesis.

5

Night was fading over the mesa of Los Alamos in the mountains of New Mexico. Yaca, a young Indian with long black hair and shining eyes, seized the last moments of darkness to slip silently through the pines and thickets towards the hiding place in the hollow of a rock from where he would watch unseen the activity of the white men. Yaca lived far away in a lonely pueblo in the high mountains. He had formed the habit of coming almost every morning to the plateau where the scientists performed mysterious rites.

There was no apparent reason for that strange conduct. He had gone there the first time by chance, following the tracks of a porcupine. When he saw the research centre, he had instinctively squatted down and watched. Since then he had come back as though drawn by a magnet.

He had no purpose except to look. Though he did not understand the activity of the human beings who haunted the mesa, he attributed a religious meaning to it. Little by little he had come to worship these personages, whose calm, silent manner was such a contrast to the ways of other white men he had known. From these men there emanated an impression of serenity and kindness that delighted him and inspired him with respect. It seemed to him that the strange occupations of those scientists, who sometimes raised eyes glowing with ecstasy to the skies, were in some way related to the thousand daily miracles of Nature. He spied on their every move, and to live in their shadow gave him a curious thrill.

Each morning, before daybreak, it was an exhilarating game for him to slip through the barbed-wire fence that surrounded the camp and outwit the sentries' vigilance. To tell the truth, the surveillance was not very strict, the government thinking the secret sufficiently guarded by the arid desert of New Mexico. Besides, Yaca had often been seen by the scientists, but they were not alarmed by his presence and did not report it to the military authorities who were responsible for security. From his appearance they considered that he was not dangerous. They sympathized with simple and primitive people. Sometimes they gave him a glance of friendly understanding and a tacit accord had been established between them: they tolerated his curiosity and Yaca never tried to draw any nearer. To adore from a distance was enough for him.

He took up his stand not far from a brick pyramid as high as a house, which was surrounded by a network of apparatus and wires. For several weeks that had been the principal theatre of operations. An instinct had warned Yaca that something was going to happen this morning. Wrapping himself in an old torn blanket, he curled up and waited for the light. Soon he heard the sound of voices, raised his head and saw two figures approaching in the growing dawn.

'Oh, Rosa, do you think it's going to succeed?'

'I'm sure of it, Enrico.'

Yaca's instinct had not deceived him. This was not an ordinary day. He did not understand their words, but his intuition was confirmed by the two strangers' voices. The man's voice trembled as if he had a fever. The woman's was passionate.

'I'm sure of it, Enrico,' Rosa repeated. 'Think of the first success. You have found the essential thing. One month ago an atom of uranium appeared.'

'One atom only!'

'One atom, it is true, but a synthetic atom, an atom created by you, more important in its minute matter than tons of metal found in their natural state in the Universe.'

'That's true,' Luchesi admitted. 'But today it's a question of creating billions.'

'That will come. Your theory is correct and the calculations are exact.'

Luchesi replied—and Yaca trembled at the sound of his voice. He had heard such tones at the dawn of a day of work only on two or three occasions and, each time, a miracle had taken place. He had seen the frenzy that seized his gods after they had bent their heads over the instruments of the cult. This morning Luchesi's tone betrayed an excitement as intense as a month before; and Yaca remembered that the day after the experiment, the scientist had suddenly danced up and down, arms raised towards the sky, an attitude in strange

263

contrast to his habitual reserve, shouting words the Indian had remembered: 'An atom! An atom!'

At this moment Luchesi was saying: 'You are right, Rosa. My calculations are exact and my theory is correct. The chain reaction is going to be produced as I had foreseen. Two atoms will be born of the first atom created. Those two will produce four and so on and so on. I should have more confidence.'

They stood silent and motionless before the pyramid of bricks which rose like a temple on the desert plateau. All of a sudden Yaca turned his head. He had heard a familiar voice which warned him of the arrival of another sage. He was well acquainted with the inhabitants and that ringing laughter could come only from Professor Sborg. Even before he saw him, Yaca pictured to himself, with a sort of filial tenderness, the Norwegian's gigantic frame and red eyebrows.

In his turn Sborg had been obliged to leave his country when it was invaded by the Nazis. His escape had aroused the admiration of the scientific world. Arrested by the Gestapo, he had escaped at night down a rope ladder and had succeeded, after many vicissitudes, in making connections with an Allied submarine. He brought with him the latest results obtained by the European laboratories, in particular the German laboratories, which continued to work for pure science. Following the example of other scientists, Sborg had found a safe asylum in America and the opportunity to continue his researches. The United States was collecting scientific celebrities as it had formerly collected European art. A Nobel Prize was the best certificate of authenticity and was particularly sought after.

At Luchesi's request, backed by Almayer, to whom the general management and organization of the enterprise had been entrusted, the majority of those famous guests had been gathered together at Los Alamos, far from crowded cities, in the peace and isolation of the desert, to collaborate on 'the project.'

Yaca noticed that Sborg's laughter was lighter and more ringing than usual. That strengthened even more his feeling that something out of the ordinary was about to happen. Soon the Norwegian's tall figure came into view. He was accompanied by John Almayer. Both men hailed Luchesi and his wife joyously.

'A great day, Luchesi,' cried Sborg with another burst of laughter. 'A miracle reworked, in a way: the multiplication of the loaves of bread.'

Luchesi smiled. Even John Almayer let himself go in a fresh burst of laughter.

At Los Alamos, in spite of the hard work, in spite of the austerity of the studies, there was nothing grim about the atmosphere. In fact, the scientists' mood was pleasant—'jovial' would be the more exact term. The exalted character of the work did not at any moment prevent the free play of sentiments and, among the latter, humour held a prominent place. In the heart of that atmosphere of smiling humanity which had gradually developed in the peaceful mood of the mesa, the greatest atomist in the world, Professor Sborg, was famous for his buoyant gaiety, his tendency to facetiousness and his inexhaustible stock of amusing anecdotes. All the chroniclers of the Los Alamos era insist on that turn of mind as on a remarkable fact. Certain of them even report that you could follow his trail by the people convulsed with laughter he left behind him.

Besides, there was often a boyish love of pranks in the behaviour of all those celebrities. Enjoying, for the first time in their lives, a deep sense of liberty, freed of financial worries and of the necessity of teaching boring classes, relieved by the military administration of all annoying details of daily life, they were not far from considering the mesa an earthly paradise. At times they behaved like college boys on vacation. Above all, the knowledge that they were working on a noble enterprise, with practically unlimited means, filled them with a strange passion and a sense of euphoria. Their genius was roused beyond its usual pitch. The partial success already obtained had been just so many thrilling steps on the triumphal path whose successful outcome they could not foresee. The result was a perpetual state of quasi-intoxication which showed in their constant good humour as well as in a youthful desire to play tricks.

Yaca, a silent and smiling witness, was present at those sometimes simple and sometimes subtle games that he did not always understand, but whose spirit he sensed from the outburst of exuberance when they pulled off a good joke. He liked the scientists' pleasantries as much as their grave and serious air when they were in the midst of a delicate experiment. They helped to strengthen his conviction that these were good.

The scientists' caustic humour led them one day to put the button at the mesa gate under weak electric tension; but this time the victim was General Groats, the military administrator of the camp and not Professor Sborg, with whom the others had hoped to get even for the many tricks he had played on them. The General pressed the button, leapt into the air in a series of involuntary capers—and flew into a towering rage.

It took all of Almayer's tact and authority to convince him that they had not tried to injure his dignity and that he was only the unfortunate victim of too much isolation. The General's roar of rage could be heard all over the camp. Yaca crouched down on the ground, taking good care not to show so much as the hair of his head. That day he understood that this personage in uniform was dangerous and that he did not belong to the race of jovial gods.

'The multiplication of the loaves of bread,' Sborg repeated. He liked to call attention to his witticisms. His words illustrated the spirit of the experiment they were about to perform that same day, according to calculations made by Luchesi and which the work of certain German laboratories appeared to confirm. One or several atoms having been created by cosmic energy, a reaction known as 'chain' must build up spontaneously through the action of natural forces. From those first elements other atoms must be born and their number increased, following a geometric progression whose series was limited only by the range of their apparatus and the rapidity of the supply of energy. If the practical test confirmed the theory, millions, perhaps billions of atoms of uranium must develop inside the brick pyramid and register their presence on the apparatus. There was no question as yet of seeing those atoms condensed in a block of visible and solid metal. To reach that future stage would require still more time and work.

'Everything is ready,' said Luchesi, now serious again.

They were waiting for several assistants who soon arrived: a group of physicists comprising some of the finest brains in the world. Yaca's heart beat fast as he saw Luchesi mount a platform opposite the brick pyramid, like a priest making ready to celebrate before the altar.

The physicists went to their posts. Each man knew exactly what he had to do. They stood, silent, in a semi-circle around the pyramid. From time to time, obeying a gesture or a brief indication from Luchesi, they moved a lever or pressed a button. All the apparatus was now in the open—the tent that covered it having been removed—and there was nothing to obstruct Yaca's admiring gaze.

Sborg and Almayer, mere spectators, stood a little behind. Near them General Groats, whom they had invited as a courteous gesture, looked anxious and ill at ease. This ceremony was too reminiscent of certain spirit seances he had attended when he was a junior officer.

For that matter, the same analogy would have occurred to

any lay observer. He would have been prepared by the words *materialization* and *disintegration* that cropped up in daily conversation. Today those silent men, their eyes fixed, hands folded, looked like a group of spiritualists gathered around a gigantic table, awaiting a supernatural apparition.

'It's going well,' said Luchesi. 'The current is on.'

A needle had moved on a central dial. That meant that torrents of invisible energy, taking their source in interstellar abysses, were beginning to converge on the pyramid, drawn by the condenser which Luchesi and Rosa had perfected. Power scattered in space gradually concentrated in the battery. The air was clear. The altitude favoured the experiment. The needle moved imperceptibly, continuously. All eyes were now focussed on a cinematographic screen on which appeared a close-up of a Wilson chamber, an apparatus used for testing atoms by means of the condensation they produced in a damp atmosphere.

For a long time the screen remained grey and misty. General Groats paced up and down, casting irritated glances at the group of physicists. He had been invited to several seances of this sort and, in his opinion, nothing useful or remarkable had ever come of them. The day Luchesi shouted: 'An atom! An atom!' and rushed into Rosa's arms and when, afterwards, his friends had hurried to embrace him, the General thought they had all gone crazy. In spite of the explanations they gave him, he could not attach any importance to a tiny flash of white mist that vanished as soon as it appeared on the screen and roused such enthusiasm among the scientists.

After an hour of patient waiting, Luchesi suddenly remarked in a dull tone:

'This is the beginning of the materialization. We are at the same point as the last time. An atom is about to be born.'

'Spirit, are you there?' cried Sborg. But he realized, from his colleagues' grave faces, that this was not the moment to jest and went back to observing in silence.

The phantom, whose materialization they were awaiting, manifested itself in its own way, as it had done one month before, by tracing a white flash on the screen that looked like a slender trail of mist.

'Now the chain reaction should start, if my calculations are correct,' said Luchesi in a voice that trembled with emotion.

'It will start,' Rosa declared firmly.

Several levers were pushed over and the miracle occurred. On the screen there appeared, first, two furtive traces, then four, then a bunch, a spray and finally fireworks that became more and more dense. On the central screen, the needle had dropped back to zero and the Geiger counters, which confirmed the presence of free atoms, crackled and gave forth a steady humming.

'Billions of atoms,' murmured Luchesi.

'Billions . . . Nonsense!' said General Groats, exasperated. 'Where are they?'

'Around you, General,' explained Almayer. 'The moment they are born they disappear, invisible in space. They are not strongly enough concentrated yet to form into visible uranium, but the principle of the chain reaction has been established. One of these days, very soon now, I predict that your eyes will see the created metal and your fingers will touch it.'

The General shrugged his shoulders. He was not convinced. The experiment was almost over. The roar of the counters, which had attained a maximum degree, now began to slow down and soon there were longer and longer intervals between the snapping and crackling. A few sporadic flashes still appeared on the screen, which had now become smooth again. The instruments stopped moving and were silent.

The maximum energy the machines could produce had been transformed into atoms of matter. Luchesi came down from his platform to be greeted enthusiastically by his friends. Then Professor Sborg came forward, waving a package he had been holding behind his back. Tearing off the wrapping, he triumphantly produced a bottle of Chianti. It was a delicate homage to the Italian physicist's native land and Luchesi, deeply moved, clasped his hand.

They toasted one another warmly and emptied the bottle. Then, flushed with their first success and in haste to continue their researches, they headed for their laboratory. Yaca waited until they had disappeared. Then he crawled through the bushes, crossed the barbed-wire fence and set out on the road home, still hypnotized by the sight of the atomic fireworks. To him the ceremony he had just witnessed was like one of those magic seances the wise men of his tribe held at certain seasons, when they covered their faces with hideous masks, painted black and white stripes on their bodies and danced frenziedly in their efforts to enter into communication with the spirits of Earth and Heaven. But the immobility and majestic calm of the scientists had impressed him much more than the contortions of his primitive brothers. His new gods, he knew, moved in a higher sphere. Lost in a series of exalted dreams, Yaca returned to his pueblo very late that night.

Before he set to work, Luchesi wiped the sweat from his brow; then, smiling, he looked at his wife and his eyes shone with pride.

'You see, Enrico,' said Rosa, 'you were wrong to doubt.'

'I admit it. It had to be. But, Rosa, do you understand the metaphysical importance of this experiment? Do you know *why* certain atoms multiply like amoeba?'

'Because you are a great scientist, Enrico.'

'No, Rosa. I am nothing. They do that because Nature herself, which we are only helping, is essentially constructive. Creation calls forth creation. That is the cosmic meaning of the chain reaction. People have long since intuitively divined that sublime arrangement of the Universe and have popularized it in an admirable saying: "Help yourself and Heaven will help you." '

Rosa nodded.

'God does not throw dice as the great Einstein says,' she murmured. 'He always works according to a creative plan.'

6

The thousand little details of the crucial experiment, as the scientists called it, were studied first with great interest, then in calculated detail so that there would be an aura of grandeur about its realization that would make a profound impression on the spectators.

Place and time were debated in a conference in which the leading scientists, members of the Cabinet, the military and the President of the United States participated. The place was determined with almost mathematical precision by historic circumstances, chance and imagination playing a part only in the final choice between sites of equal interest. It was very clear that it could only be somewhere in Japan, the one enemy still fighting against science and the law $E = mc^2$. Japan offered the scientists the last opportunity to prove the superhuman power of the formula by bringing about the immediate end of a bloody war through an irrefutable public demonstration. To government officials it represented the last chance to justify, by a practical result, the gigantic sums allocated to Luchesi's project.

For technical reasons—cosmic rays are more penetrating in the higher atmosphere—they had to proceed at a certain altitude. For publicity reasons—the effect to be made on the world—the wonder must have the greatest possible number of available witnesses. It was unthinkable that the demonstration could be carried out above armies or navies. With some reason, the scientists did not consider the military valuable witnesses. Soldiers were obviously the least qualified to grasp the import of a *constructive* act. It was therefore essential that the last stage of this long labour and research should take place in the air, above an important city, the density of an enlightened population insuring both the number and quality of the testimonials. This conviction was shared equally by all members of the conference, but chance also played a small part. When the names of different cities were being proposed, Professor Einstein, wishing to take some notes, fumbled in his pockets for pad and pencil and pulled out a scrap of yellowed paper on which was written a strange word in the middle of algebraic signs.

'Hi-ro-shi-ma,' the scientist deciphered.

It was the paper on which he had noted the name of the city that had given him a memorable welcome some years before. It had remained in the same pocket since that day.

'What did you say, Professor?' asked the President of the United States.

'Hi-ro-shi-ma,' Einstein repeated thoughtfully.

Pleasant memories, long suppressed, awoke. He saw himself walking under green arches while a rain of white blossoms fell from the sky. Deeply moved, Einstein described those pictures to the assembled men who listened respectfully. When he had finished, the President thought for a moment and then turned to the scientists.

'Hiroshima seems to me a very favourable point for your experiment, gentlemen,' he said. 'In memory of the reception they gave the greatest scientist in the world, I suggest that we choose this city.'

'That would make me particularly happy,' Einstein approved. 'I have nothing against the people of Hiroshima, in spite of their present aberration. On the contrary, I would be delighted to see them repaid a hundredfold for the kindness with which they overwhelmed me.'

No one offered any objection and the city of Hiroshima was chosen.

The choice of time was quickly settled. Everyone agreed that noon was the most propitious hour, the time when the Japanese crowd was thickest on the streets. Luchesi and Almayer were distressed at the thought that some of the citizens might miss the spectacle, particularly the women, busy at their household tasks and the very young children. They therefore suggested that the people of Hiroshima should be informed of the wonder that was going to take place in the sky above them; but here they ran into government opposition, for which the President gave the following reason:

'No, gentlemen! If your creation of matter is politically and philosophically as important as you claim, it must come as a complete surprise and its effect on the imagination of the masses will be increased a hundredfold.'

What he did not admit was that the Cabinet and the military did not share the physicists' optimism. General Groats had reported that he had seen nothing reflected in the sky during a preliminary experiment, that the scientists had put a few grains of white dust in the hollow of his hand and had told him it was synthetic uranium. But he could not be certain of anything with that bunch of dreamers, whom he sometimes suspected of being prestidigitators. The President was not eager to risk the reputation of the United States by announcing an operation whose success seemed to be problematical.

The conference over, the scientists returned to Los Alamos to work on perfecting the final details. Yaca, who hardly ever left his hiding place, saw in their eyes a flame that sparkled and flashed more and more as the great day approached. Einstein himself came to spend several days on the plateau. Though he had little liking for practical demonstrations, this one seemed to him so important that he felt he must encourage the scientists by his presence during the last hours. Accompanied by Sborg, he went from laboratory to laboratory, from workshop to workshop, and had the functioning of the innumerable mechanisms explained to him.

The original Idea, conceived by his brain, had little by little led to these subtle inventions from the keen minds of his followers. He admired their ingenuity good-humouredly, though a little condescendingly. Now and then he smiled and murmured to himself: 'Exact theories may be verified by experiments, but there is no road leading from experiment to theory.' Yaca, overcome with astonishment and awe at the sight of the great scientist, lived in his shadow during all of his stay in Los Alamos. For him each of Einstein's movements had miraculous importance. Now and then he even grew bold enough to try to catch his eye. From afar the Indian witnessed numerous private talks between the great man and Sborg. He noticed that Einstein's eyes glittered maliciously after those secret meetings and that his movements, ordinarily so quiet, betrayed an inner fire. Yaca suspected that those two men must share a secret. He was convinced of it when the Norwegian scientist's great hearty laughter rolled out more boisterously than ever.

During the three weeks that preceded the great event, neither Hiroshima nor the country round about it were bombed. The scientists had insisted upon this truce by the military command. The philanthropic character of their enterprise would not conform to an atmosphere of terror.

7

Far away on the horizon a black speck appeared above the sea—a solitary plane flying towards the land in the cloudless sky above Hiroshima. As it drew near the city, people stared in surprise at its unusual appearance. At the request of the scientists, the plane had been painted green, the colour of hope, and white doves were poised on the wings. Not a breath of air stirred. The city drowsed in the peace of the soft Nippon summer.

The leading physicists from Los Alamos were part of the expedition. Luchesi had claimed that he needed all his collaborators. That was not quite true, for the moving of a single lever would automatically release the whole series of operations, but he felt that he had neither the courage nor the right to deprive his friends of the final apotheosis. Each of them was eager to witness the definitive success, the triumphal reward of many years of superhuman efforts. Einstein alone was absent, his age and his health preventing him from flying at high altitudes. A radio telephone connected him with the plane.

'Let them do as they please,' the President had told the military command. 'This whole thing, from the beginning, is the business of scientists. We understand very little about it. It is the result that interests us.'

As the plane's crew had been ordered to follow Luchesi's instructions, whatever they might be, the pilot did not protest when the scientist ordered him to descend a few hundred yards above Hiroshima, fly over the city several times and dip his wings to make the white doves sparkle in the sunlight. After remarking that the plane ran the risk of being shot down, he obeyed. Luchesi shook his head and smiled. He felt in his heart that the guns of the D.C.A. would not go into action.

His instinct had not deceived him. The Japanese did not fire on them. They were stunned, completely disarmed by the sight of the solitary green plane, decorated with strange birds which they took for a supernatural apparition. When the

272

plane had circled several times, Rosa noticed that the streets were crowded with people who showed no signs of panic.

'Look, Enrico,' she cried. 'They have guessed it. They are with us.'

It seemed, in fact, that by some mysterious telepathy the excitement and enthusiasm of the passengers had been communicated to the people of Hiroshima below them. The citizens raised wide eyes to the sky and stood motionless in expectation of a miracle.

'Look, look, all of you! Look with all your eyes!' shouted Luchesi as if the crowd could hear him. He was beside himself with excitement. The next moment he had himself under control. He must keep calm to direct a series of delicate manœuvres. He ordered the pilot to climb some twelve thousand feet. The plane rose in majestic spirals.

'It's almost time,' said Almayer in an unsteady voice.

Luchesi released the energy condenser which, held up by a little balloon, soon floated in space. The plane began to make a wide circle around it.

Sborg grabbed the telephone that connected them with Einstein and murmured in one breath:

'It's time, Master.'

Einstein's voice sounded strangely calm in contrast to the anguished feverishness of his followers.

'I am not worried. The experiment can only confirm an *exact* theory.'

Luchesi then spoke to his wife softly.

'Rosa, it is thanks to you that I have been able to undertake and complete these researches. You have as large a part in this as I have. You must be the one to press the lever.'

'No, Enrico. All the honours are yours. This one in particular.'

'But don't you see—I can't! I'm at the end of my rope!' Luchesi groaned. And he collapsed on a bench, unable to move. All the scientists were livid, paralyzed, as ill with emotion as Luchesi. They could just manage to say:

'It's up to you, Rosa!'

In some exceptional circumstances, certain women have more nervous resistance than men. Rosa pressed down the lever firmly. Immediately from a loud-speaker came the countdown.

'Ten, nine, eight, seven . . .'

Luchesi managed to make a despairing motion with his hand. The pilot understood and cut off the engines. The plane began to glide—silently. John Almayer's emaciated face was more deeply lined than ever. Even Sborg, his face distorted, could not utter a word.

'Six, five, four . . .' came from the loud-speaker.

Luchesi brought his hand down on Rosa's shoulder and forced her to press her head near his against the porthole.

'Three, two, one . . . zero!'

As once upon a time, no doubt, the heavenly trumpets saluted the sudden explosion of the primitive atom, thus marking by an august signal the birth of the Universe, so the microphone solemnly announced the zero hour of the new age created by the genius of men. But human creation was unaccompanied by any noise. On the contrary, silence, a silence more impressive than the most monstrous of tumults, filled the serene sky over Hiroshima.

Not a sigh was heard inside the plane, which continued to glide silently in an atmosphere untouched by any breath of air. So intense, so profound was Nature's silence and calm for the first minutes of the new era that the pilots thought something had gone wrong. But the men of science knew very well that the most sublime realizations take place in meditation.

The plane turned and banked. Almost in unison the scientists suddenly cried out in triumph. Their eyes, eagerly scanning space, had noticed a first flash a little below the condenser. A ray of sunlight had been reflected by . . . by something, an object, a substance that had not been there a moment before. There was another brief flash. Then, slenderer than a blade, as light as the petal falling from a rose, it whirled in the air, glinting in the sun like a crystal. It was a synthesis of the power scattered about the world, symbol of wisdom, patience, genius and love of mankind—a thin leaf of uranium floating slowly down in the dazzling sky over Hiroshima.

For a moment, hypnotized by the appearance of the created particle so high above the town, the scientists could not take their eyes from it. Then each man reacted after his own fashion.

John Almayer grabbed Luchesi and Rosa and, sobbing, held them in his arms in a frantic embrace. Spallino danced a wild jig which made the plane rock alarmingly. But Sborg's action caused the crew even more anxiety. He rolled on the floor, banging his head against the wall, unable to repress his hysterical laughter which twisted his giant's body in tremendous spasms.

For a long time none of them was able to speak. Their emotion finally found release in a unique formula.

'$E = mc^2$!' breathed Almayer between sobs. '$E = mc^2$!' repeated Luchesi, seizing Rosa's hands. '$E = mc^2$!' stammered the latter. '$E = mc^2$!' shouted Spallino, waving his arms like a windmill. '$E = mc^2$!' groaned Professor Sborg, his laughter rumbling through the cabin.

After this crisis of pardonable madness, Luchesi grabbed the telephone, obtained a relative silence with great difficulty and, in a strangled voice, managed to inform Einstein of their success.

'$E = mc^2$, Master! Condensed energy takes form and colour! A created substance, visible, palpable, has appeared in the sky over Hiroshima. You were right: we were right!'

'I never doubted it,' replied Einstein simply.

The slender leaf of uranium was still floating slowly down over Hiroshima. It had descended only a short distance during those moments of joy and excitement. The shimmering of the pure metal made it possible to follow its traces every second.

With their nerves somewhat relaxed by Einstein's calm control, the scientists watched the continuation of the operation. The pilot had started the motor again and was keeping the plane on a level with the leaf.

'Creation cannot, must not, stop there,' said Luchesi. 'The chain reaction must take place here as it did at Los Alamos. But am I really seeing right? . . . Look there, and there . . . and there . . .'

It was true. In the space which the particle of whirling substance seemed to light up like a torch, two identical objects were now shimmering. The uranium leaf had a twin sister of a virgin matter as fine and pure as the first, which accompanied it, zigzagging in its graceful fall over Hiroshima.

The silence the scientists now observed was broken only by an exclamation of Sborg's:

'Four!'

Four leaves were now whirling above the city. But the Norwegian had scarcely spoken when eight white points sparkled in the sun. The miracle of the chain reaction had happened again. The scientists now vied with one another in announcing the new and fantastic proliferation.

'Eight!' exclaimed Spallino.

'Sixteen,' cried Luchesi.

'Thirty-two, sixty-four!' shouted Sborg.

It was soon impossible to follow with their eyes that cascade of miracles. It was as if successive waves of diamonds and pearls emerged every second from nothing, apparently engendered by the pulsations of an invisible brain. A constantly expanding cloud of translucent butterflies floated in the clear sky over Hiroshima.

Some of the objects brushed against the body of the plane as it circled.

'Why . . . ,' exclaimed Spallino, 'they're blossoms.'

Professor Sborg's laughter rang out again, but now stripped of any hysteria and loaded with malicious nuances.

'Uranium blossoms,' he said. 'A delicate thought that came to Einstein when he remembered the enthusiastic reception he had been given. I succeeded in making it possible. Once the principle of creation was discovered, it was not very difficult to force energy to mould itself according to our desire and the metallic substance to take on the form of blossoms. Thus we flatter at the same time the reason and the artistic sense of the Japanese.'

The scientists exclaimed enthusiastically and complimented the Norwegian on his ingenuity.

'Look,' said Rosa, pointing to the ground. 'They understand! They're acclaiming us! Not a single soul will forget this day!'

It was true. The Japanese had understood the significance of the supernatural cloud and the whole population was pouring out into the streets. The crowd's initial intuition, its presentiment of a miracle, had gradually been transformed into scientific certainty but without losing its religious character. Their intellectual satisfaction was as obvious as their sensual enjoyment of the ecstasy in which all the citizens now joined.

Hypnotized by the radiant cascade that was sweeping slowly towards them, their minds dazzled by the clarity of the equation $E = mc^2$, which the wise men of the town were chanting in chorus like a hymn, the people of Hiroshima were living an hour of sensual voluptuousness and intellectual joy no other community had ever known. Arms were stretched towards the sky in an impulse of gratitude, hope and love. Old men fell on their knees, thanking the gods for granting them the grace of this spectacle. They made the little children kneel beside them and join their hands in a gesture of adoration.

Impossible as it might seem in those glorious moments of uninterrupted joy, each second of which seemed to crystallize in a supreme happiness, even more dazzling heights, even more ecstatic moments were in store for the inhabitants of Hiroshima.

The first was when the cloud, constantly growing larger, had attained such magnitude that it covered the city and the surrounding country like a giant mushroom. Then all the sky of Hiroshima, as far as the eye could see, was filled with myriad blossoms, more delicate than the springtime blossoms of their own cherry trees, but reaching such a density as to decompose the solar light into a thousand fantastic fires and fairylike rainbows.

Then came the moment when the crowd, all senses alert, heard for the first time in the calm air the music of that divine rain. The harmony of sound that then struck the ears of Hiroshima could not be compared to that of any earthly melody. Only in their dreams do artists, their nerves taut, confusedly perceive the vague echoes of similar accords and on awakening seek in vain to recapture them. There was a constant undertone, a murmur of limpid streams, the whispering sound that wings of seraphims must make when they glide side by side in infinite space, and above this rustling, more subtle than an undulation of the impalpable ether, came at irregular intervals notes divinely pure, like the quivering of a thin crystal, made by the blades of virgin uranium as they touched each other in their slow whirlings.

At last came the moment all wished for fervently, the scientists in the sky as well as the people on earth, the moment in which, like a supernatural snow, with the softness and delicacy of butterflies coming to rest after a long flight, the first flakes of created material fell on Hiroshima. It was then that ecstasy reached its zenith. It was inconceivable that soul and body could withstand such a revelation of voluptuousness.

Now, if the fall of heavenly manna had long been awaited impatiently by the well and strong of Hiroshima, it was with an emotion a thousand times more intense, with a passion close to delirium that the poor and the sick of the city longed for it. The sick, the wounded had all been carried into the streets.

And look! Here under the eyes of the assembled multitude when the first wave touches earth, when those unfortunates feel the breath, the soft contact of the virgin substance, a new chain of miracles is produced, like an echo of the cascade of wonders caused by the scientists in the plane. And now one of the unfortunates, one of the war wounded, the lower part of whose body is paralyzed, flings away his crutches, raises both arms to the sky and begins to dance a triumphal dance.

And here are others who follow his example, more and more of them, as the rain of divine uranium falls heavier and heavier. The blind, who from the beginning of the manifestation turned terrified faces towards the clouds, are now trembling as the magic leaves brush their dead eyes. Their features relax, their faces break into smiles, their eyes quiver under the caress of the light. And their concerted acts of thanksgiving add their fevered notes to the aerial symphony. This is the sun of infinite gratitude that rises over Hiroshima.

Look! The paralyzed walk, the blind see, the deaf hear; wounds heal, dead flesh comes to life again. At the dawn of the glorious new era Providence has taken a hand and will not be inferior to the good will of men. Nor does it limit its intervention to a few, as so often happens, but multiplies to infinity its miracles, causes the instant abatement of all suffering, shows at last the generosity it holds in reserve to reward the efforts of those who have known how to solicit it properly and the faith of those who have not doubted.

Before this spectacle, the enthusiasm of Hiroshima exploded. In a short time the city put on again its holiday decorations. Poles decorated with banners were raised, streamers were strung across the street, flags were raised and on thousands of standards the formula $E = mc^2$ was written in enormous characters. The marvellous blossoms covered the ground like a carpet of diamonds. Children gathered them and let them rustle through their hands. Little Japanese girls arranged them in their hair like precious jewels. And at that moment, to add to the fairylike scene, the scientists flung into space glittering bunches of multi-coloured sparklers that fanned out in the cascade of marvellous lights like an aurora borealis above the blessed city.

Why did not Hiroshima's experience end on that apotheosis of glory? Why, in this world, do the noblest enterprises often end in a result which does not reflect the purity of the initial intention and is even in direct opposition to the generous principles that inspired them? Why does so much love give rise to so much disorder? Much later, in evoking the tragedy, John Almayer, a cultured man of letters, murmured sadly the verses of Milton which he imagined to be spoken by some demon:

> '. . . . .*If then his providence*
> *Out of our evil seek to bring forth good,*
> *Our labor must be to pervert that end,*
> *And out of good still to find means of evil;*
> *Which ofttimes may succeed. . . . .*'

But this was a simple commentary and could in no way pass for an explanation! The preceding questions having remained unanswered, history must be satisfied to report facts faithfully.

Luchesi showed the first symptoms of anxiety when he noticed, after an hour, that uranium was still falling ever thicker and thicker and that the chain reaction gave no sign of slowing down.

'It would be time to stop the experiment,' Almayer murmured.

Luchesi showed him the lever which he had put back to zero. He had stopped directing the operation, but Nature was now filled with a creative passion that apparently nothing could appease. Every second saw an incarnation of energy into matter double that of the preceding second and the cosmic source appeared to be inexhaustible. For some time now the aeroplane had been compelled to go to a very high altitude to avoid the created substance.

On Hiroshima the cascade of uranium blossoms became thicker and thicker, darker and darker. The sparkling and brilliance had gradually dulled as, obedient to an inexorable law, the number of uranium blossoms increased. Mathematics ruled the phenomenon and its implacable rigour was reflected in each of its sensitive manifestations. No ray of light was now able to penetrate the darkening cloud, a compact mass of dull, heavy substance falling remorselessly on the city, making the ground tremble.

On the streets the layer of uranium had by now reached to the waists of the inhabitants, even to their necks. The scientists' instruments showed, for a few moments more, some little children whom their parents lifted above their heads. Soon even they were buried under the fallen uranium, and in a very short time the synthetic matter had swallowed up the highest houses. Thus Hiroshima disappeared.

When the city had been completely submerged, when the fury created by Nature had exhausted itself, when, after a period of gradual clearing, the last blossoms whirled about on an immense lake of metal from which not a ripple emerged, when the scientists discovered that not a trace of Hiroshima remained, they were silent, lost in thought for a long time. Luchesi sighed.

'Who could have foreseen what has happened?'

'No one, Enrico,' said Rosa.

'And yet,' said Luchesi uncertainly, 'I feel as though I shared an indirect responsibility.'

'*I was the one who pressed the button,*' groaned Einstein's voice in the microphone. Sborg had already informed him.

But they all cut him short indignantly and did their best to comfort him. Sborg had no trouble in proving to the Master that neither he, nor Luchesi, nor any of the physicists had anything to reproach themselves with.

'Our conscience is clear,' he concluded, 'and that is the essential thing. Our intentions were pure. Our ideal was to create.'

'That is true,' said Luchesi with a last glance towards the ground. 'God knows I didn't want this!'

(Translated by Elisabeth Abbott)